UNBLINDED

UNBLINDED

D. Michael Hallman

Reality Road Press
Houston, Texas

ISBN 979-8-9856035-0-7 (Hardcover)
ISBN 979-8-9856035-1-4 (Softcover)
ISBN 979-8-9856035-2-1 (eBook)

Library of Congress Control Number: 2022900712
Names: Hallman, D. Michael, 1954- author.
Title: Unblinded / D. Michael Hallman.
Description: Houston, Texas : Reality Road Press, [2022].

Subjects: LCSH: Blindness--Fiction. | Blind--Fiction. | Blindness--Treatment--Complications--Fiction. | Medicine, Experimental--Psychological aspects--Fiction. | Blind--Psychology--Fiction. | Medical research personnel--Fiction. | Drugs--Testing--Fiction. | Clinical trials--Fiction. | Human experimentation in medicine--Fiction. | Medical fiction. | Detective and mystery fiction. | BISAC: FICTION / Thrillers / Medical. | FICTION / Medical. | FICTION / Crime.

Classification: LCC: PS3608.A548397 U53 2022 | DDC: 813.6--dc23

Reality Road Press
Houston, Texas

Contents

I. *AFTER*

WHEN SHE TIRED OF LISTENING to music or audiobooks through her headphones, Kathy Wright liked to listen to the noises in the hallway outside her room—footsteps, muffled snatches of conversation, the creaky wheels of carts going past, the clatter of utensils on trays. She most often heard the footsteps of nurses or other employees. They usually passed at a normal pace, but occasionally someone walked with unmistakable urgency or even ran—one might expect emergencies in a hospital now and then. The faster the footsteps, the louder the voices that went with them, but with her door closed, Kathy could catch only snatches of conversations.

She noticed doctors and nurses tended to walk more officiously than visitors, striding purposefully down the corridor. She often heard them before they even turned the corner about ten yards down from her room; at her door, many would rap sharply, then enter without waiting for a response. She learned to recognize a few of the regulars who came by to check on her just by the sound of their footsteps, even though most of the medical staff wore soft soles. The heavier heel-and-toe clacking of hard soles or the sharp tapping of high heels usually heralded outside visitors, who walked with more hesitation, stopping often—probably checking room numbers to get their bearings. Her father once told her all hospitals were designed like mazes to keep patients and visitors lost, cowed, and docile, grateful whenever they found anyone who could point them in the right direction.

This morning, after an aide removed her nearly untouched breakfast tray, Kathy was lying propped up in bed, wondering how many doctors would come by today, when she heard the tapping of high heels coming rapidly down the corridor and up to her door, where they stopped. A visitor? Not likely. Whoever it was had approached without hesitation.

But high heels? None of the female doctors who had come by before wore high heels. Maybe an administrator coming to discuss insurance matters or discharge plans? Whoever it was knocked, then waited until Kathy said, "Come on in" before entering.

"Good morning. I'm Dr. Rachel Abramowicz; I'm a psychiatrist. I'd like to speak with you if that's okay. I was told there wouldn't be anyone else in your room, so we would be able to talk alone here."

"A private room is a luxury, isn't it?" Kathy laughed. "Good insurance, plus parents with money. I'm very lucky, I know."

"Do you mind if I pull up a chair? I'd like to sit a little closer."

"No, go right ahead. Sit anywhere you like." Kathy winced at the grinding scrape and sharp thump as the doctor pulled up a chair and sat down. As soon as she settled in, there were two distinct "plops" as she pried off her shoes and let them drop to the floor.

"Gotta get those heels off, huh?" Kathy grinned.

The doctor gave a short laugh. "I should have known better. I have to go to a dinner right after work, and I thought wearing them to the office would save time. I should have just carried them with me and worn flats. It was a much longer walk to this wing than I remembered."

As the doctor shifted in the chair to get more comfortable, Kathy spoke. "I've been expecting someone like you. I know why you're here."

"And why do you think I'm here?"

"It's pretty obvious, isn't it? You want to know if I should be in a mental hospital because I'm a danger to myself or others. I think that's the phrase they use. You want to know if I'm still suicidal. No one listens to me when I tell them I never was in the first place."

"Just to be clear, no one I've talked to has said anything about putting you in a psychiatric hospital, and no one thinks you're a danger to anyone else. We're obviously worried that you might be a danger to yourself. You say you were never suicidal in the first place, but you intentionally drank something you knew was poison. Could you help me understand that?"

"I doubt it. I mean, I'll try, but I don't expect anyone to understand it. You don't have to worry I'll try it again, though. I got what I wanted."

The doctor shifted in her chair. She wasn't sure which was less comfortable—the chair or the situation. "What was it you wanted?"

"Didn't they tell you anything? Isn't it in my chart or something? Or did they want you to get it straight from me? Okay. But you're a physician, you know what methanol does. What I wanted should be pretty obvious."

The doctor said nothing; she had to hear it from Kathy. The silence between them seemed to take on weight—ten, fifteen, twenty seconds passed before Kathy finally spoke, her voice edged with anger.

"I wanted to be blind again, all right?"

II. BEFORE

1. Breakthrough

Pre-Trial

As Vice President of Testing and Development for Cardon Clinical Testing, Greg Wright was always looking for promising new drugs to test. The company contracted with universities and drug companies to conduct clinical trials for drugs that were candidates for F.D.A. approval. Getting a drug out of the laboratory and through clinical trials took more resources than most scientists could command, and even large drug companies often found it cheaper to outsource the work to a specialized firm like Cardon.

When he answered his phone one Monday, he heard the familiar voice of Laurel Ketcham, head of the Technology Transfer office at Southeast Texas State University.

"Greg, this is Laurel Ketcham. How are you?"

"Fine, thank you. You didn't even have to say who you were, Laurel; I know your voice by now. We get so much business from you guys, we should probably set up an office over there. How are you?" He pulled out his pen and held it poised over a notepad on his desk. Laurel liked to get right to business; he knew the pleasantries would be brief.

"I'm fine. Look, I think we've got something you'll be very interested in. One of our faculty members has developed a drug that—get this—has actually regrown optic nerves in blind rats...."

He sat up straight in his chair, as if jolted by electricity. "You mean....?"

"Yes! They can see again! It works in monkeys, too! We've kept it under wraps a while for more testing, but we think it's ready for a Phase 1 trial. I thought about you right off." She paused a beat or two. "How is Kathy?"

"She's fine." *And still blind, and you know it. No wonder you thought of me first.*

"Good. I know it's a long way from F.D.A. approval, but this drug could be great for her someday. And for a lot of other people." She paused. "Could you meet with us on Wednesday, say around 2:30? Paul Lazarus will be there, too. It's his drug."

"For that, I'd come over right now."

"That'd be fine with me, but I don't think Paul could be ready on such short notice. I told him to keep Wednesday afternoon open. He's tied up in his lab a lot. It's just him and one lab tech, maybe a student or two. He's reported just enough progress over the last few years to keep his funding, but he's been flying under the radar for a while, working pretty much by himself for at least five years now. I've only heard him give two seminars in all that time."

"Okay, Wednesday at 2:30, then. Your place?" He almost added, "Or mine?", but cracks like that seemed to put everyone on edge these days. He flipped his desk calendar to Wednesday, and saw he would need to reschedule a meeting. Nothing as important as this.

"Right. But don't talk to anyone else about this, okay? We're not ready to go public yet."

"Okay. I'll come alone."

"Good. Thank you. This'll be a great opportunity for all of us." She paused. "I should probably warn you about Paul."

"Warn me? About what?"

"You've heard of Asperger's, right?"

"High-functioning autism, yeah. You know that's not an official diagnosis anymore."

"All I know is, it's Paul. When I first met him, I couldn't get a handle on him. He just didn't seem interested in what I was trying to do here. So I talked to his best friend on the faculty, David Eamon. He told me Paul might be the smartest guy in the whole medical center, and David knows everybody here, believe me. David brought the Asperger's up. I don't know if it fits completely, but it makes sense of a lot of it."

"Such as?" Greg drummed on his desk with his pencil. He was quite used to scientists who lacked social graces.

"If you say 'Hi' to him, he'll nod to you, but he won't speak and he won't smile. If you want to talk to him, you have to start the conversation. He will almost never say the first word. I understand Paul's wife had to come on to him the first time they met; he was just standing off by himself at a reception for new faculty, and probably never would have said a word to her if she hadn't. Once you get him talking, he can be quite charming, but you have to make the effort. He has a nice dry sense of humor. A bit on the cynical side, but that's an occupational hazard. He does keep his work to himself. Getting anything out of him when they were trying to put together the patent application for this nearly drove our lawyers nuts. So be ready for that."

"I can see why he'd try to keep it close until he got a patent. This could make him very rich."

"I honestly don't think he gives a damn about that. The only thing that came up in the money discussions is, he insisted we write his lab tech into any royalty agreement."

"Sounds like a pretty decent guy to me."

"Decent. Yeah, I'd say that. But it doesn't make him any easier to know. Just thought I should warn you."

Once he hung up, Greg wished he had asked more questions. A drug for blindness? Really? He tried to keep up with any advances in treating blindness. Most people in the field focused on gene therapy, though he knew there had been some progress in using combinations of growth factors to restore damaged optic nerves in rats. But though nerves had regrown in some cases, they hadn't functioned normally. You had to do more than just get the nerves to grow, hard as that was; they also had to form the right connections between the eye and the brain. If Laurel was right, this Paul Lazarus had made a major breakthrough, and he'd done it on the sly. Was he *trying* to avoid a Nobel, or what?

Greg called his assistant, Peggy Wilmott, and asked her to send him any recent papers by Paul Lazarus she could find in PubMed. He needed to see what this guy had been up to.

2. *"This could be big...."*

Pre-Trial

AT THE MEETING ON WEDNESDAY, Greg Wright, Laurel Ketcham, and Paul Lazarus sat at a table in a small conference room near Laurel's office. Paul's smile when he introduced himself was tight-lipped. Greg wondered if he'd been pushed into this meeting before he was ready. That Lazarus hadn't yet published anything about a breakthrough suggested a degree of paranoia. He obviously wasn't the type to shout "Eureka!" when he made a big discovery.

Laurel skipped any preamble: "As I told you the other day, Greg, Paul here has a drug that can cure blindness caused by optic nerve damage. It's derived from a protein he found that triggers optic nerve development in embryonic rats, and it works miracles in both adult rats and rhesus monkeys that have damaged optic nerves. Before treatment, they're blind, and afterward, they're not! We think it's ready for a Phase 1 clinical trial to test for toxicity before we try larger doses to see if it works the same in humans. I don't have to tell you how much this drug could be worth. We'd like to see if Cardon would be willing to fund a Phase 1 trial in exchange for a share in the licensing. It might take a year or more to get N.I.H. funding for Phase 1, but if we start a Phase 1 trial now, we could use data from it to apply for N.I.H. funding for Phase 2 and 3 trials to find out if it works or not. But you'd be in on the ground floor if you paid for Phase 1."

Laurel leaned back slightly in her chair and looked at Greg with the air of someone holding four aces. Almost a smirk. Of course Cardon would pay.

Greg couldn't just fold, though. She had to show her hand. He nodded. "Obviously, none of this is published yet. Paul, I've read your recent papers, and they skirt around the edges of what you have here, but they don't claim any major breakthrough. How long have you been sitting on this? Do you already have the patent?"

Before Paul could say anything, Laurel responded, "Not yet, but the process is well along. We submitted a provisional application as soon as we knew it worked in rats. But it will be some time...."

Paul's face darkened. He almost spat back, "We haven't been sitting on it. I didn't want to go public until we had everything nailed down. I have a very small lab; I didn't want some drug company with deep pockets to jump in and come up with their own version of this before ours was ready. So I haven't published it yet. But sitting on it? No."

Greg quickly said, "Sorry. Poor choice of words. I didn't mean to imply you weren't doing anything with it."

Paul waved a hand toward Laurel, almost dismissively. "I'd at least have had something in press by now, but the lawyers made us wait."

No one spoke for several seconds. Laurel's eyes darted from Paul to Greg and back. "We filed for a patent more than a year ago. Paul had to modify the natural protein to make it work as a drug. That took—what, Paul? Two years?"

"Closer to three."

She continued. "The protein from embryos was broken down before it had time to work in adults, so Paul had to modify it to make it more stable without hurting its function. The protein that works in adults differs from the one he found in the fetus. It's clearly patentable."

Greg wanted Paul to answer, not Laurel. He started firing off questions like a Grand Inquisitor while looking directly at Paul, scribbling down notes as Paul spoke.

"What's it called?"

"We don't have a catchy name for it yet, just OGF83, because I had to make 83 modified versions before I found one that worked in adults. 'OGF' means Optic Growth Factor. Proteases found in adults but not the fetus would cut the unmodified protein up before it had time to do anything. I attached different side groups to amino acids around the protease binding sites until I found a combination that blocked the proteases but still caused nerve growth."

"What makes you think it'll work in humans?"

"Once we knew what to look for, we found that both rhesus monkeys and humans had the gene for the same protein rats have. We think it's made during the same period in human fetal development as in rats, but we obviously can't test that. We think it works the same way in humans as in rats and monkeys."

"How *does* it work?"

"It seems to be the initial trigger for development of the optic nerve. It's only produced for a day or two during embryonic development in rats. It's a subunit of a protein that's produced all during brain development, but only the cleaved-out subunit specifically stimulates optic nerve growth. The main protein is 586 amino acids long; the critical subunit, just 53. Amazingly short for something that important."

"Something that small can't be the only thing causing optic nerve growth."

"No, but it seems to be the master key that unlocks the whole process. In adults, it seems to turn on genes that revert neurons back to stem cells, so they start dividing again."

"Does it grow anything besides optic nerves?"

"Not in live animals, as far as we can tell. In cultured cells, it stimulates neurons more generally, but in animals, there seem to be regulatory factors you don't find in cell cultures that restrict it to the optic nerve."

"How big is the dose? Do you inject it or what?"

"That's what we've mostly been working on the past year. It's very small, picograms in rats, nanograms in monkeys, but it changes with the route of administration. It's smallest if you inject it in the cerebrospinal fluid, but you don't want to do that in humans if you can help it. It can cross the blood-brain barrier, so we've tried other ways to get it in. IV injection is okay, but a nasal spray works best—the dose is smaller, and you get the drug closer to where it's needed, right through the nasal mucosa and into the brain."

"How long before you see results?"

"From five to six weeks in rats, about two months in monkeys. You get measurable cell repair within two weeks; restoring full nerve function takes longer. Once the drug gets things started, the process seems to regulate itself."

Greg rubbed his right index finger back and forth across his lips for several seconds before he spoke. "I'll take your proposal to my boss. I think he'll go for it. We don't usually pay to run trials, people pay us for that, but this could be a blockbuster. We'll want prior approval on publications. We try not to interfere with publishing basic findings, but don't put out any press releases yet. Paul, I'd like to come by your lab so you can show me what you've got. This could be big, really big, if it works in humans."

* * *

On his way back to Cardon, Greg could hardly keep his mind on his driving. The drug seemed to cure rats and monkeys with no discernible side effects—they appeared normal in every way. And the gene that encoded the unmodified natural protein was virtually identical in rats, monkeys, and humans, which enormously improved the odds that the modified protein that worked in animals would also work in humans. A cure for blindness! A lot of it, anyway—possibly any case caused by damage to the optic nerve. His own daughter had gone blind when her optic nerves mysteriously began to degenerate—why, no one knew. They had a name for it: idiopathic optic atrophy. Fancy words that meant no one knew a damn thing about what caused it. Doctors ruled out one potential cause after another and were finally left with—nothing. Nothing to explain it. Nothing to do about it. No way to fix it.

When a horn blared behind him, Greg was startled to find himself stopped at a green light, and for an instant he didn't know where he was. He had no memory of getting there. He suddenly realized he was in downtown traffic at rush hour, lurching from light to light. As he drove through the now-yellow light, he wondered. *Does Kathy still remember colors? Red or yellow or green? What a blue sky looks like? She was just a kid when it all faded away and left... what? When she turns toward a sound now, what's in front of her? Just a black void? Things she remembers seeing? Does she imagine what things look like? Or are images all just gone now? Why don't I know that? She told me ages ago she still barely remembered how some things looked, but now? I can't remember the last time we talked about it. Have we grown that far apart? We're just so used to her being blind....*

Right there, stuck in traffic close to gridlock between Lafayette Avenue and Sam Houston Street, Greg knew that Cardon had to take on this drug, and Kathy had to be one of the first people to get it.

3. *"I'd like her to have the chance...."*

Pre-Trial

A WEEK AFTER GREG PRESENTED his report on OGF83 to Lon Cardon, the founder and C.E.O. of Cardon Clinical Testing, the company entered negotiations with Paul Lazarus and Southeast Texas State University to work out contract details for a Phase 1 clinical trial. The company agreed to cover all costs of a trial of ten patients, with up to a year of follow-up to assess any adverse effects. In exchange for funding the trial, Cardon would receive 5% of the University's net revenue from OGF83 for five years after the Food and Drug Administration approved it. It was a gamble on the company's part—few drugs ever received F.D.A. approval, and it might not come for several years. But all signs from the Lazarus lab were favorable, and the fact that rats, rhesus monkeys, and humans all had the gene for OGF83's parent protein strongly suggested that if the drug worked in the first two, it would also work in humans. An initial investment in the neighborhood of $1 million could potentially earn the company many times that. Even if the drug failed utterly, Cardon's tax lawyers could probably turn the million-dollar hit into a write-off. The reward-to-risk ratio was too high to pass up.

To begin the process of planning the clinical trial, Lon met with Peggy Northrup, the head of the Clinical Trials Unit, and Jim Russell, the physician who would oversee the day-to-day operations of the trial. They sat around a table in the small conference room just outside Lon's office, along with Greg, who at this point knew more about the drug than anyone else at Cardon. Greg chaired the meeting and spoke first.

"It may seem like we're here to plan a standard Phase 1 clinical trial, but we're not. The drug we'll be testing could be the biggest breakthrough in treating blindness since cataract surgery. I'm not exaggerating. It's not just a treatment, it's an actual cure. It's hard to say what percentage of cases this drug could help, but there are probably more than a million blind people in the U.S. alone, so even if it helps just a fraction of them, that could be thousands every year. And all we have to do to get in on it is follow ten patients for a year to make sure the drug doesn't cause any problems. But we can't use healthy volunteers like we normally would in a Phase 1. This drug works in the brain and affects nerve growth, so we can't risk giving it to healthy people. In animals it only seems to affect the optic nerve, but we can't guarantee that in humans. So we'll be testing it in blind volunteers, people who could actually benefit from it if it works. And they'll need neurological exams and brain imaging to make sure nothing goes wrong, so it'll cost more than Phase Ones usually do. And we'll have to look for benefits, too because very small doses work in animals, and that may hold for humans, too. We just don't know. So this trial's a bit different than usual."

Peggy Northrup spoke up. "So we can't go to our usual sources for Phase 1 volunteers. Where do we find the patients?"

"I've already talked with a few ophthalmologists at Southeast Texas State Medical School. They've signed on as co-investigators, and they'll refer patients to us who would be good candidates for this. I told them we'd be looking for patients with blindness caused by either trauma to the optic nerve or some form of optic neuropathy, whether they know the cause or not."

Jim Russell asked, "Will this drug do anything for common types of blindness, like diabetic retinopathy or glaucoma?"

"It might. Especially glaucoma, since that damages the optic nerve if it's not treated. But people with diabetic retinopathy or glaucoma get treated with lasers or surgery or drugs. We want to make sure that if there are any side effects, they're from the drug we're giving them, not something else."

Russell nodded. "Makes sense."

Lon Cardon took over at that point. "Let's start getting a protocol down on paper. Peggy, you start working out a budget. We're paying for this in-house, so keep it reasonable, but make sure we don't short-change the testing and follow-up. You probably need to get with Jim and whatever doctors we bring in as co-investigators. Run the budget by me once you get it. Jim, pick your team out and start working on the protocols.

Greg can give you the list of eye doctors he's talked to, so you can get with them and get a list of potential patients. You'll have to talk with a neurologist to figure out what MRI's or CAT scans we'll need. Let's all meet here in two weeks to see how things are going." He paused. "That's all I have. Oh, Greg—good work bringing this in."

As the meeting ended, Greg hung back until Peggy and Jim had gone. "Lon, I have a favor to ask."

Cardon looked at him over the top of his glasses. "It's about your daughter, right? I know you're excited about this."

"After what I saw the other day, it would be hard not to be. Those animals can see again, and they couldn't before."

"It's impressive as hell. But you know as well as anyone how many drugs don't work out once you get them in trials."

Greg looked down, scratching his forehead. "You're right, I know. But this…." His voice trailed off. "You know what caused Kathy to go blind, don't you? 'Idiopathic optic atrophy'. All that means is they didn't know. Her optic nerves just wasted away. That's exactly the kind of thing this drug might help."

"And you want to get her in the trial. Why don't you wait for Phase 2, when we know the drug won't hurt anyone, whether it helps or not?"

"I think it might be harder getting her in then. They'll be looking for N.I.H. money for that. There's no government money in this one."

"So?" Lon's brow furrowed.

"So we don't have to play by their rules. At least not entirely. We make the rules for this one."

Lon's face hardened. "And they'll be the same rules we always follow. I'm not sure what you're asking here."

"We broke the usual rules when we decided to use blind volunteers and not healthy ones. We've already gone that far. I'd like to get Kathy in, and assuming we got the contract for Phase 2, I think the N.I.H. might call it a conflict of interest…."

"I can see where it could be."

"But would it be, really? Peggy and Jim will be in charge of the trial. I was only here today because I brought the drug to the company. Once the trial starts, I won't have anything to do with running it. I'll be back looking for other drugs to bring in."

Lon pursed his lips. "True. But we still have to get this by the Human Subjects Board at Southeast Texas State."

"I don't think there'll be any problem. I work with the Board there all the time when we collaborate with their faculty. They know I don't actually work on our trials. I'm just a liaison." *Besides,* he thought, *all they do is evaluate our protocols, they don't vet participants. Kathy's name doesn't even need to come up.*

Lon sat back in his chair and brought his hands together, fingertips touching. After several seconds, he said, "All right, as long as they're okay with it. You really won't have anything to do with running the trial. But I'll want to talk to your daughter if she decides to enroll. It has to be her decision."

"Of course. I would never try to force Kathy into anything." He smiled. "As if I could. Kathy doesn't do anything she doesn't want to, believe me. Thank you. I really appreciate this."

He left and shut the door behind him, pumping his fist in triumph once he was alone in the hall.

III. THE TRIAL

4. "Please don't call them 'subjects'"

Cardon staff—Week 1

It was almost three months after the project was green-lit before they were ready to bring in patients. The week before, Jim Russell, the physician and researcher supervising the trial, gave a presentation to a group that included everyone at Cardon assigned to the trial, including statisticians and data collectors. Peggy Northrup, Lon Cardon and Greg Wright were also there.

Paul Lazarus was there, too, but as a biochemist with no medical degree, he would not be directly involved with the trial. Attending as well were three collaborating ophthalmologists who had identified eligible patients and were signed on as co-investigators. None had worked on clinical trials before, but they had seen the protocols and signed confidentiality agreements. They would be available in case the drug actually showed any signs it was working at Phase 1 doses. Two collaborating radiologists who would handle the MRIs and CT scans were both on hospital duty and couldn't make the meeting.

After some introductory remarks about the enormous potential of OGF83, Russell outlined the trial. "This is a Phase1 trial, so we only have ten patients. But they're no less important than if this were a Phase 3 trial with hundreds of them. If the drug doesn't pass Phase 1, it'll never get any further. So we have to get this right."

The smile he'd worn during his praise of OGF83's potential was gone now; this part was dead serious.

"Our patients are 18 to 43 years old. They've all been blind for at least three years, some much longer. Six represent known genetic causes of blindness, like Leber's Hereditary Optic Neuropathy. Two are trauma cases. The remaining two had idiopathic optic nerve atrophy, so we don't know what caused it. We avoided cases linked to other diseases, like diabetes; we didn't want people undergoing other treatments while they're getting our drug. It would just muddy the waters.

"We'll start with a very small dose and follow the patients for three months. If everything's good then, we'll give them a bigger dose. If there's no significant toxicity after three more months, we'll try a third dose with another three months of follow-up. But if we see any signs of therapeutic effects, we may skip the third dose and start getting ready for a Phase 2 trial. If anyone shows either clinical improvement or signs of toxicity, the timetable could change. For example, let's say we see significant clinical improvement in someone at a low dose. Then we wouldn't try a higher dose in that patient. We don't really expect to see clinical effects, certainly not with the first dose, but it could happen. Total follow-up will range from three to twelve months, depending on what we see and whether we have to stop early or not.

"We'll examine patients—and please, don't call them 'subjects'—every week for the first six weeks after the initial dose and after any change in dosage. We might go to every other week after that if we don't see any problems. If anyone actually shows signs of recovering vision, we have their ophthalmologists on call. We found our patients through them, and they're all very interested in this drug, as you can imagine."

Carl Stark, one of the collaborating ophthalmologists, raised his hand. "You know I'm just here for eye exams, but I was wondering, how are you testing psychological effects? You are looking for psychological effects, right? Since this thing works in the brain...."

"Very good question, Dr. Stark. We've tried to anticipate everything we can. Our questionnaires and interviews will help us assess things like changes in mood and any signs of depression or anxiety. We have a clinical psychologist on call if anyone develops serious problems. So we *will* be keeping an eye out for those. ... Any more questions?"

Everybody looked around, but no hands went up.

No more questions? Okay. The first two patients will get the drug on Monday, then we'll do two more each day for the rest of the week. We'll bring them in separately, as usual; we don't want them comparing notes about symptoms. If they have any side effects in common, we should be the ones who find out, not them; that's our job." He flashed a smile, but everyone understood he was not joking.

He went on. "We're really looking forward to Monday. Paul, it's your drug. Anything you'd like to say?"

Paul Lazarus stood up, but didn't walk to the mike; the room wasn't that large. He hadn't expected to be put on the spot, and his face flushed red.

"Only that I'm as excited as you are. We've seen what this can do in animals; there's no reason to think it won't work in humans, too. I think we're all going to be part of something that will help a lot of people. I can hardly wait to see." He looked around the room and grinned—the first time most of those in the room had seen him smile. "No pun intended."

5. Patient 1

Kathy Wright—Pre-Trial & Week 1

Kathy Wright could barely remember a time when she could see. She had been a normal healthy child until a month or so past her third birthday, when her mother, Shara, saw her trip over one of her toys—ironically, as Shara would later note, a toy piano. It wasn't just the fact that Kathy tripped that made her mother notice; it was the way she tripped: The toy was sitting in the middle of an otherwise clear floor, and Kathy simply walked into it; she wasn't even running. It took her parents another two or three weeks to realize for certain there was something wrong, that Kathy had to be looking directly at something to see it.

Her pediatrician confirmed Greg and Shara's fears, and sent Kathy to an ophthalmologist with expertise in childhood eye diseases. Her visual acuity was poor, and monthly examinations showed her eyesight growing worse, with her peripheral vision steadily narrowing. They could find nothing wrong with her eyes; the problem was neurological. Her optic nerves were rapidly degenerating—no one knew why, nor did they know where it might stop. Would it take just her sight, or would the degeneration spread? Would she grow deaf, too? Would it affect her intelligence? To her parents' relief, extensive testing didn't turn up any other sensory or cognitive abnormalities as her blindness progressed. Blindness in their only child was bad enough, but they would deal with it.

Kathy could still distinguish light and dark until she was nearly seven, but functionally, her vision was gone by the time she turned six. Long after she could no longer even tell day from night, Kathy would rub her eyes hard many times a day to see the yellow, green, and blue flashes and patterns—phosphenes—that would drift erratically across the blackness in response to the pressure. Finally even those were gone.

Always precocious, Kathy was surprisingly quick to adapt. Books in Braille replaced the picture books that were once strewn about her room. She started piano lessons when she was seven—taking after her mother, herself an excellent player—and added organ lessons before she was ten. Music was her anchor. The piano and organ stood solidly in place in the living room, monolithic and unmoving, always dependable—one key, one note, ever and always, world without end, amen. She would make sure of that—whenever the baby grand slipped even slightly out of tune, she would tell the tuner which notes were to blame, and whether they were sharp or flat. Living in a world of touch and sound, undistracted by sight, she became a first-rate musician, finally graduating from Worthingham College, a private college about 75 miles away, with a double major in music and English. Her time at the school was her primary experience with living more or less independently—or at least away from home.

At her mother's behest, she moved back home after college while she pondered her career options. The only job she could find in music—through her mother's connections—was as the organist at Holy Trinity United Methodist Church, at a queenly $1000 per month. Not that she needed much money, living at home as the untouched trust fund her parents had set up for her when she lost her vision grew steadily.

But another opportunity soon opened up to Kathy through her mother's connections. One of Shara's friends, Moira Callahan, often heard Kathy practicing piano and knew how good she was. Moira's daughter, Leila, recently graduated from Rice University with a major in music, was supporting herself mostly by giving singing lessons, though she also had a few piano students. But Leila's ambition was to establish herself locally as a cabaret singer. She was looking for an accompanist; she didn't want to both sing and play the piano in her act. Shara and Moira arranged for Leila to come meet Kathy, hear her play, and see whether a partnership might work.

Leila had misgivings; she had never been around anyone blind before. After introductions, their mothers left them in the living room to get acquainted.

Leila spoke first. "I'm kind of embarrassed to ask this, Kathy…."

"Don't be. Everyone's embarrassed around me at first. I'm like anyone else. I just can't see, is all."

"Do you have any trouble getting around?"

"Well, I can't drive, if that's what you mean by getting around. But I can find my way around, walking. The nice thing when you're blind is, everyone gets out of your way. They don't want to get whacked with a cane, I guess. I can swing this thing pretty hard." She waved toward the white cane that was leaning against her right leg as she sat.

She can joke about it! "Sorry. A silly question, I guess."

"Not really. Don't apologize. It takes some getting used to, being around me, I know. I warn you now, a lot of people think I'm bossy. I often have to tell people how to do things for me. You've heard that blind people can do anything sighted people can, right? Well, that's bullshit. Sometimes I do have to get people to do things for me. Often I *could* do them myself, eventually, but it saves a lot of time if someone else does. Needing someone to drive me, that's the big one. When they finally start selling these self-driving cars I keep hearing about, I'll be first in line. If someone'll show me where the line starts." She laughed.

Leila hesitated for several seconds before asking, "Would you mind if I asked you another question?"

"Let me guess. What's it like being blind?"

"Well, basically, I guess, yeah, but really it's about, how you do things. How do you do all the day-to-day things I can't imagine even trying to do blindfolded?"

"Wow, that's way too big a question for a simple answer. Hang around me for a while and see. Short answer, you learn to rely on the senses you still have, mostly touch and hearing. You have to plan out a lot of things that other people take for granted. Like making sure things you use are exactly where you expect them to be, and in the right order."

"Did your other senses become, like, super-sharp?"

"I get that one a lot. Here, let me show you something. Got a quarter?"

"Um, just a minute. I left my purse on a table over there." She got it and rummaged around in it. "Okay, here."

Kathy rubbed it between her thumb and forefinger, then slowly ran her first two fingers over one side. "Okay, this is just a standard quarter, with George Washington and an eagle on it. You got one of those state quarters?"

"Just a minute. Let me see…. Here."

Kathy repeated the process, her brow furrowed. Finally she spoke. "Virginia. Right?"

Leila looked at it. "Yes! That's amazing!" She rubbed her own fingers over it. "I mean, I can feel the uneven surface, but that's all."

"It's a parlor trick, really. After I memorized them for all fifty states, they started putting them out for territories and national parks and stuff, and I decided 'Okay, fifty's enough.' What they tell me is that I can't feel things any better than you do, but since I have to get everything I can out of touching something, I'm focused on it a lot more than you are. You could learn to do it, too, if you wanted to. That's what they tell me, anyway. Same with hearing. I don't hear any better than people who can see, I just pay more attention, so it seems like I do. If you have it, sight seems to overwhelm everything else, all the subtleties you can pick up with your other senses. If you're blind, you have to use what you're left with. I'm so grateful I can hear. I can't imagine being both blind and deaf. I don't even like to think about it." A shudder ran across Kathy's shoulders.

"Were you ever able to see? You don't mind me asking, do you?"

"No, it's okay. Everybody's curious. Yes, I could, but I barely remember. I could actually still see some in preschool, but everything was pretty much gone by first grade. I try to call things up now and then. I think I remember my mother's face, but I can't be sure. My father's, no. He was away at work too much, I guess. I think I remember some colors, like the blue sky, but it's hard to tell. What I remember might not be blue at all."

Leila had to screw up her courage before she asked her next question. "My mother is amazed that you always seem so upbeat. I mean… I'm not sure how to put it…."

"Yeah, I know. Blind people ought to weep and gnash their teeth, huh? Why aren't we all bitter about it, right? Some are, I know. But what use is that? I went blind a long time ago. Now it's just part of who I am. Not the most important part, either. Sure I feel sorry for myself sometimes. It's so unfair, right? But fair or not, it just *is*. I'm way luckier than most blind people, I know that. My parents have money, and nobody to take care of but me, so I've never lacked for anything. Except eyesight. The only thing I feel bad about sometime is that my mother gave up teaching when I started going blind, so she could take care of me. She went back to it as a substitute for the four years I was in college, and she still does a little of it now. She gave up a career for me. I feel bad about that, but that's about all. I'm pretty happy with how I've turned out."

"You went away to college?"

"Yeah, Worthingham College. Small. Good music department. Near San Antonio. Not too far, but far enough so I was on my own for the first time. Well, I had three housemates. They treated me like any other student. When I took up drinking and sex, they were happy to help. I backed off pretty quick, though. On the drinking, anyway." Kathy grinned wickedly.

Leila suddenly felt she'd been far too intrusive. She had to change the subject. "My mother says you're a terrific pianist."

Kathy shrugged. "I won't brag. I'm not bad. Why don't we go over to the piano? What would you like to hear?" Kathy stood and walked straight across the room to the piano, carrying her cane, but not bothering to swing it. She obviously knew the route.

"Um, something by Cole Porter? 'Begin the Beguine'?"

"Oh, come on! Give me something harder than that!" Kathy played the first few bars with no hesitation at all. "I know a lot of Cole Porter!"

"Okay, um, 'I'm the Villain'."

Kathy hesitated, looking puzzled. "You got me there. I know a lot of Cole Porter, but I've never heard of that one. That's Cole Porter?"

"Yeah, sorry, that was mean. It was from his first musical, in 1912, which I wrote a paper on for a Special Topics class, American Popular Music before World War II. Hardly anyone's heard that one."

Kathy laughed. "Oh, that's cheating! But I can take it! C'mon! Name another one. Maybe something a *little* less obscure, though."

For the next half-hour, Leila rattled off one Cole Porter song title after another, some well-known, some less so, while Kathy played a verse and the chorus of each. She knew them all.

After a while, Leila couldn't hold back. "You really *are* terrific!" All her misgivings had vanished. "How'd you like to play in a hotel lounge three nights a week, Tuesday through Thursday? I can't pay much, though. I only get $250 a night, and *I'd* be hiring you, not the hotel."

"You make a living out of that?" Kathy sounded dubious.

"Well, no, mostly I teach, voice and piano. But I'd like to get established as a singer, and it's a start. It's not all Cole Porter, of course. Cabaret songs. Some modern stuff. Up through Celine Dion, at least."

"I usually pick up a song after two or three listens. I could do it. How much are you offering?"

"Um, seventy-five a night? No, a hundred. I can afford that. I mostly live on what I make teaching. This is a side gig now, just to get me started as a singer. But it's regular work."

"A hundred a day, huh? Well, the money doesn't mean that much, really. I need *some*, of course, but I live here rent-free. Mom and I are pretty close. Eventually I'll move out and my trust fund will kick in. I won't be rich, but I'll have enough to live on. My folks made sure I wouldn't be left out in the cold world alone and blind. And broke."

"So a hundred's okay?"

"Yeah, why not? I make some money as a church organist on Sundays, and that doesn't pay much either. Less than you, actually."

"Oh, this is great!" Leila abruptly came over and hugged Kathy, which startled her—Kathy could hear Leila coming, but people seldom tried to hug her, so she wasn't expecting it. "I'll get you some set lists and we can work out some rehearsal times. I have to see what my teaching schedule looks like. And your schedule, of course, with your church stuff. You can start as soon as you feel ready. I'm both playing and singing right now, but I really want to focus on just singing and building a stage presence. That's worth more to me than keeping all the money."

"Okay! Partners!" Kathy suddenly stopped. "Oh! What I said about driving earlier…. You can drive me there and back, right?"

"Sure, of course. It'll give us more time to get to know each other."

So Kathy had a second job. For four hours each Tuesday, Wednesday, and Thursday evening, Kathy was Leila's pianist at the Blue Room Lounge, a midlevel hotel lounge with pretensions. They brought in "name" talent for the weekends, but wanted a regular performer during the week. Professionally, Leila Callahan performed as Lila Kallen— more euphonious, and she didn't want people calling her "Layla".

Because Kathy was self-conscious about getting to and from the piano on a cramped stage between sets, she would stay at the piano and play through the break. Then she would venture away from the cabaret repertoire, sometimes into straight jazz, where she tended more toward Bill Evans than Thelonious Monk.

Kathy wasn't playing Carnegie Hall, but she had come a long way, and being blind hadn't stopped her. So when her father told her about the OGF83 trial, she had misgivings about enrolling. She didn't believe any drug could do what they claimed this one did. Take a drug and wipe out more than twenty years of blindness? It seemed way too easy. Though it wouldn't be a huge blow to her if it didn't work; she honestly wasn't sure how much being able to see would improve her life. But her parents wouldn't be around forever. They encouraged her to be independent even as they sheltered her. She had her trust fund, as yet untouched, and she would likely never face any real financial hardship. She was happy with her two jobs, low pay and all. But the lounge gig could end at any time if audience tastes changed, or the hotel manager decided they weren't bringing in enough business, and Kathy knew it would be hard to find another Leila. So with a referral from Dr. Stark, her childhood ophthalmologist, she made an appointment to meet with Dr. Russell, the director of the trial. Her mother drove her to the Cardon building; her father was at a pharmaceutical meeting, looking for any promising new drugs in the pipeline.

The first thing Kathy noticed was the faint antiseptic smell of the building. She imagined the premises were immaculately clean—they not only smelled clean, they sounded clean; there were echoes in the corridors when they walked, with hard surfaces everywhere. When they entered Dr. Russell's office, she felt carpeting beneath her feet, and the clacking of their footsteps ceased. As soon as Kathy heard Russell's voice, she knew she'd never met him. Her father didn't often have anyone from work over to the house. She wasn't sure if Russell knew of her connection with Cardon through her father; she decided not to bring it up.

"Ms. Wright, we're about to begin a Phase 1 clinical trial of a drug that in animal studies has shown tremendous promise in curing blindness like yours that was caused by damaged optic nerves. I have to go through the informed consent form with you. There are several pages to it, but it's important that we go through them all."

He basically read them verbatim; Kathy could tell, because she had a Braille copy. She had gone through the entire form already, but rules were rules; she couldn't just say, "Yes, I've read it, just show me where to sign." Only after going through the whole form did Russell depart from the text in what turned out to be a combination warning and low-key sales pitch, neither of which Kathy felt she needed.

"Right now, we just want to make sure the drug is safe. We're starting with a very small dose and we'll increase it to something that should be at least close to a therapeutic dose, based on animal experiments. We don't really expect to see therapeutic effects at this stage, particularly at first; we don't expect any patients to recover their vision. You may well get no benefit from this trial. But whether you do or not, you will be eligible to participate in later trials when we'll use larger doses that are more likely to do some good, though there are no guarantees. If we should find any adverse effects at this stage, we'll stop immediately, and take any steps needed medically to alleviate any problems. But there is some degree of risk. Do you understand everything I've said?"

"Yes, I do. I know how clinical trials work." She stopped herself there; she had been about to say she knew about them because of her father.

"Yes, I expect you do. Your father brought this drug to us. But you knew that."

So he did know, she thought. *I guess I shouldn't be surprised.*

Well before she had come there to sign the forms, Kathy had already decided to enroll. She would do it for her father. He blamed himself for her blindness, even though, with a Ph.D. in Molecular Biology, he knew quite well that it would probably take both him and Shara to pass some gene for blindness on to Kathy—since there was no blindness in either of their families, it was unlikely a dominant gene was involved. No one was to blame, and there was no point in anyone feeling guilty about it. But her father couldn't convince himself of that. For him, Kathy was willing to take a chance with the drug, even though she didn't think it would work, and even though, at some level, she genuinely didn't care whether it did or not. She was quite happy as she was.

She signed the consent form because she thought it would make her father happy. But she didn't get her hopes up.

6. Patient 9

Trey Osborne—Pre-Trial

FROM THE TIME HE WAS born, Augustus Oswald Osborne, III, was known as Trey, for obvious reasons. Growing up, he often wondered what compelled his parents to inflict his father's and grandfather's name on him. Had his father, who went by "Ozzie", forgotten what other kids would do with it, starting with Trey's two older sisters? They would usually call him Au-*gust*-us, with a rising inflection on the "gust". For variety, it was sometimes "*Oz*-wald", with the rising inflection on "Oz". They would tease him until he cried, which was fun until he got bigger—once he started crying, he was just seconds away from exploding with rage. Tears were streaming down his cheeks the time he hit his oldest sister in the head with a glass bottle. *She* cried, then.

When he outgrew the crying, you could still tell when he was close to his breaking point—he would *spit*, an explosive eruption of saliva directed at the ground, as though anger itself was a taste too vile to contain. If he then yelled, "Shut up!" it meant he was straining to control himself. One more word, and he would explode in violence. As he grew older, he gained more self-control, losing his temper less often. But it was always just beneath the surface.

Trey's grades all through school were good, but not brilliant, though he always did well in math. He grew to six feet and 180 pounds by his junior year of high school, and played on the football team. He went on to major in Industrial Engineering and minor in Geology at Lamar University, and was still in his final semester of school when he was offered a job as a process engineer at Lenevar Field Services, a family-run firm providing equipment and technical support for the oil industry. The pay was good and the work was just what he had trained for. He liked his work;

he liked his life, mostly, though his marriage didn't work out—married at twenty-three, he was divorced by the time he turned twenty-eight. But the parting was amicable, as these things go, and there were no children to complicate things. A decade out of school, he had few complaints.

But at thirty-two, in his tenth year at the firm, he suddenly developed blurred vision. Trey thought he needed glasses. He went to an optometrist, but was surprised to be immediately referred to an ophthalmologist, who in turn called in a neurologist for consultation. The problem was not only Trey's eyes, but what lay behind them. He showed retinal cell and optic nerve atrophy, which turned out to be due to an inherited disease called Leber's Hereditary Optic Neuropathy—LHON. Passed on only through the mother, the disease mainly affects males in their teens and twenties; Trey's case was of unusually late onset, but once his vision started deteriorating, it progressed with fearsome speed. While many with the condition retain some vision their whole lives, within eighteen months, Trey could only distinguish light and dark. Within another year, he lost even that.

Long before he was totally blind, Trey's vision had deteriorated so much he could no longer work. The firm, which prided itself on treating employees "like family", generously agreed to support his retirement on disability. Though his income dropped considerably, he wasn't forced into penury.

Trey did not adjust well to his dark new world. Rather than stepping into the light with a white cane and drawing the pity of passers-by, he kept to his house as much as possible. He routinely put in ten to fifteen miles a day on a treadmill, sometimes more, with the radio blaring talk and more talk, his take on the world growing ever closer to his mood.

One thing he refused to do was give up either his driver's license or his car, even after he was totally blind. Blindness wasn't a reportable condition in Texas, and Trey's license had come up for renewal while he could still barely pass the vision test. The license was good for six years, and he could renew it online once, if he lied about his vision. Trey would keep his license as long as he could; to give up that or his car would be like giving up, period. He kept his car in the garage and renewed his insurance whenever it came due; the insurance company had no idea he was blind.

Trey was walking on his treadmill one afternoon when the phone rang; it was Dr. Patel, the ophthalmologist who diagnosed his LHON.

"Mr. Osborne, a doctor I know asked me if I had any LHON patients who might want to participate in a clinical trial of a drug that has actually restored sight in animals, and I thought of you. They'll be testing a few people to see how well patients tolerate the drug. The doses are low and there's no promise it will work at all. But if the drug doesn't cause any problems, you'll qualify for a later clinical trial using higher doses. I don't know much about the drug, but it had astounding effects in animals. If you're interested, I'll give Dr. Russell your name and...."

Trey broke in. "Yes! Yes! Tell him yes!"

7. "Unblinded?"

Trey—Week 1

Two weeks later, after a phone interview established that Trey met the criteria for the trial, Dr. Russell himself came by Trey's house to explain the trial to him and obtain his consent to participate. Russell found the austerity of Trey's house both impressive and depressing. It seemed to be decorated in Early Monastic; it nearly had echoes. *It couldn't have been this way when he could see; he must have gotten rid of a lot of stuff when he went blind. Nothing to trip over. Less to take care of.*

Russell set his phone up to record video of him reading the informed consent form aloud, with Trey following along in a Braille copy—as far as Russell could tell, anyway. Halfway through the first page, Trey interrupted.

"I trust you. I don't think you'd read one thing and give me something else to sign."

"Just this one time, don't trust us, please. We take informed consent very seriously." Russell paused the recording.

"It sounds it. A bunch of lawyers wrote this, right?" Trey grinned. Russell noted that Trey grinned after everything he said; it looked as though he was baring his teeth. Almost vampiric.

"Yes, there were lawyers. There's always lawyers. But this protects you, too."

"If this drug does what it's supposed to, I won't need protecting. You won't, either."

"We're not promising anything. We have high hopes. But one thing this form protects us from is getting our hopes too high. We really have to go through it." Russell started the recording up again.

"Okay, well…." Trey did not read Braille well. He pretended to follow along, but he just ran his fingers over the raised dots. They were indecipherable to him at the speed his fingers were moving. When Russell finished, Trey signed the form in the places Russell indicated.

"Do you have any questions?" Russell asked.

"Not really. I think the form was pretty clear. It may not work in people at all. But you say it works in rats and monkeys, right?"

"Many drugs that work fine in animals don't work in humans. So no guarantees. This is a Phase 1 trial to make sure the drug isn't harmful, so you'll start off on a very low dose. We won't try to find a dose that actually works until Phase 2, and you'll be eligible for that. The thing with the first two phases is that every patient is guaranteed to get the drug. Patients in the third phase might get the drug, or they might get a placebo. That's determined by codes assigned by someone who never sees the patients. That's called a double-blind design. Nobody knows who actually got the drug until the trial ends, when both patients and investigators are unblinded."

"That's what you hope the ones who get the drug will be, right? Unblinded?" Trey grinned wider than usual, pleased at his own play on words. "But you won't go to Phase 3 unless somebody gets better before that?"

"Someone would have to show improvement in Phase 2, yes. Not necessarily Phase 1. The dose in Phase 1 might be too small."

"If someone in Phase 2 doesn't get better, it wouldn't make any sense to keep trying, would it? That person, I mean."

"Not necessarily. People can be on different doses. Someone on a lower dose in Phase 2 might not respond, while someone at a higher dose does. But look, if even one person in Phase 2 responds at a higher dose, I promise we'll go back and give that dose to everyone. You wouldn't have to go to Phase 3 and risk getting a placebo. I can't put that in writing, but we won't abandon patients who trusted us enough to try the drug before we know if it works. But we have to get through Phase 1 first."

"Okay. I think I got it. Let's get started. I'm happy to be your guinea pig. Bet you haven't tested those yet, have you?" Trey grinned once again. And once again, Russell thought of a vampire.

8. *"Something just happened!"*

Kathy—Week 7, Wednesday, A.M.

THERE WAS LITTLE CHANGE FOR the first six weeks after Kathy got the drug. She had a few mild headaches, but Tylenol stopped them, and no one could be sure the drug was causing them anyway. Then, on a Wednesday morning, Shara passed by her daughter's room about six a.m. and found her already awake and dressing herself in the clothes Shara had helped her select and lay out the night before. The room was dark; Shara turned on the light. Kathy never bothered with lights; why would she? At the click of the switch this time, though, something changed—the void in front of Kathy's eyes was different.

"Oh my God! Something just happened!" Kathy stopped in the middle of buttoning her blouse, her mouth agape. She opened her eyes wider, as if she might see if they were open wide enough.

"What? You saw something? What was it?" Shara's heart seemed to stop; she could barely draw a breath.

"The light! I saw it when it came on! Just… just the light. Just the change. I can't describe it. But I saw it! I saw it! The difference…."

Shara almost knocked Kathy over as she enveloped her in a bear hug; Shara's cheeks were already wet. Kathy was too shocked to cry just yet. There hadn't been any sign that her eyes were changing, that anything was different, until suddenly everything was.

"Do the light again! Do it again!" Kathy cried.

Shara let go and stepped away. Kathy heard two clicks in rapid succession; the usual void reappeared, then flashed into something different, something less dark. Now Kathy had tears streaming down her cheeks to match her mother's.

"Do it again! Where's it coming from? Turn me toward it!"

Her mother gently touched Kathy under her chin, and tilted her face upward.

"Hold it there, baby. Let me get the light again."

Two clicks, this time not so rapidly. The void returned, then flared into light on the second click—brighter, more intense this time, as she faced the light directly.

Kathy was frankly sobbing now. "I can see the light! I can see it change! I can see it!"

"Can you see anything but the light? Can you see me? I'm waving my hand in front of you. Can you see my hand? Any shadow?"

"No, nothing but the light.... Call Dad in! We have to show him! And we have to call Dr. Stark. He said call him if my eyes changed, no matter when."

"Oh, Kathy!" Shara wrapped her arms around her daughter and squeezed so tightly Kathy could barely breathe, letting up only when Kathy finally had to push back. "Sorry! This is so... I just can't believe it! Let's get your father!" Shara stepped to the door and called down the hall, "Greg! Come here, quick! Kathy's seeing light! She's seeing!" Then she said to Kathy, "I'll get Dr. Stark. His number's in my phone. We'll call him right now! I can't believe it! It's working! The drug's working!" She rushed from the room to retrieve her phone.

When Greg Wright got to the room, Kathy was wiping her face dry. She was grinning now, not crying. Greg, normally stoic, had tears enough for them both.

"Oh, Kathy, I didn't even let myself hope this. I thought later, maybe, if we're lucky, when you got a bigger dose."

"Dad, I'm not seeing anything yet. Just light. Changes in the light. Maybe that's all it'll be. But you're the one who gave me the chance."

He took her right hand in both of his and squeezed. "It won't stop here. I know it! I'm sure of it."

Two hours later, Kathy was in Stark's examination room. Using a small light, he separately tested each eye. She could tell when the light was on or off. She could even see the light move—but not always because Stark was moving it; her eyes moved around on their own. Further tests established that she could as yet see nothing except the light itself and some change in its intensity—but she hadn't been able to see anything at all before. When she left, Stark told her to call him immediately, day or night, if she noticed any other changes in her vision. He then called Jim Russell at Cardon.

"Jim? This is Carl Stark. I know it wasn't supposed to happen, but Kathy Wright from the trial is suddenly seeing light now. She was completely blind before, no response to light whatsoever. I wanted to verify the change before I called you. It's real. I don't care how small the dose was, the drug is working."

9. *"I want to be a bad girl tonight"*

Kathy—Week 7, Wednesday, P.M.

Kathy could barely concentrate on her playing at the club that night. It was fortunate she wore dark glasses. They kept out most of the light, but stray light crept in on the periphery now and then, just often enough to remind her of the change in her eyes, and just often enough to distract her. She hit wrong notes in a few songs, but Leila got past them. She glared at Kathy with each missed note, but realized each time how useless that was. She put her mouth near Kathy's ear between the first and second sets and said in a not-quite-whisper, "I know you're excited, and I'm thrilled for you, but don't leave me hanging out here!"

Kathy could still barely contain herself after the show as they sat at a table in the lounge for a drink. They were about to leave when a man who looked to Leila to be in his thirties came over.

"Could I buy you both a drink? I really liked the show."

Before Leila could reply, Kathy said, "Sure. Sit with us! We're celebrating!"

"What are you celebrating?" he asked, signaling for a waitress, as he pulled out the chair next to Leila and smiled at Kathy before it struck him that she was blind, and locking gazes would not be part of the seduction.

"Oh… life!" Kathy said. "Life is good. Better than my playing was tonight!" She giggled. She wasn't ready to tell a stranger about the clinical trial, the drug, the change in her eyes.

Leila had really wanted to leave after one drink, but Kathy was oblivious; Leila said nothing. The man introduced himself as Bob Watterson.

"I'm in computers. You know, we're working on a voice-recognition interface for websites that you'd probably find really useful. It's not quite there yet, though." It was better than just blurting, "I see you're blind", but it had roughly the same effect.

"I use those all the time", Kathy said. "Kind of reinventing the wheel, isn't it?"

"Ours will be better. Easier to integrate into existing websites. I can't really talk much about it. But I doubt you'd want to hear about it, anyway. Too boring."

"Ooo, you don't know what a sucker I am for technical talk!" Kathy laughed. "I won't make you give away your trade secrets. Bet I could get them out of you, though!"

Leila was more startled than Watterson. *That's not Kathy! Flirting with a stranger? What's got into her?*

"So, you're doing this for blind people?" Kathy looked serious now.

"Not directly", said Watterson. "But it would certainly be useful for them."

"How are you so sure? Know any blind people?" said Kathy.

"Not really, no. But you wouldn't have to type out commands. That would be useful for you, wouldn't it?" Watterson's embarrassed look was lost on Kathy.

"Let me tell you something about that", said Kathy. She was soon telling him about problems she faced as a blind woman in a visual world, describing some of her necessary routines.

He seemed to find her descriptions mesmerizing. "I never realized how blind people would do things like taking a shower or getting dressed or finding food on a plate. That's fascinating."

Kathy shrugged. "You'd get bored if I kept on."

"No, I wouldn't. Really."

"Prove it then. Let's talk some more. Would you like to take me home? With you, I mean."

Leila was shocked at Kathy's boldness, though probably not as much as Watterson was. Leila quickly said, "Are you sure? I can drive you like always."

Kathy said, "No, that's all right. I want to do something different tonight."

Leila said, "Mmm", trying not to sound disapproving, then said, "I have to go to the ladies' room. I'll be back in a minute." As she got up, she beckoned for Watterson to come with her.

Nodding to Leila, he told Kathy, "And I need to go to the men's room. I'll be right back. Don't go anywhere."

Kathy gave a short, mirthless laugh. "Don't worry. I won't wander off."

Leila and Watterson stopped in the hallway by the restrooms. Leila was blunt. "Look, you seem nice enough, but we don't know you. It's really not like Kathy to go off with a stranger she's just met. I really don't like this."

Watterson's eyes narrowed. "She's an adult. If she wants to go with me, why shouldn't she? You're not her mother, are you?" He smiled, but did not look amused.

"No, I'm not her mother." Now it was Leila's eyes that narrowed. "But I am her friend. How many blind women have you ever picked up before? Any? I need to look out for her. I don't trust strangers, and I can see them. She can't."

"Shouldn't that be her decision? We're not strangers now. She's been telling me about herself. How long would we have to talk before we're not strangers? She trusts me enough to take her home. You think I'd hurt her or something? I'm not a serial killer, you know."

Judging from the look on his face—narrowed eyes, clenched jaw—Leila wasn't so sure of that. Each stared at the other. Then Leila spoke. "Look, you may not like this, but could I see your driver's license?"

He replied coldly. "You're right, I don't like it, and you don't have the right to ask. But if it'll make you happy, here." He pulled out his wallet and flipped it open to show his license.

She pulled her cell phone out of her purse and snapped a picture of it, then one of Watterson. When she checked to make sure the pictures had come out, she looked at his address and realized she knew where the street was.

"Sorry. But I have to watch out for her." Suddenly feeling like an over-protective mother grizzly, Leila looked down, blushing. *If Kathy knew, she wouldn't like this one bit. But if anything did happen, I'd never forgive myself.*

Watterson knew he'd won; he could afford to be magnanimous. "You really don't have to worry about her. She'll be fine with me. I think she's fascinating."

Leila went back to the table, without using the restroom, making it back before Watterson. "Don't you think you're moving a little too fast, Kathy? We don't know this guy. He seems nice, but we don't know anything about him."

Kathy said, "Leila, you're not my mother. I know you're just trying to look out for me, and I appreciate it, but I'm going with him. Nothing's going to happen to me."

"It better not. I'll kill this guy myself if it does." She tried to lighten the mood. "It's not just that you're my friend. You know how hard it would be for me to break in a new pianist."

That had the desired effect; Kathy laughed. "Don't worry. I won't leave you. Think how hard it would be for me to find a new singer." But just so Leila wouldn't misunderstand, she added, "But I *am* going home with him tonight."

Just then Watterson returned to the table. Kathy smiled at his arrival. "My place or yours?" Before he could answer, she said, "It'll have to be yours. My parents are at mine. I don't suppose your parents are at yours?" She laid her right hand on the table, palm up; he cupped it with both hands.

"No, no. Just me." He smiled, more at his incredible luck than at Kathy, who couldn't see it. The gods were kind tonight.

Leila got up to leave. "Well, I'm going home now." To Kathy, she said, "I'll pick you up at the usual time tomorrow. Call me if you're not home then."

"I'll be home by then. I can't wear this same dress tomorrow."

Leila tried not to frown as she nodded to Watterson, but she did look him directly in the eye for an extra second. "You be careful." It was more a warning to Watterson than an admonition to Kathy. Then she left.

Kathy put her purse on her shoulder and took her cane in her left hand as she stood up. "You can guide me."

He tried to take her right hand, but she pulled it back. "Not that way. You'll just pull me along, and it's awkward. Slide your hand inside my elbow so we're arm-in-arm and guide me. Let me know when we're coming to a step or a curb. You know clock face directions? Twelve o'clock in front, six behind, all that? Use those. Don't just say, 'Left' or 'Right' or 'Over there'. And for God's sake, don't point. People do it all the time. I only know because every time they do, they laugh and tell me."

They made it through the door and outside, with Bob stumbling more than Kathy did. He wasn't used to this. When they reached his car, he wasn't quite sure what to do.

"Hold my cane, would you? You can put your hand on top of my head so I don't bump it on the roof; just don't push down hard. Once I'm in, I can usually find the seat belt, but you can help me if I can't."

When they were both in, Kathy said, "I'm bossy, I know. You have to be when you're blind. People want to help you, but they don't know how. A lot of times, they make things worse, but they mean well. I hope you won't mind if I tell you how to help me." She laid her hand on his thigh; she could clearly feel his erection.

"Not at all. Correct me whenever you need to." He swallowed. He wasn't used to this; he usually had to work a lot harder. "Okay. My place, then?"

As they were pulling out of the parking lot, Kathy had her first flash of anxiety. She really *didn't* know this guy, and had no idea where they were going; he could be taking her anywhere. "Wait. Let's go to a motel instead. Not the hotel here. There must be one close by. I'll pay, if that's a problem." She suddenly felt it might be better to be someplace where there would be other people around, rather than alone with him in a strange house. At least someone at the motel would know they were there together.

"Are you sure? Are you worried about going to my place? I can take you home if you're having second thoughts."

"I don't want to go home. I want to go to a motel." She could tell he was miffed, but any explanation would just insult him. She squeezed his leg. "I want to be a bad girl tonight. I've been good way too long."

He rose in his seat a bit as she ran her hand back and forth along his cock, now rock-hard. "I think we can find someplace close by." His voice was slightly hoarse, which made her smile, though he couldn't see it; he didn't dare take his eyes off the road.

With the change in plans, he took a sudden left at the next light just as it turned red. He didn't notice the car a half-block behind him make the same turn, right through the red light. Leila now knew they weren't going to either his house or Kathy's, and she didn't like it.

She tried to stay within a few car lengths of them. It was both good and bad that traffic was light—good, because it made it easier to follow them; bad, because it would make her more conspicuous if Watterson bothered to look. *But why would he even think anyone was following him?* She laughed aloud, feeling ridiculous for playing detective. But she followed them anyway—this was far too out-of-character for Kathy. Kathy went out with men; sometimes she even fucked men—but always men she had gotten to know first, usually through Leila. For better or worse, Leila had become Kathy's gatekeeper—almost everyone Kathy went out with now, she met through Leila, and if Leila didn't like someone, they either didn't get to Kathy in the first place, or they weren't around her for long. Leila was beautiful, Leila was talented, and Leila would cut men off at the knees if she didn't want them around. She could drop a seemingly casual remark in a tone of voice that could make men shudder. Kathy seldom complained if someone suddenly stopped calling or showing up at the lounge, since the men Leila disliked didn't usually impress Kathy, either. Leila and Kathy both liked men, but they clearly loved each other, and if it was less than erotic, it was more than platonic.

Watterson pulled off the freeway after just two miles, heading toward a strip with several motels side-by-side. When Watterson pulled up to one, Leila drove past it, then doubled back. She parked in a space about fifteen cars down from his from which she could see the lobby door. She turned off the ignition, slid down in her seat, and waited.

Some of Kathy's euphoria had worn off by then. Letting a stranger pick her up was exciting, but violated every instinct she had. She'd had sex, mostly back in college, but always with someone either she knew, or a friend did. Casual sex was like flying blind, and walking blind was hard enough. Living blind required discipline, demanded it. Want to get something off a shelf? You'd better know which shelf, and what's on it, and where. Casually lay something down without thinking and you might never find it again. Want to let a stranger pick you up for sex? Better hope you picked the right stranger. You sure can't judge him on looks. *I think this guy's all right, but right now, I kind of wish Leila was here.*

Some of Kathy's customary caution began to assert itself. She went into the lobby with Watterson with her cane in her left hand and him steering her by the right elbow. If people at the front desk knew she was blind; they might be more likely to watch out for her.

Watterson asked for a room for one night. "We'll be leaving early in the morning."

Kathy spoke up. "Do you have one on the ground floor? It would be easier for me." She lifted her cane a few inches; the clerk should know what a white cane meant.

He said, "Umm... okay. Room 116. Left out the door and just around the corner."

"Thank you. We only need one key. I won't be wandering around on my own." She smiled. She didn't want to just blurt out that she was blind. The clerk would have to be blind himself not to see it.

As Watterson steered her through the door of the room, she had already decided they wouldn't be spending the whole night there. She hoped he wouldn't mind, but she would wait to tell him until she was sure she had him in a good mood. If he had any doubts about what she wanted to do, she made it clear immediately. "Show me where the bed is. It's so nice we don't have to unpack anything."

"Wait a second. I need to find the lights."

She gave a short laugh. "Sorry. I forget other people need those." She was startled a bit when the light came on; she wasn't yet used to the fact that she could tell now. She hadn't said anything about that to Bob. If he noticed her slight flinch when the light came on, he didn't say anything.

When they got to the bed, she turned and reached out to touch him. "You can help me with this dress."

* * *

Leila waited two or three minutes after Kathy and Watterson vanished around the corner before she got out and went to the lobby. The desk clerk said, "Welcome to the Westchase Inn. How can I help you?"

"That man and woman who just came in...."

"Do you know them? Are they expecting you?"

"I know them, yes. They aren't really expecting me. Are they just here for the night?"

"I'm sorry, we can't give out information about our guests."

"Look, you saw she was blind, right? She's a friend of mine. I don't really know this guy she's with, and I'm a bit worried. I usually know her friends." She fished around in her purse and came out with two twenties and a ten dollar bill. More than she could really afford and probably overkill, but she needed his cooperation. "Are you working all night?"

"I get off at eight. But I can't tell you anything about a guest. I'll get in trouble."

"She's blind, all right? All I want you to do is call this number...", and she grabbed a motel notepad lying on the counter and scribbled her stage name and her cell phone number on it, "... when they check out, no matter what time it is. I'll pay you fifty dollars. That's all you have to do. I just want to make sure she gets home all right."

He hesitated. "I'm not supposed to."

"Look, what could it hurt? I'm her friend, I'm trying to look out for her. If she weren't blind, I wouldn't be asking; she could take care of herself. All I want to know is when she leaves. That's all. I know how long it should take her to get home. I can check on her then."

"What if I get off before they check out?"

"Then call when you're ready to leave and tell me she's still here. The money's yours either way. Please take it and tell me you'll call." She pushed the money and notepad across the counter, and read his name, Howard, off his name tag.

"Okay. If she's still here and you come back after I get off, don't tell anyone else about this, please. I could lose my job."

"Of course I won't. You're helping me. I wouldn't get you in trouble."

When her phone rang minutes after 2:30 a.m., Leila didn't have to drive from her house to Kathy's to watch for her, her original plan. Instead, she'd put her seatback down as far as it would go and dozed in her car in the motel lot. Not the best place to spend the night, but when she looked at the dashboard clock, she saw she wouldn't have to.

The desk clerk wasted no time phoning her. "Hi, this is Howard, the night manager at the Westchase Inn. They didn't stay very long. They dropped the key off a minute ago."

"Thank you very much, Howard. I really appreciate it." She raised her seatback, but kept her head down as she watched for Watterson's car to pull out. She followed, again keeping about two cars back, feeling more conspicuous now with few cars around. She only turned to go home when she saw him turn onto Kathy's street. It would be too obvious if she followed them right up to Kathy's door, and she really didn't want to be spotted. She wouldn't care if she pissed him off, but she didn't want Kathy to know she'd been following.

* * *

Leila fought back the urge several times that day to call Kathy, but figured she would have slept much of the day, the same as her. Leila didn't have to get up till 1:00 to handle two voice students in the afternoon, and was grateful she had a light schedule that day, though she couldn't afford one like that every day.

When she drove over that evening to pick Kathy up, she didn't want her to suspect anything. "Did you go home with him?" she asked.

"No. I decided I'd rather be somewhere there were other people around."

You have no idea, Leila thought.

Kathy continued. "We went to a motel. We only stayed a couple of hours. Then he took me home."

Leila wasn't sure she wanted to ask anything more, but decided "How'd you like him?" wouldn't be prying too much.

"The sex was fun. He was nice, but we don't have much in common. That stuff about his work helping the blind was bullshit. He just wanted to get in my pants. I'm not sure I'd want to see him again. I think he'll probably call. Hell, after the blow job I gave him, I know he will." She laughed. "I'll have to figure out what to tell him when he does. I hope he doesn't come by tonight."

"I have to say I was worried some. Neither of us knew him. I'd never seen him before. He's not one of the regulars. Were you ever worried about him?"

"Not really. Maybe a little, I guess. Enough not to want to wake up in his house, not knowing where that was." She laughed. "It's not like I was worried about him taking advantage of me. I wanted to take advantage of *him*." She paused. "I hope I didn't snap at you last night. I know you were just trying to look out for me. I really *don't* know why I did it. You just don't do things on a whim when you're blind. Everything takes too much planning."

Leila reached over and patted her leg. "You didn't snap at me. Don't worry about it. I promise not to scare off every boyfriend you get."

"All my many suitors." She laughed.

As she parked for work, Leila thought, *If this is how she's going to act when she's got just a little vision back, I hope she'll hurry up and get the rest of it.*

10. "Phosphenes!"

Trey—Weeks 8-11

For the first two months, nothing really changed for Trey, except that he had frequent headaches. They weren't severe, and they responded to aspirin or ibuprofen, but he was certain the drug caused them. Gradually, he noticed something peculiar—more and more, the headaches were accompanied by something like a light show. He became aware of yellow spots—usually circular, but occasionally oblong or irregular shapes—that would float randomly across a black field. He could see the shapes even when his eyes were closed or covered with his hands. In fact, if he pressed against his eyes, the number of spots would increase, and their color would grow more vivid, more intense; then separate lights would coalesce into one glowing spot with hazy borders.

"Phosphenes!" Dr. Patel exclaimed, when Trey called to report the floating shapes. "Light patterns usually caused by manually stimulating the retina—rubbing your eyes, say. Other types of stimulation can do it—some drugs can cause them. Some blind people experience them even when they can't actually see anything, but if your optic nerve isn't functioning at all, you won't get them. If you're seeing them now, it means your optic nerve is recovering! We need to call Dr. Russell."

"You think my sight is coming back?" Trey gripped the arm of his chair and leaned forward.

"We'll have to wait and see how far this goes. But this really is promising! We always hoped for something like this, but we didn't expect it yet—the dose was so small. But it seems to be working, or starting to."

For several days, Trey found himself touching his closed eyes, pressing them, rubbing them the way he used to when he first woke up in the morning, back when he could still see. He wanted both to experience the sensation of light and to see if it would change as the days went by. Within a few days, colors besides yellow began to appear—purple first, then green. He had to fight an incessant urge to rub his eyes—he was afraid he'd damage them.

A little over three weeks after the phosphenes appeared, Trey's brother, Bob, came by on a Sunday evening to help Trey with his bills. Either Bob or Trey's oldest sister, Silvia, came over once a week to help him handle those. Trey preferred Bob—he never completely forgave his sisters for tormenting him when they were kids—even though he sensed Bob wasn't comfortable around him. Bob carried the same mitochondrial mutation Trey did, and expected to end up like him. But LHON is a fickle and unpredictable disease, and regular eye exams had shown no problems with Bob's vision so far.

Bob let himself in with his own house key, as usual. Most of the house was dark—Trey had no need for lights. Bob had put a few lights on timers, to keep the house from looking unoccupied. But it was dark in the bedroom-turned-office where Trey piled his mail on a desk each day for Bob or his sister to sort through later. Trey was on his treadmill in the living room.

"Trey, I'm here!" Bob called out loudly.

Trey knew the route to his office by heart and could walk there as fast as anyone with eyesight could. Bob got there just behind Trey; he groped inside the doorway for the switch and turned on the light.

The dark field in front of Trey, all of it, immediately turned gray, many shades lighter than the blackness that was always there. Trey, stunned, grabbed the doorframe with his left hand to steady himself.

"Oh my god! I saw it when you turned the light on! I can see the light now!" He paused. "Nothing else, just the light. It changed color. It's lighter; grayish, not white. Turn it off! Let me see it again."

Bob clicked the light off for a fraction of a second, then on again.

"Yes! Yes! Everything went dark, then light again! I saw it!"

"Wait here a minute," Bob said. "I'll be right back." He had long ago placed a flashlight by the front door, so he would always know where one was if the house was dark when he arrived. When he returned, he pointed the light at Trey's face and turned it on.

"I saw that! What did you do?"

"I shined a flashlight in your eyes. Here, I'm moving it back and forth. Can you see that?"

"I think so. ... Wait a minute. Move it to one side, then slowly across in front of me. ... Okay. I could see a slight change in intensity moving from left to right, I think. Is that what you were doing?"

Bob thought for an instant Trey had it backward. "No. Wait, yes, from *your* left to right. It took me a second there. I was thinking *my* left and right. We should call your eye doctor."

Bob pulled out his cell phone; Dr. Patel's office and cell phone numbers were listed in his Contacts. He brought up the home number, pressed the call button, and put the phone in Trey's hand. "Here. You should be the one to tell him."

11. "There's something in front of me...."

Kathy—Week 10, Tuesday, A.M.

For two weeks, Kathy's progress seemed to stop with being able to tell light from dark. She began to think that was all her recovery would amount to. But on a Tuesday, just one day after an eye exam showed no further change in her sensitivity to light, Kathy opened her eyes when the alarm went off at seven a.m. and was shocked—the formerly dark field in front of her was now filled with shapes and colors. The suddenness of it was breathtaking. Her vision seemed to have sprung forth all at once, fully formed, like Athena from the head of Zeus.

Her scream had something of both alarm and delight in it. Her mother came running from downstairs. "Kathy? What is it? What's wrong?"

"I can see! I can see! ... I think... I can see. But I can't make out what anything is. I see something in front of me when I open my eyes. But I can't tell what anything is, or how far away it is. I reach out my hand thinking I'll touch something, and it's not there." She was sitting up now, her legs dangling over the side of the bed. She waved her arms in front of her the way she did only when she was completely disoriented and trying to find the nearest wall or object. That only happened if she drifted off to sleep in a chair and woke up suddenly, or when she woke up in the middle of a dream. Those were the only times her blindness brought her close to panic. "There's something in front of me, but I can't touch it. Is that you, Mom?" She reached out toward something that seemed to be changing shape in front of her, and felt her mother grasp both her hands.

Kathy was horrified to realize her mother was right in front of her, close enough to touch, but she could see nothing even vaguely resembling the image of her mother she had tried to hold onto when everything else had faded out. Kathy tried to call up that image every time she heard her mother's voice or felt her touch. She was never sure if it was one she had actually seen or one she simply imagined, but she clung to it fiercely. Had all those dark years cost her even that?

She realized tears were streaming down her cheeks; perhaps that was why she couldn't see anything clearly. She asked for something to wipe her eyes with. Shara sat down next to Kathy and pressed a wad of tissues into her hand, then put her arm around her and pulled her closer. "Are you okay? This is wonderful! You can actually see again?" She knelt in front of Kathy, her hands on Kathy's knees, and gazed up at her face, looking for some glimmer of recognition in her eyes. But they moved around, unfocused, restless as ever; Shara could not lock eyes with Kathy, try as she might.

Kathy separated the wad of tissues into two bundles and pressed one tightly to each eye. She said nothing until the tears stopped, then carefully opened her eyes and tried to focus on Shara, who was peering into her face. Kathy saw only a jumble of colors and indistinct shapes. Everything seemed to be moving, though she knew her mother wasn't, because she had both hands on Kathy's knees, waiting for her reply.

"I don't know what I'm seeing! Everything's so confused. I can't keep my eyes open! Everything is moving so much. You're not moving, are you?"

"No, I'm right here. It's your eyes, honey. They're still moving around on their own, like they've always done. Don't panic. I'm sure you'll get control of them. Right now, they're not moving together, so of course you can't focus on anything. It'll be all right. I'm here." She hugged Kathy. "Don't be afraid. Close your eyes and get dressed like you normally do. I'll get my phone. Your father left for work early today. I won't call him until he gets there; he might run off the road if we tell him about this while he's driving. We'll call the study doctors first. This is wonderful!" She went downstairs, where she'd left her phone; it had several numbers in it, including Dr. Stark's. Besides being Kathy's doctor when she went blind, he was the lead ophthalmologist for the trial.

When Shara dialed Stark's number, his assistant answered. Shara explained why she was calling, and the assistant couldn't hold back her own excitement.

"She can see now? Oh, wow! Dr. Stark's in a meeting, but I'll go get him. He'll want to talk to you right now! Hold on, please, I'll be right back."

Shara was on hold less than a minute before Stark came on the line. He was excited, too; he skipped a greeting altogether, and his words came rapid-fire. Shara was startled when his voice came through and he immediately asked a question, without any pleasantries.

"When Kathy went to bed last night, all she could do was tell light from dark, and this morning she can see?"

"Oh! Sorry, doctor, I didn't know you picked up. Yes, that's what happened. But she can't see normally yet. Everything's a jumble of colors and shapes that won't hold still."

"Did she say anything about the light hurting her eyes?"

"No, she didn't. She *is* having trouble keeping her eyes open, though. She says everything's confusing. Everything's moving."

"It's probably nystagmus. Her eyes have been moving on their own for years. It may take her some time to control them. She may also have trouble with strabismus for a while, where each eye focuses on something different. Tell her not to worry. It'll get better. Look, I'd like to examine her as soon as possible. Today if we can. We'll send someone to pick her up if you need us to. If what she's seeing bothers her, tell her it's okay to close her eyes. Dark glasses may help. She can even wear a sleep mask or blindfold, if she wants to. It might help with her exam if she doesn't try to use her eyes much until we can look at them."

To him, she's a guinea pig, Shara thought. She could understand that. The more they could learn from Kathy, the better. "We can come today, if Kathy's okay with it. You don't have to send anyone. I'll drive her in. I want to be with her anyway. Let me see what she says. Or you can talk to her now. She's right here."

"That would be great."

Kathy had little to add, except to say she would come as soon as she could get ready. She didn't tell him she hoped he could reassure her. She felt overwhelmed and, to her surprise, afraid. She had been convinced at first that the drug wouldn't work at all, and then that it would do no more than let her tell light from dark. Now she could see—but something wasn't right. Kathy had sometimes tried to imagine how wonderful the world might look if she could see; she never dreamed it could be so terrifying.

12. *"I can't make out your face...."*

Kathy—Week 10, Tuesday, P.M.

DR. STARK PUT KATHY THROUGH a complete battery of eye tests. Some were maddeningly difficult—her eyes would not stay still very long. But with persistence, Stark managed to determine that her pupils responded normally to light, that the intraocular pressure inside her eyes was within the normal range, and that her retinas appeared normal. He couldn't measure her visual acuity completely, because she was unable to focus even one eye on anything very long, or to focus both eyes at the same time. After years of disuse, her eyes seemed to have their own agenda; they stubbornly refused to look where she wanted them to.

Based on the experiences of people with congenital cataracts who had their vision surgically restored after years of blindness, her problems weren't surprising. The drug had restored neural connections lost for two decades, but whether it restored them correctly was anyone's guess. The visual cortex in Kathy's brain may have been reprogrammed to handle other tasks once visual input from the optic nerves ceased when she was still a child. She was now past the age by which the development of the brain was usually considered complete, though the more scientists learned about it, the longer the period of development seemed to get. The brain's full capacity to repair and reprogram itself is not yet known. While OGF83 had regrown neurons in Kathy's visual system, no one could say whether the new cells would function normally. The drug seemed to restore normal vision in lab animals, as far as that could be measured. But rats and monkeys can't tell you what they're seeing.

The experience of patients after congenital cataract removal had shown that sight and seeing are not the same. After the surgery, people had eyes that functioned normally, but they still had to learn how to see, how to integrate visual information with the information they got from their other senses to form a coherent picture of the world—a hugely difficult task for people who had never seen a picture.

Stark wanted Kathy to know what she was facing. Literally overnight, she had gone from blind to sighted, but her brain hadn't caught up with the change. Maybe it never would. She had the capacity to see, but learning to use it might take a long time and a lot of work. No matter how well Kathy had thought she understood that before, now that she had actually seen what she faced, Stark expected her to be both fearful and depressed. He didn't want to make it worse, but he didn't want to sugar-coat it, either. After completing all his tests, he sat directly opposite her. She tried to keep her gaze fixed on him, but her eyes stubbornly wandered, refusing to focus on anything long enough for her to get a clear image of it.

"You know you're going to have to learn how to see again. It might not be easy."

Kathy could tell where the sound was coming from, but could not fix her eyes on his face. "I know. It might take a while to get used to this. Right now, it would be easier to just close my eyes and walk around blind the way I'm used to. I know where everything in the house is; I don't need to see it. It's been a long time since my parents moved the furniture because I was bad." She laughed. "Just kidding. It was only last week." She grinned. "No, really, they've never done anything like that."

Stark laughed. "I'm glad you can keep a sense of humor about it. I think that'll help you a lot. I don't know how long it will take you to get control of your eye movements, especially since your blindness was neurological. In the early days of cataract surgery, adults who had congenital cataracts removed faced the same problem you have; they usually overcame it in a matter of days, weeks at most. They usually had a problem you don't seem to have—for a while after the operation, they were blinded by light; it was very painful. You seem to have missed that. Maybe your eyes were adapting to light during those weeks before you could see, when you could tell light from dark."

Kathy tried to focus on his face as best she could. "It does hurt when I open my eyes, but I don't think it's physical. I think it's more psychological. I see things, but I can't make any sense of them. I only see fragments, colors and shapes... and they're always moving. Nothing will stay still! You know what hurts most? I thought I remembered my mother's face. I tried hard to hold onto that all while I was blind. But this morning, I knew I must be looking right at her, and what I saw didn't look anything at all like what I remembered, or thought I remembered."

His voice softened. "You haven't seen your mother in over twenty years. She wouldn't look the way you remember even if you did manage to keep a mental picture of her all those years. You'll recognize her again soon, I'm sure of it. Recognizing faces is something hard-wired in the brain. Babies can do it. I'm sure you'll get it back, once you get control of your eyes again. Give it a few days, and see if it doesn't start getting better." He smiled, but Kathy couldn't see it.

A distressing thought occurred to her. "I can't make out your face right now, either, and you're right in front of me, too."

"I'm not surprised, not the way your eyes are still moving. Would you like an eye mask to wear when you feel overwhelmed? I'd like you not to wear it all the time—in fact, I'd like you to use it as little as possible. Only when you feel like you *have* to block everything out, to get a little rest. The more you use your eyes, the faster you'll learn to control them. The world will look less scary then."

"I sure hope so. Because it's really scary now." She twisted her hands together nervously.

"It'll get better, I promise. Do you think you could come in every day for the next week or two? You have priority over all my other patients, except emergencies; we'll even reschedule some patients if necessary. Pick whatever times work for you. I'll have my receptionist set it up. We'll send someone to pick you up if you need it. There's so much we can learn from you by watching how your vision develops. You can do an enormous amount for science."

And for your career, she thought, but kept that to herself. She couldn't blame him.

13. "We're in new territory here"

Trey—Weeks 10-15

For several weeks, Trey's visual world contained no objects, only areas—light and dark patches with hazy boundaries. He could tell when he came to a doorway or window, or when something blocked part of his visual field.

Even this limited recovery was exciting. It galled Trey no end that he had to keep it largely to himself. The trial patients had been required to sign Non-Disclosure Agreements before they got the drug. Among other things, they were specifically asked not to post anything on social media, and not to let their families do it, either. Cardon wanted to keep control of any news that might come from the trial, good or bad. The company knew people would talk to family or friends if anything happened; they asked that the patients be discreet about it and ask anyone they did tell not to spread it around.

So when Trey got a phone call from Al Guttmacher, the only person at Lenevar Field Services who still kept in touch with him now and then, he had some qualms about telling him the news, such as it was, but felt he could trust him to keep it close.

"My God, Trey, you think your sight's coming back? This new drug can actually do that?"

"Let's not jump the gun. I can tell light from dark, that's all. But I couldn't even do that before, so there's hope. They told us the drug's restored sight completely in rats and monkeys. Only that was at higher doses than what we're getting right now. They want to be careful until they're sure the stuff isn't going to poison us. So don't go telling a lot of people, okay? They don't want to have to apologize for getting people's hopes up if we all start dropping dead all of a sudden. There's no guarantee we won't." Trey laughed.

"Sure, I understand. You must be pretty excited, though. You hear about miracle drugs, but they never seem to work out like people hope. Or else they cost an arm and a leg, even if they grow you one back. They always say, 'Insurance'll pay it,' but premiums keep going up. Insurance people must get sick every time they hear about a new drug being approved. They know it'll be expensive."

"That's probably true. But hey, I'm glad you called. How're things at Lenevar?" Trey wasn't sure how much he wanted to know. He was kind of pissed off that only Al still bothered to call him up now and then. *You'd think I was contagious.*

"Not good. Oil prices are still way down. I think I'm hanging on by a thread. They've laid some people off, and that may not be over yet. The company still has a few big contracts, and it's been through this kind of thing before and come out okay. I've managed to hang on this far, knock on wood. I'm not buying anything big for a while, though. At least I got my car paid off."

"Well, hang in there. It's good to hear from you. I haven't heard much from anyone else there. Though I guess I've been gone a long time now, huh? Wonder how many people still remember me? I guess the ones still hanging on would. When a crunch comes, the newbies usually go first. You've been there a while." After a short pause, Trey said, "I've got to go now, but good to hear from you. I'll let you know if anything changes." But he wasn't at all certain that he would.

* * *

About three weeks after the call from Al Guttmacher, Trey's recovery suddenly accelerated, his vision getting better literally by the day. As the borders around light and dark areas grew more distinct, features within the areas gradually appeared.

Oddly, though the first sign of his recovery was the appearance of phosphenes in different colors, as objects began to appear Trey largely saw them in shades of gray as his vision recovered from the periphery in. He had lost central vision first; now it seemed he would get it back last. This was disconcerting. The urge to look directly at something to see it better was irresistible, but initially things were more blurry at the center of his visual field than at the edges. It wasn't until objects directly in front of him began to come into better focus that color began to creep back in. First a greenish cast appeared in some gray areas, mostly near the edges, but green objects soon appeared. When he first saw some large green expanses outside, it took him a few seconds to realize he was looking at lawns. A few days after, he started seeing shades of red and yellow; another week and blue appeared. For several weeks until everything came into focus, Trey's world looked like a painting by Monet.

The speed with which his vision returned was dizzyingly fast after three years of darkness. In just a few weeks, ghostly grayish shadows with fuzzy boundaries became distinct shapes with different colors that then turned into chairs and tables, trees and cars, knives and forks and spoons. And faces. Trey was astonished when he first saw his face in the bathroom mirror; he looked much older than he expected. *Being blind must have done that.*

During this period, Dr. Patel came by Trey's house several nights a week to assess his progress, while Trey went to Patel's office near the Medical School each Monday morning at eight-thirty for more thorough testing. One of the data collectors working on the trial would pick him up and take him home. It was during one of the Monday morning sessions that Patel raised a disturbing possibility when Trey asked a simple question.

"How long do we keep doing all these tests?" Trey's voice betrayed a hint of impatience.

"We'll still need to keep them up after the trial ends. Leber's is a mitochondrial disease, and you still have the mitochondrial mutations that cause it. The drug doesn't change that. I don't want to sound discouraging, but we can't be sure the disease won't come back. If it does, the drug might be able to reverse it again, but we don't really know. We're in new territory here."

14. Exposed

Paul Lazarus/Lindsey (Lin Xi)—Week 15

EVEN WITH OGF83 BEING TESTED in humans, Paul needed to keep working on his experiments in animals, trying to discover just what OGF83 triggered that stimulated optic nerve growth—there was no way such a small protein could do all the work by itself. So he continued to make OGF83 in his lab following the protocol he had developed with his lab technician, Xi Lin, known to everyone as Lindsey. In surname-first China, her name was Lin Xi; that was reversed when she came to the U.S. and her surname became her "last name" on official forms. She clung to her original name after a fashion by adopting "Lindsey" as her "American name", almost always using it when introducing herself.

After receiving a Bachelor of Medicine degree in China, she came to the U.S. for a Master of Public Health degree, hoping to use that to help her get a hospital residency once she passed the U.S. Medical Licensing Exam. She got sidetracked after passing the first two parts of the three-part exam when she discovered she preferred research work in a laboratory to clinical work on patients. Working part-time as a Student Research Assistant while Paul established his laboratory, she quickly proved invaluable performing delicate surgery on laboratory rats. She was so skilled that while she was still a student, Paul got the University to sponsor her for a coveted H1-B visa, reserved for foreign workers who could do jobs for which there were not enough qualified U.S. citizens available. He later persuaded the school to support her application for Permanent Resident status and a green card. She dropped out of the M.P.H. program, and stopped pursuing a U.S. medical license, and was rapidly promoted from Laboratory Technician to Senior Laboratory Assistant. Paul considered her a colleague, and included her name on every paper that came out of his lab.

Paul and Lindsey worked well together, even though he sometimes had difficulty understanding her accent, still heavy after she had been in the U.S. more than a decade. Because of that, Paul rarely spoke to her about anything except work. He knew almost nothing about her personal life, but assumed she had one.

Tonight Paul needed to make a new batch of OGF83 for his next round of experiments. He had already isolated the unmodified protein, then attached the chemical groups that stabilized it and made it useful as a drug. Now he needed to adjust the pH of the buffer solution it was in from alkaline to neutral by carefully adding a few drops of hydrochloric acid at a time to the beaker and watching as the needle on the pH meter slowly swung from nine to seven. It was important not to let the pH drop below seven. If the solution became acidic it would form a gas containing molecules of OGF83. The finished drug was administered in an aerosol spray in humans, but as a controlled dose squirted directly into the nasal passages; if the solution formed a free-floating gas, there would be no way to control the dose.

The procedure was routine; Paul had done it dozens of times. It was one of the few tasks in the lab he would not delegate to Lindsey. Though the process was carried out in a fume hood, making the chances of ever inhaling the compound minimal in any event, he felt that if anyone were to run the risk, it should be him, not Lindsey.

Everything went as expected until Paul's finger slipped on the valve of the titration flask containing the acid and, instead of a few drops, a stream of hydrochloric acid splashed into the buffer. The needle on the pH meter immediately swung all the way down to five.

"Goddamn it!" Paul moved too quickly in closing the valve, knocking the titration stand sideways and overturning the beaker containing the now-acidic buffer solution. This would not have been serious had the spilled buffer stayed under the fume hood, where any escaping gases would be vented to the air above the building, but Paul had set up the apparatus too near the front of the hood; almost half of the buffer spilled from under the hood and splashed onto the floor.

Hearing the commotion, Lindsey rushed over to see what had happened.

"No!" Paul shouted. "No! Stay away! I let the solution turn acid and knocked it over. Get out until I get it cleaned up. Close the door behind you."

It was too late. Both Paul and Lindsey smelled something sharp and acrid; both had probably inhaled not only the buffer, but some amount of OGF83. How much, Paul had no idea. He grabbed several absorbent pads from the nearest bench top and slapped them on top of the spill. Time was critical. He mopped the floor with the pads and threw them in the fume hood. He then started mopping up what he'd spilled inside the hood itself. But in his hurry, he leaned too far into the hood; the acrid odor filled his nostrils again. He had been exposed to the fumes twice in the same accident.

He stuffed a bench pad into the beaker to soak up what little buffer solution remained in it, then stuffed all the pads and his gloves into a biohazard bag, taped it closed, and dumped everything into a biohazard container for disposal. Once he had everything cleaned up, he considered whether to report the accident to the Safety Office as required. But he hesitated. Lindsey probably hadn't inhaled a significant dose. She was at least six feet from the spill at her closest approach, and she left the lab within seconds once he told her to get out. He doubted even he had anything to worry about, despite being exposed twice. The acidity of the solution probably inactivated the drug. Reporting the accident would just lead to a tedious investigation and even more tedious monitoring of both of them for possible effects.

He decided it would be better not to report it, but he had to clear the decision with Lindsey. She simply shrugged; to her, it was just another routine spill, nothing to worry about.

Paul still needed another batch of the drug, so he set the apparatus up again. This time, he tried to go through each step as carefully as if he were doing it for the first time.

15. *"...Some pretty astounding results"*

Paul—Week 16

JIM RUSSELL HAD GIVEN PAUL periodic updates by phone since the trial started, but their frequency had slipped as time passed. When first Patient 1 and then Patient 9 had shown signs of recovering vision, Russell immediately notified Paul, but he waited until both had regained actual vision before he called Paul in for a more complete briefing one Monday afternoon.

"So what's it look like now, Jim? You said you had some pretty astounding results."

Russell looked down at his notes. "Let's get the less astounding ones out of the way first. For everyone, the only consistent negative side effect is still headaches. They're usually mild and fade over time. They were bad enough in Patient 3 that he said he probably couldn't go on to the second phase, though if his vision improves any, he'll try to stick it out. But he hasn't shown any measurable response yet. So far, Patients 2, 6, and 10 show no response, either, and only mild headaches. But six patients have shown measurable improvements. Patients 4 and 7 can tell when you turn a light on or off—not perfectly yet, but they couldn't do it at all before. Patient 4 can do it about seventy-five percent of the time and Patient 7 hits it about ninety percent, so they're not just guessing. Patient 5 could tell light from dark even before we started, but now she can see different colors, at least the main ones—red, yellow, blue, green, the primary ones. She can't distinguish shapes yet, but she can detect when colors cover only part of her visual field—that is, if you show her a red circle and a yellow square at the same time, she can see the different colors, but she can't tell you the shapes. Patient 8 is showing some color perception, but it's odd, and we're not quite sure what's going on."

Paul frowned, cocking his head slightly. "'Showing some color perception.' How's that different from the one who can see colors? She's seeing different colors but getting them wrong?"

Russell smiled like a magician about to unveil his greatest trick. "Actually, she's not seeing different colors—she's not even responding to light and dark so far. She's hearing them."

"Hearing them? What?"

"She didn't lose her sight until she was in her thirties. She still knows colors very well, though she's had no perception of any since she went blind. Now she's seeing colored flashes when she hears sounds. Some sounds, anyway—a thunderclap is bright orange, she says, but a handclap is green. Music is pulsating shades of violet. She says the flashes appear in front of her, like she's seeing them—she's not just imagining colors in her head, she's actually perceiving them somehow. She also sees colored phosphenes when she rubs her eyes, which she couldn't before."

Paul was still thinking about the sound/light connection. "She has some form of synesthesia...."

"Yes. So the drug may be causing some cross-talk in the neural pathways. It's not clear where this could go. We don't know if any other senses will become involved yet. Will tastes have colors? Smells? We have to follow this up. What we're really focused on right now, though, is the two patients I called you about earlier. Are you ready for this? They can both see again!"

"Just like before they went blind?" Paul looked puzzled, his glance darting back and forth, as if he were looking for the answer.

"Not quite, not for Patient 1. She lost her eyesight as a child and she's twenty-six or twenty-seven now, I forget, so she was blind a long time. Her brain's had a lot of time to rewire itself, so she probably has a lot more to relearn. Patient 9 started losing his sight in his early thirties, and he's only been completely blind about three years."

"But they both have eyesight back?" Paul was having trouble making sense of this.

"Patient 9, almost completely. Patient 1, not yet. She's seeing a jumble of shapes and colors, and has trouble separating them. She can recognize some individual objects, but only under controlled conditions. She still has trouble focusing. She's also having a lot of problems with depth perception. She can't judge distances. She sees everything as two-dimensional, even though both her eyes work. Her brain just doesn't seem to be processing spatial information. This is something we wouldn't be surprised to see in someone who'd been blind since birth. In the early days of cataract surgery, doctors operated on adults who had congenital cataracts and had never been able to see anything. Most of them had no concept of space. They had to learn to see spatially. Some never did. It's a bit more surprising in her case. We know she could see spatially at one time, but she's apparently lost that. Carl Stark is working with her to see if she can get it back. But it's not an overnight thing."

"So, what, she's walking into walls?"

"More like she isn't walking because she's afraid she *will* walk into walls. She won't walk with her eyes open. She says everything looks like it's directly in front of her, close enough to touch it, though there's nothing there when she tries to. She gets around better with her eyes closed, using a cane like she was still blind. Carl's trying to get her to walk with her eyes open, but he can't just take away her cane."

Paul was silent for several seconds, his brow furrowed. He let out a long breath before speaking. "I think we might have a problem."

Russell was surprised. "A problem? You've cured blindness! It's not perfect, but still…."

"The problem is, we weren't supposed to yet. There's no reason the drug should've worked yet. We calculated the first dose so it wouldn't. On a per-kilogram basis, the first dose was equivalent to one that caused only partial nerve growth in monkeys, not enough for them to get their vision back. Not a single monkey."

"Humans aren't monkeys."

"Exactly. That means the drug's not acting in humans the way it did in monkeys. The second dose we calculated is equivalent to one that restored sight in about twenty percent of monkeys. The third dose was large enough to bring it back in about seventy-five percent. That was going to be our baseline dose in Phase 2, and we would go up from there. But counting the partial responses, we've got better than twenty percent response at a dose that shouldn't have worked at all."

Russell's puzzled look didn't change. "I still don't see why that's a problem."

"Think about it. We deliberately made the dose too small to work—we thought. But it's working. That means the drug isn't behaving in people like it does in rats and monkeys. We don't know what it could do."

"Come on, Paul. It's doing exactly what you want! It's regrowing people's optic nerves."

"And if we're lucky, that's all it's doing. But we don't know that. How are your other tests coming out?"

"We haven't found any problems so far. See? The drug's doing fine. Better than fine."

Paul shook his head. "Better than fine worries me. I don't like it that it's not acting like we predicted. I need to think about this. And Jim?"

"Yes?"

"You need to look harder for side effects. That woman with synesthesia bothers me. The drug seems to be doing more than it's supposed to in her case. It's affected more than just her optic nerves, and we never saw any evidence for that before."

Paul left, looking distracted. Jim Russell shook his head as the door shut. *Damn! He comes up with a cure for blindness, and you'd think he just lost his dog.*

16. "We've all been blind about this"

Trey—Week 18

Patients in the OGF83 trial were brought in to Cardon periodically for physical examinations, questionnaires, and interviews, all designed to detect any problems that might be traced to the drug. The procedures took half a day, but Trey did not find them onerous at first. As his vision rapidly improved and he emerged from darkness, he was elated, and that feeling lasted several weeks. But he gradually grew aware of a disquieting undercurrent, a foreboding, something wrong he couldn't quite see, something just beyond the range of his restored vision.

It finally struck him one morning as he shaved that no one, least of all him, had really planned for what might happen if the drug actually worked. *No one thought it would work so soon. They normally use healthy people in the first trials, so whether the drug actually works or not doesn't matter. They're still thinking that way. They didn't expect anyone to get their sight back yet, they told us that. It didn't occur to them it could be a problem if you did. They figured you'd just go back to your life, only now you could see. But it's not that simple. I'm living on a disability pension. What happens if I'm not disabled anymore? What do I do then? Can I just go back to what I was? How would I do that? We've all been blind about this.*

When the data collector who came to pick him up that morning tried to make small talk, Trey responded mostly in monosyllables, thinking of what lay ahead. A physical exam. An interview by Dr. Russell. Then some questionnaires—read to him, because nobody had ever expected any trial patients to be able to read printed questionnaires. *They're so locked into this, they insist on reading me the questions when I can read them myself. Just follow the protocol.*

The physical was routine—no further problems since the early head-aches, which had faded out. After he got through the questionnaires—they were the same as always—Trey was ushered into Russell's office, where the doctor was staring at a computer screen. Russell looked up and smiled broadly. "Trey, you haven't had any problem at all adjusting to getting your sight back, have you? That's not true of everyone. I think it's been easier for you because you'd only been blind a few years when the trial started. Some of the—"

"Wait a minute," Trey broke in. "'That's not true of everyone.' Other people got their sight back, too?"

"Well, I can't really talk much about other patients, but yes, some have responded to the drug. One almost as much as you, but that one hasn't adjusted nearly as well. That patient had been blind much longer than you. In your case, the parts of your brain that handled vision probably hadn't changed much. I imagine you could still remember images from before. You hadn't forgotten people's faces, had you?"

"No, not really. Not even the ones I wish I had, like my ex-wife's."

The doctor laughed somewhat ruefully, Trey thought; he must have been through a divorce, himself. Russell looked at the computer screen again. "According to Dr. Patel, your visual acuity has gotten much better of late. I don't know if it'll get all the way to 20/20, but it's getting closer. The drug's worked for you far better than anyone dared to hope, though we still need to look for any side effects. Physically, everything seems great. How's your state of mind right now? Have you noticed any mood changes since the initial excitement of getting your sight back? Any feelings of depression or anxiety?"

Trey paused, shifting uneasily, then looked straight into Russell's eyes. "Well, one thing's been worrying me a lot."

"What's that?"

"I retired on disability when I couldn't see well enough to work any-more. Now I can see again. I'd like to go back to work, but what with the oil bust, my old job's probably gone. I heard the company downsized after I left, and oil prices are still down. I doubt if anyone's hiring much in my line of work right now."

"You're worried you might lose your disability pension and be stuck with no job."

"Yeah, a lot. I was finally starting to accept that I was blind, and all of a sudden I can see again. I feel kind of like Rip Van Winkle when he woke up. Everything kept moving, but I didn't. I got left behind."

"But you're better off now than you were, aren't you?"

"Of course. Why would you even ask that? No one was happier than me when my sight came back. But nobody thought it would happen this soon. Everybody said, 'Wait till Phase 2'. For me, Phase 2 is here. I have to figure out what's next."

"Well, we're not ready to go public yet. The trial's still going on. But when all this is over, you're going to be famous. I bet you'll get offered book deals, public appearances. I don't think you need to worry about going broke. You could be a motivational speaker!"

"Really? What could I say to motivate people? Be good, work hard, and wait for a miracle drug? I don't want to be the poster child for a new drug. I'd like my life back, and I have a chance now. How do I start? You have a career counsellor for this?

"We hadn't really planned that far, I have to say. That's not something we've had to worry much about before, you know? Especially in Phase 1 trials. We're usually testing healthy people then. In trials with sick people, if the drug works, they get better or survive longer, and everybody just goes on from there. I can see where blindness might be a little different. I understand your concern. But I wish you'd look on the bright side here."

Trey grew annoyed at Russel's bland obtuseness. "Look, I don't want to sound like I'm whining. But I was an engineer. We have to anticipate things before they happen, not wait until they do. Designing a project, you ask, 'Okay, what's the worst case here?' You learn that every decision you make early on affects what you can do later. I'm only trying to figure out what's going to happen now. I thought if I was lucky, I might get part of my vision back, maybe just tell dark from light, and I'd get the rest back in Phase 2, after a bigger dose. But we're way past that already."

"Look, as far as your disability goes, don't worry, I'm not going to call up your old company and tell them, 'Hey, you remember Trey Osborne, who retired because he went blind? Well, he can see again.' That's between you and the company."

"That's very nice of you," Trey said, with more sarcasm than he intended, "but you think this isn't going to get out before you're ready?

People talk. I know I told someone from where I used to work that I was in a trial, though I said we didn't expect much. I think I talked to him around the time I was just starting to see light, before I knew what was about to happen. Who knows who he might have told? I didn't swear him to secrecy. I didn't see any reason to, I didn't give him enough detail to really tell other people about it. That was a while back...." He paused for a few seconds. "You know, I just realized he hasn't called me since then." He paused again. "Maybe he's not as good a friend as I thought.... I really haven't talked with anyone from the company besides him since just after I retired. A lot of them said, 'Let's stay in touch,' but we didn't. It works both ways. I mean, I haven't called them, either. You know, when you stop working with people, you realize how little you really had in common with them. Just work, and then that's gone. And I'd gone blind on top of that, and that cuts you off even more. People act like they're afraid it's contagious. After a month or so, almost nobody called anymore. But I didn't call them, either." Another pause. "You know, I'm not trying to cheat anybody. I'd like to go back to work, but I don't know if I can un-retire. I could get stuck with no job and no other income."

Russell squirmed uncomfortably in his chair. He tried to adopt a more sympathetic tone—it wasn't something that came naturally. "Nobody expected the kind of response you've shown. The dose you got was below the therapeutic dose in any of the animal studies. We thought the drug was a long shot in your case, anyway, because none of the animals it worked on had anything like Leber's. I'm as eager as you are to know what's going to happen."

Trey sighed, as if resigned to the unfairness of it all. "Yeah, I can appreciate that. It's not you I'm pissed off at, you know. But when this is all over, you get your name on a paper, and I try to go back to a job that may not be there anymore."

"I understand that. I'll help you if I can. But I don't really know what I can do right now."

"I don't, either." Trey drew a deep breath and let it out. "Sometimes success can knock you on your ass, can't it?"

17. All the Way to Meltdown

Paul—Week 18

PAUL TRIED TO PUT THE lab spill behind him, but it kept nagging at him.
He looked for anything out of the ordinary, but—what? They'd tried the
drug in controls, healthy animals, but had seen nothing abnormal. If
you already had functional optic nerves, the drug didn't grow new ones.
The animals went about their business. As did Paul. He did notice every
twinge, every fleeting pain, every momentary lapse of concentration or
memory, every misplaced pen or key ring or cup of coffee, but nothing seemed out of the ordinary. Yet he worried. The incredibly strong
response in two trial volunteers should have buoyed him immensely—
but he couldn't help thinking that they probably hadn't received much
more of the drug than he had when he spilled it. In humans, OGF83
was apparently capable of working at vanishingly small doses. Neither
he nor anyone else had expected that. But in his own case, he couldn't
pin any specific symptoms on the drug. Maybe he hadn't inhaled any of
it after all—maybe all he'd inhaled was the smell of buffer. Maybe he'd
been lucky. All he could do was go about his work as usual. Not all of
it involved his lab. He had other responsibilities as a faculty member.

The Graduate School of Medical Sciences at Southeast Texas State
was not large—it had about 50 full-time faculty members. Overshad-
owed by the Medical School, the Graduate School seemed to suffer from
an inferiority complex, though the administration kept trying to find
ways to make it stand out more. In the state legislature, the University
of Texas and Texas A&M got most of the attention, and the lion's share
of the money. The rest of the state's public universities fought over what
was left, and Southeast Texas State won few battles. The University's
resources were limited and unevenly distributed. The Graduate School

didn't even have its own building. It was housed on four floors in the West Wing of the Medical School building; most people in the medical center thought it was part of the Medical School, and since more than half the faculty had academic appointments in both schools, it nearly was. Kurt Herzenmacher, the head of Molecular Biology, was the Graduate School's biggest name. Accordingly, he had the biggest lab and the most resources, which he zealously guarded. Because of that, he had more influence than anyone else—even the Dean—on any school policies that affected the distribution of money, lab space, and students.

Like most of the faculty, Paul didn't care for Herzenmacher, who only cultivated friendships with people who might do him some good. Paul, like many on the faculty, felt that Herzenmacher got as far as he had less for what he knew than for whom. Science may be more of a meritocracy than many other fields, but even in science, money tends to follow money. Someone who's gotten ten grants often has an easier time getting an eleventh than someone with one grant has of getting a second one, and not always because the one with the most grants has the best ideas.

Paul tried to stay out of any arguments about the distribution of resources within the school, but it was precisely because of his perceived neutrality that the Dean of the Graduate School asked him to chair an *ad hoc* committee to examine the way money was apportioned among departments for students. All incoming students had to serve internships in two different labs their first year, and departments with more money could offer more internships. The smaller departments wanted internship funds to be centralized, so they could better compete for students. If three students wanted to intern in Pharmacology, but the department only had money for two, one of the three had to find another department. The larger departments, particularly Molecular Biology, strongly opposed having a central fund. Paul's committee was to devise at least three different plans for apportioning money for students among the departments, which the faculty would vote on.

It was exactly the kind of thing Paul hated to do. Just getting committee meetings scheduled was a pain in the ass; devising alternative plans for distributing the funds was like having a boil there lanced. They came up with three new plans, plus the status quo—four options to consider.

It took three months to work out the details. The committee—though primarily Paul—then distilled descriptions of the four plans into a six-page document. The Dean sent it out to the faculty a week before the quarterly general faculty meeting, strongly emphasizing the need for everyone to read it before the meeting, because they would be choosing which of the four plans to adopt.

There were 47 faculty members at the meeting, probably all of them astounded by the turnout. It was all but unprecedented to have that many at any meeting, even "mandatory" ones—no one could remember anyone ever suffering any consequences for missing a mandatory meeting. How to apportion funds for students was clearly a subject of wide interest. After a few preliminary remarks, the Dean gave Paul the floor. He had a few slides to show, but the essentials of the four plans were laid out in a single table; everyone had been given a printed copy.

Paul outlined each plan, briefly summarizing the arguments for and against each one, sticking close to the wording in the table; he then said, "Our committee recommends Option 3. It will give more slots to the smaller departments, and while it will take a few from the larger ones, it doesn't take away as many as the other plans would. It's fairer than what we have now, and it will strengthen the smaller departments in the long run. Overall, we think it's the best one for the school."

A voice from the back of the room broke in—Herzenmacher. "Wait a minute, what's this Option 3 again? I haven't had a chance to look at all of these."

Paul tried to keep an even tone. "Kurt, you know your department has the most to lose if we make any changes, and you haven't looked at any of the plans? Our report went out a week ago. It's only six pages long, including two tables and a figure. Didn't you read it? The dean said it was important for everyone to read it before this meeting."

Herzenmacher's reply was almost sneering. "I don't have time to read everything I get in my e-mail."

Paul didn't go from normal to a boil—he went all the way to meltdown, instantly. His face twisted into a snarl, and his voice rose in volume as he spoke, ending at a level no one in the room had ever heard at a faculty meeting, no matter how heated the discussion. "You mean to tell me we sent out a document you could probably read in fifteen minutes about the most important vote this school has taken in years, one that will affect your department more than any other, AND YOU DIDN'T EVEN BOTHER TO LOOK AT THE GODDAMNED THING? WHO THE FUCK DO YOU THINK YOU ARE?"

Everyone in the room looked shocked. Shouting in faculty meetings wasn't rare, but never like this; this was off the Richter Scale. This was a Paul no one had ever seen before.

Herzenmacher leaped to his feet. "You pissant little one-grant wonder! Do you even have tenure? Who do you think *you* are, talking to me like that?"

Paul just said, "Fuck yourself," quietly, but directly into the microphone, then turned and walked out. He tried to slam the door behind him, but the hydraulic piston that automatically closed the door wouldn't let him.

* * *

David Eamon from Biochemistry, Paul's only close friend on the faculty, was the first person to show up at his office. "Damn, Paul. Where did that come from? No one but Kurt likes Kurt, but no one's ever talked to him like that. Not in public, anyway."

"Maybe it's time someone did. What did the son of a bitch expect? Did he really think the school would just go with whatever plan benefits him most?"

"Probably. It always has before, hasn't it?" David smiled, but it was basically the truth, and neither he nor Paul thought that was funny.

"It's time someone called the smarmy bastard out. How'd the vote go?"

"The issue was 'postponed for further discussion.' You can bet Kurt will pay attention next time. And he'll round up more allies, though I think almost all of them were already there."

"He doesn't have allies, he has lapdogs."

"Well, he'll have all of them. We'll have to see how many we have." As he left, he put his head back in the door. "The dean's on her way."

Dean Helen Bailey Sanders was an M.D., Board-certified in Internal Medicine, who also had a Ph.D. in Epidemiology. She had been affiliated with Southeast Texas State since her residency. The balance she maintained between clinical work and research had shifted decisively toward the latter during the thirty years since, so as her role at the Medical School diminished, her profile at the Graduate School rose, and she was appointed Dean seven years ago. Though not known for her personal warmth, she managed to avoid making serious enemies, which made her the consensus choice as Dean over Herzenmacher, who had been the betting favorite, but, to the shock of many, was passed over. He had pissed off too many people.

She knocked on Paul's door, then walked in before he could respond, shutting the door behind her. She didn't bother to sit, putting her hands, palms down, on the top of his desk and leaning far over it as she spoke. Her tone was not friendly.

"What was that all about, Paul? Proud of yourself now? I wanted to get the vote out of the way today. Now we have to postpone it several weeks, at least."

"I'm sorry it came to that, but if Kurt hadn't looked at the proposals, he would have gotten the vote postponed anyway."

"*I* postponed it, not him! If we'd had the discussion I wanted, I'd have called the vote regardless of what Kurt wanted. But things got too heated after you left. Damn it, Paul, I was depending on you to make the case for Option 3. I thought it would carry. But we ended up with two factions snarling at each other. Trying to ram a change through under the circumstances would only hurt the school. I think it had enough votes, even if Kurt had enough people to make it close. But I can't have a civil war in the school. So *I* called for the postponement, not Kurt. I still think Option 3 will carry, but now he'll have time to rally opposition. Nobody much likes him, but a lot of people are scared of him." She sat down then.

"I'm sorry the way things turned out, but I can't guarantee it wouldn't happen again. The son of a bitch just set me off."

"Well, it won't happen again. Look, I appreciate the job you did on the committee. The report was really good. To summarize everything as well as you did in only six pages—that's not what we usually get around here. Brevity is a lost art. But I'm going to have someone else chair the next meeting. I haven't decided who yet. Someone else on the committee."

"I won't argue with you. I don't even have to be there, if I can get my vote counted."

"I don't have any problem with you coming to the next meeting; I just don't think you should chair it." She got up to leave, but turned and locked eyes with him, her look stone-hard. "Paul? Anger management. You need to work on it. I wouldn't have guessed."

Well, that could have been worse, Paul thought, *but when have I ever exploded like that? In front of everybody! I don't do things like that.*

18. "How long do I have to be miserable?"

Kathy—Week 19

Kathy's daily eye exams stopped after just two weeks; they were exhausting even Dr. Stark. Her vision improved so little from one to the next that Stark moved them from daily to weekly. Kathy had plateaued. Once she learned to control her eye movements and showed some gains in visual acuity, her progress seemed to stop. Her depth perception was all but nonexistent. The only thing that changed was her mood—it went steadily downhill. Part of every exam was a pep talk by Stark urging her not to give up. He felt certain she would improve, despite the lack of any corroborating evidence.

At the end of one exam, Stark and Kathy sat facing each other across his desk as she tried to focus her eyes on him. Everything was blurred; his white coat seemed to blend with the wall. His face was tan, and stood out more, but his eyes were just dark patches on it, his mouth an amorphous slash that changed size when he spoke. Stark seemed as far from her as the wall, though she knew he couldn't be.

His summary was succinct. "I can't see any change at all since last time. Your acuity's the same, and probably your depth perception. It's hard to tell about depth perception when you can't see anything clearly. You're not getting any worse, at least. There doesn't seem to be anything wrong with your eyes—they're responding to light normally. Your brain just hasn't caught up with them. We can't rule out that you're progressing at least a little. It's just very hard to measure right now. We'd be able to get a better idea if your acuity would improve a little. What do you see when I move my hand like this?" He waved his right hand in front of her.

"I can see something moving. I'll have to take your word that it's your hand."

He suddenly thrust his hand straight out toward her face. She did not flinch. She saw something change in front of her, but it did not register as something coming at her, something she should avoid. He gave a short, abrupt "Mm", and she heard a pen scratching on paper in front of her.

"Please", she said, "Can't you tell me what's going on? If my eyes are working like you say they are, why can't I see like I'm supposed to?"

"We think when people go blind, parts of the brain normally used in seeing get shifted to other functions. That's where people got the idea that blind people compensate for their lost vision by developing super-sharp senses of touch and hearing. Their ears aren't any better than other people's. They seem to hear better because they're paying more attention to sounds, and maybe they're using more of their brain to process what they hear.

"Look, nature doesn't waste anything. You've heard the old crap about people only using 10% of their brains? That's garbage. If we only used 10% of our neurons, that's how many we'd end up with after evolution got through with us. It takes too much energy to maintain something if you're not using it. When animals adapt to living in caves, they eventually lose their eyes altogether. Use 'em or lose 'em. It's happened with fish, salamanders, crustaceans, others I can't think of now. … Insects!" Stark suddenly exclaimed, pointing a finger, though the gesture was lost on Kathy. "I can't believe I forgot insects! Animals that far apart in evolution, they all lose their eyes if they live in caves. It's too expensive to keep things around if you never use them. If you're carrying around billions of neurons, you're gonna damn well use them for something.

"If you're blind, you're not using your visual cortex for seeing anymore. What happens to it? If you start using it for something else, what happens if you get your sight back? I think your brain is going to have to reprogram itself, reorganize itself, to take in this new visual information, and that may not be easy, especially for an adult. But I think it can happen. People who've had strokes often recover some of the functions they've lost, even if they can't replace the neurons they lost. The brain puts old neurons to new uses, or it comes up with workarounds. I think yours will, too. It'll just take time."

"But how much time? How long do I have to be miserable? How long will it take for my brain to straighten itself out?" She gave up trying to keep her eyes focused. Everything in front of her started moving again.

"I'm afraid I can't say. No one can. You just have to be patient and keep working at it. You have made progress. When your sight first came back, you couldn't focus your eyes at all. That was easier to fix than your other problems, but it didn't happen overnight." He held his hands up before him, his fingertips nearly touching, then suddenly spread them apart, imploring—a gesture again lost on Kathy. She saw movement, nothing more. "Please don't give up. Don't be discouraged. I know it's hard. You just have to keep working at it. If you do, I really believe it'll get better. I'll do whatever I can to help. I know your mother will, too. You're not in this alone."

For a moment, Kathy was reminded of an evangelist. *He really does believe. It really matters to him. Maybe he's right. He could be right. But....* "I'd feel better about all this if you'd ever had a case like mine before. You haven't, have you? You don't really know if I'm going to get any better, do you? Maybe this is all the eyesight I'm ever going to get. If that's true, I'd just as soon not have it at all. It's not helping anything."

Stark tried to look directly in her eyes, but realized they were wandering again. At least now both were looking in the same direction. "You're right. I don't know. No one does. I don't think there's ever been a case quite like yours before. No one else in the trial responded to the drug the way you have. I've heard of spontaneous recovery from idiopathic blindness, though I've never seen a case myself. We can't explain the recoveries any more than we could explain the blindness. It's possible you'd see more improvement if we increased the drug dose. That's in the trial protocol, but we haven't got that far yet. We don't want to push the dose up until we're sure there's no toxicity at the lowest dose. Don't lose hope yet. I think you'll get better, if you keep working at it."

She sighed. "Yeah, that's what everyone tells me. I can't see any signs of it, though." She paused. "That wasn't a joke, by the way." She smiled weakly.

19. The Swimming Pool

Paul/Lindsey—Week 19, Sunday

WORK IN A RESEARCH LAB is rarely consistent with fixed routines. For Paul, the only thing constant from day to day was the five-thirty alarm. He arrived at the lab by seven and often left long after dark. His main strategy for keeping his weight down was forgetting to eat. Paul tried hard to use the swimming pool at the University's recreation center at least three times a week, even if he couldn't keep to a fixed schedule. It kept him in reasonable shape, and just as important, it turned off the noise in his head for a while—time in the pool was the closest thing to meditation he knew of. He tried to think only of what lap he was on, though stray thoughts about the lab often crept in.

The Sunday after the faculty meeting, Paul was swimming in the last lane of the pool, next to the deep end, when he noticed a chunky woman in a leopard-print bikini splash into the deep water and thought she looked familiar. He couldn't see clearly through his goggles and it took him another lap before he realized it was Lindsey. He'd never seen her at the pool before. He had definitely never seen her in a bikini.

Lindsey didn't have the body for a bikini, but Paul couldn't stop looking. She obviously wasn't used to swimming. She stopped each time she reached the side and held on to catch her breath. Her belly fat made a crease across her stomach halfway between her breasts and navel while she hung onto the wall. Paul's first thought was, *maybe she shouldn't wear a bikini*, but he found her strangely attractive. When she stretched out while swimming, the crease vanished, and her belly looked solid, not flabby at all. Stretching out to swim accentuated her breasts. Paul was astonished; she seemed ready to burst out of her skimpy top. *I had no idea she had tits like that.* The only thing he'd ever seen her in was a lab coat.

He tried to be discreet about staring. Several times he took an extra stroke between breaths, just to see her better. Her long black hair, tied in a ponytail and streaming behind her, just added to the attraction. He tried to slow down to match her pace and keep her in sight longer, but found it difficult. It would have been too conspicuous for him to stop each time and start back across when she did, so he couldn't stay in sync with her very long.

This is ridiculous. She's not that pretty. But damn, I didn't know she looked that good in a bikini.

He hoped she wouldn't finish before he did, and she didn't. After his final lap, he paused for a moment, and then, almost involuntarily, ducked under the lane divider and swam toward her in the deep end, where she was once again clinging to the side. Lindsey looked startled when he approached, and he realized she probably didn't recognize him in his goggles. And she'd never seen *him* half-naked, either.

He grabbed the side of the pool and grinned. "I didn't know you swam."

She blushed, though the glare of the sun and the fact that her face was already red from exertion made it hard to see the added flush of pink. "I'm trying to lose weight."

He was surprised to hear himself say, "You don't need to. You look good in that." He wasn't sure whether he'd crossed a line he shouldn't have. But he meant it.

She blushed even more, her neck and shoulders flushing now, and he couldn't think of anything to say to make things less awkward. The best he could come up with was, "Maybe we'll run into each other here again." He was astonished to find himself wanting to suggest that they arrange to. Not trusting himself enough to risk saying anything further, he pulled himself out onto the edge of the pool and said, "Well, see you in the lab tomorrow," then walked around the pool to get his towel.

What the fuck? I've always liked thin women, that's why I married one. I've never thought about Lindsey like that before. It's not a good idea to start now. For a lot of reasons.

He smiled and gave her a quick wave as he headed for the locker room, hoping no one would notice his erection. He blushed, himself, when he looked down. *Maybe I shouldn't wear a Speedo.*

20. Carried Away

Paul/Lindsey—Week 19, Tuesday

THE TUESDAY AFTER THEY MET at the pool, Paul and Lindsey worked late in the lab, trying a new technique for extracting mRNA from cultured neurons. Paul let her do most of the work, especially the pipetting of chemicals in microliter quantities; she had much better hands for it than he did. Trying to observe one step of the procedure more closely, he rested his left hand on her shoulder and leaned over her, becoming aware for the first time of a slight aroma of either perfume or shampoo. Leaning over further, he placed his right hand on the benchtop. She put the pipettor down, placed her gloved right hand on his, and kept it there, half-turning to face him.

They looked at each other for a few seconds, and without a word, they were suddenly locked in an embrace and kissing. Her hands found his belt and zipper; she pulled his zipper down and reached in, her gloves still on, and pulled out his cock. She quickly slid down in front of him and took it in her mouth.

Paul's eyes widened and his jaw dropped. He wasn't about to push her off, but couldn't figure out what to do with his hands. He didn't want to grab her head; she didn't need any directions from him. He finally let his fingertips rest on her shoulders and leaned back against the lab bench. It didn't last long; he came within minutes. She stood up, bracing herself with both hands on his hips, and they both headed immediately to his office, neither saying a word. Once there, they undressed urgently, tossing their clothes aside, letting them fall where they would. Paul stopped her when she was down to her bra and panties; he wanted to take those off her himself. Both were black—silky, not lacy. Paul had to wait to get his erection back—pure physiology; he couldn't be more turned on than he was—so he went down on her on the carpet. It was awkward; he kept hitting his bare buttocks on a cold filing cabinet, but didn't let it break his focus. By the time she reached orgasm, he was hard again. They squirmed to a position where they had more room and fucked—still wordless, just grunts and moans. He rolled off her when he came; she turned her back to him and they spooned for a few minutes, Paul stroking her breasts and belly the whole time. Neither spoke. Finally she said quietly, "We have to finish." They dressed in silence and went back to the lab. Once they'd completed the procedure—the interruption didn't hurt anything, as far as Paul could tell, though it wasn't in the protocol—they left, separating in the parking garage. The only thing Paul said was, "See you tomorrow." She replied, "Good night."

Driving home, Paul tried to sort out his feelings. Guilt, mainly—he had never cheated on Sharon in the twelve years they had been together. Fear, too. What if she ever found out? And how would this affect working with Lindsey? Was this a one-off, simply a sudden lapse in judgement for them both? Had he been bottling up some feeling for her for years? Or even just since he'd seen her at the pool? He'd been aroused, yes, but it wasn't the first time the sight of a near-naked woman at the pool had done that; most of the women who'd given him hard-ons had better bodies and wore skimpier bikinis than Lindsey. Maybe it was only a matter of seeing her body when he'd rarely seen her without a lab coat.

But he couldn't deny how invigorated he felt. It wasn't just the afterglow of the sex. What was most exciting, most gratifying, was the sheer spontaneity of it. He and Sharon lost that long ago. The feeling of having sex on a sudden, surging impulse because it seemed necessary *now*, right *now*, with no planning, no preparation, no forethought—that somehow felt almost as good as the sex itself. At the same time, he knew that his doing *anything* that impulsive, let alone something as shatteringly wrong as that, was totally unlike him. He could hardly believe he'd done it. The instant his lips touched Lindsey's, he seemed to become someone else entirely, someone he didn't even recognize. And that scared the hell out of him.

He was glad Sharon was out when he got home—she was teaching an introductory psychology class on Tuesday and Thursday evenings at the local community college, since she only had a part-time slot as an instructor at Southeast Texas State. Her inability to find a full-time tenure-track position at the University was a major source of frustration, and put a strain on their marriage.

He took a shower to wash off any traces of sex, any lingering scents he might have picked up from Lindsey, remembering what he had heard as a teenager at his first job, at a McDonald's. One of his managers, a retired sailor, often bragged about his sexual exploits in various ports, but said he couldn't do any of that now, because if he was ever with another woman, his wife would smell it on him—every woman could do that, he said. Paul never believed it, given the frequency of infidelity, but it seemed best not to take any chances. The shower also helped him calm down and compose himself, so when Sharon came home, he could act as if nothing out of the ordinary had happened. He wondered whether that might soon be true.

When Sharon came home and asked how work had been, he just said, "Nothing unusual. I think the new RNA method might work."

He didn't know what to expect when he got to work the next morning. As usual, Lindsey was already in the lab when he arrived. She was working with a graduate student interning in the lab, showing him the method she and Paul had worked on the previous night. She obviously felt comfortable with it already, which was typical—Lindsey mastered new laboratory techniques much faster than Paul.

Having the student in the lab much of the day kept Paul and Lindsey from talking about what had happened. When the student finally left for a class, Paul had no idea what to say. He fumbled for words.

"Look, I don't know what came over me last night...."

"Me neither. But I liked it."

"We both got carried away. I didn't even ask about, um...."

"Don't worry. I use pills. My parents still want me to marry Chinese; they think I'm pure. I'm not. But I don't sleep around. I don't have anything you could catch."

Paul blushed. "I-I hadn't thought anything like that. Really."

She seemed far more self-assured than Paul. "I had. I know you're married. I don't want to mess that up. And I like working for you. But...." She paused, for several seconds. "Last night felt so good." She looked directly at him without the smile that was her default expression when she spoke, and put her right hand on his knee. Paul felt awkward, but did nothing to remove it.

"It felt good to me, too." There was a long, uncomfortable pause. He finally just put his hand on hers, though he wasn't sure why. "Well, um, let's see what we need to do in the lab."

It was the only thing he could think of to say.

21. *"...There might be a problem with the drug"*

Paul—Week 20

For the next week, Paul avoided starting anything in the lab that could keep him there late. He wasn't sure how to handle this thing. Before they ended up naked on his office floor, he had never looked at Lindsey as anything but a supremely competent lab tech, one he was lucky to have working for him. Now every time he looked at her, he thought of her tits or how it felt when she sucked his cock. He felt that if they were alone together, he would immediately start undressing her. He felt certain she wouldn't object. Paul wasn't someone who had ever surrendered easily to impulses. Now he couldn't trust himself.

What changed? Not just me, but Lindsey. What's got into us both?

Then he remembered the spill.

We were both exposed, probably me more than her, but we don't know how much we inhaled. Could OGF83 possibly do this? It didn't seem to affect behavior in animals, but we didn't look at behavior much. They seemed fine, and we left it at that. If it is the drug, what then? Ten people have gotten larger doses than we probably did. Are any of them having problems? Should I warn Jim Russell? I wouldn't want to risk shutting the trial down over a vague suspicion. I need some advice. Maybe David could be more objective than I can.

When David Eamon dropped by his office that morning, Paul motioned for him to close the door, and began talking before David even sat down.

"David, there might be a problem with the drug. I'm not sure. Maybe you could tell me what you think. A few weeks ago, I spilled a batch and breathed some of the vapor. I can't be absolutely sure I breathed in the drug; it may have been nothing but the buffer. But I think some of the drug was in the vapor. Probably not much, but we don't know for sure, and any exposure might be significant."

"Did you report the spill?"

"No. You're the first person I've told. Lindsey was there. No one else knows about it. She may have been exposed, too, though she almost certainly got a smaller dose than I did."

"So you think the drug might be affecting you now, but you're not sure?" He chuckled. "What, can you see better now?"

Paul, frowning, wondered if David was taking this seriously. "No, I wish. I think it might be affecting my behavior. I've given in to some sudden impulses lately."

"Like your blow-up in the meeting? Hell, Paul, Kurt deserved it. *I* was pissed off at him."

"Yeah. He deserved that. But when have you ever seen me blow up that way? I don't do things like that."

"It was a bit out of character, I'll give you that. But if that's all you're worried about, anyone can lose their temper."

"But that's not all. I... the other night, I... Lindsey and I had sex. In my office. It just... happened. We never did it before. We haven't done it since. I think she'd like to, though. ... Hell, I'd like to. But I don't want to. I've never cheated on Sharon before. It just happened. That's what I mean about giving in to sudden impulses."

David frowned; he was Paul's friend, but Sharon's, too. "Damn, Paul. I don't know what to say. You think it was a one-time thing?"

"I don't know. I don't know what to think. I think I'd like to fuck her again, but I don't really want to, if that makes any sense. It could screw everything up. My job, my marriage.... Would I do it again? I don't know. I really don't. If the impulse came...."

"Fight it. The school doesn't like supervisors getting involved with their employees. At least she's not a student. That would really be trouble. How do you think she'd take it if you said it was a mistake, a one-time thing, and you couldn't do it again?"

"I don't know." Paul looked away. "I can't even guarantee it won't happen again. If it was just an impulse...."

"Then you need to control it. I mean it. You could get in all kinds of trouble. Not just here. What do you think would happen if Sharon found out? Why would you keep doing something you seem ambivalent about?" Paul didn't want to answer the first, and couldn't answer the second. He squirmed in his seat. David went on. "You know I won't say anything about this to anyone."

As David was leaving, he stopped in the doorway. "Look, if you feel like acting on an impulse and you need someone to talk you out of it, call me."

Paul said nothing. They both knew it wouldn't work that way.

22. *"He's becoming a problem, isn't he?"*

Trey—Week 21

AT HIS NEXT EXAM, TREY seemed so morose and uncommunicative that Donna Martinson, who handled interviews for the trial, finally threw up her hands and excused herself. She went to Jim Russell.

"Dr. Russell, I think you're going to have to finish up with Mr. Osborne. I can barely get him to answer the questions."

Russell sighed. "He's becoming a problem, isn't he? All right. I'll be there in a minute."

When Russell walked through the door of the interview room, Trey looked surprised.

"Dr. Russell! Miss… umm… the woman who does the questions just excused herself. She didn't say she was going to get *you*. Did I say something that upset her? I didn't mean to. I hope she doesn't think I was mad at her."

Russell sat down across from Trey. "Miss Martinson just thought it would be better if I did the rest of the interview. She was having some trouble getting you through all the questions. I think she got through most of them, right? We'd like to get through all of them, but we can stop for now if they're bothering you." He paused with a quizzical expression, arching his eyebrows. "Is there something else bothering you today? Does it have to do with what we talked about last time? You wanting to go back to your job?"

"Maybe. I don't know. I've just been down lately. Not as happy as I should be, considering I can see now. I don't know why I'm not adjusting better." He shrugged and shook his head, waving one hand toward Russell, palm up. "I didn't adjust very well to going blind; you'd think it'd be easier to adjust to seeing again."

Trey turned his head slightly and seemed to look off in the distance before he continued. "For a while after my eyes went, I was probably kind of a jerk. I had a girlfriend then. I met her after my divorce, she didn't have anything to do with that. Not that it matters now, I guess. Anyway, we'd been going out about a year before my eyes went. She stuck with me for about six months after that. She left because she couldn't stand me feeling sorry for myself all the time, and I guess I did. What can I say? That's a hell of a thing to get used to, you know? In my job, I traveled a lot—I'd been to Alaska, the Middle East, Malaysia, about everywhere you could go in Texas and Oklahoma. Not desk work, not most of it. Seeing what we could get from tapped-out wells, things like that. I helped put in rigs out in the Gulf, helped design and build and test them. Even apart from work, I spent a lot of time outside. Once that was gone, I just felt stuck at home all the time. Even after three years of being blind, I wasn't getting out much. I withdrew from everything, really." Trey looked down at his hands, and for the first time, Russell felt sorry for him.

Trey went on. "I used to be a pretty good dancer before I went blind, you know? That's how I met my girlfriend. I suppose you'd call it depression, what I went through. I'm not sure I'm over it yet, even though I can see now. Because of what we talked about last time, I still kind of feel like I have to hide, you know? At least until I can figure out where the money'll come from once people find out I can see again."

"Have you thought of trying a therapist? We can help you find one."

"No. Not… not really. I think it's pretty understandable why I would have been depressed when I went blind. I mean, who wouldn't be? I'm just feeling, I don't know, uncertain these days. I don't think taking a pill or talking to somebody's gonna change that."

"Is there some friend, some family member you can talk to? Someone to just be around for you? We hate to see you come in so unhappy. You're the biggest success story we've had in this trial so far."

"Yeah, I ought to be happy about that, right? I'm not acting like a good poster child. I'll try to do better by the time you're ready to go public."

Trey abruptly stood up. "I'd like to go home now, if that's okay. Do you mind? If I don't see Miss… Martinson, could you tell her I'm sorry? I didn't mean to upset her."

Russell had hoped to get back to the questionnaires, but he said nothing, just nodded. *Easier to let him go for now. Maybe he'll snap out of it before next time.*

23. *"It's not getting any better"*

Kathy—Week 22, Tuesday

IF "LEARNING TO SEE" WERE a graded class, Kathy knew she would flunk it miserably. Her visual world was a tangle of shapes and colors. Nothing was what or where it seemed. During one test, she knocked an apple off a table when reaching for it, then tried to pluck one out of a picture; they looked the same. Apples are apples, unless they're not.

Identifying the simplest objects was an ordeal. During one test in a dark room, Dr. Stark showed her a ball, half red and half blue, sitting on a table under a spotlight.

"How many objects?"

"Two. They're half-circles. Or half-spheres. I can't tell which."

"Which is closer?"

"The red one. I think. That's hard. They're not far apart."

"Close your eyes a minute. Here." He handed her the ball. "Now look at what you have."

Kathy gasped. "It's a ball! How come I couldn't see that? It's just two different colors."

"One object, two colors, yes. Let me put it back on the table." He took the ball from her. "Now what do you see?"

She stared hard. "I think it's a ball now, but only because I touched it. I can't honestly say I see it that way. I think I do. But I might be fooling myself, because I know what it is."

"Okay, close your eyes again." He replaced the ball with a cube, half blue, half yellow. "What do you see now?"

"I think it's two things again, that's really what it looks like. Squares… or cubes, I guess. They look flat, though. The yellow one looks closer, it really does. But you're just trying to fool me, aren't you? It's just one thing, isn't it?"

"Yes, it's just one thing. Here." He handed her the cube.

She turned it over and over in her hands, looking at it, trying to see it—looking and seeing were not the same. She finally spoke. "What it really is, is just another data point, isn't it? That's what I am, too, right? Just another data point."

Stark was taken aback. "No, Kathy, no. How many years have I known you? You were a little girl when I first saw you. You could still see then, but your sight was going fast, and we couldn't stop it. You're not just data to me, you know that."

"I'm sorry. That was a lousy thing to say, I didn't mean it. That's just how I feel sometimes when we do this." Two tears rolled down her cheeks. "Let's stop for today, okay? I'm a little tired."

"Okay. We'll try some more next time. Don't give up."

Stark didn't write anything down about the exchange until Kathy left.

* * *

Kathy's gauge of distance when she was blind had simply been, how many steps away is it? When she closed her eyes, that still worked. When she opened them, the world was a morass of hazards hidden by her nonexistent depth perception. She tripped. She fell. She bloodied her nose on a half-open door, blackened her eye on the corner of a cabinet. Opaque glasses now both covered bruises and blocked her vision; wearing them was a relief. She could use her cane without being self-conscious.

The day after her session with Dr. Stark, her mother had Kathy close her eyes while she led her along a meandering path through the house to the living room, where the piano was. Shara kept Kathy talking so she couldn't count steps. They stopped.

"All right. You can open your eyes now. How many steps would it take you to reach the piano?"

Kathy felt relieved; this was easy. "One. It's right in front of me."

"But we're standing in the doorway. Close your eyes and count your steps while you walk to the piano."

Kathy shook her head. "I already know how many. It's five. I've walked from here to the piano thousands of times. It's always five." She grimaced. "But it looks like one step and I'm there!"

Shara tried a new tack. "Okay. Close your eyes and hold your hands about a foot apart."

"A foot?" Kathy remembered all the conversions. Twelve inches is a foot. Three feet is a yard. A mile is 5280 feet. But that was just math and memorization. She couldn't picture the distance in her mind. She held her hands up about five or six inches apart. "Is this it?"

"Not quite. But close." Shara thought for a second. "How far is it from one side of your room to the other?"

"Eight steps."

"So how wide is your room?"

Kathy was exasperated. "Like I said, it's eight steps."

"That's how many steps across it is. How wide is it?"

Kathy was genuinely puzzled. She could define "wide", but she couldn't picture it. "I don't know what you mean."

"How many feet across is it?"

"Eight, I guess. Isn't a step about a foot?"

"No. Your room's about fifteen feet across."

Kathy thought this over. "So I'm about ten feet from the piano right now?"

"That's about right."

Kathy's voice showed genuine alarm. "But it looks like one step and I'll run right into it! That's why I don't want to open my eyes when I walk!"

Shara patted her shoulder. "I know, honey. We'll just have to keep working at it."

Kathy closed her eyes and walked to the piano, and kept them closed as she practiced. She had been crushed to find that trying to play the piano with her eyes open was a disaster. When she tried to watch her hands as she played, they seemed to belong to a stranger; her eyes could not keep up with her fingers. Passages she had played hundreds of times became minefields of missed notes and clashing discords. She soon gave up; if she wanted to play, she had to keep her eyes either closed or covered.

That evening, as Leila was driving them to work, Kathy confided in her one real friend besides her mother.

"Leila, I don't know how much more of this I can stand! I wish I was still blind. I mean it! It's not getting any better."

"Come on, Kathy. Try to be patient. I'm sure it'll come back to you like it was when you were a kid. Can't you remember anything from when you could see before?"

"I used to think I could, but I don't know anymore. I thought I had an image of my mom in my head all these years, but maybe I just made it up. All I know is, I don't recognize her face now when she's right in front of me. The only reason I know it's her is because she's usually the only other person in the room. If you and Mom were both there, and didn't speak, I don't know if I could tell you apart. ... We could try it. But if I can't, I'm not sure I really want to know." There was silence for half a minute before she resumed. "I don't mean to dump this on you. Especially right before work like this."

"That's okay. Maybe we can change the set. Go for the darker stuff, heartbreak and lost love and all that." She laughed, but Kathy became visibly upset.

"No! Stay with the set you've been doing. I won't have any trouble with that. I don't need to be any more depressed than I already am."

Leila reached over to pat her arm. "Okay. Okay. I was just joking. You know I wouldn't do that to you. ... Have you told those guys from the study about this? Do you think the drug has changed your mood?"

"They know I'm unhappy. They think it's just because of all the trouble I'm having seeing. I hope that's the cause, but I don't believe that's all it is."

"Well, that's what they'd want to believe, isn't it? They wouldn't want to think the drug is the problem. They've got to be seeing dollar signs in all this. I mean, they have a cure for blindness! They wouldn't want to think it's screwing up your head. If they could say your problems are being caused by your trouble seeing, that would be a lot better for them. If you think it's more than that, you need to tell them."

"That's just it. I don't know if it's more than that. I just know it's a lot harder than I thought it would be."

Leila pulled the car into the hotel parking lot. "Well, no matter what, you know I'm here for you." She squeezed Kathy's knee. "And here we are. It's showtime, folks!"

24. On a Clear Day...

Kathy—Week 22, Wednesday

THE FOLLOWING EVENING, KATHY WAS playing solo during Leila's between-set break. She felt awkward and self-conscious leaving the stage, so she would stay at the piano and play through the break. This gave her twenty minutes or so when she could be creative and play anything she wanted, as long as it didn't rile the audience. All the management cared about was having a large and happy crowd.

For tonight, she chose three short pieces arranged for solo piano by Bill Evans. As something of a sardonic joke, she started with "On a Clear Day (You Can See Forever)"; her generally somber mood these days hadn't killed her sense of humor. She followed that with two darker pieces, "Midnight Mood" and "Here's That Rainy Day". Each would last about five minutes, so she would have time for all three.

Her playing of "On a Clear Day" and "Midnight Mood" essentially duplicated the original Evans recording. But about three minutes into "Here's That Rainy Day", where Evans lightened the mood, Kathy took her own tack, moving both the melody and bass line down an octave and slowing the tempo. The piece became as melancholy as Kathy; she felt as if it were raining in her soul. Suddenly the piece was hers, and hers alone. She circled back in it and began taking the song places it had never been before. Tears started down her cheeks; it was good she was wearing dark glasses. She wasn't aware of the tears, or the diners, or the waitresses, or the busboys, or anything at all but the music. She slowed the tempo even more, and moved her left hand further down the keyboard, into the lowest octave; she slowed the bass line down further still, letting the overtones ring, creating dissonance no mere lounge pianist would ever touch. A few diners noticed, and paused in their eating, wondering at the turn the music had taken. Kathy had left the original arrangement far behind now; she was letting the song take her where it wanted to go, and she kept playing, bent low over the keyboard, horribly out of position, until she suddenly felt Leila slide up against her on the bench and heard a whisper in her ear. "Kathy, your playing's fantastic, but we have to do the set."

Kathy was horrified. She had no idea how long she had been playing. Leila slid a short distance down the bench and put her hand on Kathy's leg, letting her find a way to end the song gracefully. When Kathy brought it to a close, Leila walked to the microphone and said, "Ladies and gentlemen, my pianist, Kathy Wright! Wasn't that wonderful?" Those diners who hadn't been paying attention were probably mystified, but everyone applauded, and Leila started her set. As it went on, Leila seemed to be rising to a challenge Kathy hadn't intended to make; Kathy thought Leila had never sung better.

Kathy apologized afterward. "Leila, I'm so sorry! That's never happened before! The music just took over. I couldn't stop! How long did I go on?"

"Not that long. Really. Maybe an extra five minutes. I hated to stop you. I've never heard you play like that. You seemed lost in your own world. Did you know you were crying? I wish I could have let you go on, but I'm not sure the audience was ready to hear anything like you were playing. I know you're good, but, Kathy, you were on a different level out there! I couldn't have kept up if I'd been trying to follow along, believe me; I had no idea where you were going with it."

"I'm sorry, I really am. I'm supposed to accompany you, not go off on my own. I don't know what came over me."

"It's all right. I mean it. You don't have to keep apologizing." She laughed. "Just don't get any better, okay? I'd have to pay you more! Come on, let's call it a night."

25. Upstairs and Down

Kathy—Week 22, Thursday, A.M.

THE FOLLOWING MORNING, KATHY WENT downstairs to breakfast the way she always did these days, with her eyes closed. Trying to walk with them open only confused her, as her eyes told her she was about to collide with a wall at every step, while her hands or cane said otherwise. In the house, of course, she never needed her cane; once she oriented herself in a room, she knew exactly where every obstacle or piece of furniture was. She could have walked the whole way downstairs backward. In deference to her mother, she tried to keep her eyes open while she ate her cereal, but she couldn't help cheating. Kathy hoped Shara wouldn't notice that every time she raised her spoon from the bowl, she closed her eyes as it neared her lips. It was less messy that way—she spilled more when she tried to see what she was doing.

Shara had to run some errands after breakfast. When she left, Kathy was still at the table with a cup of coffee, half-listening to the news on the radio, thinking mostly about what she needed to do before work that evening. She decided the first thing she would do was make herself walk up the stairs to her room with her eyes open. She had gone up and down them a thousand times when she couldn't see at all; now she would force herself to look, to let her eyes guide her back to her room.

When she was blind, stairs never bothered her, which often surprised people who didn't know her. Stairs were regular and predictable. Kathy routinely breezed up and down them with a facility that would startle those who had never seen her do it before. She would hesitate on unfamiliar stairs, but once she knew how many steps there were, she knew exactly how high and how often to raise her feet when going either up or down. The first few times, she would consciously count the steps, but in a very short time she no longer had to—she would somehow know when she reached the top or bottom of a flight, with no missteps. Whether she did this through subconscious counting or some sort of intuition, she couldn't say.

She had been dismayed to find how much her newly restored sight hindered her walking, and this was true nowhere more than on stairs. Once she started looking down at her feet to see where to place them, her nearly nonexistent depth perception threatened to trip her up. She couldn't tell how far above the surface her foot was. Going up stairs, she would continually stub her toes on the next step up; going down, she would be thrown off balance whenever she jarred her foot forcefully on the next step down because she expected it to be lower than it was. If she looked up or straight ahead, instead of at her feet, it didn't help, because she couldn't judge horizontal distances any better than vertical ones. Her eyes refused to tell her that the next step up was closer to her than each successive one—each step looked as far away as every other one. Wherever she looked, she seemed to face a flat screen, a world with only two dimensions. It was much easier to pretend she was still blind and walk with her eyes closed, though she knew she would never learn to use her eyes if she kept that up.

She was determined this time to take the stairs like everyone else did, with open eyes. She stood at the foot of the stairs for several minutes, trying to will herself into seeing the steps receding from bottom to top, but the topmost step still looked just as near as the bottom one. Her eyes told her that if she held her hands straight out, she would touch the eighth step up, yet when she put out her left hand as far as she could reach, there was nothing there—as she knew there wouldn't be, despite everything her eyes told her.

She took a deep breath, placed her right foot on the first step and her right hand on the rail, and started slowly upward. The contrast between what her eyes and her extended left hand were telling her seemed overwhelming. With every step, she seemed to be walking into the flat scene in front of her but never getting there, as though she were trying to step into a picture that was always just out of reach. *You'll have to learn how to see*, Dr. Stark said. Her confident *I know* seemed hollow now. This was terrifying. As far back as she could remember, every step she had ever taken had been into the unknown, into the nothingness usually marked out by her swinging cane. Now she seemed to be walking into something solid, her eyes telling her one thing, her hand another. She knew her eyes were lying—if she couldn't feel anything in front of her, then nothing was there. She could close her eyes and do this the way she had for years—she knew how high to lift her foot, how far forward to move it, how far down to put it to feel the solid stair again. She had never needed her eyes to tell her that, and what they were telling her now was that if she lifted her foot and swung it forward, it would crash into the next step up.

I need to watch when I walk; I've got to learn this. She forced herself to look, barely daring to blink, though she had to whenever tears turned the wall she saw in front of her, real or not, into a blur. *Lift, forward, down; lift, forward, down.* She had not had to think so hard about what she was doing for years. With her eyes open, she moved far more slowly than she would have blind. She made herself look ahead, each step taking an agonizingly long time. Each time she lifted her foot, she thought, *I'm going to run into the wall, it's right there*, and then, *No, I won't, there's no wall there.* About halfway up, she realized she was crying. *This is ridiculous. You've done this a thousand times! How can this be so hard?* If she couldn't make her eyes see the world as she knew it to be, what use were they? Vision was a trick, a trap, a cruel mirage. If she couldn't trust it, what use was it?

When she finally reached the top, there were tears streaming down both cheeks, and she could taste blood on her lower lip; she'd bitten it without realizing. She turned and sat down on the top step, put her face in her hands, and sobbed. She was still sitting there when Shara came home two hours later.

26. "I saw a wall that wasn't there"

Kathy—Week 22, Thursday, P.M.

KATHY KNEW SHE HAD TO pull herself together before Leila came by to pick her up for work. She could barely explain to her mother what had happened; she retreated to her room and didn't come down for lunch. She put on her darkest glasses and made no effort to use her eyes the rest of the day. Though she made it to the top, the staircase had beaten her; one defeat was enough for one day. Both she and her mother were almost silent during dinner, each discouraged in her own way.

That night, after the second set, Leila and Kathy sat in the bar talking, as they often did to unwind. Kathy, as usual, drank only one half-strength margarita; she long ago learned that too much alcohol didn't mix well with being blind, and as long as her sight stayed as useless as it was now, she still regarded herself as blind. She was trying to describe to Leila her disheartening walk up the stairs that morning. She didn't expect Leila to understand. How could she? How could anybody? Who could imagine that merely walking up a flight of stairs could be torture? Kathy wasn't seeing the same world everyone else did—hers was filled with objects that weren't what or where they seemed to be. Everything she saw was right in her face, leaving her no room to move, to breathe. She had to shut out the world she saw so she could live in the only one she knew, the one she could feel and hear and touch and smell.

A thirty-ish dark-haired man was sitting on the stool next to Kathy, listening. He looked vaguely familiar to Leila; she thought he was probably one of the regulars. He leaned toward Kathy and broke in, with the self-confidence of someone who had drunk just enough to make him think he was charming.

"I'm sorry, but I couldn't help overhearing. What you were saying reminded me of a rhyme I heard when I was a kid:

As I was walking up the stair,
I saw a wall that wasn't there.
It wasn't there again today.
I wish that wall would go away.

Or maybe it was a man he saw on the stairs. I don't remember."

He grinned, obviously feeling clever. The grin vanished abruptly when he got half a margarita in his face. Kathy didn't have to aim; she flung the drink toward his voice.

He sputtered in protest, but the bartender, Linda, who had been listening to Kathy, too, immediately stepped in.

"You need to leave. Now. You have no idea what she's been through."

He started to object, but she cut him off. "Now! Don't make me call security."

He turned away and walked off with his head down, looking more sheepish than angry. He did say to Kathy before he left, "I'm sorry. I didn't mean to upset you. Really."

The bartender said, "Do you want another drink, Kathy? No charge."

"Thank you, Linda, but no. I think that'll do it for tonight. I'm sorry I made a mess for you."

"I'll clean it up, don't worry. He just thought he was being funny. I don't blame you. I'll back you if he complains and they say anything about you flinging a drink at a customer. I don't think he'll complain, but if he does...."

"Thanks for stepping in, I appreciate it. I shouldn't have done it. I've been upset all day. He just set me off. I'm sure he wasn't trying to be a jerk. I'd apologize if he were still here."

Linda said, "No, he deserved it. I can't imagine what you're going through. If it'd been me, I'd've thrown the glass at him, not just the drink. Though he's not usually the jerk he seemed to be just now. He comes in fairly often. His name's Eric. I thought he had a thing for Leila, but maybe it's for you. Too bad he said something stupid the first time he got up the nerve to talk to you."

Leila spoke for the first time. "Well, that's one less fan we have to suck up to. Too bad. He obviously has good musical taste." She finished her own drink in one swallow. "Come on, Kathy. Let's go home. It's been a long day."

27. "Are you mad at me, Mr. Osborne?"

Trey—Week 23

AT HIS NEXT CLINIC VISIT for the trial, Trey found himself more irritable than ever. *I'm sick of all these questions trying to get at how I feel. I feel pissed off, is how. We've done all this to death.* About halfway through the first questionnaire, he stopped the interviewer. "Could we get some new questions? We go through the same ones every time. My answers haven't changed in the last month. Why don't we just say, 'Nothing's changed since the last time', and get it over with?"

Donna Martinson, the interviewer, said, "I think some of your answers have changed over time. We need to be consistent at each exam so we can see exactly what changes do occur. May I go on?"

"All right. But what are all these questions trying to get at? Why don't you just ask me, 'How do you feel?' 'What's your mood been like?' 'Is everything going okay?' Instead of all this, 'In the past week, have you felt hopeless at any time?' Or whatever." He was visibly angry.

She kept her tone even, though she was now irritated, too. "We are trying to find out how you feel. We just have to go into a little more detail than that. And we have to stay consistent."

"Why is that so important? If my mood changes, why can't I just tell you that? All this is becoming a goddamn waste of time. Sorry. I didn't mean to snap at you." He held his hands up, palms toward her, genuinely contrite.

She frowned. "Are you mad at me, Mr. Osborne?"

"Not at you, no. At this whole process. Now that I have my sight back, why is the rest of this necessary? What do you expect to find?"

"We don't know what to expect. This is a first-stage clinical trial. We want to know that the drug isn't toxic. If there are any side effects, we don't know what form they might take. We have to consider all possibilities. We know all this can be boring, especially since the drug has already worked for you. But we have to try to evaluate everyone the same way, whether the drug works for them or not. The questionnaire we're going through now is so we can see if the drug might have any psychological effects."

"It seems to me you've found out what you need to know. When I signed the consent form, it said I could withdraw at any time, right? I think I'd like to withdraw." He surprised himself, saying that. He hadn't come in with any intention of quitting.

She was nonplussed. No one else had quit the trial, not even the patients the drug wasn't helping. "Yes, you can withdraw anytime. We would rather you didn't. Would you please talk to Dr. Russell first?"

"Sure, I'll talk to him. But I don't think he'll change my mind."

She hurriedly went to find Jim Russell. She had to call him out of a meeting, but this was an emergency, and he agreed when she explained the situation.

When he came into the room, he rushed past his greeting before Trey could respond. "How are you doing, Mr. Osborne? Ms. Martinson tells me you want to withdraw from the trial? Do you mind if I ask why?"

"No, I don't mind you asking, but I have the right to withdraw at any time, don't I? That was in the consent form I signed."

"Yes, you have the right to withdraw at any time. But very few people drop out of a trial when a drug's worked for them. The drug's been a spectacular success for you, hasn't it?"

"Of course it has. I mean, I'm looking at you now, right? I'm grateful for that, don't get me wrong. But all these tests and questions are annoying. You know I can see again. What else do you need? And I am kind of pissed that you never got back to me about those questions I brought up when I first started seeing again."

Russell looked genuinely puzzled. "Questions? Oh, you mean about your disability pension and your prospects for going back to work? I meant it when I said that was an issue between you and your employer— former employer. We're not required to report anything to your former company. In fact, we can't. Your trial results are medical records, and strictly confidential—we couldn't report them to anyone without your permission, with the few exceptions listed in the consent form. None of those apply here. Your former company has nothing to do with the trial, so there's no reason we'd report anything to them."

Trey gave a dismissive wave of his arm. "That's only part of it, to tell you the truth. I don't see any point going through the same questions, over and over again. It's a waste of time."

"Mr. Osborne, there's so much more we could learn from you. You're almost unique, you know. You're the closest thing to a complete cure the drug's produced. You shocked everyone."

It didn't even register with Russell that he had just referred to Trey as a "thing", but it infuriated Trey. "So I'm the best thing you've got, huh? Well, now you know the drug works. What else do you need?"

"We still don't know about all the possible side effects; some could develop later. That's why we have to keep going with the exams and questionnaires. We're supposed to follow patients for a year. Even though you got your eyesight back after the first dose of the drug, you could still develop side effects. The protocol calls for two more doses, but you obviously don't need them, and they wouldn't help you any, so we would skip them in your case, unless your eyes regress. We'd still like to follow you for the whole year."

"Yeah, well, I think you've found out all you needed to know. I would like to withdraw. I have the right. You said so yourself."

Russell tried one final pitch to keep Trey in the trial. "Yes, you can withdraw. But you know, we can't be sure your recovery is permanent. You still carry the underlying mitochondrial defect that caused your blindness in the first place. If you were to start losing your sight again, the second and third doses in the protocol might help. Even if you don't need them, all your eye care is free while you're in the trial. That's a real benefit, don't you think? It really would be to your benefit not to quit. Maybe we could modify the exam and questionnaire schedule in your case, have you come in less often. I hope you'll stay in the trial. What we learn from you could help thousands of people."

Trey could see the irrefutable logic in everything Russell said. There was every reason for him to stay in the trial, except one—he didn't want to. He was sick of the prying questions, sick of being a guinea pig. "I don't see it. What you've learned from me is that the drug works for my disease. What else do you need from me? I don't want to do this anymore. I want to withdraw from the trial. Is there a form for that?"

Russell hesitated. He'd seen plenty of people drop out of clinical trials before, but never someone who'd been helped by the drug. It made no sense. But he couldn't force Trey to stay. Maybe dropping out would only be temporary. He'd realize pretty soon it was a mistake. They needed to leave the door open for him to come back, but Russell couldn't stall any longer. "Yes, we have a form. I'll get it. You know, if you withdraw, you can change your mind later. I hope you will. Maybe after you've thought about it a while...."

"I won't change my mind. Look, I'm grateful for what you've done for me, I really am. But I still want to quit. I don't expect you to understand why. I'm sorry."

"Would you like to think it over, sleep on it? It's a big decision."

"No. I've made up my mind. Please get me the form."

Trey was determined to quit. He wasn't sure why. All he knew is that he was sick of the whole thing. Wasn't that enough?

28. "I think the drug might have something to do with it"

Kathy—Week 25. Sunday

Twice more in the next two weeks, Kathy found herself getting carried away by the music she was playing between sets. Each time she managed to cut her improvisational flights short before Leila was ready to start the second set. Kathy then enlisted Leila to help her if she were to get carried away again. If Kathy was still playing when Leila was ready to start the second set, Leila was to touch Kathy's shoulder as a signal for her to bring the piece to a close. Kathy might not need the reminder, but it would be there if she did.

Kathy had so far experienced no problems with her playing in church, where there was no one like Leila close by. With the choir or congregation involved in a hymn, it was easy to stick to whatever pieces the music director had planned for the service. Kathy did get to pick what she played while the congregation was settling in. About fifteen minutes before the service began, Kathy started playing to help put people in the mood for worship. The music should help quiet people down, not stir them up, so she would play something from the canon that was melodic and usually, to her taste, fairly innocuous. But she was playing for the congregation, not herself. Kathy knew Baroque composers for the organ were famous for their improvisational skills, but it was modern practice to stick to the score, so Kathy did, though the score was in her head, and not in front of her.

One morning about a month after her first flight of improvisation at the Blue Room, she was playing Buxtehude's *Wie schön leucht der Morgenstern, How Lovely is the Morning Star*, one of her favorite pieces—she much preferred it to Bach's version, which sounded muddy and clotted to her. About three minutes into the song, in a passage where an eight-note motif in the right hand seems to be chased by the same motif in the left, she suddenly departed from the score and began spinning off variations, though probably no one in the congregation realized it. Astonished by what she could do with just eight notes, Kathy improvised for several minutes before moving to the next section; she quickly left the score behind there, too. She was overwhelmed by the waves of sound that washed over her; tears began to stream down her cheeks, though she was smiling ecstatically. The morning star was lovely indeed; *everything* was lovely. She almost felt touched by a God she didn't really believe in. Dimly aware she was straying, with effort, she managed to return to the score, but each time, she quickly spiraled off into music no one had ever heard before. She was in ecstasy, almost orgasmic, with her head far back, her face turned to the ceiling, her body swaying as she played.

And then she became aware of a hand on her shoulder, and the urgent voice of the music director in her ear. "Kathy! Kathy! Ms. Wright? The service was supposed to start ten minutes ago! You have to stop... are you crying? Are you all right?"

Kathy stopped abruptly. "Oh my God! What was I doing?" She tried to keep her voice down, but was certain people in the first row, at least, could hear her. "I'm sorry. I got carried away.... I'm all right. You can start the service now. It's okay—I'm okay. I'm sorry. You can start the service."

She couldn't have been more embarrassed if she'd suddenly realized she was sitting at the organ naked. Without ever opening her eyes behind her glasses, she turned her head toward the choir and nodded, smiling ruefully. She wanted to be somewhere far, far away. Anywhere but here. Only she had at least another hour to go and several hymns to play, and nowhere to hide.

After the service, neither the minister nor the music director, mystified by what had happened, said anything to her about her lapse, but one member of the choir walked over before Kathy left the organ and said, "I wish they hadn't stopped you. That was lovely."

Afterward, Kathy said nothing to her mother in the car until they were almost home. Then she said quietly, "Mom, I'm scared. I think I'm losing control of myself. I think the drug might have something to do with it."

29. The Void Inside

Kathy—Week 25, Wednesday

THE WEDNESDAY MORNING AFTER THE incident at church, Kathy woke up and knew immediately that something was terribly wrong. All she wanted to do was burrow beneath the covers again and never wake up, but she knew a lifetime of sleep wouldn't help. It's not that she felt bad—she felt nothing at all, as if every emotion had been drained from her. How do you express the ache of total emptiness? She was utterly blank, everything in her an enormous void. She existed only in this very moment, but this was no nirvana, not even close. She had no feelings, no plans. No past. No present. No future. Nothing. There was nothing inside her, nothing at all. No reason to get up. No reason even to exist. It was as though a black hole had sucked in every thought and feeling and collapsed on itself, leaving nothing behind.

When she opened her eyes, the inevitable cacophony of color and shapes she faced every morning was there. She could make nothing useful of it. She closed her eyes to shut it out.

She reached over and pressed the button on her talking clock and found that her alarm wouldn't go off for another seventeen minutes. Somehow, the precision of the clock reading saved her, the knowledge that time existed and would pass as always, even if she felt apart from it, suspended in an awful and endless present. She sat up on the edge of the bed, making no move to keep the alarm from going off; she knew her mother would come in once it did. To her mother, the alarm wasn't a wake-up call—she would have been up for at least an hour already—it meant that Kathy was up, and Shara would come in to greet her, and it would be a good day.

Kathy wouldn't take that away from her, though she knew it would not be a good day. There were things she had to do, and she had no will to do any of them. Getting dressed. Going down to breakfast. Practicing. That afternoon, Leila was coming over early, because she wanted to add a new song to her repertoire, and they needed to rehearse—or Leila did; Kathy could already play it, after listening to a recording three times.

Kathy knew her mother and Leila depended on her. She had no right to let them down; she would get up and force herself to do what she had to. For them, not her. All she had the energy to do right then, though, was sit at the edge of her bed with her eyes closed to block the visual clutter.

When the alarm finally went off, she did nothing to stop it. Normally Kathy couldn't stand the sound and would shut it off before the annoying beep sounded more than three times. Her mother knocked twice at the door, then came in, puzzled at the alarm still going. Seeing Kathy sitting on the side of the bed and making no move to shut off the noise made Shara's brow furrow. She moved quickly to the bedside table and stopped the alarm.

"Kathy? Are you all right? What's wrong, honey?"

From somewhere inside, Kathy managed to summon the energy to answer. "I'll be okay," she said, though she didn't believe it. "I woke up before the alarm went off. I'll be okay."

"Are you sure?"

"Yeah, it's all right. I just need to wake up all the way. I'm okay."

"Come down to breakfast when you're ready. I made some pancakes."

Kathy managed to smile, though it wasn't easy. She nodded in reply.

"You come on down when you're ready. Are you sure you're okay?"

She nodded, though she knew she wasn't okay, she wasn't anywhere near okay. She couldn't muster the energy to speak.

Shara, unsure, decided not to press too much. "Okay. I'll be in the kitchen."

The only movement Kathy had made the whole time was to nod her head, and she sat immobile for another ten minutes before a convulsive sob shook her and she felt tears streaming down her cheeks. The spell was broken. She would be okay, for now. She never knew before how a flood of misery could come as such a relief, but feeling miserable was infinitely better than feeling nothing at all. Without opening her eyes,

Kathy had stared into a void far more terrifying than anything she ever faced when she was blind.

She finally got up and got dressed, listlessly. She would do what she had to do to get through the day.

That was the first time Kathy experienced the soul-crushing weight of true depression, the awful paradox of feeling bereft of all feeling. It would not be the last.

30. Fighting with the Night

Trey—Week 25, Wednesday

TREY HAD SERIOUS MISGIVINGS ABOUT quitting the trial, but what more could he gain from it? An eagle's eyesight? X-ray vision? He could already see the world perfectly. What he couldn't see was his future, and he didn't think the trial would help that.

Trey was surprised how little the miracle of regaining his sight had changed him. Instead of dancing down the street each day, reveling in all the sights he once took for granted, he largely shut himself in as before. The main change in his habits was that when he used his treadmill, he watched television instead of listening to music or an audiobook. When he went outside at all, he mostly kept to his backyard. Until he could figure out where he would get money from if he lost his disability pension, the fewer people who knew he could see again, the better. Trey's house had grown largely dark once he lost his sight—only his brother or sister and a once-per-week aide turned on lights that weren't hooked to a timer, and only a few were. Trey seldom turned on lights in the front of the house, and he kept the blinds closed.

His uncertain financial situation and career prospects left him fearful and agitated. If he lost his disability pension, the pittance he got from Social Security wouldn't even cover his mortgage, and would certainly stop soon after. Sooner or later, he would need a job, but where? The fracking boom had initially been great for Cardon's business, but its success bred failure once abundant oil and natural gas made prices sag. Oil field service companies like Cardon got hammered. Trey searched online job listings and grew more desperate by the day. There were jobs everywhere but in the one field he knew.

Trey heard of people getting busted for fraudulently retiring on workman's comp with things like back problems, then getting caught dancing or skiing and ending up in prison. But he wasn't trying to scam anyone—he had been certifiably blind. Two doctors had examined him and said it was permanent, with no possibility of recovery. Was it his fault no one had considered the possibility of a miracle? And who knew if the miracle would last?

On a Wednesday just over two weeks after he withdrew from the trial, alone and anxious, Trey peered through the slats of the blinds in his living room window as it began to turn dark outside. The woman from two houses down was walking her dog, a yapping little black-and-brown bastard that his brother told him often shit on the front lawn. Bob had words with the woman once when he told her she needed to pick up after her pets. Trey didn't even know his neighbor's name, though he knew the dog's—Buster; the woman often talked to him loudly enough for Trey to hear inside, though apparently not to discipline the mutt or keep him off people's lawns. Trey would as soon talk to the dog as the woman, and he had never got on with dogs. He now had a strong urge to go out, but waited until the woman was out of sight before he left the window and carefully opened the front door a crack. He studied the street, making sure it was empty, working up the nerve to step out, when he suddenly realized a walk wouldn't do it. He had to get *out*—of the house, the neighborhood, maybe the whole city, who knows? The house suddenly felt like a jail cell. He would break out, escape. He would take his car and drive… somewhere. Anywhere. He had no idea where.

He wasn't sure how good his night vision might be. In daylight, with most of his neighbors at work and the neighborhood streets largely empty save for letter carriers and lawn crews, he had slipped out in the car a few times, driving more slowly and cautiously than he ever had before he lost his sight. He had broached the subject of driving to both Dr. Patel and Dr. Russell. Both said there was no reason he couldn't get his driver's license again whenever he felt ready; he would certainly pass the cursory eye test at the Department of Public Safety. He hadn't told them he never surrendered his license after going blind in the first place.

It was quite dark now, cloudy, with the moon just a sliver. Trey looked out the garage door windows to make sure the street was empty before he opened the garage and carefully backed the car out. He first meandered slowly through the neighborhood to check his night vision. In the empty streets lit only by streetlamps and his headlights, he had no difficulty. He decided to try the main roads, though he wouldn't risk freeways yet. He turned left out of the neighborhood, waiting much longer than he would have in the past to let two cars cross by in front.

He headed generally north and east, tacking toward the edge of town. He had no real destination in mind; he just drove, roughly alternating right and left turns onto cross streets he wasn't familiar with, still heading northeast. He quickly found that night driving in traffic took hard concentration. Every light he saw had a halo around it, a bright haze that made it hard to see anything past the light. Oncoming cars appeared to be just headlights floating above the road, the mass of each car lost in a white blaze that turned red as the car's taillights appeared alongside and then receded in his rear-view mirror. It was disconcerting. If a pedestrian were to cross in front of him, Trey was afraid he wouldn't see him at all through the haze and halos of the cars and streetlights; he would run right over him. *I probably shouldn't be out here. Too late, now.* Just as he was about to turn back, the traffic thinned out. Soon there were fewer approaching cars to make him squint to penetrate the haze of light so he could see what was in front of him. He could drive in this. He was glad he wasn't on a freeway, even though oncoming traffic would be further away; he wasn't ready to drive that fast.

On a freeway, though, he would have at least known where he was. After it passed under a viaduct, the street he was on merged with another and changed names, and soon he no longer knew exactly where he was. He had never been in this part of the city before. It was now after ten p.m. on a weeknight; the area was nearly deserted. He soon passed through a run-down, semi-industrial area of metal buildings surrounded by eight-foot fences topped with barbed wire angled inward, more suited to keeping people in than out. He drove on and soon found himself in an area where old houses—many of them mere shotgun shacks, all the rooms lined up one behind the other—stood in darkness that was broken only by dimly lit windows and feeble porch lights. The whole neighborhood looked as if the power company were afraid to send crews in even to put up streetlights. Trey realized he must have passed the city limits. He was sure that eventually he would run into one of the freeways that looped around the city, so he kept driving. He soon came to what seemed to be a foundering business district full of darkened shops and garages, many derelict or abandoned. There were a few open convenience stores with names like Kwik-Buy and Grab-n-Go squatting at corners, and a number of bars and cantinas scattered along the road. It occurred to him that maybe he could stop for a beer while he decided whether to turn around or go on; maybe he could even ask someone for directions. He had let his cell phone contract lapse when he went blind, since he rarely went out; now he carried a prepaid phone for emergencies, good only for making calls, not getting directions.

He decided to stop somewhere to sort things out. Anyplace would do, as long as they spoke English there. He passed two places with Latino-sounding names, then pulled into the parking lot of a bar where a buzzing neon sign read "Carl's Lounge", with the "e" flickering on and off as if trying to decide whether it was worth the trouble to stay lit.

He parked as close as he could to the only floodlight in the potholed parking lot. As he walked to the door, he thought the place looked faded even in the dark. *This neighborhood must be where old bars go to die.* Once in the door, he realized he had forgotten how dark bars could be; it took his eyes a good ten seconds to adjust, even after his drive in the dark. Once they did, the dim light was an advantage; it didn't leave everything enveloped in haze the way headlights did. The only reasonably well-lit area was in a room off to the side with two pool tables, a game going on at each. A jukebox played a generic country song Trey had never heard and would forget as soon as it ended, to be followed by another and another, world without end, at least till closing time. There were maybe fifteen people in the bar, most of them in the room with the pool tables, either playing or watching. Several people looked over when he entered, then immediately turned back to whatever they had been doing.

There were eight low-backed stools at the bar; five were occupied, three at one end, two at the other. Trey took off his jacket and hung it over the back of the middle unoccupied stool, sat down, and ordered a Budweiser. He drank it straight from the bottle, staring vacantly into space, focusing on nothing, hardly needing his restored vision. As his thoughts wandered, he decided there was no point in asking for directions; it would only make him feel more stupid than he already did for getting himself lost. He would figure out how to get home when he was ready to leave. With nothing but his thoughts to distract him, he finished his beer faster than he intended. He wasn't ready to leave yet, so he ordered another, paid for it, then went to the bathroom to piss, certain that with the bartender there, no one would bother his jacket or beer.

When he came back, there was someone on his stool, his beer had been pushed further down the bar, and his jacket was on the floor.

Fury welled up in him like scalding magma, starting from the knot in his stomach and spreading upward, making his heart hammer in his chest and his teeth clench so tightly his gums hurt. That his beer had been moved made it clear his jacket hadn't fallen off the stool by itself. The tattooed bastard sitting in his seat deliberately dropped it on the floor. Trey's first impulse was to smash the son of a bitch's head in, but he could see the motherfucker was taller than him and maybe thirty pounds heavier, though much of the extra weight was fat that hung over his belt, not muscle. He had longish hair and a beard, wore a denim jacket and jeans, and had the general look of a biker, though he wore no colors on his jacket. Trey knew he couldn't let this pass. He also knew he wouldn't win a straight-up fistfight; it had been years since he'd been in one, and he doubted that was true of this fucker. He would have to bide his time and watch for his chance. Without a word, Trey picked his jacket up and brushed it off, then put it on, and sat down on the next stool over. The son of a bitch looked over at him, probably hoping he would say something, but Trey ignored him, clasping his beer in both hands and nursing it for the next half-hour or so. The SOB ordered two more beers in that span and finished them both. He ordered another, then went to the bathroom, leaving his open beer on the bar; he was either daring Trey to touch it or had decided he was too much of a pussy to try.

Trey waited less than half a minute after the door shut to follow him in. The son of a bitch was standing at the lone urinal, looking up toward the ceiling; he didn't turn to look as the door opened, and gave no indication he knew it had. Trey walked toward the lone stall to the left of the urinal as though nothing was wrong, until he was directly behind the asshole. Then he suddenly lowered his shoulder and launched himself at the bastard with all his weight. He slammed his right shoulder into the man's back, trying to hit him as hard as he had ever hit anyone on a football field when he played strong safety back in high school and was known as a vicious tackler. As the man crashed into the wall, caught too much by surprise to cry out, Trey pulled back and turned square on so he could grab the son of a bitch by his hair with both hands, then jerked the bastard's head back a few inches before smashing the man's face into the wall with all the strength he could muster, bracing himself with his right leg to get more force into it.

The urinal hung on a back wall made of cinder blocks covered by a sickly green coat of paint. The asshole got a grunt out before his face hit the wall, blood splattering from his smashed nose. He wasn't out cold, but he was too stunned to react as Trey twisted the man's head around sideways, planted both feet to get more leverage, and this time smashed the left side of the motherfucker's head against the wall as hard as he could. The thud his head made when it hit the wall was louder this time than before, and Trey was surprised the bastard's head didn't break open like a dropped watermelon. The impact opened a gash and left a new splatter of blood on the wall. Trey couldn't tell if the blow had fractured the man's skull, but it did knock him out. He fell heavily against Trey, who backed away and let him slump onto the piss-splattered floor.

As he looked down at the man's bloodied face, a brief flash of something close to panic replaced the rage he felt when he launched his attack. He had wanted to hurt the son of a bitch; now he wasn't sure he hadn't killed him. He had to get out of there and as far away as he could. He took a deep breath and considered his next move. He needed to get away before anyone else walked in, and in a bar, someone would have to take a piss before long. He could leave the man where he lay, sprawled in front of the urinal, but if anyone came in the bathroom now, Trey would be caught. He wasn't sure whether he would be charged with murder or aggravated assault; he didn't intend to find out. He would shove the limp body into the toilet stall and close the door, maybe buying him a little time before anybody discovered the guy, dead or alive. As Trey grabbed the man's limp body under the arms to drag him to the stall, he realized for the first time that the man was armed– he had a .32 caliber semi-automatic pistol holstered in his left armpit. A surprisingly small gun for such a large thug, Trey thought. He crammed the gun into the pocket of his jacket, to make sure the bastard wouldn't have it if he came to. He dragged the man, a dead weight Trey could barely manage, to the stall and backed in, awkwardly pulling him onto the toilet, then pulling the man's legs up to get him all the way inside. His head lolled back against the wall, slack-jawed, his smashed nose still oozing blood, some of it running into his open mouth. For an instant, Trey thought he should shove the fucker's head into the toilet instead of sitting him on it, but this was no time to be creative; he needed to get the hell out of there. He reached up and wiped sweat out of his eyes with the back of his hand; whether the sweat was from his exertion or his fear of getting caught he didn't know. As he stepped out of the stall and slammed the door shut, his foot came down on something hard—a bloody tooth. He kicked it into the stall and backed away. The door started to come open; he slammed it shut again and watched it pop right back open. He pressed against it more gently hoping it would stay shut, realizing there was no way he could latch it from the outside. He quickly grabbed a paper towel and wiped the door where he thought he had touched it. He knew he had to get out before somebody came in to piss. If the son of a bitch in the stall was dead or didn't come to, he might stay undiscovered for hours, as long as the stall door stayed shut—*nobody* would use that toilet unless he absolutely had to. If only that damn door would stay shut. On a sudden inspiration, Trey closed the door and repeatedly folded the paper towel he was holding until it was small enough to wedge between the stall door and the frame. Maybe that would hold it closed for a little while. Trey had done what he could; now he just had to get out of the bar.

He forced himself to walk out calmly, heading straight for the door at what he felt was a normal pace, fighting his instinct to hurry, knowing it was critical to get as far away from the bar as possible before either the guy woke up or somebody found him. Right now, nobody was heading toward the bathroom or paying any attention to Trey. Thankful he had already paid for his beers, he realized he was leaving behind two bottles with fingerprints on them. Maybe the cops wouldn't try all that hard to find someone who assaulted a thug who almost certainly had a criminal record, at least not if the thug was still alive. If the son of a bitch came to before anyone found him, Trey suspected he wasn't the kind of person likely to call the cops himself. Not even about his missing gun—Trey doubted the guy could legally carry one; he looked like someone with at least one felony conviction in his past.

Trey made himself walk to his car at a normal pace, then tried not to pull out of the parking lot too fast, watching the bar door in his rear-view mirror to make sure nobody came out as he was driving off. He turned right at the first corner down; only then did he hit the gas hard. He turned left at the first four-lane road he came to, figuring that would probably bring him to the Beltway sooner or later; it did. The traffic was thinner by this time; once he got on the freeway, he kept to the right lane, so the oncoming cars were far enough to his left that the haze from their headlights didn't bother him too much.

His heart pounded and his hands shook. But a curious feeling of elation welled up as he got further down the freeway and became more certain that nobody was after him. He couldn't help grinning. *Showed that motherfucker, didn't I? Not so damn tough now, is he?* It would feel so good to do something like that again if he ever ran into another asshole like that. Then he remembered the gun in his pocket and found himself thinking it might be a good idea to hang onto it, just in case.

31. "I don't think they're worried enough"

Paul—Week 25, Wednesday, A.M.

PAUL WAS SURPRISED WHEN GREG Wright called his office one Wednesday morning about six months into the trial. Paul had talked to him only twice before. The first time was when Wright called to tell Paul about his daughter, Kathy, and ask whether he thought she would be a suitable candidate for the trial; Paul saw no reason why she wouldn't be. The last time was soon after that, when Wright called to say Kathy had enrolled in it and thanked Paul for his support.

"Is there something wrong with the trial?" Paul said, when Wright identified himself. "When I talked to Jim Russell not long ago, he said everything was fine."

"I'm not sure if anything's wrong or not. That's why I wanted to talk with you. I haven't cleared this call with Jim, by the way. I'd appreciate it if you didn't mention it to him. I wanted to ask you about some possible side effects my daughter might be having. I can't say for sure the drug is causing them."

"What kind of effects? Jim never gives me much detail when we talk, but he hasn't mentioned any really negative effects except headaches. He told me two people have shown strong responses. Is your daughter one of them?"

Wright gave a short laugh. "You could say that. She actually got her sight back. Kind of. Her eyes seem to work fine– that part was spectacular. I don't think her brain has caught up, though. She's having a lot of trouble making sense of what she sees and she can't tell how far away things are when she does see them."

Paul tried to be reassuring. "That's not unheard of. In the early days of eye surgery, a lot of people who had congenital cataracts removed had to learn how to see. Some never got the hang of it completely. They had a lot of problems with depth perception."

"Yes, I know. That's definitely part of it. What I'm wondering about are psychological effects, behavior changes. Did any of your animals act strange?"

"No. Not that we could tell. They all seemed normal afterward. Of course, we can't know what's going on in their heads. We can't say there weren't subtle changes we didn't pick up on. That's why we've been cautious with this trial, starting off with a very low dose. They ask about psychological effects as part of the protocol. What's going on with your daughter?"

"It's not easy to pin down. She's been seriously depressed. It's possible that's caused by all the trouble she's having trying to see, but I think it could be more than that. She tells me she's had some serious mood swings—from way up to way down, though she's down a lot more than up."

"Not everyone who's ever regained their sight has been completely happy about it, especially at first. It's a serious adjustment to make. The ones who have a hard time usually get over it. Sometimes it takes a while."

Wright almost snapped back at him. "I know about all that. I've been looking into this, you know? I've tracked down some of that literature. I'm not sure it applies to what I'm talking about here." He paused, and his tone softened. "Did you know my daughter plays piano in a hotel lounge three days a week? The Blue Room at the Regency Square? You know it? Never mind, it doesn't matter. The singer she works with told me that one night a few weeks ago, Kathy got so caught up in the music she was playing between sets that it kind of ran away with her. Leila had to cut her short. The same thing happened last month at church when Kathy was playing the organ before the service started. She got completely carried away and kept playing after the service was supposed to start. They were so surprised, they let her go on for ten minutes before the minister had to stop her so he could start the service."

"She keeps playing, even when she knows she should stop?"

"When she gets carried away, I don't think she knows she should stop anymore. And Leila told me something else. I asked her if she'd noticed anything else different about Kathy. She told me Kathy had been more… unpredictable lately. She didn't want to say any more than that, but I kept at her, and finally she told me that right after Kathy's eyes started getting better, she let a stranger pick her up at work. Leila said she'd never done that before—Kathy's always been careful who she goes out with. Leila said her going off with a stranger wasn't like Kathy at all. I almost had to force Leila to tell me about it, but she's worried, too. My concern isn't that Kathy had sex. Blind or not, my daughter's an adult, and she makes her own decisions. According to Leila, though, the thing with this one guy just came out of nowhere, and Kathy's always been more careful than that."

Paul sat upright in his chair and almost dropped the phone. *Impulsive sex? So it's not just me. Or me and Lindsey.*

Wright continued. "But all that's happened when she wasn't depressed. Sometimes her mood is so black, I wonder if she hasn't thought about hurting herself. She hasn't said anything like that. But both Leila and my wife have noticed how depressed she can be now. I've seen it, too. It's just not like Kathy."

Paul wasn't sure what to say. "We didn't really assess behavior much in the animals we worked with. We didn't notice anything odd, though. I wonder if some of your daughter's mood swings aren't related to her eyesight problems. It seems to me her depression certainly could be. I mean, I don't know, I'm no expert there." He hesitated a few seconds. "You know, this may have no connection with what your daughter's going through, but I'll tell you something I've only told one other person about. I had an accident in the lab, and I think I was exposed to the drug—probably not much, but we know you don't need much to see an effect. And lately I've had some trouble being impulsive, myself. And now with what you tell me—I don't know. Maybe this is something we need to look into. You haven't talked to Jim Russell about your daughter's problems?"

"I haven't, no. Kathy goes in for testing regularly, though, and I'm pretty sure she's told him about being depressed. I'm not sure about the runaway playing incidents. They embarrassed her. Even though my wife was at the church when it happened, Kathy didn't want to talk about it. It wouldn't surprise me if she didn't tell Jim about them, either, though I don't know. I like Jim, but if she did tell him, I think he'd be inclined to downplay anything that can't be clearly linked to the drug. Our company has a lot at stake here—I don't have to tell you how much money this drug could be worth. I think everyone's more worried about physical side effects than psychological ones. They're easier to pin down, and easier to fix. Since Kathy is having so much trouble seeing, they probably figure her depression's a natural response, so if it's caused by the drug, it's indirect and they can discount it."

"Look, I don't know if the drug has any psychological effects, but based on my own experience and what you're telling me, I think it might. Would you mind if I talked with your daughter? Would she be okay talking to me?"

"I don't think she'd mind. I'll ask her. I don't think she'd have any problem if you wanted to talk. She knows who you are."

"If she knows I made the drug, she might blame me for all this, you know? Could you tell her I'd like to talk and let me know if that's okay with her?"

"Sure, I'll do that. Thanks for listening to me. Maybe the drug's not to blame, but we need to know if it is."

"Yeah. I'll call Jim Russell and ask if they've noticed changes in anyone's behavior. It's a reasonable question. I won't say anything about you calling or mention anything about your daughter if you don't want me to."

"I think it'd be better if you could keep my name out of it for now. If you say anything about Kathy, he'll know where it came from. Maybe you could just keep things kind of general when you talk to him? They need to look into this. I'm worried about my daughter, and I don't think they're worried enough."

Paul sat at his desk for some minutes after the call, thinking. If he hadn't been worried enough before, himself, he was now.

32. Within Reasonably Normal Bounds

Paul—Week 25, Wednesday, P.M.

WHEN PAUL CALLED JIM RUSSELL'S office, his assistant said he wasn't available and asked if she could take a message.

"Tell him Paul Lazarus would like to talk with him."

Russell called back within minutes. "Paul! What can I do for you?" Russell tried to keep an annoyed edge out of his voice. He had told his assistant not to bother him unless it was dire, but she knew Paul had high priority

"Sorry to bother you. I wanted to check on the trial. I've been wondering—have you seen anything that might suggest any neurological side effects? Any behavior changes?"

"Neurological? Would you count headaches? It can definitely cause those. Sometimes severe, but they usually get better over time. In all but two patients, they eventually faded out completely. In one of them, they're still bad enough that he probably won't go on to Phase 2. But behavior changes? Not that I know of. Why? Have you seen anything in your animals that would make you suspect something?"

Not in animals, in people, Paul thought, but was careful not to say it. "No, we haven't seen any obvious behavior changes, not even in our longest survivors. We also haven't seen any brain changes in necropsies. Besides the optic nerve, of course. I'm talking about the kind of thing it would be hard to test in animals, though. As far as we could tell, all our animals behaved normally after treatment. Only you can't ask animals what they're feeling. I've been worried about what the trial subjects might be feeling, whether they're normal, that's all."

Russell did sound annoyed now, like an impatient teacher with an exceptionally dull pupil. "Participants, please. Or patients. We try not to think of them as subjects. Semantics, I know. We never refer to them as 'subjects', so we won't slip and call them that when we're talking to them. They don't like it. Sorry, I don't mean to preach."

"That's okay." *Subjects, patients, participants. We treat them like guinea pigs, whatever we call them.*

Russell was definitely in lecture mode now. "You know we ask a lot of questions about how they're feeling, whether they've noticed anything different, if their behavior has changed in any way." *Paul's seen the protocols. Why's he acting like he doesn't know any of this? Why this sudden interest in patients' behavior?*

"Have you found anything?" Paul was certain the answer would be "No", whether it was true or not.

"Nothing unexpected. All the ones who haven't shown any response have been depressed about it to some extent, though we told them from the start we weren't expecting any therapeutic response at this stage, certainly not with the first dose. But nobody goes into a trial without hoping it'll help them. Even if we tell them the chances are remote, each one hopes he'll be the one. There's always disappointed patients in any trial. People get depressed if a drug doesn't work. We've seen that here, sure. That's normal."

"Nothing else?" Paul pressed further.

"Well, I have to admit the two patients who got their eyesight back haven't quite reacted the way we thought they would. One of them is having a lot of trouble adjusting, much more than we anticipated. Her eyes function perfectly, but her visual cortex hasn't caught up. She sees images, but can't make sense of them."

"I think I know who that is." As soon as he said it, Paul mentally kicked himself. If Jim figured he was talking about Kathy Wright, he could easily guess who Paul had talked to. *Way to protect your source, dumbass.*

Russell sailed right past the slip. "You know I can't say who, but she's reported being depressed. That's understandable. I mean, she can *see*, just not the way she hoped. You'd expect her to be depressed."

"That's all, just the kind of depression you might get from being disappointed? No manic depressive mood swings or something?"

"From normal to depressed and back, sure. But nothing bipolar. No wild manic highs followed by terrible lows, if that's what you mean. She's been pretty depressed at times, sure. The problems with her eyesight are extremely frustrating, so that's not surprising. The way things are now, she can't use her eyes; she keeps them closed or covered most of the time. It's no wonder she's depressed—she's functionally blind, even though her eyes work. Think how that must be. I'd be depressed, too. You think you know who she is—has she been talking to you?"

"No, just to someone I know. He believes some of her mood swings may be worse than you think. I don't know much more than that. You might ask if she's had anything unusual happen the next time she comes in. But please don't tell her you've been hearing things from other people."

"I think we can push our questions a little further without giving anything away." Russell's gaze fell on the protocol manual for the trial— almost 500 pages, with all the appendices. *As long as we can do it within the protocols. We're not changing them now.*

"You mentioned the other person who can see not reacting the way you expected. What happened there?" *Someone else is acting strange? Shit.*

"Hard to say, really. He dropped out of the study. I'm sorry I didn't tell you about it before; things have been hectic around here. He was free to quit, of course, but he didn't give us a clear reason, and he hasn't responded to any of our attempts to contact him since. He got really angry at his last exam. Said he was tired of answering the same questions over and over, going through the same tests. I can see his point, but that's part of the deal in a clinical trial. He seemed genuinely pissed off, though. Rather ungrateful, you know? I mean, he got his sight back without any problems at all. Of everyone in the trial, he's the one we'd most like to follow up. But I couldn't talk him into staying. We're trying to get him back. So far, we've tried phone calls and letters, with no response. I don't want to pressure him too much, but I might have to go by his house myself, see if he'll at least answer the door."

"He got pissed off and dropped out, even though he can see again? That doesn't sound like a normal response to me. Could the drug cause that, you think?"

"It's certainly not what we were expecting. But it would be hard to blame the drug for making him act like an asshole. Nobody else has. It would be a big help if we could get him back. … Anything else I can tell you?" Russell was clearly tired of the conversation; the last sentence had a sarcastic edge to it.

"No, not right now, anyway. I'm just worried the drug might have psychological effects in humans that we couldn't see in animals."

Paul couldn't see it, but Russell raised his eyebrows. "That's all there is to it? I can understand you worrying about it, but you shouldn't. We're trying to watch out for things like that. We want this drug to work as much as you do. We don't want anything getting past us."

"I know. Just let me know if anyone else starts acting odd, okay? I'll sleep better once we're sure the drug isn't changing people's behavior."

"Don't lose too much sleep. I think everything we've seen so far is within reasonably normal bounds, except maybe the one pissed-off guy. I'll keep trying to get him back in the trial."

"Okay. But if he really is pissed off, you might want to be careful. Don't just drop by without warning; we might never get him back." After the call, Paul sat for several minutes, staring into space, wondering why he felt compelled to give that last advice. He decided his explosion at the faculty meeting might have something to do with it.

33. "What would you look for?"

Paul–Weeks 25-26

PAUL FELT LIKE A MAN with his head on a block, waiting for the axe to fall. He was convinced there was something wrong with OGF83—but what? If it was doing anything it wasn't supposed to, it was taking its time and being damned subtle about it. When David Eamon, came by his office about eight the next morning, Paul decided it was time to get some advice.

"David, I think I fucked up. I didn't look hard enough at the animals we treated with OGF83. They got their eyesight back, and that's all we cared about. They seemed normal, but I don't know, maybe they weren't really normal, and we just missed it." Paul bent and twisted the fingers of his right hand nervously, making his joints crack and pop.

"What should you have done? Put them through mazes?" David smiled for an instant. "What kind of tests could you give them? What would you look for?"

"I don't know. What do I know about animal behavior? They didn't cower in their cages or try to bite. No more than usual, anyway. At least that's what the animal techs said; I didn't handle them very much myself. Lindsey did all the surgeries and drug dosing and implanted electrodes for signal testing. The people in Animal Care did the feeding and cleaning and kept records. Nobody said anything about any odd behavior." Now Paul started cracking the joints on his left hand.

"The people in Animal Care would have noticed anything strange and told you about it. I'm on the Animal Care and Use Committee, so I see them a lot. They know what they're doing."

"But I didn't. We were so thrilled with the positive results that we didn't look hard enough for negative ones, and that's my fault. I should have known better. We just assumed that because the animals looked normal, they were normal, and we thought the drug would behave the same way in humans as it did in monkeys, at least. Maybe not rats. Rat physiology's different. But it seemed to work fine in monkeys. It regrew optic nerves just like it did in rats, and everything looked fine. But maybe it wasn't. We need to find out more about what else the drug might be doing." He had started back in on the fingers of his right hand.

"Okay. We need to know what else the drug might be doing in animals besides growing new optic nerves. Do you have any funds you could use for some tracer studies? We should track it in the brain and see where it's going."

"Yeah, I have some money I could use. We'll have to keep the number of animals down, though, especially monkeys. Can we get expedited approval through your committee?"

"I think so. We have labs around here that do tracer studies routinely. They'll have templates for the approval forms we can tweak pretty quick. Let me ask around to see who could help."

* * *

A week later, David, who seemed to know every scientist at the Medical Center, had arranged for Paul to meet with Larry Wisniewski, who used Positron Emission Tomography scans to track metabolic activity in the brain to study different diseases and treatments. They quickly worked out a protocol. Wisniewski would label a batch of OGF83 with a radioactive tracer, and Paul would give the labeled drug to a dozen rats and two rhesus monkeys from Janey Rose's lab in the Physiology Department. Paul would use healthy animals to save time—cutting an optic nerve, then waiting for recovery would take too long. Wisniewski would run multiple PET scans on the treated animals over a two-week period to see how the drug was metabolized—where it went in the brain and how long it took to break it down.

With David Eamon's connections on the university's review committees, Paul was able to get expedited review and approval of the study within a couple of weeks. Three weeks after they planned it, the study was underway. Now they just had to wait.

34. Road Rage

Trey—Week 25, Wednesday

OVER THE NEXT FEW DAYS, nothing turned up in the news about anyone being found dead in the bathroom of a bar. Trey assumed the guy either came to on his own with a very bad headache, or had been found and taken to a hospital. Trey was probably in the clear.

He kept replaying the whole thing in his head and coming back to the thrill he felt driving home afterward. He couldn't remember the last time he felt so fully alive. For the first time, he thought he understood the kind of people who seemed to look for fights. He hadn't exactly vanquished his foe in hand-to-hand combat, but then he hadn't been in a fight since high school. He had to be realistic about the odds and do what he could to improve them. If you're not the biggest or the strongest or the meanest, then you'd better be the smartest and find some way to get an edge. He decided to keep the biker's gun with him when he went out. It was small enough to conceal easily, carried in a pocket holster. When he drove, he put it in the console between the front seats; it's hard to draw a gun from your pocket when you're sitting.

He still avoided going out in the daytime as much as possible, but now and then it was unavoidable. The Wednesday after the bar incident, he had to go out for some groceries. About ten a.m., he looked to see whether any of his neighbors were around, then backed his car out of the garage. The gun was in the console beside him.

A car approached from the right as he turned left out of his neighborhood. It didn't look that close, so when Trey pulled out in front of it, he was startled to hear the driver blow his horn, then lay on it for several seconds after it was no longer a warning and had become an insult. Trey glared in his rear view mirror. The car moved to the right lane and pulled up beside him. Trey looked over to see a stocky man with a mustache giving him the finger and shouting something. At forty miles per hour, Trey couldn't hear anything the guy was saying. He figured "Fuck you!" and "Asshole!" were in there somewhere. If the son of a bitch had driven off then, Trey would have let it pass, but he kept pace for two blocks, then three, and stayed there, glaring, still mouthing words Trey couldn't hear but could easily imagine.

What's with this guy? He didn't even have to swerve when I pulled out. He wasn't that close. Trey felt a surge of fury. *You stupid son of a bitch. Watch this!* Almost in one motion, he popped open the lid of the console, pulled out the gun, flicked the safety off, and used his trigger finger to push the button on the console that lowered the passenger side window. The other driver lowered his own window and shouted something Trey couldn't make out. Trey raised his arm, holding it stiffly out to the side, the gun pointing directly at the other driver, whose furious expression was replaced by one of shock and then terror in the space of an instant. His eyes popped wide open, and he stopped shouting as his mouth formed an "O". He reflexively braked. Trey anticipated that; he didn't want the son of a bitch to get behind him and see his license plate. So Trey hit his brakes, too, and the cars stayed side-by-side as both slowed. Realizing that braking wouldn't help, the man hunched low over the steering wheel and stomped the gas; his car surged ahead. Trey let him pull away, then abruptly turned left at the next side street. *I need to get home; the fucker's probably already on his cell phone dialing 9-1-1. I'll do without the groceries for now.* He headed home, his heart pounding.

Bet that stupid son of a bitch thinks twice before he blows his goddamn horn next time. He just had to be an asshole. I'm sick of assholes.

That night, Trey felt ready to take on anyone and anything. He knew shooting that horn-blowing bastard would have caused nothing but trouble, but knowing that he *could* have made him feel the way he had after he kicked that biker's ass. He couldn't focus on the TV as he ran on his treadmill. His mind was racing, and his legs followed; he ran harder and longer than ever before. He felt good, better than ever. He could run a marathon if he wanted; he could do anything. *Now that I can see again, I can get my life back. All I have to do is get my old job back. It wasn't my fault I had to leave. I only retired because I went blind, and now*

I'm not blind anymore. They have to take me back! It'd be discrimination if they didn't, wouldn't it?

I'll skip the bureaucrats in Personnel and go straight to Steve Linscombe. I liked working for him, and I know he liked me. He was more a co-worker than a boss. He'll want me back, and he'll have some pull at the company.

Trey would surprise him, show him how completely he'd recovered. He knew how and when to do it, too. For as long as Trey had worked at Lenevar, Steve would go in to work every Sunday morning about 8 or 8:30, when the building was virtually deserted. A few others usually showed up in the afternoon, but Steve was the only one you could count on to be there every Sunday. Trey knew that, because he would often go in on Sunday mornings himself, sometimes arriving before Steve did. He couldn't remember ever working on a Sunday morning without seeing Steve there.

By the time he finished on the treadmill, Trey was convinced that paying a surprise visit to Steve Linscombe on Sunday was absolutely the right thing to do. He didn't have to worry about his future, he'd simply pick up where he left off. He could hardly wait till Sunday.

35. Things Fall Apart

Trey—Week 26, Sunday

WHEN STEVE LINSCOMBE PULLED INTO the Lenevar lot that Sunday about eight, he was surprised to find another car there. Usually, no one else was around that early on a Sunday, which is precisely why he liked to come in; he could get some work done without interruption. He parked, and as he got out, so did the other driver. Linscombe was stunned to see Trey.

"Trey? Is that you? How can you be here? How can you drive? You're supposed to be blind!"

Trey grinned. "Not anymore! Believe it or not, they tested a new drug on me, and it worked! I can see now! I can even drive!" He waved toward his car.

"How is that even possible?" Linscombe stood uncertainly for a moment, shifting his weight from one foot to the other. There was no protocol for this—a disabled ex-employee who wasn't disabled anymore, come back for… what? But he couldn't turn him away. "Come on in. Tell me what happened." He couldn't think of anything else to say. He already had misgivings. *What does he want? Why is he here? He could have come by my house, or called. If he wants his old job back, he knows I can't hire him; he'd have to go through Personnel.*

Trey could barely contain himself once he sat down in Linscombe's office; his words came out in bursts, as if fired from a machine gun. He kept brushing his hand across his forehead as though he were brushing back a lock of hair, though his hair was already combed back. "A shock, isn't it? I wanted to surprise you. I want to get my old job back. I don't know what to do with myself now. I've got to do something. I can't just sit around doing nothing now that I can see again. I never knew how much I'd miss my job until I couldn't do it anymore. Being blind is a drag, let me tell you."

Linscombe could barely follow. He was still getting over the shock of seeing Trey—and Trey seeing him. Trey's rapid-fire sentences and agitated manner made Linscombe uneasy. Why come to him? He had been Trey's supervisor, and that was all; they hadn't been close. He hadn't tried to contact Trey once he left. He couldn't remember ever asking anyone how Trey was after that, and he wasn't sure anyone else at Lenevar had kept in touch with him. But here he was, and his timing could not possibly be worse. With oil prices and rig counts down, and a lot of exploration on hold, the oil services industry had been hit hard. Lenevar's revenues plummeted, and there had been two rounds of layoffs in the past 12 months, with a third imminent. There was no job for Trey to come back to. But Linscombe had to keep the conversation pleasant for a few minutes while he figured out what to say.

"It's good to see you again. And really good that you can see me! When did all this happen? How long have you been able to see?"

"I got the drug last April. They were looking for side effects, so they started with a dose nobody thought was big enough to work yet, but they guaranteed me a spot in the next round, when they'd up the dose to find one that works. Nothing happened for a month. Then I started seeing light flashes when I rubbed my eyes, then I got to where I could tell dark from light, and then I started to see things again. It took about four months, all told. I see almost 20/20 now, and I'm starting to go nuts. I can see again, but I don't have anything to do. I can't just sit around. I don't want to start all over somewhere new. I was good at what I did, but I've been out of it for nearly four years, and I'd have to explain why if I looked for a job somewhere else. I wouldn't have to explain anything here. You know me, you know what I can do." Trey was still talking so fast, Linscombe could hardly keep up.

Linscombe put his left hand over his eyes, massaging his temple with his thumb, grimacing behind the cover of his hand. "Trey, you know I don't do the hiring here. I can't give you your old job back; I don't have the authority. If I could, I'd be happy to. But a lot has changed since you left. You know how bad business is now, don't you? Oil prices are way down. We've had to let people go, even some who were more senior than you. I hate to say it, but right now, I don't think there's a job here you could come back to. I'm sorry."

This was like a kick in the gut. Trey had convinced himself that there was absolutely no way he wouldn't get his job back. "Damn, Steve, that's not right! I only lost my job because I went blind. This is like when a starting quarterback gets hurt, right? When he comes back, he's supposed to get his job back."

"Come on, Trey. This isn't football. The company's barely hanging on right now. Oil prices will go up sooner or later, but no one knows when. We lost money the last three quarters, even cutting things to the bone. Maybe we could take you back when we start hiring again, but I don't see how we could do it now. And...." He paused, hesitating to bring up what had occurred to him as he was speaking. He would have to tell the company Trey wasn't blind any longer. They were scrambling to survive the worst downturn they'd ever faced. They couldn't afford to subsidize Trey if he wasn't disabled anymore.

"And what?"

"You know the company committed to covering your pension, even though it didn't have to. Hell, we don't even offer a straight pension anymore; new hires get 401(k) plans now. Not many companies this size ever had full pension plans for employees, but this one did, and that was a huge commitment. The company stepped up for you when you had to retire. Now that you're not disabled anymore, I don't know if the company can keep paying you like it has been. We're having to cut expenses wherever we can, just to stay afloat. You have to get permission just to make hard copies of anything, to save on paper."

"Come on! You can't cut me off like that! No job and no pension? What kind of shit is that?"

"Maybe we could give you a severance package, like we do with people who are laid off, so you wouldn't just be cut off all of a sudden. Give you, I don't know, six months to find a job. I think we could work something like that out." Linscombe knew he didn't have the authority to promise anything like that, but he had to tell Trey something. He thought the company would go along with it; Trey had been a good engineer.

"Come on, Steve. I'm not asking for a handout here, just my old job back. I just want to work. My life stopped completely when I went blind. You have no idea. I had to start *everything* over. Now I have a chance to get back to normal. I'll never get back those years when I couldn't see. I don't want to start over again at a whole new job. That's not fair. Something great happens to me, and suddenly I'm screwed? That's not right. No way that's right."

"I'm sorry, Trey. You're right, I *don't* know what you went through. But I know what this company is going through now. We're barely keeping our heads above water. I'd really like to help you, but I doubt we can give you your old job back, not right now, anyway. Maybe when oil prices go back up…. In the meantime, we're hurting. We'll probably have to let more people go, if things don't pick up soon."

"Goddamn it, Steve. I'm not asking for a handout."

"I know you're not. This is just a bad time."

Trey was silent for several seconds, his gaze on the floor. When he looked up at Linscombe, his expression had changed, as though some spark behind his eyes had gone out. When Trey stepped out of his car just minutes ago, he was excited, animated, almost flying. Now he seemed to have shrunk two sizes. He looked up, his eyes shifting rapidly from side to side, as if he were looking for a way out.

Linscombe felt he had pushed a button he didn't want to. When Trey spoke, his voice sounded flat and tired. The sudden change was scary. "Look, no one here except you knows I can see again. Maybe you could just not say anything while I look for a job. I could at least keep my pension while I look. If things are as bad as you say, it could take me months to find a job somewhere else, it's been so long since I worked. All I know is oil. If I have to find a job in some other field, it'll be even harder. Unless it's some minimum wage job. I can't get by on that."

"Come on, Trey. Don't ask me to lie. I have a responsibility to this company."

With more vehemence than he intended, Trey immediately shot back, "You wouldn't be lying! All you'd have to do is not say anything!"

"I don't see that as not lying. What if it comes out that I knew you could see and didn't say anything? That could cost me *my* job. They might even think I've been covering up for you. How do they know you didn't fake it somehow, pay off some doctors or something to say you were blind? How come nobody's heard of this miracle drug? Wouldn't they be parading you in front of TV cameras? If you suddenly show up here again, everyone will figure you were faking it from the start, unless you can prove it's this drug that did it. Did anyone else take it? Can they see again?"

Trey felt a flash of panic. "What do you mean? You think I faked it all? They can't say anything in public about the drug yet. They said there were still legal issues with the patent. We had to sign Non-Disclosure Agreements before they'd give it to us. I shouldn't even be telling *you*."

There was a hostile edge to Linscombe's voice now. "Whatever, I can't cover for you. I'd be risking my job. You can't expect the company to keep paying you if you're not disabled. If you haven't thought about looking for work anywhere but here, you need to. The money they're paying you now might keep somebody from being laid off."

Trey shot back instantly, his voice rising in volume. "Yeah, by cutting *me* loose. I didn't do anything wrong, goddamn it. I took a chance on a new drug. No one knew if it would work. I'm not gonna let myself get screwed just because it did."

"I'm not trying to screw you. But I can't cover up for you. I won't lie for you."

Trey bolted to his feet, his face contorted in a snarl. "Goddamn it, Steve! I come here to get my old job back and you hit me with this? I don't get my job back, plus you take away my income?" He leaned far over the desk, both hands on the desktop. "I'll be goddamned if I'll let you do that!"

Now it was Linscombe's turn to snarl. "Are you threatening me? I think you need to leave!"

Trey stood up straight and closed his eyes tightly. His expression changed from a snarl to a grimace, his face twisted in pain. He seemed to be fighting something inside, trying hard to hold it back. And then it came.

He spat. It wasn't aimed at Linscombe. Trey turned his head to his left, and a gob of saliva spattered on the floor.

Linscombe was outraged. He shot out of his chair as if launched from it. "What the fuck is wrong with you? Jesus! Get the hell out of here! Now!"

Trey's face was still twisted in a grimace; his fists were clenched. He was fighting to hold something in, something that would engulf them both if he let it out. Closing his eyes even tighter, he shouted, with a voice that rose in pitch on the second word, "Shut *up*!" Then he opened his eyes and said slowly, in a lower tone, "Don't say another word!"

"Don't tell me to shut up!"

That was the trigger. *Not one more word.* That flashed through Trey's mind at the same instant Linscombe shouted, when it was too late to speak, too late to warn him one last time. Trey erupted. In that instant, without thinking at all, he plunged his right hand into the pocket of his jacket and came out with the gun he had taken from the barroom thug. The safety was off—he would regret that when he thought about it later. There was already a round in the chamber, and that, too, would bother him when he thought back on it afterward. If he'd had to thumb the safety off or chamber a round, he might have had second thoughts about pulling the trigger. Too late now. Linscombe had no chance to react, not even to say, "No!" or throw up his hands. There was a sharp, explosive bang, shockingly loud; Trey flinched as he pulled the trigger, scrunching his neck, but he couldn't miss at that range. The bullet pierced Linscombe's chest and passed through the right side of his heart. He sat down in his chair suddenly, falling back into it as if his feet had been pulled from under him. He grunted in pain and for a few seconds looked at Trey with a wide-eyed, slack-mouthed expression of surprise. Then he seemed to look right through Trey at something very far away. He slumped over to his right, his arm dangling limply over the arm of the chair. A bloodstain spread over his chest, and his khaki pants turned dark around his crotch as his bladder emptied.

For a second, Trey thought of calling for help, but knew it was useless. He stood looking down at the gun in his hand, as though surprised to find it there. *Shit. Shit. Shit. I didn't intend this. What now? Turn myself in? Say it was an accident? It was. But if you pull a gun and it goes off, they'll never believe you didn't mean to shoot it. Even if they did, you'd still go to jail. Claim self-defense? No one would buy it, even if it's true in a way—he'd take away my living, how could I let him do that? I had to stop him. But no one would buy that.*

No. No one's going to find out I did this. Nobody knew I was coming here, not even Steve, so he couldn't have told anyone. No one could have heard the shot; there's no one else in the building—no cars in the parking lot but ours. I'll wipe off everything I might have touched and leave.

His mind was racing. *Could I make it look like suicide? No. No note. They'd investigate and they'd know he didn't shoot himself. No gunpowder on his hands. So they're gonna look for a killer and a motive. Probably an employee he had a fight with, or someone who got laid off. But not me. With Steve dead, no one at Cardon knows I can see, except maybe Al Guttmacher. No one else here bothered to keep up with me after I left. I think I talked to him when my eyes started getting better. But I don't think I could see yet. We haven't talked since then. If Al told anyone about the drug, the cops might check me out, but I'll worry about that later.*

Maybe I could make this look like a botched robbery—Steve surprised a burglar. That might throw the cops off, so they don't look too hard at ex-employees. Why would anyone want to break in here, though? Maybe Steve ran into the wrong person in the parking lot, someone who saw an easy victim. Maybe the cops wouldn't buy it, but they'd have to consider it. If I can get them to look for someone with no ties to Lenevar, it's worth a shot.

Trey realized he had just made a grim pun of sorts, and chuckled aloud. *I must be one sick bastard.*

Trey went to work, starting with what seemed obvious. He ripped two tissues out of a box on Linscombe's desk and hastily wiped up the gob of spit on the floor. He tossed them in a trash can, then laughed ruefully. *Right. Wipe up the evidence, then leave it here.* He fished the tissues out of the trash and stuffed them in his pocket. He pulled more tissues out of the box and tried to think of anything he might have touched. *The desktop, certainly.* Not sure where he put his hands when he leaned over it, he wiped the whole desktop. He tried to think of what else he might have touched. *The arms of this chair. The doorknob?* Linscombe had opened the door, not him, but he wiped both knobs anyway, then stuffed those tissues in his pocket, too. He pulled two more from the box and used them to open three of the four desk drawers, rifling through their contents, careful to use tissues. The bottom right drawer was locked, so he touched Linscombe's body for the first time, pulling his keys from his pants pocket, grimacing as he fished around in the pocket of the wet pants. He opened the locked drawer using tissues; nothing but files. The same was true of two filing cabinets he also had to unlock; he left one drawer open on each. Then he pulled Linscombe's wallet from his right hip pocket and his smartphone from his shirt pocket. He had to wipe some blood from the phone. It was dangerous to carry away anything with Linscombe's blood on it, but he would get rid of the bloodstained tissues as soon as possible. He was pleased to see that the phone was one with an accessible battery; he pried the phone open and took the battery out. He had plans for that phone. And the wallet.

He went back over everything, wiping the handles on all the desk and file cabinet drawers again. He wiped every flat surface in the room, and objects like a stapler and a pencil sharpener, even though he hadn't come anywhere near them. He wiped Linscombe's keys and put them on the desk. Wiping everything might make it look all the more like a robber determined to cover up every trace. He wiped the plastic and metal parts on Linscombe's chair. As he scanned the office to see what else he could do to make it look like the scene of a robbery gone wrong, he suddenly heard the metallic clank of the building's front door opening. He froze, and heard a second thunk as the door closed. Footsteps clacked on the lobby floor, drawing closer, then stopped for several seconds. Trey reached into his pocket, his hand tightening on the gun. The footsteps started again, this time receding down the corridor on the opposite side of the lobby from Linscombe's office, fading out without Trey hearing any door open or close. Trey exhaled; he hadn't realized he'd been holding his breath.

He was no longer alone in the building. He fought back an urge to run. No. He had to be calmer than ever now. *Okay, let's think this through. How could Steve have surprised a burglar? How could a burglar get in the building?* The front door was the only logical entry point. What few windows the building had were small and high up on the walls; it would be almost impossible for anyone to get in through one of them, even with a ladder. Trey knew from years of working in the building that the heavy fire exit doors were all wired with alarms. No, the front door was the only way. But whoever came in had seen an intact front door. For Trey to fake a forced entry there by breaking the glass, he would have to find whoever just came in and kill him, too. *No, forget that.* Too bad; an interrupted burglary would be more plausible than a robbery that started in the parking lot. Whoever came in could be almost anywhere in the other wing of the building, and hard to find. Trey didn't feel he could hunt someone down to shoot him. He had no doubt he would shoot anyone who found him in the building. It would be a matter of survival. But he couldn't go looking for them. *I'm not a cold-blooded murderer, goddamn it.*

Trey had to get out of the building without being seen or heard. He opened the office door a crack and listened; somewhere down the opposite corridor, he heard a door open and close. He remembered what he had always considered a flaw in the building's security system—you had to use a keycard to enter the building when it was locked, but you could exit without one. He was glad of it now; he didn't need Linscombe's keycard to get out. He put his head out the door and looked up and down the hallway. Nobody there. He took one last look around the office to see if there was anything he'd missed. It occurred to him he hadn't wiped the framed pictures on Linscombe's desk of his wife, April, or his college-age daughter. He had skipped them because he didn't want to look at them. He'd liked Steve. April, too. He'd never met the daughter. *Too bad it came to this.* He reluctantly wiped both pictures, and was surprised to find blood on the tissue after he wiped April's. There was blood on Steve, and on the chair and the floor beneath it, but he hadn't seen any spattered anywhere else. Trey slipped out the door and quietly closed it behind him, wiping the doorknob before leaving. His soft-soled shoes made little noise on the polished lobby floor. He slowly backed into the exit bar to open the door without touching it with his hands. Once outside, he turned and, again using tissues, grasped the outer handle to let the door shut quietly, rather than let it close automatically with a loud, metallic "thunk". He looked carefully around before walking to his car, grateful that no windows near ground level overlooked the parking lot. A maroon SUV was parked three spaces down from where his and Linscombe's silver sedans sat side-by-side. Whoever drove the SUV would have seen Trey's car, but there were thousands of gray or silver cars on the road; nothing made his stand out.

Trey got into his car, shut the door as quietly as he could, and drove away at a normal speed, watching to make sure nobody came out of the building as he drove off. He took a roundabout way home while pondering how to get rid of everything from Linscombe's office.

Once home, he flushed all the tissues he had crammed into his pockets down the toilet. He stripped down in front of the washing machine and put in everything he'd been wearing except his belt and shoes, then ran the washer on the "Heavy" cycle. Standing naked at the kitchen sink, he used soap and water and an old toothbrush to scrub his belt and shoes, paying special attention to the soles. He took a knife and scored each sole several times, in case he had left any footprints at the scene.

He then took a long and thorough shower. He had to get rid of the gun and Linscombe's wallet and phone, but that would have to wait until dark. Meanwhile, he put on latex kitchen gloves and methodically wiped the wallet and phone, even the battery, with a cloth soaked in rubbing alcohol. He had shot Steve Linscombe in a flash of anger, without even thinking, but he was thinking very clearly now.

36. *"I haven't been 'Jimmy' since I was ten"*

Jim Travis—Week 26, Sunday

When Steve Linscombe hadn't come home or called by seven p.m., his wife, April, called both his office number and his cell phone and got no answer. This wasn't like Steve. If there was something holding him up at the office, he would always call. When he went in on Sundays, he was invariably home no later than five, usually sooner. At 7:45, worried, she drove to his office and found his car still in the parking lot. No other cars were there. The front door was locked, and there was no doorbell or buzzer, no way to alert anyone inside short of pounding on the door. She called his supervisor, Darrin Hammond, then sat in her car, waiting, for an interminable twenty minutes, dialing Steve's office and cell numbers alternately every few minutes.

As Hammond drove there, breaking speed limits all the way, his first thought was that Linscombe might have had a heart attack or a stroke, though he was only in his early fifties. As he pulled into the parking lot, April shot out of her car and rushed over. He barely got his own door open before the frantic woman grabbed his arm.

Her words tumbled out in a rush. "Something's wrong. I know it. This isn't like Steve. He always calls. He's got to be in there. I was going to call an ambulance, but thought I should wait for you. Should I have called an ambulance?"

"No, how would they get in without busting through the door? Nothing looks wrong out here. I'm sure they'd have waited until someone from the company came. We'll call one if we need to, but let's go in first and see what's going on. Don't rush ahead of me when I get the door open. Let me go first."

He used his keycard to get in, and switched on the lobby lights; only the dim night lights had been on. He had to hold April's arm to keep her from racing ahead as they went down the corridor to Steve's office. There was no answer when he knocked on the door; he pulled April back from the door and told her to stay behind him. He tried the door and found it unlocked; he opened it carefully and looked in. The lights were still on. He said, "Steve?" and then, "Oh my God!" Linscombe was slumped in his chair, his head lolling to one side, and Hammond had seen Linscombe's vacant eyes and blood-soaked shirt. He immediately backed out and shut the door, forcing April back.

Hammond grabbed April by the shoulders, crouching so he could look her straight in the face. "April? I'm sorry, but I think Steve's dead. You can't go in there, I'm sorry. There's nothing we can do for him. It's too late. We've got to get the police here, and we need to get outside. We don't know who's in the building. Come on. We've got to go."

April tried to rush past him, but he grabbed her and held her back by hugging her against him with his left arm as he pulled out his cell phone and dialed 911 using his right thumb. He had to shout to make himself heard over April's cries of "Steve! No! Let me see him! I have to see him!" Hammond had to wrestle her down the hall and into the lobby, giving up all thought of leaving the building; they would have to hope no one who didn't belong was still there. He got her onto a bench in the lobby, and she seemed to lapse into shock, sobbing quietly. He sat hugging her while they waited for what seemed like an hour, but was really less than ten minutes before a policeman and then an ambulance arrived, sirens wailing.

When the ambulance arrived, the paramedic in charge took one look in Steve's office and said, "This one's for the medical examiner." The uniformed officer who had gotten there first said, "Yeah, he's on his way. We've got a guy from Homicide coming, too."

The guy from Homicide, Detective Sergeant Jim Travis, showed up about twenty minutes later. The uniformed cop knew him slightly, enough to know Travis didn't make a point of his rank with fellow cops unless there was any doubt about who was in charge. The cop gestured down the hall and said, "In there, Jimmy." Travis stopped short. "I haven't been 'Jimmy' since I was ten. Just 'Jim'. Anybody besides the EMT been in there?"

"Just me and the guy who found the body. On the bench over there. He had the sense not to go in, and he kept the wife out. I didn't touch anything. Neither did the ambulance guy. He didn't have to. That guy was dead all over. No need to look for a pulse."

Travis scowled, hoping the wife hadn't heard that. Travis could be as flippant around death as any cop, but not in front of the relatives. He had been a cop for eighteen years, a detective for eight. Not a back-slapper, he wasn't universally liked by his fellow cops, but he was widely considered the best detective on the force, even by the other detectives. His case clearance rate had been the highest in the Homicide Division for six years running.

Travis waited in the lobby for a Forensic Technician, Mirielle Fernandez, to arrive. He had asked the dispatcher, Don Templeton, for her as soon as he was called for the case. "Don, Jim Travis here. I need a tech. Is Mirielle up this shift?'

"She's on call, but she's due up second, after Corey Ford."

"Can you move her up? I need the best one we've got."

"Come on, Jim. You always need the best one we've got. We try to stick to the chart. Corey's okay."

"Okay's not good enough. You know I always want Mirielle."

"You and almost everyone else." Templeton paused. "All right. I know you like her. I'll do it. But if Ford gets wind and bitches about it, I'm gonna send him straight to you."

"The responsibility's all mine. Don't tell him unless he asks, though, okay?"

Travis had worked with Mirielle at several dozen death scenes; he always asked for her because she was as thorough as he was. She arrived about fifteen minutes after he did.

Her first words were, "Don said you asked for me, so he jumped me ahead of Corey. I was hoping for a quiet Sunday."

"Me, too, but you know how these things work out. You know I always ask for you."

"Why is it you gringo cops all ask for me, and all the Latino guys want the bottle blonde?"

"Joanie? They ask for Joanie? Is that right? I did not know that. Can't be for her tech skills. She's okay, but that's all. You run rings around her. So does Corey. They know she likes women, don't they?"

"Yeah, but they all think they can turn her around. You're not chasing after me, are you? You know that could lead to a hostile work environment." She was grinning.

"I'm a cop. The whole world's a hostile work environment."

"Yeah, that's what I hear. So why is it you really ask for me?"

"I ask for you because you're the best, Mirielle." He'd told her that many times. She made him say it again at every crime scene they worked together.

She was still grinning. "I know."

"That I ask for you because I think you're the best, or that you're the best?"

"Both. So what we got here?"

"Not sure. Workplace shooting, no suspects. That's about all I know so far. Those two over there found the body. Let me talk to them for a minute before we go in. You get your gear on and your kit ready while I do that. Then wait in the lobby while I do a walk-through." Travis never told his evidence techs much, even if he'd been over the crime scene thoroughly before they arrived. He wanted them to see the scene with no preconceptions.

Travis briefly questioned Darrin Hammond about what he had seen and what he might have touched in the office; they moved out of earshot for April Linscombe, who was red-faced and still dabbed at her eyes now and then, though she wasn't crying audibly anymore. Travis appreciated it that Hammond had touched nothing but the door handle and had the sense to keep the wife out. *Lord knows what she might have fucked up.*

Travis asked Hammond whether anyone else had been working in the building.

"I don't know. No one else was here when I arrived. We can find out if anyone else used their keycard to get in today and when they got here. Our head of security can access the keycard records. But you don't need a card to get out, so we won't be able to tell what time anyone left."

Including the killer, Travis thought. "Are there any lobby cameras?" he asked, though he was already certain there weren't.

"No, sorry. We never saw the need. This isn't the kind of business anyone would be likely to rob, you know? No money around here, ever. Payroll's all done direct deposit. Even petty cash gets handled with a card."

"Didn't think there were any cameras. Just had to make sure. Thanks."

Hammond said, "We've got some other people here now. I called to let them know. One of them can stay with her—" he gestured toward April Linscombe—"while I go with you."

"No, sorry. It's a crime scene. No one goes down that corridor without my say-so."

"But the company—"

"I don't care. It's a crime scene. Right now, it's *my* crime scene. No one goes in until I say they can. Don't want to throw my weight around, but I will if I have to. We can't risk losing any evidence. Don't worry. If you've got company secrets in there, they'll still be secret when we're through. If we have to take anything, we'll catalog it and let you know. Pass the word to your people, okay? That whole corridor's off-limits. I'd block off the whole lobby, but it's too late for that."

As always, Travis first did a walk-through alone, leaving Mirielle to guard the corridor entrance. She wasn't a cop, but no one questioned the authority of a woman in a haz-mat suit. Moving slowly, Travis looked closely at everything, but touched nothing. After looking around the office, he went outside the building, walking slowly around it, inspecting every door and window, looking closely at the ground or pavement around each possible entry point. Despite the apparent ransacking of the office, he doubted that this was a robbery or burglary of any kind. There was no sign of forced entry at any point outside the building or at Linscombe's office door. He knew from a single glance the position of the body was all wrong for a robbery. If Linscombe were being robbed, why would he be at his desk? Travis was certain Linscombe knew his killer.

Travis returned to the office and made another slow walk-through, Mirielle following this time. Travis sometimes leaned over to get a closer look at something, but was careful not to touch anything. He noticed Linscombe's work badge still attached to his belt by a short lanyard, so the killer hadn't taken it to get out of the building. That might be significant. A stranger to the building might not know you didn't need a keycard to get out and might have taken Linscombe's before realizing he didn't need it. The killer was someone familiar with the building.

After his walk-through, Travis let Mirielle photograph the entire scene, then waited with her in the lobby until the Medical Examiner arrived. His examination of the body was *pro forma*, if not perfunctory, and took less time than Travis thought seemly. But after examining several hundred bodies over the years, this M.E. had the procedure down cold, as it were. After examining the chest wound, he checked the body for rigidity and blood pooling and measured its temperature. He didn't need a calculator to work out the time of death; he'd seen enough corpses like this one to know what the calculations would show.

His summary to Travis was succinct. "The cause of death was a single gunshot wound to the chest. The body wasn't moved from where it fell, and it's a small office, so the shot was from close range. We can work out exactly how close from gunpowder residue on his clothes once we get him back to the lab. The bullet is still in the body; it didn't go through it and into the back of the chair. Not a powerful gun, could even be a .22. We'll find out at autopsy. Death was pretty quick. There's a lot less blood than you'd expect; he didn't die by bleeding out. That bullet hit exactly the right spot. I'd say it was all over inside of a minute. I'd put the probable time of death somewhere between 8:30 and 9:30. You need to look for anything on the body, or can we go ahead and take it?"

"We'll need to go through his pockets first. Won't take long."

Travis called in Mirielle. "Let's find out what he had on him when he died. We should check his work badge for prints, and anything else left on him that might hold a print. Someone went through his desk and file cabinets. They might have gone through his pockets, though it would have been messy with all the blood, piss, and shit."

The body had been sitting in urine and excrement for hours and the odor in the office and the corridor outside it, now that the door was open, was rank. Getting the body out of there would help a lot, but the seat was still wet. The smell would be there as long as the chair was.

When they went through his pockets, one thing argued strongly against a botched robbery: They found no wallet or cell phone, but he had sixty-three dollars in his left front pocket. Not something a robber would have left behind. Travis assumed Linscombe carried a wallet, the cash in his pocket notwithstanding—there was no driver's license on the body, and most people would carry at least that with them. Linscombe's wife was too distraught to question now; he would ask her later if her husband carried a wallet. She told the first officer on the scene that she tried calling her husband's office and cell phones, so Travis knew a cell phone should have been with the body.

When the M.E. had removed the body, Travis said to Mirielle, "All right. Let's see what we can find." He didn't say anything about his conclusions from his walk-through; he would let her form her own opinions.

Wearing a full protective suit, gloves, and a cap, Mirielle went over the whole office very slowly, using a magnifying glass in places and looking carefully under the desk and chair. She turned the lights off and looked at everything using a portable ultraviolet light. The dried bloodstains on the floor around the chair were easily visible under normal light, but she noticed some small, faint, whitish spots on the floor at the front of the desk and just underneath it, with a few tiny spots on the front of the desk itself. She spent several minutes on her hands and knees, examining them closely, looking for any pattern. She rose to a kneeling position. "Somebody spit here."

Travis crouched down to look. "Spit? Somebody spit on the floor?"

"I'm pretty sure, yeah. We'd have to test to be sure, but they wiped most of it up. There's a barely visible smear where they wiped it. If there was a big gob there when they did, they got almost all of it. There's a little spatter on the floor under the desk. And there's a few spots on the front of the desk. The bad news is, there's not much left. If I swab every spot, there may be just enough to either do a saliva test or try to get DNA—probably not both. If that's the case, go for the DNA, but there's no guarantee we'll get enough for a profile, if we get any at all. A whole gob of spit would give you lots of DNA, but all these tiny spots combined might not give you enough to test."

"I thought you guys only needed one cell to get DNA from these days. There wouldn't be one cell in it?"

"Don't believe everything you hear. That 'one cell' stuff only works if everything's perfect. In theory, you could amplify one cell's worth of DNA into a lot more. The problem is, if you've only got one cell in a sample, you could easily miss it completely. We'll see what we can do. But we don't know that this has anything to do with the murder. Who would spit on an office floor? And why?"

"Assuming the murderer did, this probably means we're not going to find much in the way of fingerprints or anything else here."

"Why?"

"If he knew enough to wipe his spit up, he probably cleaned everything else up, too. We'll just have to see how thorough he was." Travis looked in the trash can. There was nothing in it but a crumpled letter and an advertising flyer for an oil industry conference. "If he wiped it up, he took it with him when he left."

Travis was right. A thorough examination of almost every solid surface in the office you could touch without standing on a ladder turned up no fingerprints complete enough to be useful. Travis figured even the few partial prints would almost certainly be from Linscombe. They would check, of course. And they would collect latent prints from the front door and various points in the lobby, too, as well as in the bathrooms down the hall from Linscombe's office. Any they found, though, would most likely be from Lenevar employees who had nothing to do with the killing. Unless they could get some DNA from the few scattered saliva droplets, which Mirielle doubted, whoever the killer was had done a good job of covering almost all of his tracks. A Luminol test showed a very faint blood track, mere droplets at each step, running from behind the desk, through the doorway, and out into the hall, but the trail grew fainter with each step and disappeared completely about twelve feet down the corridor, as if whoever made it had faded further into invisibility with each step before vanishing altogether.

37. Covering Tracks

Trey—Week 26, Monday & Tuesday

TREY HAD TO WAIT FOR nightfall to dispose of the most critical evidence that could tie him to Linscombe's death. In the time he had to make his plans, he thought of ways he would not only cover his own trail, but put the police on someone else's, at least for a while. Once the false leads he was going to plant dead-ended, the police would be confused and there would be nothing left to connect him to the murder.

He would ditch the gun first. About a half-hour's drive outside town, a backroad Trey knew of crossed a tributary creek of the Colorado River. The creek was normally about 20 feet wide there, though it could swell considerably after heavy rain. The bridge across was so low that the roadbed was often underwater when the creek flooded, though the four-foot guardrails were seldom completely submerged. A bigger river would be better, but he didn't know of any water crossing that was as easy to get to and yet as isolated as that one. There were woods on both sides of the creek there. At night, there was little traffic, and no one would be likely to see him stop on the bridge and fling the gun into the creek.

Trey got there that night about ten. As he neared the bridge, he saw headlights far behind him, so he drove past the bridge and turned off on a road about a mile away. He waited until the car passed, then drove back; it took him just seconds to get out, and fling the gun about 30 feet out into the middle of the creek. He wore latex gloves when he handled the gun, and made sure he heard the splash. Though the creek was normally no more than eight to ten feet deep at that point, the location was isolated and the gun would soon either be buried in the creek bed or so covered with algae as to be unrecognizable.

Now for the cellphone. It was close to midnight when Trey pulled into the parking lot of a motel he had passed on his way to the creek. He drove slowly through the lot, looking for any out-of-state car parked in a dark area. He spotted a minivan with Oklahoma tags parked in the shadow of an RV from Michigan. Either would do, but the minivan was more sheltered from view. He parked in a space slightly further down. Still wearing latex gloves, he hunched over in his seat and, by the feeble beam of a penlight held in his teeth, put the battery back in the phone and turned it on. He got out and crept to the back of the minivan in a crouch. He felt around underneath it near the exhaust pipes to find a bare area. He tore a strip of duct tape off a roll and laid it down sticky-side-up, then took the cap off a small tube of epoxy glue and squeezed most of it onto the back of the phone. He laid the phone face down on the tape, then pressed the glue-smeared phone onto the bare area. The tape would hold it there while the glue dried. The phone would ping every cellphone tower it passed until the battery died. If the police tried to track it, great; that's exactly what he wanted.

He drove back home then; he would deal with the wallet tomorrow.

* * *

The following morning, Trey risked going out in daylight to drive to a park where homeless people congregated. There was a makeshift camp in a patch of woods just outside the park boundary, making the camp hard for the city to clear out. The homeless who stayed there didn't usually bother people in the park; mostly, they dispersed to nearby intersections to panhandle. Trey brought the wallet with him in a Ziploc bag. He had removed Linscombe's driver's license, the only thing in the wallet with his address on it, and wrapped it in a paper napkin for disposal. When he stopped to get gas on the way to the park, he fished the napkin with the license wrapped in it out of his pocket, feigned blowing his nose in it, then dropped the napkin and license in a trashcan by the pump. If anyone ever looked at the footage from the security camera there, they wouldn't think twice about someone tossing a napkin full of snot into a trash can.

When he got to the park, Trey walked around for a few minutes until he found a bench not far from the woods where the homeless camped;

there was no one nearby. As he sat down, he pulled the wallet in its plastic bag out of his back pocket, opened the bag and let the wallet slip out onto the bench beside him. He sat for several minutes to make sure no one around was paying any attention. A bicyclist passed by about ten yards away; Trey turned away as though he were looking at something off in the distance, so the rider wouldn't get a good look at his face.

When the bicycle was out of sight, Trey casually stood up and walked away, leaving the wallet behind. If anyone—maybe one of the homeless campers—found it and tried to use the credit cards, it would lend credence to the idea that Linscombe had died in a botched robbery. There were no pictures or anything with Linscombe's address on it in the wallet, making it less likely that anyone who found it would play Good Samaritan and look for the owner.

On his way home, Trey stopped at a hairstyling shop he had never been to and got a buzz cut. He wanted to look different than he had during any of his recent crimes. He was in this all the way now. But who could prove it?

38. None of It Added Up….

Travis—Week 26, Monday

THE MISSING PHONE AND WALLET notwithstanding, Travis didn't buy the robbery idea for a minute. Too many things didn't fit, and the sixty-three dollars in Linscombe's pocket was almost the least of them. What thief would hang around some deserted offices on a Sunday morning looking to rob someone? Nothing nearby would likely bring an armed robber into the area. It seemed unlikely anyone would have deliberately followed Linscombe there to rob him; he drove a Camry, a nice enough car, but it was five years old, and hardly marked him as someone likely to carry a lot of money. The car itself wasn't touched. Linscombe's wallet and credit cards and his cell phone were taken, but neither the cards nor the phone had yet been used. There was no sign of a break-in at Lenevar, and nothing seemed to be missing from Linscombe's office. Whoever tried to make it look ransacked did a half-assed job. Some drawers had been opened but not disturbed. Then there were the traces of saliva on the floor and the front of the desk. What robber would spit on the damned floor? None of it added up to a robbery.

So then what? Had Linscombe been involved in an affair, one that his lover or her husband decided to break off permanently? That would have to be looked into. But Travis thought it more likely that the whole thing had to do with the price of oil. Like every other company in the oil services industry, Lenevar had been hit by the oil bust and laid people off. Maybe someone who lost his job took it out on Linscombe. That seemed more plausible and gave Travis a working hypothesis.

On Monday, Travis called for an appointment with the CEO of Lenevar, Leonard Ravenel. Travis had no reason to suspect him, so he didn't want to show up at his door unannounced, waving his badge. Ravenel's assistant quickly found a slot that afternoon. As Travis drove over, he found himself musing over the confluence of "len-ses" here—Linscombe, Lenevar, Leonard. It suddenly struck him that "Lenevar" was "Ravenel" backward. *That's one way to name your company.*

Lenevar was not a large company; according to its website, it was family-owned. The main administrative offices were in a smaller building separated by a covered walkway from the building Linscombe had been killed in. The only way in which the administrative building was more opulent is that it was carpeted, though Travis thought the carpet had seen better times. The guard at the front desk looked vaguely familiar—an ex-cop?—but said nothing when Travis showed his badge. Ravenel's assistant appeared about a minute after the guard phoned. She ushered Travis to Ravenel's office, which wasn't much larger than Linscombe's. Travis got right to the point. "Mr. Ravenel, I'm Detective Sergeant Jim Travis. I'm investigating the murder of Steven Linscombe. I'd like to ask you a few questions."

Ravenel looked like he might still carry a slide rule, Travis thought. He wore a tie with a short-sleeved shirt; no jacket in sight. He came out from behind his desk and pumped Travis's hand.

"Of course, Detective Travis. Or is it Sergeant? I'm sorry I didn't talk to you yesterday. They called me, but I wasn't able to get here until after you left. I was flying back in from Dallas; the plane didn't land until after 9 p.m. They met me at the airport with the news, and I came straight in, but it was late when I got here. We're all shocked by this. Everyone here knew Steve. This is not a large company. Almost everyone knows everyone else." Ravenel pushed his glasses up his nose and gestured Travis toward a seat. "I'll be happy to answer any questions I can. But I have to ask you—should I be worried that you want to question me? Do I need a lawyer here?"

"No, sir, that won't be necessary. You're not a suspect. You weren't even in town." Travis sat down, while Ravenel returned to the chair behind his desk. Travis wanted his cooperation; it would make questioning his employees much easier. "We don't have any suspects yet. Whoever did it tried to make it look like a robbery gone wrong, but some things don't fit with that. We thought another possible angle was a conflict with an employee, or a former employee. That usually involves someone with a grudge killing his boss. Bosses usually fire problem employees, not kill them." Travis gave a tight-lipped smile. "Do you know if Mr. Linscombe had any recent clashes with anyone he worked with?"

"None that I know of. You'd have to talk with his supervisor or the people he worked closely with. No reports of any problems made it to me. You can talk to the people in his unit to ask if there was any trouble between Steve and anyone else, but I've already asked around a little myself, and nobody could think of anyone Steve had any problems with here. It wasn't unusual for him to come in on weekends, by the way."

"Thank you. I was going to ask that. I would like to talk with his supervisor and anyone else he worked with. It would be nice if I could do it here. If we find a suspect, we'd bring them in for more questions, but right now, I'm just looking for information that might be useful. I want people to feel it's an interview, not an interrogation. Once you get people in the station, they're less likely to talk and more likely to lawyer up. The smart ones, anyway, which is what I'd expect to find here. You've got a lot of engineers, right?"

"Yes, most of us here have a college degree, often more than one. So you think it's likely there's a grudge involved."

"It's a possibility. Has anyone been fired recently that you know of?"

"No. If they had been, I'd know about it. As I said, we're not a large company. We haven't fired anyone for cause here in a while. We have been forced to lay off about sixty people in the last two years, since oil prices crashed. We may have to let a few more go if prices don't go up soon. We're doing our best to keep layoffs down, and we've been pretty generous with severance pay. No one's happy to be let go, obviously, but I haven't heard of anyone making threats."

"Was Mr. Linscombe involved with the layoffs in any way?"

"Not directly, no. He lost a few in his group, and he would have had some input on who went and who stayed, but not the final say. And he wouldn't have been the one to tell anyone they were being let go. That would have been someone higher up."

"I see. I'd like to start by talking to your current employees and see where that goes. If nothing turns up, I'll want to talk with former ones, particularly any who were fired for cause, especially if they worked for Mr. Linscombe, and anyone who got laid off, even though Mr. Lins-combe wasn't directly involved with that. Maybe someone was mad at the company and he just happened to be there. It would help if I could look at your records for the last five years or so for people who lost their jobs, whether they were laid off, fired, or just quit. We won't need a subpoena, will we?"

Ravenel looked surprised. "Oh, no. We want you to find whoever did this. No one will feel safe around here until you do. We've stepped up security already, and we're looking at what else we might need to do because of this. You can look at our records as far back as you need to. We've been in business thirty-three years now."

Travis thought of the lone guard in the lobby and wondered what their stepped-up security might look like. "Thank you, I appreciate that. I think five or six years back would do. Most people don't hold grudges that long."

"We can easily get you a list of the people we've had to let go, and their files. I'm pretty sure we could have that for you by tomorrow afternoon at the latest. I'll take you to Catalina Hernandez, who runs our Personnel office." He paused. "We still think of our employees here as people, not 'Human Resources'."

"Along with people who've left for any reason, even if it was voluntary, I'd like to look at anyone who might have faced disciplinary action, even if they're still here."

Ravenel pushed his glasses up again. "We'll give you whatever you need. We haven't had many formal disciplinary proceedings, though. We usually handle problems face-to-face. We haven't had many problem employees at all. Most of the people who've left here either left voluntarily or because of layoffs. This is a pretty good place to work."

"I'm sure it is, from what I've seen."

"Would you like us to set up a conference room for you to use? Or would you want to talk in people's offices?"

"We can talk in people's offices, if they have them. If anyone doesn't, having a small room available would be nice. I could also use it to go through personnel files, if that's not a problem. These will be interviews, not hard-ball interrogations. If I turn up a suspect, I'll question them down at the station later. I can't make anyone talk. If you make any kind of announcement, please don't say anything that would make people think they have to talk to me or else. That wouldn't look good in court.

Anyone can refuse to be interviewed, and anyone can insist on having a lawyer present, though I guarantee I'll look very hard at anyone who does either. Anyone who looks like they might be hiding something goes to the top of my list. That's not a good place to be. I will be recording the interviews, but I don't want people to think I'm an adversary. I'm just looking for information right now. I want people to feel as comfortable talking to me as they can, under the circumstances."

"That sounds fine. I'll have my assistant set everything up. Is tomorrow afternoon okay to start? You can stay as long as you need to."

"That would be fine. Could I talk to your assistant and tell her what I need?"

"Of course. I'll take you to her office."

As he drove back afterward, Travis found himself thinking, *I hope I don't get spoiled by this. I hardly ever talk to people this eager to help.*

39. "I guess I can cross him off my list"

Travis—Week 26, Tuesday

WHEN TRAVIS ARRIVED AT LENEVAR on Tuesday afternoon, Catalina Hernandez told him he could have come in sooner; they could have given him everything he needed by Monday afternoon. She clearly wanted to let him know how well she ran her office, and Travis was impressed; it wasn't the kind of bureaucracy he was used to dealing with. He thought Ms. Hernandez, who appeared to be in her mid-thirties, was young to be head of a department, but quickly decided she got where she was because she was damn good at her job.

Travis had spoken with Darrin Hammond, Linscombe's supervisor, on Sunday, so it was easy to start this round with him. He had Hammond go through his story again. Hammond remembered April Linscombe's call as coming just before seven this time, instead of around eight, but a few further questions were enough to get the timeline settled. People's estimates of time at a murder scene were often the first thing to get squirrely with repeated tellings; trial lawyers loved to pounce on any discrepancies. Hammond would be hard to shake, though. He was level-headed, his story could be checked, and his conduct at the scene on Sunday had been impeccable—April Linscombe could have easily wrecked the murder scene if he'd let her in her husband's office.

Roger Letourneau was next. Letourneau had been Linscombe's previous supervisor; Hammond succeeded him when Letourneau got promoted. Travis had to remark on the picture behind Letourneau's desk—he was proudly holding up the head of an elk that had a very impressive spread of antlers.

"You like to hunt, I see. That head would barely fit in this office."

Letourneau's face lit up. "Yeah. That one's in my den. Probably wouldn't go over that well in here, though quite a few hunters work here. A lot of women go, 'Ewww!' when they see that picture the first time. I got that one on a job in Montana. Great hunting up there! In Texas it's mostly deer and hogs, unless you go in for canned hunts on game ranches. Which I don't. Good fishing, though. A lot of our jobs here are out in the Gulf, if you like fishing. Rigs draw fish like coral reefs do."

"I've fished near a few. Good for snapper." Travis had gone fishing in the Gulf maybe twice. You use what you can to establish rapport.

"Oh, hell, yeah. You can get a lot more than snapper, though. I hooked a six-foot marlin once. Couldn't keep it, though. Too small."

"Did you ever go hunting or fishing with Steve Linscombe?"

Letourneau's smile faded. "The reason you're here, huh? No. I don't think Steve did much of either, if any. Pretty much a family guy. I don't know many wives that are into hunting. I know there's some out there. Mine's not. But that's kind of the point of hunting, isn't it? Get out with the guys?"

"I guess so." Travis didn't hunt, himself. The only gun he ever fired was his service pistol, when he had to qualify. He'd never had to draw it on the job. He'd known cops who would pull theirs at the slightest provocation; they made him nervous. "Did you know Mr. Linscombe well?"

"Not really. He didn't hunt or fish, so we didn't have much in common except engineering and oil. He didn't drink much, either. Family man, like I said."

"So the quiet type? Didn't make many enemies, I gather." That was what Travis was really after.

"Not that I know of. I wouldn't know that well, though. He worked under me. This is not like the military, you know, where officers and enlisted men don't fraternize, but I don't really do a lot with the people I supervise. Have 'em over for cookouts now and then, maybe. Mix with 'em a little at the Christmas party. That's about it. Someday you might have to fire them or lay them off, you know? Never easy, but a little easier if they're not friends. I think Steve was kind of stiff, too. Just my impression. He kept you at a certain distance, you know? I'm not a hugger, myself, but I don't think Steve was even much for shaking hands. But I never heard anyone complain about him."

"I see. So you don't see him making either friends or enemies, huh?"

"Yeah, you could put it that way. The Ravenels—the daddy's retired; his son runs it now—try to treat people here like a family, but it don't always work. Great when the money's coming in, I guess, but when you gotta lay people off, well then you're laying off family, right? Not so easy, then. And maybe it puts a little more pressure on people to get along, paper things over instead of dealing with 'em up front, you know? Some of the worst fights I've ever seen were in families. Had a neighbor once who shot his brother."

"Kill him?" Travis always took a professional interest in murder.

"Oh, yeah. They put him away for about ten years. Thought it would've been longer." Letourneau looked almost pensive.

"How's this family culture work here?" Travis had certainly seen more than his share of family violence since he moved to Homicide. Being family didn't guarantee civility, that was certain.

"They do want you to fit. I think some people don't feel comfortable with it, and don't stick around long. If you're not a team player, you won't feel that welcome. But look, I can't knock it too much. I've done pretty well here. Some of that 'We're all family' stuff may hurt the company, though, especially now, with oil prices down. They're probably paying out more in severance than they can really afford, you know? And they've always offered generous retirement benefits, maybe too generous. I don't do the books here, but I think they're barely hanging on right now. I keep my resume up to date, you know? And I made sure I built up some savings. I think things could go south here pretty quick." He paused and put his left hand to his chin, his index finger extending across his lips, almost as though he were shushing himself. "I'm not sure how much of this I should really be telling you. I'd appreciate it if you wouldn't say anything about it to anyone else. I don't suppose any of it's likely to help you find whoever killed Steve."

"Maybe not, you never know. I appreciate your telling me. I'll keep it quiet, of course."

After a few more questions, Travis ended the interview. He had not gotten much on Steve Linscombe, but he'd learned something about the company's situation. Travis knew times were tough in the oil industry, but things were apparently more financially precarious at Lenevar than he would have guessed.

Travis interviewed seven other current employees who either worked in Linscombe's unit now or had in the past. None could remember his ever having any serious problems with anyone at the company, themselves included. And none had been in the building on Sunday, according to the keycard records, though it was possible for several people to enter together with just one opening the door. The engineer who came into the building shortly after the murder Sunday, Harold Brown, had never worked directly with Linscombe, though he recognized Linscombe's car in the parking lot. Brown was another Sunday regular at Lenevar, often arriving just as Linscombe was leaving. Brown hadn't paid any particular attention to the other car in the lot that morning. All he could say about it is that it wasn't a truck, SUV, or minivan, and it was almost the same color as Linscombe's—silver or gray. He did notice the other car was gone when he left about two hours before the body was found. He neither saw nor heard anything out of the ordinary while he was there.

Catalina Hernandez had given Travis the personnel files of sixty-eight people who left the company involuntarily over the past six years, mostly through layoffs, and another nineteen who left voluntarily or retired. Almost every employee who faced any formal disciplinary action during that period was in one of those two groups, mostly the first one—layoffs seemed to offer an opportunity to get rid of problem employees. The infractions for which workers had been disciplined were all pretty standard—too many absences, or being late too often. No thefts or embezzling or assaults on co-workers. Turnover at Lenevar was low as long as oil prices were high. The layoffs had occurred in two groups about six months apart. He started with their records, sitting at a table in a well-lit conference room that was larger than he really needed. He also had no need for a projector screen or whiteboard, though both were there. Or the fourteen chairs—two would do. He found the coffee machine they set up for him in one corner a thoughtful touch. Ms. Hernandez asked only that he lock the door behind him whenever he left the room—they didn't want personnel files lying around in the open.

Travis got through about half the records that afternoon, and finished the rest on Wednesday, after which he would begin the tedious process of tracking down and interviewing everyone on his list. As he carried the last of the personnel files back to Catalina Hernandez's office, Travis wished there was some tangible way he could express his appreciation for the company's cooperation. People—usually Ms. Hernandez—had stopped by the conference room several times each day to ask if there was anything he needed.

"Ms. Hernandez, you and your whole staff have been very helpful; I really can't thank you enough. I can't think of anything more I'll need here, but if I do, I'd like to call you directly, if you don't mind."

"Of course. We're sorry you had to be here, but we're glad we could help. I hope you find whoever did it. I hope it won't turn out to be anyone who worked here. I've never seen anyone here who struck me as someone who could kill somebody. Especially someone like Mr. Linscombe. We didn't cross paths very often, but he was never anything but nice to me."

Travis didn't want to say anything offensive or flippant, but he hoped the murderer *would* be someone who had worked at Lenevar. "People can surprise you sometimes. I've learned to keep an open mind about who is or isn't capable of something." He turned to leave, then suddenly stopped and turned back around, his right hand up as though to stop Ms. Hernandez from leaving, though she was still at her desk. "I would like to ask about one employee in particular, though. I don't know if you'd remember him, but you had one guy retire on disability a few years ago. Augustus Osborne? Did his disability have anything to do with his work here?"

She smiled; Travis thought she was stifling a laugh. "You mean Trey. Yes, I remember him. *Nobody* called him by his real name; you can see why. No, he had some kind of inherited disease; it had nothing to do with his job here. But I don't think he would be the man you're looking for."

"Why not?"

"He retired because he went blind."

"I see. I guess I can cross him off my list. Thank you." As Travis walked to his car, he thought the "I see" might have come across as some kind of sick joke. He hadn't intended it.

40. "You look like you want to defend yourself...."

Trey—Week 26, Saturday

TREY KNEW GETTING RID OF the gun he killed Linscombe with had been necessary, but now he needed another one. Maybe more than one. Instead of buying from a licensed gun dealer, he decided to buy from an individual seller at a gun show—no background check, less hassle. He searched the internet for upcoming gun shows and found one being held that weekend in Houston—not too far, not too close. He didn't want to run into anyone at a local gun show who might know him, particularly anyone from Lenevar.

That Friday, Trey withdrew two thousand dollars from his bank. He intended to keep a low profile, get in and out fast, and pay cash. When he drove to Houston Saturday morning, he wasn't sure what to expect; he'd never been to a gun show before. He wore clothes he thought would help him blend with the crowd, wearing a baseball cap because he thought it was the kind of thing you'd wear at a gun show. He wasn't wrong, he saw when he got there; no suits and ties, lots of baseball caps. A few cowboy hats; that was overdoing it, he thought. A lot of camouflage. Camouflage everywhere, though it stuck out like neon in the crowded convention center. Duck hunting camouflage. Jungle camouflage. Desert camouflage—he stifled a laugh when he saw that. *Not in east Texas, sport.* No camouflage for snow, at least.

Trey was surprised at the number of women there, though most seemed to be with husbands or boyfriends. No children. Lots of gray hair and thinning hair under all those baseball caps. People wandered through, inspecting the vast array of merchandise: guns and knives; gun parts—barrels, stocks, magazines; ammunition; gun cleaning kits;

even clothes—mostly t-shirts, most with slogans. Anathema to Trey, who kept his opinions close—why wear them on your chest? Trey assumed most people were idiots; a t-shirt with a message just took out the guesswork.

A few people came with their own guns, walking in with rifles slung from their shoulders or guns on their hips. *Why? To show they own guns? Almost everybody here owns a gun. Most of them more than one. These guys look like the kind of lunatics we're supposed to keep guns away from. Maybe they're trying to sell them?* That seemed unlikely; most of the private individuals who were selling what they brought were at a line of tables along a back wall, and Trey headed straight there.

Those along the back wall seemed to divide into those selling rifles or shotguns and those selling handguns, though a few had both. Most sold the same guns you could find in any sporting goods store or gun shop, except for one man who had only antiques and another who specialized in vintage M-1 rifles. Trey ended up buying all his guns from a weathered-looking garrulous guy named Clint, who was probably in his mid-sixties, judging from his talk, but looked as if he could be pushing ninety-five. He had a wide array of guns; Trey asked how he'd amassed a collection like that. Turned out Clint had once owned a pawn shop, and cherry-picked unredeemed guns over the years. He didn't much like the kind of people who pawned their guns, but people who bought them were okay. Clint quickly latched on to Trey.

"You don't look like the type of guy who'd pawn a gun. You look like you want to defend yourself from the type of guy who'd pawn a gun, right?" He laughed.

Trey just smiled.

"You shoot a lot? Or you just want to?" Clint asked.

"Used to." Trey said. It wasn't a lie. He'd occasionally hunted deer with his father, until the old man fell out of a tree stand and broke an ankle. Trey had even tried deer hunting with a handgun once, with no luck. He had sold off his guns when his vision started to go.

"Out of practice, huh? You should keep it simple for self-defense. A revolver's what you want. Works first time, every time. Not as many bullets to work with, but if you hit what you aim at, you only need one."

"They're a bit harder to shoot, aren't they?" Trey was just playing along; he'd fired revolvers before.

"Airweights are. These guys here have some heft. They're still small, but these older ones have steel frames, not aluminum. And none of that plastic stuff they use now. Here. Feel this."

He handed Trey a .38 Special. It did have heft.

"See? These guys don't jump around in your hand. You can fire these all day and not feel like someone's been beatin' your hand with a hammer. They stay on target, unlike them lightweight ones. You got vermin you need to get rid of, these'll do it. Or varmints. Either one." He grinned. The way he spat the word out, "vermin" were clearly the two-legged kind.

"Older though, right? Kind of expensive, aren't they?" Trey looked dubious.

"Naw, these are workin' guns, not museum pieces. I'm just sellin' off some of what I've picked up over the years. You know how it is with guns. You can't get just one. They like company. Sometimes I think they breed while you ain't looking. Except they always seem to cost you money. Same as kids do, I guess, even though breedin' them's free." He grinned again.

Trey didn't find him as funny as Clint found himself, but his guns were clean, they worked, and they were priced cheap. Maybe Clint had fallen on some hard times. "What else you have?"

When Trey left the show an hour later, he took with him two .38 Smith & Wesson snub-nosed revolvers of different vintages and a newer Ruger 9 mm compact semi-automatic, plus ammunition for them, and had money left over. He wasn't sure why he felt the need for even one gun, much less three. It did seem to him he had run into more assholes lately than he ever had before. The world looked darker now than it did when he was blind.

Best to be ready for it.

41. "You think he can see again?"

Travis—Week 27

TRAVIS DECIDED TO START WITH the most recently laid-off Lenevar employees, rather than those fired for cause. From a practical standpoint, the recently laid-off employees would probably be easier to find; most would still be in the area.

He found no likely suspects or potential leads in his first seven interviews. None of the seven had worked directly with Linscombe; only two had known him slightly. Linscombe had been the immediate supervisor of the eighth person he talked to, though. Alan Guttmacher had worked at Lenevar for eight years, but the project he was on had been cancelled when oil prices dropped under \$50 a barrel and stayed there. Prices had recovered some since then, but too late to save Guttmacher's job. He hadn't yet found another one. His Lenevar file showed no disciplinary infractions at all, and his annual evaluations, all signed by Linscombe, were highly positive—glowing, actually.

Guttmacher was not surprised when Travis showed up on his doorstep on a Friday with his badge and asked if they could talk.

"I've been expecting someone to come by ever since I heard about Steve. Come in. My wife's at work. The sole breadwinner now." He was wearing a jacket and tie, which Travis found surprising. The engineers he'd spoken with had all been dressed more casually—jackets, maybe, but no ties. Guttmacher may have noticed the look of surprise that flashed across Travis's face.

"If you're wondering about the coat and tie, I have an interview today. Can't say I expect much from it, but you never know."

"I'm sorry about your job, Mr. Guttmacher. From what I've been able to learn, your boss had nothing but good things to say about your work there."

"I know. We had to go over my evaluation every year, so I know what was in my record. Unless they had a secret file for the bad stuff." He laughed. "No, I know better. Steve was a good boss. I have nothing bad to say about him."

"If there was a secret file, they kept it from me, too. Mr. Linscombe clearly appreciated your work. How long was he your supervisor?"

"About six years, I think. I started out under... umm, George Shearing. Had to think of his first name. He was an older guy, Mr. Shearing to us. When he retired, Steve got his job. They moved him over from another project. He was less formal. He told us to call him Steve."

The questioning was routine from there. Guttmacher had never had any problems with Linscombe, nor could he think of anyone else who might have. Guttmacher had been visiting with a brother-in-law the day of Linscombe's murder, and that would have to be checked out, but his story was straightforward and contained nothing suspicious in it. Finally Travis had only one other possibility to explore.

"Mr. Guttmacher, was Steve Linscombe the person who told you that you were being laid off?"

"No, no, that was Darrin Hammond, Steve's boss. Look, I didn't even blame *him*, much less Steve. I wasn't the only one laid off; they weren't singling me out for anything. It was just oil prices. Almost everybody else on my project got laid off, too. Two senior guys got transfers to other sections. I certainly didn't have anything against Steve. I was shocked when I heard he'd been killed. I even went to his funeral, you know."

Travis did know. He had been there himself, and had a list of all the names from the funeral parlor guestbook. A police photographer had also discreetly photographed everyone at the graveside, so Travis knew that Guttmacher had left after the service at the chapel. Nothing strange there—many more people had gone to the service than the burial.

"We don't have any reason to suspect you. We're just talking with former Lenevar employees to see if anyone knew someone who might have had a grudge against him."

"I understand that. I really hope you catch whoever did it. Steve was a good boss, the best I've ever worked for. He was just a good *person*.

I really thought of him as a friend. It's not like I was over at his house a lot, but I was there a few times."

"We'll catch the guy, sooner or later." Travis paused. "Just one more question. Have you been in touch recently with any current or former Lenevar employees who might have known Mr. Linscombe?"

"Mmm, not many. Especially anyone still there. You know, a lot of people treat being laid off like it's contagious. They really don't want to be around you. Even people you thought of as friends. Not everyone, but some." He scratched his chin while he thought for a few seconds. "Let's see… Linda Hollingsworth. I've talked with her a few times. She was the only woman on our project. She got laid off, too. I thought maybe they'd keep her on– you don't see that many female engineers in the oil business. But she lost her job, too. She's already found another one, though. Companies want diversity now. Not that she isn't good, she is. But I doubt if most people who got laid off when I did have jobs yet. Not in oil, anyway. Let's see, who else? Darrin Hammond, of course. He's still there, so you've probably talked to him."

"Yes, I have."

"Anyone else?" Guttmacher asked himself aloud, looking up at the ceiling, trying to remember. "Hmm. Let me think—oh. Yeah. Trey Osborne. He goes back a ways, but he knew Steve."

Travis thought the name sounded familiar, but had to think a few seconds before he remembered what Catalina Hernandez had told him. "Trey Osborne? Didn't he retire when he went blind?"

"Yeah. But you know, the last time I talked with him, he told me he'd taken an experimental drug, and he thought he might actually be getting some of his eyesight back, believe it or not. I really should have checked with him again before now to see how that was going. His eyes were only slightly better when we talked, but he'd been totally blind for a while."

This was an unexpected twist, though Travis wasn't sure what to make of it. "You think he can see again? How long since you talked to him?"

"I don't remember. It's been a while. Three or four months, maybe? I don't remember for sure. Must have been longer than that. I don't think I'd been laid off yet. He told me his eyes had improved, though he still couldn't see. He could only tell dark from light. But he hoped he'd be able to see again before too long. I figured he'd call me if he got any better, but I haven't heard from him, so maybe he didn't. I feel bad, though. I should have called him. I just got caught up in my own problems when I got laid off, I guess."

"Do you know how he got this drug?"

"He was in a clinical trial, but I don't know the details. Somebody at the medical center found a drug that cured blindness in rats, and they were testing it in humans. Trey probably told me the guy's name, but I don't remember it."

"That's not something I'd heard of before. I guess I should talk to Mr. Osborne."

"Well, I'm sure he doesn't have anything to do with this. He retired four or five years ago. Maybe more than that. I doubt if he'd seen—I mean, talked to Steve anytime recently."

"Probably not. But thank you for the information."

Now Travis would have to put Trey Osborne back on his list. It probably wouldn't lead to anything. What were the chances the guy had gotten his sight back completely? Wouldn't something like that have been all over the news? Even if he could see now, what could he have had against Steve Linscombe? But it couldn't hurt to follow up on it. No real leads had turned up yet.

42. "Can you see anything yet?"

Trey—Week 28, Monday

Alan Guttmacher had to scroll through the contact list on his phone to find Trey's number. His talk with the detective had reminded him that he hadn't spoken with Trey for some time. He didn't know whether Trey knew about Steve or not. He probably did, but it wouldn't hurt to call him. He dialed the number; after five rings, it went to voicemail.

"Hey, Trey. This is Al. I know we haven't talked for a while. I just wanted to know how you're getting along. Can you see anything yet?" He paused. "I know you must have heard about Steve Linscombe. A cop came by here to ask me about him, which reminded me it's been awhile since we talked. I'll call you back later, or you can call me. You know my number. Okay, I'll talk to you later."

Trey heard the call when it came; he had long ago started letting all his calls go to voicemail, returning those he felt like answering. He'd probably return this one, but he needed to think about it first. He rubbed his finger across his lips, his chin resting on this thumb.

Okay, this tells me two things: Al doesn't know I can see again, and I might be hearing from a cop soon. When did I last talk to Al? He asked if I can see anything yet, so I couldn't see then. I'll tell him I'm still blind. He won't know. If he comes over, I can fake it; I've had lots of practice being blind. If the cops don't know I can see, I won't be a suspect, but they might want to ask me if I knew anyone who didn't like Steve.

Do the cops know about the drug trial? How much could Al tell them? Couldn't be much, I don't think I even mentioned the company running the trial, just that I was in one. I doubt if the cops know much more than that. They would know I retired from Lenevar because I went blind. Did Al say anything to make them suspect I could see again? What did he tell them? His message didn't actually say he mentioned me to the cops, but if he hadn't, why would the cop's visit remind him we hadn't talked in a while?

Will the cops just show up at the door, or will they call first? I need to make sure there's nothing in the house that would tip them off—nothing laying around I might have been reading. I need to wear dark glasses and carry my cane when I answer the door.

Trey waited until Monday evening to call Al.

"Al? Hey, it's Trey. I got your message. What's going on?"

"Trey! What's going on with *you*, I should ask. What's happened with your eyes?"

"They didn't get any better, I'm afraid. They actually got worse since the last time we talked. That's why I haven't kept in touch. It was too depressing to talk about it. I really had my hopes up for a while." All the lies tripped right off his tongue.

"Damn, Trey. I'm sorry to hear that."

"Yeah, thanks. ... You know, I can't remember how much my eyes had changed the last time we talked."

"You could tell dark from light. Did your eyes get any better than that before things started going backward?"

"Yeah, they did. I was just starting to be able to see shapes and tell when something was moving. But I've lost that. The doctors warned me it could happen. The drug might grow my optic nerves back, but it wouldn't fix what caused them to degenerate in the first place." Trey figured he was already lying when he said he'd stopped getting better; might as well keep going.

"Damn. That's a shame. How are you holding up?"

"What can I say? It sucks. But I'm okay, really. No one thought the drug would work at this stage, anyway, the dose was so small. They're talking about giving me a larger dose now. That might make a difference." *One lie leads to another.*

"Did the drug work in anyone else?"

"I don't know. The trial people never told me about anyone else. ... I'm okay, really. We knew it was a long shot." He paused. "I heard about Steve. That's a damn shame."

"Yeah. He was killed right in his office. How many times have we been in there?"

"Mmm. I hadn't thought about that. It is kind of creepy, isn't it? Whoever did it is still out there." There was a long pause before Trey decided to steer the talk away from Steve Linscombe. "What's going on with *you*, Al?"

"I got laid off not long after we talked."

"Really? Damn. Did it catch you by surprise?"

"There had been rumors going around when we talked, but I didn't say anything. I hoped that if I didn't talk about it, maybe it wouldn't happen. But it did. Oil prices are killing us. It's hard to tell where it's going to end."

"They'll go back up sooner or later."

"Hope it's sooner. I've been looking for three months and nothing's turned up. Some people they let go before me have been out of work nearly a year now."

"They hold on to good workers as long as they can, you know. The people they let go first are the ones they like least. I'm not surprised they might have a harder time finding jobs. I think there's a good chance you'll find one before some of the earlier layoffs do." Trey had no idea if any of that was true, but you were supposed to be encouraging in these situations.

"I hope so. I did land an interview last week. I think I might have a good shot at the job. I'm trying not to get my hopes up too much, though, in case it falls through." He paused. "But, hey, talk about dashed hopes—are you really okay? You sounded hopeful the last time we talked."

"Yeah, I'm okay. Really. I tried to keep my hopes down, too." When he paused, Trey realized he'd just contradicted what he'd said earlier about being hopeful. He decided to shift the conversation back to the police, to get some idea of what he could expect. "You got laid off before Steve got killed. Is that why the cops wanted to talk to you?"

"I think so. I guess they figured I'd have a motive, you know. But Steve didn't have anything to do with the layoff. Hell, he probably helped me hang on as long as I did."

"Probably, yeah. Tell me, did the cops take you in, or did they just come by? Did they call and tell you they wanted to talk to you?"

"No, a detective just came by and asked if we could talk. I guess he figured since I'd been laid off, I'd probably be home. Travis. His name was Travis. He didn't come off as threatening or anything. He said he was talking to people who had worked with Steve, to see if they knew of anyone he might have had any trouble with. I really couldn't help him much there. I'm sure he was feeling out my attitude toward Steve, too. But me and Steve never had any trouble. Steve's the best boss I ever had, and I said that."

"How'd my name come up? If you don't mind me asking."

"He just wanted to know if I'd been in touch with anyone else from Lenevar who had anything to do with Steve. I've only talked with a couple of people there since they let me go. I said I'd talked with you, but not in a while. He recognized your name. He knew you'd gone blind. I was kind of surprised, but I guess I shouldn't have been. I'm sure the company gave him a list. I mean, how else would he have known?"

"Yeah, I'm sure they're just going through a list." Trey paused; he didn't want to jump to his next question too abruptly. "Did you tell them about my eyes getting better?"

"I mentioned it, yeah. I hope that's okay. I didn't know they'd gotten worse since we talked. He asked if I thought you could see again; I told him not as far as I knew. He asked me how long since I talked to you. I wasn't sure, though I knew it was before I got laid off." He paused. "Sorry I haven't kept in touch. I should have called you before now."

"Don't worry about it. I haven't wanted to talk to anyone much since my eyes got worse again.... I'm glad you called, though." He genuinely was, though not for the reason Al might think. "You say he just dropped by, huh? I guess I should get the place cleaned up. Maybe keep a light on for him."

They talked for a few more minutes, each making vague promises to keep in touch with the other. When they'd hung up, Al wondered for a second about Trey's saying he should clean the place up. He'd been to Trey's house once or twice after Trey went blind and knew it was always immaculate. Blind people couldn't afford clutter; everything had to be in its place, or they couldn't find it. There couldn't be much to clean up now. *He was probably joking*, Al thought.

Trey was not joking. He had reverted to his old habits once he got his sight back. Clutter was a luxury he would have to give up for now. He needed to have everything ready when the detective showed up.

43. A Careless Glance

Trey/Travis—Week 28, Friday

WHEN HIS DOORBELL RANG AROUND four in the afternoon on Friday, Trey was startled, but knew it must be the police; it was just a matter of time. He had briefly thought about calling them and telling them to come get it over with, but he knew that would be ridiculous. He would have to wait.

Trey answered the door wearing dark glasses and carrying his cane. "Yes? Can I help you?"

Now that he was actually at Trey's door, Travis was suddenly uncertain what to do. He would normally show his badge and ID, but how would that work with someone who couldn't see it? He held them out anyway. He had thought the door would be answered by someone who could see—if not Trey Osborne, then his wife or a kid or a caretaker. *Can a blind man really live alone? Evidently.*

"Mr. Osborne? I'm Detective Sergeant Jim Travis. I have my badge here. Is there anyone home who could... verify it?"

"No, I'm alone here. What's this about? Is something wrong?"

Travis hesitated. "No, I mean, there's no emergency. You're not in trouble. I just wanted to talk to you because you used to work at Lenevar Field Services...."

Trey tried not to sound as if he'd been expecting the call. "Oh, is this about Steve Linscombe? I heard about that. I can't see your badge, but if you tell me how you heard about me, that might help me identify you."

"Of course. From employee files at Lenevar, I knew you retired because you, um, lost your eyesight—"

"Went blind, yes," Trey interjected.

"But I recently talked with a friend of yours who said you'd taken an experimental drug, and your eyes might have improved. He didn't know how much. He just said your eyes were getting better when he talked with you."

"Okay. Who did you talk to? If it's who I think it is, I'll know you're who you say you are."

"Do you know Alan Guttmacher?"

"Al, yes. Okay. He told me a detective had been by to talk to him and he'd mentioned my name. Come on in." He stepped aside and gestured for Travis to come in. "Turn on a light if you need it. I don't, so it may be dark in here. Come this way. We can sit at the kitchen table. I'll lead the way. Don't worry. I know my way around here. I don't really need my cane around the house."

So why did you carry it to the door? Travis said nothing. He followed Trey down the hall to the kitchen.

Trey groped for the back of a chair, pulled one out, and sat down. "Pull a chair out for yourself, if you would, please."

"Of course, thank you," Travis said, pulling out the chair across from Trey's. "I won't take up much of your time. I wanted to talk to you because Mr. Guttmacher mentioned you. I thought maybe if you talked to anyone else at Lenevar, you might have heard something about how things were going there. Maybe something about Mr. Linscombe."

"Sorry I can't help you there. It's been a long time since I talked to anyone at Lenevar besides Al."

"Mr. Guttmacher said your eyes had improved. Can you see anything at all now?"

"I can tell dark from light. That's about it." Trey kept his face turned toward Travis, tilted slightly upward, as if he thought Travis were a few inches taller than he actually was. He tried to keep his eyes from fixing on anything, in case Travis could see them through the dark glasses.

"Oh. Do the lights help at all? They were off in front, but I notice your kitchen light was on."

Fuck, Trey thought. *I let that slip.* "I can see when the light changes suddenly, like when you turn a light on. Once it's been on a while, I don't notice it anymore. I certainly don't need it. I don't remember who turned the kitchen light on. It might have been on for days. People who *can* see come here now and then, and they use the lights. Mostly my brother." *Trying to trap me?*

"I see." *Fuck*, Travis thought. *Is that something you say to a blind man?* But Trey didn't react. "So you haven't been in touch with anyone from Lenevar lately. Mr. Guttmacher said it had been a while since he talked with you. Not getting any better must have been a blow, after you got your hopes up."

"Yeah, well, they said not to expect too much. This test was just to see if the drug had any bad side effects. The dose was pretty small."

"So you're not taking the drug anymore? You said the dose *was* small."

"No, I just took it once, like everybody else. The idea was to wait a while, then go to a larger dose if there were no problems." *Why is he asking about the drug? What does he know?* Trey reached to rub his chin and touched his upper lip; there was a little sweat there.

"Did you have any problems?"

"Yeah. Bad headaches, mostly." *Why is he pushing this?*

"Were other people taking the drug? Do you know if anyone else got better?"

"There were other people in the trial, sure. I don't know how many, though, or who they are, or what happened to them. ... I don't see what that has to do with Lenevar. Or Steve Linscombe."

"No, no, you're right. Sorry. I was just curious. The idea that a drug might cure blindness is pretty interesting."

"No problem. But I really haven't been in touch with anyone at Lenevar, except Al, and not that often even with him. I didn't know he'd been laid off until he called the other day."

"I see." *Damn it, I said it again.* "Would you happen to remember the last time you spoke to Steve Linscombe? Or heard anything about him?"

"Well, I heard about him from Al the other day. Nothing before that that I can remember." *What did I say to Al about hearing the news? Did I say anything? Shit, I don't remember. Maybe I should hedge a bit.* "I may have heard something on the news about him being killed. I'm not sure... no, I must have; I wasn't surprised when Al brought it up. But I don't remember the last time I talked to Steve. Not for a couple of years, at least."

"Umm... all right." *Almost said, "I see", again.* "Well, I appreciate your talking with me." Travis paused. "That's an interesting-looking watch, if I may say."

"Yes. It actually *tells* you the time. See?" Trey pushed a button on it, and a somewhat tinny voice said, "The time is 4:38 p.m." "If you push this other button, it'll tell you the date. You can lose track of both when you're blind. Day and night don't mean much."

"I can imagine." Travis paused for several seconds, trying to think of something to say next, but drawing a blank. "Well, thank you for your time. I can see my way out, you don't have to get up." He cringed. *Damn, that was awkward. Hard to say anything right.*

"That's okay. I need to lock the door behind you, anyway."

As they walked toward the door, Travis asked, "Could you tell me who's running that drug test? That's pretty fascinating."

"A drug company, Cardon. The drug came from a guy at Southeast Texas State, though. I think his name was... Lazarus. That's it. Paul Lazarus. I never met him. But the Cardon company actually runs the trial."

"Thank you. And thank you again for your time."

"Sure. Sorry I couldn't help much."

I wouldn't be so sure, Travis thought, as the door closed behind him. He had to find out more about that drug trial, and about Trey Osborne and what the drug might have done for him. Just before he asked Trey about his watch, Travis was certain he had seen him glance at it.

44. Red Light

Trey—Week 29, Tuesday

Boy did I fuck up, goddamn it! As soon as he closed the door behind Travis, Trey smacked himself in the head with his fist. *I know he saw my head tilt. It was so slight, I didn't even see the damn watch. But I started to look, and he saw it. That comment about the watch was no coincidence. He'll contact Cardon now for sure.*

Could they tell him anything? According to the consent form, my records are confidential. I have to give permission before they can disclose my records to anyone outside the trial except my doctors and my insurance company. The police can probably get around that, but they would need probable cause. Would almost looking at my watch in front of a detective who thought I was blind be enough? Maybe.

Even if that detective knows I could see at one point after I took the drug, how would he know I still can? No one from Cardon has seen me since I dropped out. Maybe the drug wore off and my eyes regressed. They wouldn't know. That means I've got to fake it for everybody now. Go out rarely and carefully, and only at night. And make damn sure no one's around when I do.

So it was after 10 p.m. the Tuesday after his talk with Jim Travis when Trey drove home from a grocery store some miles from his house where no one would be likely to know him. He was turning left from North Greenway Drive onto the Knox Street Bridge across Green Bayou when an oncoming car turned right on red just as Trey started across the intersection. This annoyed him; what annoyed him even more was that the car stayed in the right lane and stopped at the red light at the end of the bridge, keeping Trey from turning right on red himself. That pissed him off, but when the light turned green and the driver ahead didn't move, he was ready to erupt. He tried to blast his horn, but hit the wrong spot on the steering wheel hub. Three times. It wasn't the first time he hadn't been able to blow the horn when he tried to—because of the air bag in the steering wheel, you had to hit the hub in exactly the right spot.

The green light for Knox was absurdly short, and the car in front of him didn't move at all before the light turned red again. There was no other traffic around. Trey pulled one of the .38 revolvers he'd bought at the gun show out of the center console, got out, and strode rapidly up to the car in front. The woman behind the wheel had her head bent over a cell phone she held in both hands. Texting.

She looked up, startled, when Trey hammered the window twice with his left fist. Her look of surprise turned to one of terror when she saw the gun pointed at her face. Trey pointed down with his left index finger, and she fumbled to find the switch that lowered the window.

"What the fuck are you doing?" Trey snarled. "Texting? What the fuck is wrong with you? You know the light changed?" He turned his head slightly to his left and spat explosively, as if he were trying to expel something vile from his mouth. "Give me that goddamned phone!" She hesitated a second, paralyzed with fear, then handed it to him.

"Now get your ass out of here! Go!"

She spoke for the first time. "But the light's red!"

Trey was astounded. "What the fuck? You see this?" He raised the gun barrel slightly. "Go! Before I blow your fucking brains out!"

She stomped on the gas hard enough for her tires to squeal and took off across the intersection just before the light turned green again. She came close to running over his right foot, her rear tire barely brushing his toes.

As he hurried back to his car, he could see headlights about a quarter of a mile away coming down Knox. By the time he turned right the light was red again; the car he'd seen coming sailed right through it. Trey saw no other cars as he stopped half a mile down South Greenway and got out, leaving the car running. He crossed behind it to the bayou's edge, pulling out his shirttail and wiping the phone with it. Holding it by its edges so as to leave no fingerprints, he flung it into the bayou. He listened for the splash, then hurried back to the car and drove home, circling his block once to make sure no one was around.

He was breathing hard, his heart racing, the whole way home, wondering what had gotten into him. He hadn't looked around at all before he got out with his gun. It was pure luck no one else had been around. He would have to get more control of himself the next time someone pissed him off.

He was pretty sure there would be a next time.

45. *"Anyone can spit"*

Travis—Week 29, Wednesday

At shift change the Wednesday morning after his visit with Trey, Travis stopped by the coffee vending machine outside the assembly room where the uniformed patrolmen got their orders for the day then often stopped afterward to swap gossip with the night shift cops just getting off. As a detective, Travis was seldom near the assembly room, but no one had started up the coffee maker in the Homicide offices and he needed a cup. Two patrolmen stood near the coffee machine, talking. Travis recognized Carlos Ortiz, who had been the first cop on the scene of a murder Travis had worked a few months back. Travis nodded to him as he put his money in the machine and waited for his cup to fill. He caught a snatch of the conversation.

Ortiz was laughing. "Man, I had a woman last night learned the hard way not to text and drive. She sat at a green light texting. The guy behind her got out, pointed a gun, spit at her, took her phone, and told her to go, now. She told me she'd have to run a red light, like she couldn't believe he'd make her do such a thing. I had to fake a cough to keep from laughin'. She was so hysterical I couldn't tell what bothered her most, him pullin' a gun, spittin' at her, takin' her phone, or makin' her run the red light. Probably takin' her phone. People sure love their damn phones."

Travis broke in. "Did you say he spit?"

Ortiz replied, "Yeah. Hi, Jim. How you doin'?"

"I'm fine. I'm just asking because I'm working a case where we found spit on an office floor. Couldn't get any DNA, though. Killer wiped almost everything up. Seems odd someone would spit in an office. Your guy spit at her, huh? Don't guess you collected a sample."

"No. She couldn't call it in till she got home, so I didn't talk to her where it happened. I think he really spit on the ground, not her. She was so worked up, it's hard to say. She wasn't makin' much sense. You think there's some connection with your guy?"

"Probably not, unless there's a pissed-off psycho running around who spits a lot."

"Check baseball players. Those guys spit everywhere." Ortiz laughed.

Travis kept a straight face. "Your guy fire the gun?"

"No, just pointed it. If he shot it, she didn't stick around to see."

"What'd he look like?"

"She didn't see much. Too scared, I guess. White male, maybe six foot, regular build. Couldn't see his car, either. Just his headlights."

"Thanks. Probably no connection. Lots of pissed-off people out there. Anyone can spit." Travis got his cup of coffee from the machine and started toward his office. "Later."

"Yeah, see you."

At his desk, Travis sipped his coffee and stared at the wall. *Maybe there is a pissed-off psychopath running around out there. Probably no connection with my case. But you never know....*

46. *"It might do both"*

Paul—Week 29, Wednesday (1)

Larry Wisniewski's tracer experiments went smoothly. His only complaint was having just two rhesus monkeys to base conclusions on, but Janey Rose in Physiology only had two she could spare on short notice. After the two-week run, it took Wisniewski a weekend to complete his analyses and make slides for a presentation. He arranged a Wednesday afternoon meeting with Paul, David Eamon, and Janey Rose to present the results.

They met in a small conference room. Using a projector connected to his laptop, Wisniewski put up a slide showing PET scan images of two rat brains, side by side. The areas where the drug concentrated showed up white against the darker gray of the brain. "We'll start with the rats. There's a big difference in how the drug behaves in rats and monkeys. You say it triggers optic nerve growth the same in both?"

"As far as we can tell, it does. It certainly restores vision in both," Paul said.

Wisniewski waved his hand toward the slide showing on the screen. "These are composite images for all twelve rats, superimposed. In the first one, right after we gave them the drug, you can see it concentrated around the optic nerve. But look at the intensity of the signal in the second image, thirty minutes later—the concentration has dropped off noticeably, even if you take diffusion into account. The protein breaks down fast, and the tracer gets carried off in the blood and excreted." He clicked through the next few slides, each with four images side-by-side. "Here you can see further fading of the signal at thirty-minute intervals for the next eight hours, and we made further scans at set intervals over the next three days. We used a zirconium isotope with a long half-life to get a measurable signal over that long a period, though we were drawing blanks by the third day. I'd estimate the half-life of the drug as between two and three hours in rats. Most of it never gets very far from the optic nerve, though there is some diffusion to other areas. So, that's what we found in the rats."

"And in the monkeys?" Janey Rose asked.

"Ah, the monkeys. They're different. A lot different. Since we only had two to work with, we can't estimate the half-life as well as we could with a dozen rats." He clicked to the next slide, again showing two images side-by-side.

"These are from one of the monkeys, showing the drug right after administration and thirty minutes later. The picture is pretty much what you saw in the rat—the drug's localized near the optic nerve. But the slightly lower signal intensity in the second image is almost certainly just from the drug diffusing away from the optic nerve. There's about as much of the drug left after thirty minutes as there was at the start. And that's just the beginning. Here...." He put up a slide with three brain images lined up. "These are scans at two, four, and six hours. The lit-up areas get fuzzier, but that's almost entirely due to diffusion—the drug is spreading out from the optic nerve. But if you account for diffusion when you estimate the concentration, you've got about as much drug left after six hours as you had at the start. It's not breaking down, it's just spreading through the brain. It does break down eventually, as we'll see in the next few slides with images at different intervals over the next week. We'd need to test more monkeys to be sure, but I'd say the half-life in monkeys is days, not hours. It just keeps spreading through the brain as long as it's around. In a time-lapse view, superimposing images made at different times, it lights up the cortex like a Christmas tree. Not all of it, but a lot of it." He put up a slide showing white areas across most of the brain. "What do you know about the biology of the drug?"

Paul replied. "The natural protein is identical in rats, monkeys, and humans—the same amino acid sequence in all three. There are seven DNA sequence differences between rats and rhesus monkeys, and another three between monkeys and humans, but none change the amino acid sequence, even though two of the DNA differences between rats and monkeys occur in protein-coding exons—they're silent mutations that shouldn't change the function. All the other DNA differences, between the species occur in introns, which don't encode amino acids and get cut out of the DNA before the protein gets made. None of the changes in the introns occur in splice sites or any regulatory sequences we know of. So the protein structure's the same in all three—the unmodified rat protein ought to work in humans, and *vice versa*, if you introduced it at the right time in the developing embryo. Any differences between rats, monkeys, and humans in how the protein acts must be due to differences in how it's metabolized. We've been looking at what breaks the drug down in rats, but we haven't done much in monkeys or humans. Because it seemed to work the same in all three, we figured it was processed the same."

"Mmm. Well, there's one more thing that might be pertinent." Wisniewski clicked to the next slide. "You notice I didn't show a composite view from the two monkeys combined? Look at these two images side-by-side, taken eight hours after we gave each monkey the drug. Notice anything?"

They all studied the images for nearly a minute before Paul spoke.

"They're not identical, though there's a lot of overlap. If you superimposed one on the other, you'd cover most of the cortex, but different areas are lighting up in each one."

"Right. We'd have to test more monkeys to be sure, but I think there's some degree of randomness in how the drug spreads through the brain. It concentrates around the optic nerve first, but it's hard to predict where it'll go after that. Does it stimulates nerve growth everywhere it goes? If you figure its metabolism in humans is probably closer to what it is in monkeys than rats, it might end up in places where you don't want it. It may stimulate optic nerve growth in humans just like in rats and monkeys, but after that, who knows?"

There was a long silence. Then Paul said, "We've never seen any neurological anomalies in rats or monkeys. Behavior seems normal in both, and we haven't seen any brain abnormalities in any necropsies. We never saw any noticeable behavior changes in rats or monkeys. There could be subtle ones, but it's hard to know what to look for."

"Well, if you can measure it, you might want to see if any of them are seeing sounds or hearing lights. The drug might create connections between parts of the brain that don't normally talk to each other, and it could cross sensory channels. If it specifically triggers just optic nerve growth, maybe it won't affect other parts of the brain much. But if it stimulates nerve growth more generally, it's hard to know what might happen."

Paul said, "Wow", in a flat tone of voice. "Thank you, Larry. You've certainly given us a lot to think about. We'll try to figure out where to go from here."

"I'll send you the image files. This should make a pretty interesting paper."

"The drug's in a clinical trial, so we'll have to hold off on publishing anything right now. But we'll definitely publish this as soon as we can. What you've got here is important."

Everyone was quiet as the meeting broke up. Paul and David stayed seated as the others left, When they were gone, David grabbed Paul's shoulder.

"In monkeys and probably people, this stuff just won't go away. Jesus, Paul, you didn't make it stable—you made it bulletproof!"

Paul shook his head. "Impossible. Its half-life in neural cell cultures is less than an hour. Once it binds a receptor, the neuron takes it in and breaks it down in a few minutes."

"Then some protein that's in the brain but not in cell cultures must bind to it and keep it from breaking down. After it triggers optic nerve growth, it doesn't go anywhere, it just hangs around for hours, maybe days, working the whole time. It doesn't stay bound to the receptor that grabs it first; it gets released and latches on to another neuron, and then keeps going. It doesn't know when to quit!"

Paul arched his eyebrows and looked down, biting his lower lip. "Larry wasn't measuring its activity, just its location. The drug definitely hangs around longer than we expected. It *could* be stimulating nerve growth the whole time...."

David broke in. "Maybe it doesn't always grow whole new neurons. It could just grow new connections between neurons already there, connecting ones that don't normally talk to each other."

David grew more animated. "If that happens, this thing is changing something fundamental. Look, you are who you are because of the connections in your brain. No one else has the exact same set you do. Some connections are hard-wired; we all have them, so we all react the same to some things. Nobody laughs at funerals or cries at a joke—if they do, something's wrong. Those hard-wired connections are what make us alike; the ones you make on your own are what make us all different. Why are some people smarter? They make new connections faster; they learn the first time they see something, not the third or fourth. What's memory? You make connections that last longer, and you can call them up better. Creativity? You make connections between things most people wouldn't see as related." David was standing now, waving his arms as he spoke, almost messianic.

He went on, caught up in his own explanation. "Mental illness? Some connections are hooked up wrong, or just missing. Voices in your head? Misconnections make auditory circuits fire on their own. Maybe depression is just failure to turn mood circuits on when you ought to; things that ought to make you happy just don't flip the right switch because your brain never made the right connections." He had started pacing, talking at a faster and faster clip.

"The point is, the connections in our brains are *everything*. They make us who we are. And the people who get this drug, it's changing them. It starts out regrowing their optic nerves, but then it keeps going, creating connections that weren't there before, and that could change your behavior. Maybe that's why you suddenly took up with Lindsey, and blew up in that meeting." David fixed Paul with a look that showed there was no "maybe" about it in his mind. He'd explained everything.

Paul was silent for several seconds, shifting uneasily. "So what do we do?"

"First, nobody else gets the drug, that's clear. And you better keep a close eye on everyone who already has—including you and Lindsey. Who knows for how long? We don't know what this drug might do. You better get the people at Cardon in on this, and the Data Safety and Monitoring Board for the trial. Also the University's I.R.B. and the legal office. The people in the trial knew it was an experimental drug when they took it, so you're probably covered there. And who knows? They might not even complain—besides making them see again, it might even make them smarter. But it could make someone psychotic for all we know. The really scary thing is...."

They spoke in unison: "It might do both."

47. "It's really not the money..."

Paul—Week 29 (2)

Jim Russell was skeptical when Paul called him after the meeting to tell him about Wisniewski's results, and insisted they stop the trial.

"Come on, Paul, what would be the point of that? Nobody's had a second dose yet, and we can't take back the one they've already gotten. Even if we were to stop the trial, we'd still have to follow up on everyone just like we're doing now. So why panic? We can just hold off on the second dose for now, and keep doing what we're doing."

Paul had to concede that Jim's proposal made sense. Still....

"I don't think we can keep patients in the dark if there might be something wrong with them. The Data Safety and Monitoring Board certainly needs to know."

"I see your point about the DSMB. But you know how those boards are. They'll want to shut the whole trial down immediately. We'll definitely have to go to them at some point. But do we really have enough evidence right *now* that the drug is causing psychological problems? We only have depression in one patient, and it's pretty understandable. Her eyes work fine, but her visual cortex isn't processing the signals right. We think that may improve with time. Her depression, it could just be an indirect effect of her vision problems. I think we need clearer evidence of psychological effects before we risk shutting down the trial over them. Wisniewski's findings are interesting, but they're based on only two monkeys, whose behavior apparently didn't change. We can skip the second dose for now, but I think we should make sure the drug really is causing the problems you're worried about before we raise an alarm. OGF83 isn't perfect, but it's restored vision in 20% of the people who've taken a minuscule dose. Even if it worked in only 10% of all blind people, think how much good that would do! Think how much money your school would get with even 10% success! Do you really want to jeopardize all that just on a suspicion of side effects?" Russell was calm through all of this, sounding like the voice of sweet reason.

Paul was pacing back and forth at his desk, carrying the phone with him. "Damn, Jim, listen to yourself! Are we worried more about the people taking the drug or the money we could make from it? It's hard for me to tell. That's why we need the DSMB to take a look. They don't have anything to gain or lose by shutting down the trial, but *we* do. How objective can we be? Look, even if they do shut it down, we'll still have to follow up on all ten patients just like we're doing now. We'll still be able to monitor the effects of the drug. I'm not being entirely unselfish here. If we stop the trial before there's any more damage, I think I can fix the drug so it still works but has fewer side effects. Wisniewski's results suggest it's too stable. It's hanging around too long. I think I can fix that. If OGF83 is causing problems, maybe OGF84 won't. It would be better not to wait for the damage to get worse before we stop this. If we let things go too far, we might never get a chance to try OGF84 or 87 or 100."

"Paul, if you want to be a whistleblower on this, I can't stop you. But I wouldn't be so sure we'd still be able to follow up on the subjects if they shut the trial down. No consent form is so ironclad it can stop lawyers. If the trial gets stopped early and any patients lawyer up, they'll probably insist on using their own doctors. I think we should get more evidence before we risk shutting the trial down."

Paul could see Russell's point, but he wasn't sure he could trust Russell to gather evidence that might jeopardize the trial. Maybe he could do something about that himself. He would definitely have to talk to Greg Wright's daughter to find out what was going on with her.

"Okay, Jim. I won't go to the Monitoring Board—yet. But you need to ramp up the psychological tests. And get that guy who dropped out back in the trial! We need to know what's going on with him."

"All right, we can try that. And Paul?"

"Yes?"

"It's really not just the money I'm worried about."

Paul wasn't convinced of that at all.

48. *"I wish I was blind again"*

Kathy—Week 29

"THIS IS GETTING TO ME, Leila." Kathy sat hunched over her drink at the bar after their last set on Wednesday. It was close to Thursday now, nearly midnight. Kathy was on her second drink.

"I can tell. You don't usually get full-strength margaritas." Leila had a glass of the house Chardonnay in front of her—still her first.

Kathy stuck her index finger down in her glass, slowly stirring her drink. "I know. Much less two of them. I kind of fought with my mother today. Not really a fight. She just annoys me sometime. She's only trying to help. We go through these exercises in a dark room they set up, trying to improve my focus. They had to put black curtains over the windows to get the room dark enough for spotlights, but the exercises aren't helping. It's easy to focus on one thing under a spotlight as long as everything else is dark. As soon as she turns on the room lights, though, it's back to the same thing. I can't see just one thing. It's like everything's trying to push its way into my head all at once. Sometimes I want to close my eyes and scream 'Stop!' But everything just keeps coming. I can't even describe it. I don't think I could stand it without these glasses." She put the finger she'd been stirring her drink with into her mouth, then drew it out and pushed up the nosepiece of the wrap-around dark glasses she now wore virtually every minute she was awake; they were almost completely opaque. She might as well wear a blindfold.

"Anyway, I told Mom I was sick of these damned exercises and stomped out of the room. I didn't even wait for her to turn on the lights. I already know where everything in the room is, I don't need a damn light. Mom needs a flashlight when it's that dark. Who's handicapped then?"

"Your mom's only trying to help. You said so yourself."

Kathy sighed. "I know. It gets her so mad every time I say I wish I was blind again. Boy, does she hate that! She says, 'No you don't. Your brain's had twenty years to adjust to being blind. You have to give it time to readjust now.' I say, 'How long? Another twenty years?' Oh, does that piss her off."

"Do you really want to be blind again? Don't you think you'll get something out of this eventually? I can only imagine what you're going through, but I can't imagine ever wanting to be blind."

"I couldn't either, before now. I used to try to imagine what it would be like to see, but I didn't imagine anything like this. My eyes don't help me at all. If I cover them, I can get by like I always have. If I open them, I'm almost paralyzed. I can't play the piano; my eyes can't keep up with my fingers and I botch everything. Shit, I can barely walk without stumbling. How often did I stumble when I was blind?"

Leila gave a short laugh. "Come on, now. You stumbled sometimes, and you know it."

It was Kathy's turn to laugh. "Okay, you're right. I love it that you keep me honest."

"What are friends for? But if that's true, tell me honestly, isn't there anything good you're getting out of this? Something to keep you trying?"

Kathy arched her brows. "Honestly? I have to say I'm playing better than ever, if I can keep it under control. I'm more free to create something, not just play back something I've heard before. That part's great, but it doesn't have anything to do with seeing. Is the drug doing that? Probably. But I think it also made me depressed. It's like, 'Okay, I'll give you one thing, but it'll cost you.' Is there anything good about seeing, itself? Sometimes, I have to admit, the colors and shapes and patterns I see can be so beautiful they make me cry. But maybe I'm really crying because they're so beautiful and so damn useless at the same time. My eyes don't help me at all. Almost everything takes longer if I try to do it with my eyes open. I make way more mistakes. When I reach for something, it's never where I expect it to be. It's either closer or further away than it looks. Sometimes everything seems to be right in front of me and sometimes it seems like it's halfway across the room, even if the only thing that changed is that I closed my eyes and then opened them. What can I do with that?"

Kathy leaned toward Leila across the table and her voice dropped almost to a whisper. Leila could barely hear her above the noise in the lounge. "I'm really scared, Leila. I haven't told anybody else this, but I'm worried about my hearing. I was in my room reading Braille the other day and I suddenly heard my mother's voice right behind me. I almost jumped out of my seat." Kathy leaned even closer, as her voice rose in both volume and pitch—the edge of alarm was unmistakable. "The thing is, I didn't hear her footsteps! I didn't hear her open the door or come in the room! I don't know, maybe I left the door open myself, but Leila, I didn't hear any footsteps! I always hear footsteps. You can't come in a room without me knowing it. Maybe—*maybe*—if there's a carpet you could, but we don't have a carpet." Her voice dropped in pitch. "What if I'm losing my hearing? Not going deaf or anything, but not hearing as well as I always have? What if my hearing gets dull and my eyes never get any better than they are now? Where would I be then? I'd be stuck in the middle, not able to hear like I do now, and not able to see well enough to make up for it. I'd be completely fucked. What if I'm too old for my brain to rewire itself for vision? I've heard your brain has developed as much as it's going to by the time you're in your thirties, maybe sooner. Trying to switch over from hearing to seeing could leave me stuck right in the middle of both."

Leila sensed that any reassurance she tried to give would sound empty; there was no way she could know what Kathy was going through. She reached both hands across the table and grasped both of Kathy's for several seconds.

What was going through Kathy's head at that moment is that she couldn't let her useless eyesight fuck up her hearing. If it came down to a choice between her eyes and her ears, it would be up to her to make it.

49. *"I didn't know you felt that way"*

Paul/Lindsey—Week 30, Tuesday

"Is your wife teaching a class tonight?" Lindsey asked Paul. The question seemed innocuous enough.

"Yes, Tuesdays and Thursdays. The semester still has a few weeks to go." Paul looked up from the paper he was reading in *Vision Research*. "What do we have going in the lab?"

"It's pretty quiet now. The Wisniewski lab sent over some of the rat brains for sectioning to look for abnormalities. We could work late, but we probably don't have to." She walked up behind Paul and put her hands on his shoulders, a slight smile on her face.

"Would you mind staying late? If you've got something to do…."

"No, it's fine. It won't take long to do the sections. I can have them ready for slicing this afternoon. We don't have to look at them all tonight, but I'll have them ready." She smiled more broadly.

"Okay. I can give you a hand later if you need it." He knew she probably wouldn't need it. It was just polite to offer. She would need him in the lab later, but not because she needed any help making pathology slides.

* * *

Lindsey worked on slides until about 7:30 that evening, while Paul worked in his adjoining office. A graduate student from another lab came by to get Lindsey's advice on an assay. A common occurrence—Lindsey was gifted in the lab, and students often came to her for technical advice. Once the student left, Lindsey locked the lab door, then went into Paul's office. He pulled an exercise mat from behind a file cabinet and laid it out on the floor—not much of a bed, but better than the threadbare carpet.

Lindsey shrugged off her lab coat and hung it on the hook on the back of the office door, which she also locked. She stood facing Paul, who suddenly stepped toward her and put his arms around her, kissing her hard. He moved his right hand from around her and began unbuttoning her blouse; she began to unbutton his shirt. She finished first, and moved to his pants, unzipping them and rubbing his cock before she unbuckled his belt and undid the snap, then knelt to pull off his shoes, socks, pants, and underwear, while he took off his shirt and threw it on a chair. Once he was naked, he finished undressing her, slipping her blouse off her shoulders and unhooking her front closure bra—black; she knew he loved to see her, however briefly, in black lingerie. He knelt in front of her, sucking her nipples while he unzipped and unsnapped her pants. She had lost no weight since the day at the pool, and he moved his mouth down her round belly, stopping to lick her navel. He pulled her pants off first, then slowly slid her black panties down, kissing and licking as he went. Once he reached her wavy black pubic hair, he quickly pulled her panties off the rest of the way, then tilted his face up underneath her, licking her labia until she gasped. He pulled her down on the mat and started back in on her breasts, then slid his face down her body, licking her while she put her thighs over his shoulders. They spent the next half-hour on the mat in the serious business of pleasure.

This had been routine for nearly three months. The first time, Paul had succumbed to an impulse he felt helpless to resist, but now it was harder to blame it all on OGF83. It wasn't impulsive anymore.

As they lay curled up together afterward, Paul brought up a subject he had mentioned just twice before.

"Do you think that spill we had affected us this way? Did you ever think of having sex with me before that? It just seemed to come on us all of a sudden, don't you think?"

She turned to him, her head in her hand, propped up on one elbow. "I think we inhaled buffer. I've smelled it before."

"Yes, but OGF83 doesn't have any smell that I ever noticed. The only thing we *would* smell would be the buffer."

She shrugged, then smiled. "If it is the drug, why would it make us want to fuck?" She put her other hand on his crotch. "I didn't feel any sudden, umm, what's the word? Compulsions? That I have to do something? You touched my shoulder. I touched your hand. We kissed. I thought you finally realized how pretty I am."

"I did. But we'd worked together for years...."

"So it took you a long time to see me. I broke up with my boyfriend not long before. I thought I had to lose weight to get another man. That's why you saw me at the pool and realized how hot I was. Even if I'm not skinny." She giggled, and rubbed her hand on his cock, which got hard again. "But I'm not fat, either!"

"No, you're not. And you are hot. But...." He glanced over at the clock on the bookshelf by his desk, "It's getting late."

They gathered up their clothes and started dressing. She suddenly broke the silence. "You said we've worked together for years. It has been a long time. Shouldn't I be more than a Lab Tech by now? I should be a Research Associate or a Faculty Associate. Haven't I earned it?"

Paul was taken aback. "I didn't know you felt that way. I thought you were happy. I'll see whether we can't get you a raise. We can talk about it tomorrow. I'd like to get home tonight before my wife does."

As they left, they passed a cleaning woman mopping the hall outside the lab. Paul wondered if she suspected anything. She had keys to every room. She could have walked in on them anytime. Why hadn't she? What did she know? As he tried to imagine what she would think if she walked in on them, he found himself looking at his own behavior as though from outside. *You've been taking a big risk just for sex. You don't love Lindsey. You've had your problems at home, but you still love Sharon, not Lindsey.*

The sound of Lindsey's "Good night" in the parking garage suddenly jolted Paul back to here and now. *Was she less impulsive when we started all this than I thought? I didn't know she was unhappy with her position. I don't think I like where this is going.*

50. *"You could if you tried"*

Paul/Lindsey—Week 30, Wednesday

THE NEXT MORNING, LINDSEY BROUGHT the subject of her promotion up almost as soon as she arrived. She stood in the doorway of Paul's office, leaning on the frame, and with no preamble said, "I'm already at the top of the salary scale for Senior Lab Assistant II. My pay can't go any higher. The least I should be is a Research Associate, and I do more than Faculty Associates in some of the labs here."

Paul leaned back in his chair, spreading his hands and shaking his head sympathetically. "I think Research Associate requires at least a master's degree, and you never finished your M.P.H. I'm pretty sure Faculty Associate requires a Ph.D."

"Barbara Kerkorian doesn't have one." Her voice was sharp, almost accusing.

"Oh, her, yeah. I was told she was a protégé of Bill Ross. He pretty much founded the Biochemistry department here, and chaired it for about thirty years. He kind of dragged her along with him. I think they gave her that to keep him happy; he actually wanted her on the faculty, but they wouldn't go for it. Technically, I don't think a Faculty Associate can have tenure, but that's basically what she's got. The school's gone along with it forever. Bill Ross retired years ago, but Barbara's still here."

"They could do the same thing for me. They would if you told them you wanted it."

"Me? I don't have that kind of clout. Especially since the last faculty meeting. I'm not the most popular guy around here right now."

She snorted. "Huhn! They're gonna make millions off OGF83. They'll give you anything you want."

"They won't make a dime off OGF83 if it fails in trials. If it does work, they already own it, whether I'm here or not. I just get part of the money. You, too, you know; I made sure that was in the agreement. They wouldn't cut you in for much, but you'll get something."

"I bet if you backed me, I'd make Faculty Associate."

He shook his head. "I don't think so. I think they closed the door behind Barbara. They don't do things around here now the way they did when she got here. That was a long time ago."

"You could try." Her tone was accusing.

"Look, why don't you go back and finish your M.P.H.? Then I could put you up for Research Associate. We could work around your classes."

"I'd probably have to start over."

"It hasn't been that long. The courses you already took would still count."

"Maybe. It'd still feel like I was starting over. I shouldn't have to. I've already done more than most people around here."

"I'm on your side, Lindsey, you know that. But I don't make the rules."

"You could if you tried. Everybody says the school's gonna make millions off this."

"Nobody knows that yet. I hope it does. But right now, I don't have as much pull around here as you think I do."

She shook her head. "You could do it if you tried." There was an edge in her voice he had never heard before. She turned abruptly and left before he could say anything more. He almost called her back, but decided to let it go. *Shit. This is the last thing I need right now.*

51. "I hope you can prove it, then"

Paul—Week 31, Wednesday (1)

LINDSEY SAID NOTHING MORE ABOUT a promotion over the next few days. She said very little at all, in fact, and over the next week, she managed to finish everything in the lab during normal hours and leave on time every afternoon. Paul knew she was mad at him, but hoped she would get over it.

Paul was surprised the following Wednesday when Dean Sanders called him to her office and asked him to close the door and sit down. She immediately came to the point.

"Paul, your lab technician has filed a sexual harassment complaint against you."

Paul's head jolted back. "What? Lindsey? Xi Lin?"

"Yes. She says the two of you have had a sexual relationship for three months, and that you won't recommend her for a promotion unless she keeps having sex with you."

"That's not true! She's mad because I wouldn't recommend her for a position she's not qualified for. It has nothing to do with sex!"

"So you haven't been having sex with her?"

"No, no, I mean, yes, we've had sex, but it has nothing to do with her not getting a promotion!"

She shook her head. "I'm disappointed in you, Paul. You know better than that. Whether her promotion had anything to do with sex or not, you know supervisors can't have sexual relationships with anyone who works for them. Her complaint triggers a process I'd do anything to avoid, but I have no choice. You need to stay home for a few days while we get it started. For now, you're suspended with pay. We're going to have to move her to a position where you won't be her supervisor. If there's no one but her who could run things while you're out, you need to bring all your projects to a stop. I don't know how long your suspension might last. We can't leave her in your lab."

"I don't know, maybe if I talk to her.... She wanted me to put her in for a position she wasn't qualified for. She'd need a master's degree. I told her that. I guess this is how she decided to take it out on me. I can't believe she'd do this. We can work this out."

"No. I can't let you talk to her now. The school would see that as attempted coercion. I'm going to have to turn this over to Kelsey Clarke." The Dean flashed a grimace. "She's the school's Title IX Coordinator. I have to tell you, I think she'll push this as far as she can. She's a zealot. The regulations permit an informal resolution of these cases if there's no violence or threats involved, but I'm sure she'll want something formal. She'll interview you two and any witnesses and write a report. Then there'll be a disciplinary hearing before a faculty panel. You can bring an observer, but not a lawyer, unless there's a criminal charge, which there isn't so far. The observer can't actually say anything—it's not the same as having an advocate. You need to remember one thing, Paul—with Title IX cases, you can forget about 'innocent until proven guilty'. You're pretty much guilty unless you can prove you're innocent. Not really fair, but that's how it is. I've seen it. It's not pretty. Title IX used to be mostly about making women's college sports programs equal to men's, but it's turned into a monster. I'm all for gender equality. I don't think Title IX complaints are the best way to get it, but there's nothing I can do about it. I don't get to set school policy on these things." The Dean's tone was hard throughout, though she clearly didn't think much of Title IX or Kelsey Clarke.

"I just get today to get my lab and my office straight?" Everything was moving too fast here.

"I think that would be best. You're close to David Eamon. I assume he'll be your advocate—observer, I mean. While you're out, you could have him keep your lab up, pick up your campus mail, whatever. Just give him the keys to your office and lab."

"He already has a key to the lab. He works in there, too."

"Well, good. I didn't realize he still did research. I thought he let that slide once he got tenure." Her tone was icy. For years, she had made it a point to put David on every time-suck of a committee the school had.

She looked down at some papers on her desk, and it was clear the meeting was over. Paul got up to leave.

"You know, it's not like she's saying, Helen. It was consensual all the way. I was already sorry it happened for a lot of reasons, even before this."

"I hope you can prove it, then."

As Paul walked back to his office, it occurred to him that he wasn't entirely sure whether the Dean hoped he could prove that it was all consensual, or that he was sorry it happened.

52. Suspended

Paul—Week 31, Wednesday (2)

PAUL WAS STILL THINKING ABOUT what he needed to do to get ready for what might be a long suspension when David came by. Paul asked, "Did the Dean tell you?"

"Tell me what? I haven't seen her today."

"I've been suspended. Lindsey filed a sexual harassment complaint against me. She got pissed off because she wants a promotion and she thinks I'm blocking it. I couldn't get it for her if I wanted to. She'd need a master's degree, and she never finished hers."

"Damn, Paul. Suspended for how long?" David sat down in his usual chair; he came by at least once a day, usually more often.

"Right now, it's indefinite. At least it's with pay. I'm supposed to wrap everything up in the lab today. It's good I don't have any critical experiments going right now. I do have a batch of treated rats I was going to use for some behavior studies, but I can leave them alone for a while. Could you keep an eye on them until I get back? The people in Animal Care actually take care of them; all you have to do is check on them now and then. If you could just keep an eye on the lab in general, I'd appreciate it. You'd be in there for your own stuff, anyway."

"Of course I will."

"Thanks, I really appreciate it. Also, the Dean says I'm allowed to have someone from the school as an observer at any hearings about my case. Could you do that? I was told specifically it's just as an observer, and it's not the same thing as an advocate. I don't think you're even allowed to say anything. But I don't know. I don't really know anything about the process." Paul, always in motion even while sitting, was moving his swivel chair back and forth more rapidly than usual.

"I'd be happy to, if that's where I could do you the most good. I imagine they'll call witnesses. Could I be a witness if I was your observer? I've certainly been around both you and Lindsey a lot, and I've never seen any sign of trouble between you, since you told me about your first... lapse. I might be more valuable to you as a witness than an observer, if I can't be both."

"That's a good point. I don't really know enough about the process now to tell you one way or the other. I guess we both need to read up on how it works."

"Yeah, I'll look the procedures up and send you the links. But Paul?"

"What?"

"Even if they don't allow lawyers in the hearing, I think you should probably talk to one."

53. *"...I don't even want to look at you...."*

Paul—Week 31, Wednesday (3)

PAUL SAT AT THE KITCHEN table that afternoon, wondering what he could say to Sharon. She had been out when he got home. When Paul heard her car pull up, he went to meet her at the door. As soon as he saw her, he could tell from the grim look on her face that she already knew. Before he had even closed the door behind her, before he could get a word out, she said, "Paul, what the hell is going on? Did you know your lab tech e-mailed me saying you'd been fucking her and she's filed a sexual harassment charge against you?"

Paul's jaw dropped. *Goddamn Lindsey! How could she do that?* He'd been wondering how to work up to a confession; that was useless now.

"Look, I was going to tell you. It just happened today. I was going to tell you as soon as you came home...."

She cut him off. "She just filed a complaint today. What I want to know is, how long has this been going on? She's worked for you forever. Have you been screwing her all this time?" She put her purse and briefcase down on the front table and turned toward him. Her face was crimson.

"No! Really! No. Just... just a few weeks. It was stupid. I know there's no excuse. It just happened. She... kind of came on to me one night in the lab, and I didn't try to stop it. I could have said no, but I didn't. We... we did it a few times afterward." He couldn't bring himself to tell her how long and how often he had been having sex with Lindsey. Not that the details were likely to make much difference. He knew he was already fucked.

"How could you? How dare you?"

Paul backed up a step, shaking his head. "I know. It was stupid. It was just sex. I was trying to figure out how to break it off. I don't have any feelings for her. I love you. You know that."

"Like hell I do." She nearly spat it out. "Don't even say it. How dare you say that to me now? I don't wanna hear it. That's not what you do when you love someone!"

Paul took a step toward her, his arms slightly open, but she backed away. He closed his eyes and shook his head. "I know, I know." He opened his eyes, still shaking his head, trying to look contrite. "I was so stupid! I... look, I really don't know what to say. Maybe we should talk about it in a little while, after we both... after it's had some time to sink in. Can we sit down? Let's go in the kitchen." He walked past her. She said nothing, but followed.

As they pulled chairs out to sit down facing each other, Sharon said, "I'm going to be just as pissed off in a little while as I am now. Right now, I don't even want to look at you, much less listen to any apologies." She turned her face slightly away from him as she said that, then abruptly snapped it around to face him. "All I want to know is, why? Why all of a sudden, if this really has just been going on a few weeks? She's been your lab tech for years."

"Look, I don't know if you're going to believe this, but I think OGF83 may have something to do with it." He wasn't sure even he believed it.

Sharon looked for an instant like she might laugh. She didn't. "Oh, come on! How? What could that have to do with it besides keeping you and her in the lab together all the time? You've been more married to your work than to me for a long time now."

"No, look. I... I never told you this, but I had an accident in the lab about six months ago. I spilled some of the drug and inhaled the fumes. Lindsey was there. She breathed it, too. We don't know how much either of us took in...."

"So what? It's an eye drug, isn't it? What's that have to do with anything?"

"It's a *brain* drug. It might affect behavior, too. That's not just based on me, but on some of the patients in the trial. It may have different effects in some people, but it seems to affect self-control in everyone. You give in to impulses. Remember that blow-up in the faculty meeting I told you about? That was after the spill. I'd never done anything like that before!"

"Come on! How do you go from losing your temper to screwing around?"

Paul was sounding like an evangelist now. He had the answer. Anyone could see that. "That was an impulse, too! That's the connection! You lose control of your impulses. One of the patients in the trial did something similar, she—"

"You fucked one of the patients in the trial?

"No! No. Not me!" Sharon wasn't understanding; he had to make it clear. "She let a stranger pick her up. She'd never done that before she had the drug. She's given in to other impulses, too. Another patient seems to be having problems with his temper. Those are the two I know about."

Sharon wasn't buying it. "Does the drug make you stupid, too? You know better than to fuck an employee."

"No! When you have an impulse, you don't think about consequences. You just give in to it. I think OGF83 can cause that."

"Then why haven't you stopped the trial?"

His voice rose in pitch. "I tried to! I tried to get Jim Russell to. But we can't prove it's the drug. Suspicion's not enough, and that's all we have right now."

She waved her hand dismissively. "Right. You can't blame this on your drug. You knew better. How many times did you fuck her? Were they all just impulses?"

"The first one was, for sure. After that… I don't know. I don't know what to say."

"Did you break it off before she filed her complaint? Is that why she did it?" She arched her eyebrows.

"No. I wanted to. I didn't. I…. It wasn't love. It was just… sex. That's all."

"That's almost worse. It *is* worse. I could see you throwing all this away if you fell in love with someone else, but just for sex? We have that, too, in case you forgot."

"No. I can't…. Look, I don't know what to say."

She stood up. "Well, I do. I'm going to call up Linda and see if I can't stay with her a few days. And I'm going to talk to a lawyer. I don't think I can forgive this. It wasn't just once. That would have been bad enough, but maybe I could forgive that, I don't know. But you let it go on. I don't think you can blame your drug for that. *Once* is an impulse! *Once!* Maybe! Not this! I should throw *you* out, but right now, I really don't want to stay here and be reminded of you. I'm going to call Linda now. If I can't stay with her, I'll get a hotel room, but I'm sure I can stay with her. Don't call me. I'll call you. When I'm ready. It might be a while."

She went to their room to call her friend, Linda, and pack. Paul sat down at the kitchen table, his hands under his chin, and stared off into space until long after she was gone.

54. The Worst Side Effect of All

Paul/Kathy—Week 31, Thursday

PAUL HAD ALREADY DECIDED HE needed to talk to Kathy Wright; he would approach her at her night job. She might have a harder time saying no. He would at least get to see her reaction if she didn't want to talk.

On Thursday, the day after Sharon left, Paul went to the Blue Room about 8:30 and sat at the bar; he would try to talk with Kathy after the last set. He could turn his seat halfway around and see the small stage from the left side. There was room for a baby grand piano and a microphone stand, with a small space for the singer to stand in. The singer billed as Lila Kallen, wearing a low-cut peach-colored evening dress slit to mid-thigh, was in the middle of her first set. She sang quite well, he thought, though his tastes tended more toward Classic Rock than Cole Porter. She would sway and gesture expressively while she sang, seducing the microphone and most of the men in the place, and she made good use of what little space she had onstage.

The piano was at the back of the stage, offset to the right, from Paul's vantage point. Kathy wore a black dress that wasn't low-cut. If her goal was not to draw attention from the singer, she failed. Leila could give men wet dreams, but Kathy was herself striking—tall, with long, flowing brown hair, and dark glasses that gave her an aura of mystery. Even trying to blend with the background, Kathy was formidable visual competition for Leila; Paul wondered if the singer made Kathy wear dark dresses so she wouldn't steal the spotlight. He thought you would have to put Kathy in a burka to make men take their eyes off her.

He noticed she behaved as though she were totally blind. Her glasses were dark to the point of being opaque, and a white cane lay on the floor to the right of the piano. She showed no sign of looking at the keyboard while she played; she usually seemed to be looking straight ahead, or slightly upward, though with those glasses, she wouldn't see much even with her eyes open.

Paul nursed a Fat Tire through three songs before the set ended and Leila left the stage. Kathy remained at the piano and began playing a piece he didn't recognize. Some parts stayed mostly in the low end of the keyboard's range, the notes rarely straying above middle C. While she played, he ordered another beer and asked the bartender if he could get a message to the pianist. "No problem," she said, and called over one of the servers.

Paul said, "I would like to get a note to the pianist, but she seems to be blind?"

"Mostly she is. She can see some, but I don't know if she could read a note. I can give her your message, though; I can read it to her."

He wrote on a napkin, "Could we talk after the show? Paul Lazarus—OGF83."

She looked at it. "I'll let her know." She looked up with a quizzical expression. "Could I ask what that last thing is?"

"It's kind of hard to explain. She'll know it."

The waitress went over to Kathy just before Leila reappeared for the second set. Paul couldn't tell if she gave Kathy the note, but they spoke briefly, and he saw Kathy's head turn partway toward him, though probably not far enough to see him, if she could see anything through those dark glasses. The waitress looked at him and nodded. She came over as Leila started the second set.

"She said it's okay. She's been expecting you."

"I know her father," he offered as a partial excuse, pressing a ten-dollar bill in the waitress' hand. "Thank you. Really." Paul sat on his stool and watched what turned out to be a two-beer set.

After the show, it was Leila who came over to him while Kathy remained at the piano. The waitress who delivered the note had pointed him out.

Without preamble, Leila said, "She wants you to get a table so you two can talk. I'll wait, and drive her home afterward. She told me who you are. I'll be honest—I don't know whether to congratulate you for curing blindness or tell you to go to hell."

Paul jerked back as though he'd been slapped. "Thanks for being honest. I think. I do like your singing."

"Well, thank you for *that*, anyway. Look, I don't want to be an asshole, but all this has put Kathy through hell. When she first got her sight back, she thought she would be so happy. I was thrilled for her, but it turns out seeing's not as easy as you'd think. Once she found she couldn't make sense out of anything she saw, it was like someone let all the air out. She's not just my pianist, you know—she's my closest friend. I love her very much, but I tell you, she can be a bear to be around now. Up, down—she's all over the place. Down way more than up, lately. And she can go from 'up' to 'down' in a flash. Not so much the other way. Sometimes she doesn't want to touch a piano, even when we need to rehearse something. But she makes herself practice and she makes herself come here and play three nights a week even when she'd rather just curl up and die. Anyone who can go through life blind and not be bitter about it has more guts than I do, but I had no idea how tough she really was until all this. I know your drug wasn't supposed to cause any of this, so I can't really blame you. Curing blindness should be a great thing, right? But—Goddamn!"

All Paul could do was nod.

The waitress he had talked to earlier showed him to a table near the back of the room, then brought Kathy over. Kathy carried her cane, but the waitress guided her to the table by her left elbow as if she were practiced at it. No one watching would have guessed that Kathy could see anything at all. When she sat down, she told the waitress, "Thanks, Sheryl. Could you tell Linda to get me the usual?"

Kathy spoke to Paul. "You're wondering why I do this if I can see. It's faster, believe me. I stop at every step if I actually try to watch where I'm going. I practiced quite a while before I finally gave up. It just wasn't getting any better."

He nodded before realizing that she probably couldn't see it, even if her eyes were open behind those opaque glasses. "I see. Oh, I'm sorry, I...."

Kathy gave a short laugh. "Almost everybody apologizes when they say that, once they realize they've said it. If they realize it; some never do. Don't worry about it. I say it myself sometimes. I even used to when I was still completely blind. It's kind of built into the language, you know?"

Paul had wanted to talk to her, but now that she was right in front of him, he wasn't sure what to say. She broke the silence.

"My father said you wanted to talk to me. You're both worried the drug might be affecting my behavior. The short answer? Yeah, it does."

"You can tell?"

"That I'm not feeling or acting like I was before? Of course. How could I not know that?"

"I meant that the drug was doing it. How are you different?"

"I'm depressed a lot of the time, and I never was before. That's the main difference. Funny. That's the last thing you'd expect, isn't it? A blind person gets their sight back, and they get depressed? That's the thing, though. My eyes may be taking things in, but my brain isn't. What I see is all just a jumble of shapes and colors and fragments. I have to work hard to pick out specific objects. Even if I manage to do that, I can't tell how far away anything is. That's why walking's hard. I can't tell what's right in front of me from what's on the other side of the room."

"So you're seeing everything flat, like a picture without perspective?"

"I suppose so, if I understand what 'perspective' means. It took me a while just to learn what a picture is, though I must have seen them when I was a kid. I think I get it. It's a flat depiction of something, where everything in it is the same distance away from you, even if it looks like it's not. But the 'looks like it's not' part I have to take on faith. To me, almost everything looks like it's the same distance away. Put something in front of me alongside a picture of it, I'm not sure I could tell you which was which without touching them. If you put two things in front of me, one right there and the other across the room, and tell me to touch the one closest, it's about 50:50 which one I reach for. Even if I can tell you which one is further away, don't ask me how far. Anything I say is just a guess."

Paul found himself nodding again. "You know, the trial doctors think your depression may be just a normal reaction to your not being able to use your vision because you *can't* see things spatially. They think your depression stems from that, not anything the drug's doing directly."

"How would they know? I get why they might think that, but how do they explain the highs?"

"Jim Russell didn't think you had exaggerated highs."

"Sometimes I don't think he's paying attention. I told him I'm up and down. Mostly down, yeah, but not always."

"He thinks your lows are serious depression, but your highs are probably more like normal good moods."

"How the hell would he know?" She spat back, visibly angry. "I know what my moods are like. I know what's normal and what's not."

The waitress brought Kathy a margarita. Paul still had half a glass of beer he had brought to the table; he had completely forgotten about it.

"Thank you." To Paul, she said, "Half the usual tequila. Not good to drink too much when you can't see. Ever heard the phrase, 'blind drunk'? If you're blind, you really don't want to get drunk, trust me. I know I'm not technically blind now, but I might as well be, for all the good my eyes do me. So anyway...."

"I understand you sometimes get carried away when you're playing. Is that when you're in one of your 'up' moods?"

"So you've heard about that, huh? From my father, I suppose? Or did Leila tell you? That's the only good thing to come out of this, though I have to keep it in check. My playing is better than ever. I can improvise now. I used to just stick with the song I had memorized. I still have to do that when Leila's singing, of course. But during breaks...."

"What you were playing tonight—was that yours?"

"No, it was Keith Jarrett, mostly. But I did improvise part of it."

"I noticed you were playing more at the low end of the keyboard than most people do. The low notes."

"Yeah, those parts were mostly me. The song is called 'In Front', and there are some low and midrange parts in the original, but I took them further. When I was a kid, I sometimes used to hit notes or chords in the lowest two octaves of the piano and just let them ring for as long as the sound lasted, just listening to the overtones. Sometimes I still do. I just love those sounds, they're so rich, so complex.... So I like playing in that range. I do more of it now. My playing's more adventurous. I don't know how much the audience likes it, if they're paying attention. I haven't heard any boos yet."

"So when you improvise, you're just carried away by the music? You're just following an impulse?"

"Sometimes, I guess. When I lose myself in the music."

"I'm trying to figure out if OGF83 can make you act impulsively. Have you done that any times, besides when you're playing?"

"Do I act more impulsively since I took the drug? I went to a motel room with a guy I had just met here one night. After I'd had the drug, but before I could see anything except light and dark. That was pretty out of character. I usually get to know someone first. That probably counts. Why?"

"Because I was exposed to the drug by accident, and I've had some trouble controlling some of *my* impulses since then. I'm wondering if that's not caused by the drug."

"What kind of impulses?"

"Well... I lost my temper, in front of a lot of people. And... and...." He hesitated for several seconds. "I cheated on my wife, with my lab tech. I'd never done anything like that before."

Kathy laughed, but quickly stifled it. "Sorry. You blame that on your drug? If you were going to give in to an impulse, couldn't you come up with one a little more original? Most men who cheat on their wives don't need drugs to make them do it. Maybe alcohol. A lot of them blame that."

Paul looked down, chagrined. "I know. 'The drug made me do it' is hard to get anybody to swallow. My wife certainly didn't."

"So she found out. How'd she take it?"

"She left me. I don't know yet if she'll be back."

"Oh. Sorry." She paused. "How did she find out? Did you have an impulse to tell her?"

"I had to. I got charged with sexual harassment at work." He didn't want to say that Lindsey had actually told his wife before he could. "I was suspended. I could still lose my job. My lab tech...."

"Did you force her into it? Intimidate her? Of course; you're her boss."

"No! We both wanted it. At first, anyway. We didn't say a single word the first time it happened; we just looked at each other, and then we were kissing, and it went from there. It did break the rules, because she worked for me. But the whole thing was out of character for her, too, and I think the drug's involved. She got exposed to it in the same accident I did."

"So you think the drug causes impulsive behavior? Do you think it affects everyone that way?"

"I don't know for sure. It might. That seems to be a common thread. That's why I wanted to talk to you, to find out if you've had anything like that happen."

"Maybe I have. One of my times involved sex, too, when I went off with the guy I'd just met. You could call getting carried away by the music impulsive, too. Different people have different impulses."

"Exactly!" Paul was excited. "I think impulsiveness might be the common link. I can't say it happens with everybody. Only twelve people have had the drug so far, counting me and my lab tech. What we found in monkeys is that in each one the drug started out in the same part of the brain, but it didn't always end up in the same parts. So some effects might be common to everyone, but others could be different."

"Well, maybe that explains me. If impulsiveness is what makes me get carried away while playing sometimes, then I guess I have that. But if that's the worst thing your drug did, I wouldn't have a problem with it. That would be worth it for the way it's freed up my playing. Let me tell you, when the music takes over and carries you away, there's nothing better than that. Nothing! Not even sex. But that's not all your drug's done."

"It restored your sight. Partly, anyway." Paul felt a pang of guilt, considering who he was talking to, but he felt compelled to stick up for his work.

"That's the worst side effect of all!" Kathy's vehemence shocked him. "If things stay the way they are now, I'd rather not see anything at all. I don't know, maybe Dr. Russell is right. Maybe that *is* enough to explain my depression. My eyes work, but I can't really see. But my eyesight, fucked up as it is, is the same every day; my mood sure isn't. Some days I'm fine, fucked-up eyesight and all. If I close my eyes or wear dark enough glasses, I can get by just like I did when I was totally blind. But some days, I just want to *die*. My eyes are just as fucked-up on the good days as the bad ones, but my moods aren't the same, not at all. I think it's the drug."

"Maybe. I don't know. I mean, a lot of what's happened to me lately is depressing, but I'm not really *depressed*, not in the way you're talking about. What happens on a bad day? How do you get through it?" Paul looked down and suddenly realized he still had half a beer in front of him. He took a swallow.

"Working helps a lot, even if it's just three nights a week and Sundays. It adds structure. We rehearse some during the week, when Leila wants to add a new song, and I make myself practice even when she's not around. Without all that, I'd be a lot worse off than I am. My church gig helps, too. I play organ on Sundays at a Methodist church. I structure my weekends around that. Choir rehearsals on Saturday, the service on Sunday, then organ practice after the service. If you have things you have to do and other people are depending on you, on a bad day you get up and make yourself do what you have to. Mondays are the worst. I don't usually have anything scheduled on Mondays. Then I'm on my own. My mother tries to help."

"And you never had depressions like that before the drug?"

"No, nothing like this. I mean, I'd have moods like anybody else. But not these... black holes. Depression isn't just feeling bad. It's not feeling anything at all. Nothing. You might as well not even exist. It's like a void inside you. You're just blank. When I was completely blind, there was always a void *in front of* me, but I never had one *inside* me. You don't want to do anything. You don't have the energy to move, to eat, to talk, to do *anything*. You just sit until the emptiness finally breaks. You know how you can tell you'll be okay? You start crying. I do, anyway. Crying's actually a good sign. Once you start crying, you know you'll get through it, because you can feel *something* again, even if what you're feeling is miserable. Feeling anything at all is better than that... nothingness...." She turned her head to the side, as if she were looking into the void at that very moment, then suddenly jerked it back, facing him. "Look, this is not what you were after, is it? You just want to know whether I've been impulsive, because that's what you've had trouble with. Me, too, I guess. Besides that one time I went off with the strange guy, it's only happened when I was playing something, but not every time. So far, once in church, maybe four times here. Leila only had to stop me the first time. She doesn't even know about the other ones. I realized it was happening and managed to pull myself back. I don't count times when I'm practicing and go off on a tangent, because who's to say I need to stop? I guess it happens then, too, sometimes. Does that help?"

"Yes, I think so. It's clear the drug affects people differently. But I think acting on impulse may be common to everybody. Will it get better? I wish I knew. Could I ask if you're taking anything for your depression?"

"I went to another doctor a few weeks ago. A regular doctor, not a shrink. She started me on Wellbutrin. She said it had fewer side effects than most antidepressants, so we'd start there. Is it helping? I don't know.

Maybe. It certainly hasn't cured it. But my doctor says most antidepressants take a while before you know whether they're going to help or not. Maybe it just hasn't been long enough yet. Though that's what Dr. Russell keeps saying about my eyes."

Leila came over to the table. "I don't want to interrupt you, but they wanted me to tell you it was last call. The bar's closing in fifteen minutes."

Kathy spoke. "That's okay. You can sit with us if you want to. I think I've told Dr. Lazarus everything I can." To Paul, she said, "Has this helped at all? Is there anything else you want to know?"

"No, I just wanted to see what effect the drug might be having on you, and you've made that pretty clear. But I mean, yes, yes, you've been very helpful. I wish I could be. I wish there was more I could say. I didn't intend for any of this to happen. I wish I could tell you things will get better, that your eyes will start working the way they're supposed to. But I can't. I don't know. Nobody does. As for the other effects, it's obvious OGF83 is doing things nobody expected. I'm sorry. I really am. I wish there was something I could do to help. But if we know what problems the drug's causing, maybe we can fix it so it won't cause them next time."

"Look, I can't blame you. You were trying to help people see again. How can I blame you for that? I'm sorry it's not working the way it's supposed to. Maybe you *can* fix your drug so it just cures blindness, without all the other stuff. But I meant what I said. My playing is better than it's ever been, and if your drug has something to do with that, I'm glad for that part. But it came at a steep price. You know...."

Paul arched his eyebrows. "Yes?"

"If you ever come up with an antidote, give me a call, will you?"

"You'd be the first person I'd call, I promise."

But he knew there would never be an antidote. In some people, with some kinds of blindness, OGF83 worked. It just wouldn't go away, it wouldn't stop. Paul felt sure he could fix that, but not this time. Next time.

55. *"...There may have been some side effects"*

Paul/Travis—Week 32, Monday

AFTER HIS TALK WITH TREY Osborne, with the names, "Cardon" and "Lazarus" to go on, Travis did a Google search for any mention of a drug that might cure blindness. The first thing that turned up was a *Post and Chronicle* interview with Paul Lazarus, from shortly before the clinical trial started. Cardon's website mentioned an on-going clinical trial, but gave no details. Travis called the company, going straight to "0" to get a human on the line. Once he identified himself and explained what he wanted, he was put through to Jim Russell's office immediately. Russell was out of town, but Travis was able to get an appointment for the following Tuesday, four days away.

Before going to Cardon, Travis thought it would be a good idea to talk with Paul Lazarus. He easily found his address, and about 5:30 p.m. on Monday, Paul was surprised to answer the doorbell and find a man in a suit and tie, who immediately showed him his police badge and ID.

"Hello, sir, I'm Detective Sergeant Jim Travis. Are you Paul Lazarus?"

Uncertain why a detective would want to talk to him, Paul nodded. "Yes. Is there something wrong?"

"No, sir. Nothing for you to be worried about. I would just like to ask you a few questions about a patient who took your drug for blindness. It should only take a few minutes, if you wouldn't mind."

For an instant, Paul thought he might be in trouble and wondered if he should call the University's legal department. Then he remembered that his standing with the Office of Legal Affairs probably wasn't very high right then. "No, come on in. I don't know how much I can help you, though." He led the way to the kitchen and gestured toward a chair. "Have a seat. Would you like some coffee? Wouldn't take long to make it."

"No, I'm fine, thank you. I won't take much of your time."

Paul sat down across from him. "I'm afraid I'm not really involved with the drug trial. That's run by Cardon Clinical Testing. Jim Russell runs the trial; he gives me updates now and then. I've talked about it once or twice with Greg Wright, who's a manager there. Greg doesn't work on the trial, but his daughter is in it. She's the only trial patient I've met. I probably shouldn't have mentioned her."

Travis took out his notepad. "I'll keep it to myself, don't worry." He rapidly scribbled down the names Paul had mentioned. "So you don't know anything about the other patients?"

"Only what I hear about their progress from Jim, but he never uses their names. I know in general how it's going, but I'm really outside all that. I'm not a physician, and I've never worked on any clinical trials. I developed the drug using animals. I've never done any research in humans. I can't tell you anything about the patients, because I don't even know who they are. Even if I did I couldn't say anything, because of privacy laws."

"But you're not a physician, so doctor-patient confidentiality wouldn't apply to you, would it?"

"No, but there are still federal laws about releasing medical information. You know, most hospitals won't even give information about a patient's condition to anyone outside the family because it's 'protected health information'. You could get in a lot of trouble giving it out."

"Yeah, so I've heard. By the time I see someone, their condition's not usually an issue." Travis didn't smile at what Paul took to be a grim joke. The detective went on. "I haven't talked to anyone at Cardon yet, so I'm not sure what they'll be willing to tell me. I'm just trying to find out about one man who took your drug. You say the only person you know who took it is a woman?"

"I only know about Greg's daughter because I got to know him while they were planning the trial. She was the first patient enrolled. When Jim Russell tells me about anyone in the trial, he just calls them by number—Patient 1, Patient 2, and so on. There's only ten of them. I know from Greg that his daughter is Patient 1. I probably shouldn't tell you that much, but I already told you she's in the trial."

"So you can't tell me anything else about any of the patients?"

"Maybe in general terms. I really can't talk about specific individuals, even by number. If that's what you need, you should talk to Jim Russell."

"I'm trying to find out about one specific person who may have gotten his sight back. That's all I really need to know—is he in the trial, and did he get his sight back. Your drug can really cure blindness?"

"Not always. Sometimes. Please keep this to yourself, but two people can see now who couldn't before. There's been some improvement in two or three others. It hasn't helped the rest. But you know, this first trial was just to make sure the drug wasn't harmful in humans, not prove that it worked. We started with such a small dose, we're surprised it worked in anybody. We were going to increase the dose in stages. If we can move on to a larger dose, there's a good chance it'll work in more people."

The detective in Travis didn't miss the opening. "*If* you can move on? Why wouldn't you if the drug works?"

"Well, patients were going to get a second dose if the first one wasn't harmful, but they've dropped that for now. We're not certain, but there may have been some side effects."

"What kind of side effects?"

"Psychological ones. As I said, it's not certain. They can be hard to measure, and it can be hard to tell if the drug is really causing them. You know, if you get your sight back after you've been blind for years, maybe all your life—that's a big adjustment to make. You might expect some psychological changes."

"I would expect people to be happy about it."

"Everyone thinks that, but if you've been blind long enough, you actually have to learn how to see again. Even aside from that, think about it. You've spent most of your life learning how to deal with being blind, and suddenly you can see. All your habits, all the ways you've learned to cope with things, that's all gone. You've got to start over. You'd think it would be nothing but good to get your sight back, but it's not that simple. Look at it this way—from what you've seen as a detective, don't you think there are some people who find they're better off in jail? I doubt if they really like it, but they've grown used to it. They can't seem to get by outside, but they can in jail. Maybe it's the routine, you know what's coming every day, and you get comfortable with it. I wonder if that can't happen with something like blindness. At least for a few people."

Travis bit his lower lip. "Maybe. I know some people that got out of jail and immediately did something that guaranteed they'd go right back. Hard to imagine any blind people preferring blindness, though."

"I could be wrong. But other things make me think the drug could cause psychological changes in some people."

"Like what?"

"I've never been blind, but I was exposed to the drug by accident. I'm pretty sure it's changed me." Paul surprised himself by bringing it up.

Travis raised his eyebrows. "How?"

"I think I've... lately I think maybe I've acted on impulse sometimes, when I wouldn't have before. I mean, I'm not that kind of person, you know? I've always been the kind who thinks things through first. But I accidentally spilled some of the drug and inhaled the fumes, and since then I've done some things I wouldn't have done before. I can't be sure it's the drug, but I think it might be. And look, here I am telling you all this on a sudden impulse. That's not like me."

"Have you done anything you can tell me about? I'd just like to know if it would fit in with the way the guy I'm looking at may be acting. *Could* be acting. I don't know that he's done anything at all. I'm just trying to find out whether it would even be possible for him to have done something I'm investigating. He couldn't have if he was blind. You say two people regained their sight. He might be one of them. I don't know."

"What is it he might have done?"

"Sorry, I can't say. It's an open investigation."

"I see. Well, if whatever he might have done involved a sudden impulse, I'd say there's a chance he did it."

"So the drug makes you impulsive? Makes you do things you normally wouldn't? Maybe lose control?"

"It might, to some extent. Maybe not everyone...." Paul's voice trailed off. Suddenly he looked straight at Travis. "You're right. Maybe losing control is the best way to put it. I lost my temper in a faculty meeting and said things that really pissed some people off. I certainly lost control of myself there." He paused. "I also screwed my lab tech, which screwed my marriage and maybe my career with a sexual harassment charge. I guess I lost control there, too. I've known my lab tech longer than my wife, and never looked at her twice, and a few weeks after the accident, we were fucking in my office. Something changed. She was exposed to the drug in the same accident I was." Paul slumped back in his chair, a faraway look in his eyes. "Could I have stopped it? I think so. I just didn't want to...."

"I hate to say it, but in my line of work, that looks almost normal. You really think your drug caused it?"

"I've never been the kind of person who blows up in public or screws around on his wife. Then suddenly I am. There's something wrong there."

"So where's that leave you?"

"Up in the air, right now. I'm temporarily suspended. I could get fired, even though I have tenure. I don't think they'll go that far, though."

"Why not?"

"They stand to make a lot of money if this drug works. I developed it at the University, so they own it. They'd still own it even if they fired me, but it would look bad if they did."

"Why don't you tell them the drug might have caused your behavior?"

"I can't prove it did. It would look like I'm denying any responsibility. I don't think that would go over too well. Also, my lawyer thinks we should hold that in reserve and not use it unless we really need it."

"Why?"

"Because the school doesn't know there might be a problem with the drug. They just know they stand to make a lot of money if it works. If they think there's a problem with it, they might see it as safer just to cut ties with me. That might not be so bad, really. I don't think I'd have too much trouble finding a job, maybe with a drug company. But if I left, I'd rather it be my choice. And I think I can get past this with the school. From what I've seen, scientists don't generally take sexual harassment charges too seriously. Not the men, anyway." Paul abruptly sat upright, as if he'd just remembered something. "Is any of this really useful to you?"

"I think so. If this drug really can make you impulsive, it might have some bearing on my case. Maybe not. But it looks like I'll need to talk to the people running the clinical trial. I have to know if this guy can see." Travis stood up. "I appreciate your time. I might want to talk to you again sometime."

"Sure. If you think it might do you any good."

"Thank you. Good luck with your job. Here's my card. If you think of anything you think I should know, call me, please. And if you do end up taking a job somewhere else, let me know, please."

"Sure. I hope this was helpful to you."

"It has been. Thank you."

As Travis drove away, Paul wondered if it might be worthwhile to talk with a lawyer about this. He didn't think he was in any kind of trouble with the police. His lawyer might see it differently.

56. "...The company can neither confirm nor deny...."

Travis—Week 32, Tuesday

As he drove to Cardon that Tuesday, Travis wondered how cooperative they would be. He expected at least one lawyer at the meeting, and when the receptionist ushered him to Jim Russell's office, he was not surprised to find a third man sitting off to one side.

"Detective Travis? This is Tom Fox from our Office of Legal Affairs. The company insisted we have one of our lawyers present for this meeting."

"I expected it. Let me say up-front, though, your company is not under investigation. I'm trying to get some information about someone who I believe is, or was, a patient in one of your clinical trials. Augustus Osborne, who goes by the name, 'Trey'?"

Tom Fox spoke immediately. "Detective Travis, the company can neither confirm nor deny that any specific patient is enrolled in one of our clinical trials, not without a court order or the patient's consent. We're dealing with medical records, and doctor-patient confidentiality here."

They didn't waste any time getting to the bullshit. "I see. I'm not looking for detailed medical records. I'm just trying to find out if one person is participating in your clinical trial of the drug called—", he opened the small notebook he always carried to interviews, "—OGF83. It's supposed to treat blindness?"

"We can confirm that we have an ongoing clinical trial of this drug. That much is a matter of public record, since the trial is registered with the FDA. But we can't tell you anything about any of the participants."

Travis almost rolled his eyes, but he needed their cooperation. "Not even a name? Or, since I'm already sure he was in your trial, whether the drug worked and he got at least some of his sight back? I've heard that much already."

Fox was dispassionate, almost bored. "Sorry, we can't confirm either the name or the outcome, not without a court order. Please understand, we're not trying to obstruct any investigation you're conducting. We're happy to cooperate to the extent we can within the boundaries set by law. But running clinical trials, that's what we do here. To keep the trust of the patients who volunteer for them, we have to safeguard their anonymity and the confidentiality of their medical records, and comply with all laws and regulations governing research on human subjects. We will comply with any court order to the fullest extent possible. But without one, we can't give out any information about any of the participants in one of our trials. We can't even confirm or deny that any specific individual is enrolled in one."

Sensing that Travis was about to argue, Jim Russell broke in. "I'm sorry you drove all the way out here for nothing, Detective Travis. If you get a court order, we'll do our best to give you whatever information you need."

"If I were to ask you whether a specific person like Mr. Osborne was enrolled in the trial or not, couldn't you just shake your head yes or no to indicate whether he was in it, and whether the drug worked for him? I don't need his medical records. If you're worried about giving away the results of your trial, that information would be confidential. This is part of a criminal investigation."

Fox quickly said, "No, sorry. Not even that. That's protected health information. We need a court order."

"I see. I wasn't really looking for anything more than for you to confirm a name and whether he'd actually gotten his sight back, since he's now claiming to be blind. I was hoping nothing formal would be necessary. But that's okay. I'm sure I can get a court order for what I need by next Wednesday. Could we go ahead and set up an appointment for next Wednesday afternoon?"

Before Fox could reply, Russell spoke. "I'm sure that will be fine, but I'll have to check with my assistant. She keeps track of my calendar. Tom?"

"It's fine with me. If there's any reason I can't make it next Wednesday, someone else from our office will be there."

Travis stood up. "Well, thank you very much for your time. I'll plan on next Wednesday, if you could check with your assistant before I leave. If there's any delay in getting a court order before then, I'll let you know." Outwardly polite, he was inwardly seething. *Jesus Christ! All it would take is a damn nod! Goddamn lawyers.*

57. Fraud or Murder?

Travis—Week 32, Thursday

TRAVIS CALLED SEVERAL JUDGES THAT afternoon and was able to get an appointment with one early Thursday morning, before court sessions opened. Lester Brown had been a policeman for several years before he quit to enroll in law school. Not surprisingly, he was considered cop-friendly, so when Travis requested an order granting him access to Trey Osborne's medical records, he was surprised when Brown seemed reluctant.

"Detective Travis, it's not clear to me. Are you pursuing a fraud case or a murder investigation?"

"It could be both, Your Honor. I have a strong suspicion Mr. Osborne is masquerading as blind while collecting a disability pension. He *was* blind at one time, and his disability pension was legitimate then. But he's been in a clinical trial of a drug for treating blindness, and I've received information from someone who knows him that suggests he might have recovered at least some of his vision. When I interviewed him, some of his actions made me suspect he's able to see now."

"You 'suspect he's able to see now'. That seems a bit shaky."

"Yes, sir, I'd have to agree if that was all there was to it. I'm not just going on hearsay. It's based on what I observed when I interviewed him. The clinical trial results could confirm my suspicions."

"Or not. What about the murder?"

"Your Honor, a former supervisor of Mr. Osborne at the company he retired from was killed in his office on a Sunday morning. There were no witnesses. The killer tried to make it look like a robbery, but there's a lot of evidence that doesn't fit with that. I've been interviewing employees and ex-employees of the company, to see if anyone might have had a motive for the killing. When I heard Mr. Osborne might have regained his sight, I thought I should question him. When I talked to him, I became suspicious that he was concealing the fact that he had regained his sight, and I began to suspect he might be concealing more than just fraud."

"I'm not sure that some rather vague suspicions that he had regained his sight and speculation about his possible motives for concealing it are enough to establish probable cause for a broad search through his medical records. But from what I've seen of you in my courtroom, I don't believe you're the kind of investigator who goes off half-cocked, so I'll meet you halfway on this. But I'm going to tailor this order narrowly. The company must tell you whether the suspect participated in their trial, and whether he did in fact regain his sight, wholly or partly. If he did, they need to turn over those records describing the extent to which he recovered his sight—nothing else. I don't think what you've described is enough to justify granting blanket access to his medical records."

"I see, Your Honor. Thank you. Whatever you think is best."

As he left the judge's office later with the signed order granting him less than what he had hoped for, Travis felt some disappointment. But his standard practice was always to ask for more and settle for less. *This order should get me what I need.*

58. Eyes and Needles

Kathy—Week 32

After talking with Paul Lazarus, Kathy was certain that the drug was causing multiple problems. She was also certain there would never be an antidote. They were so close to success—why try to reverse side effects in a handful of people? She would be written off as a casualty—unfortunate, but necessary. No omelets without broken eggs.

Kathy was equally certain that she never wanted to see anything again. Her vision was worse than useless. When she actually tried to watch what she was doing, she knocked things over, she stumbled when she walked. Her eyesight caused her nothing but problems.

Everyone keeps telling me to be patient. How long do I have to wait? Maybe I've been blind too long. I've been stuck at the level I'm at now for... how long? It seems forever.

I'm beginning to understand Oedipus. He didn't want to see anymore, either. But I can't do what he did. Sticking pins in your eyes? The pain would be unbearable. How would you do it? Put out both at once? Some say he used the same pin for both eyes. Could you really put out one eye at a time? Wouldn't you faint after the first one? Even if you didn't, how could you possibly make yourself do the other one?

Could I get a sympathetic doctor to blind me painlessly? No. They'd probably try to get me committed. No doctor would do it. "First, do no harm", right? But they'll amputate an arm or a leg to prevent gangrene. What if keeping my useless eyesight wrecks the hearing I've relied on most of my life? Wouldn't losing that be worse? But they wouldn't listen. They don't know what it's like.

What about chemicals? In some countries, men blind women they claim dishonored them. They throw acid in their faces, the sons-of-bitches, not only blinding them, but disfiguring them, too. Could I put acid in my own eyes with an eyedropper? Would that work? Just burn my eyes out, without hurting anything else? What would happen to my eyelids? Would I have holes in my face where my eyes were? I'd be better off using needles.

Then Kathy remembered something she'd heard once. More than a hundred people somewhere—India?—had died from drinking illegal liquor contaminated with methanol. But many who drank it and survived had gone blind. It seemed if methanol didn't kill you, it usually left you blind. It didn't take much of it, either.

She went online to research the effects of methanol, using software that responded to voice commands and a text-to-speech converter. It took her just minutes to find all about methanol– its chemical structure and properties, its manufacture and use, and, most important to her, its effects when ingested. This was toxic stuff. As little as an ounce could kill you; three would, for sure. Just over a third of an ounce could be enough to blind you. So she might have some leeway—not much; she would be running serious risk at any dose. A dose large enough to wreck her optic nerves might damage other parts of her brain, too, though that was less common. She would have to take that chance.

Both dose and timing would be critical. Damage to the optic nerve depended on the methanol being metabolized to formic acid, which took time. If you changed your mind, even with a lethal dose, you had a good chance of getting off almost scot-free if you got to an emergency room immediately. Dialysis could remove methanol from the blood before it could be metabolized, and there were antidotes. Timing was key. If Kathy drank the minimum amount likely to blind her without killing herself, she would have to wait at least eight hours before calling for help. They would be the longest eight hours of her life. She would need steel nerves—except for her optic nerves, she hoped.

She mulled the idea over for three days before deciding. A liter of methanol, 99.95% pure, cost less than thirty dollars online. If you're going to drink poison, you might as well get the best.

She ordered it.

59. Perceiving, Not Seeing

Kathy—Week 33

When the package containing methanol arrived three days later, Kathy got to it before her mother even knew anything had been delivered. Kathy heard the truck pull up and immediately headed for the door, getting there before the driver could ring the bell. If he was surprised to find a woman in dark glasses waiting at the door when he walked up, he said nothing but, "Good morning" as he placed the package in her hands. Kathy took it to her room without Shara ever seeing it. She slid the shipping box under her bed, turned on its side.

Now she had to decide how much she would take and how she would measure it out. With her almost nonexistent depth perception, she couldn't rely on her eyes to help her measure and pour it, but she had poured liquids for years without being able to see at all. She had a set of Braille measuring cups and spoons she could use. She would do it over her bathroom sink. Pure methanol would be tasteless, so she didn't need to mix it with anything to make it palatable, though drinking it in a glass of water might be easier. All she had to do was decide on the dose and the timing, to maximize the chance she would go blind but not die. Suicide would be simpler—fewer variables to deal with. But she didn't want to die; she just didn't want to see. Dose and timing would be everything.

Kathy mulled over her plans for more than a week. *Am I crazy to want this? They say if you're worried about being insane, then you probably aren't, so I don't think I am. But what if I'm wrong about the whole thing? If I kill my vision for good, could my hearing still get worse? I don't think so. My brain wouldn't be trying to reprogram itself anymore. But if I don't do it, I don't think my eyes will get any better than they are now. I can perceive things, but can't see them—nothing my eyes take in means anything. What use is that? I was better off blind before. I'd be better off blind now.*

Am I being selfish? What about the people I depend on? They were so happy when they thought my sight was coming back. If there's any possibility of getting useful vision back, don't I owe it to them to stick it out? If I could see like I'm supposed to, it would be so much easier on Mom and Dad. Their whole lives have revolved around me since I went blind, Especially Mom's. And Leila! Leila's the best friend I've ever had. She just volunteered for the whole thing. She could easily find another pianist, someone who could see, someone who could drive herself in to work every night. She can be like a mother bear sometimes, but she treats me like a partner in her career. They all love me. If keeping my eyesight would take some of the load off them, don't I have to stick it out? But none of them would want me to if they knew how miserable my eyes were making me, I know it. If they really knew, I know in my heart they'd accept my decision—but only afterward. They'd never agree to it beforehand.

It's a terrible risk, I know. What if I get the dose wrong or pass out and don't call for help soon enough? I could die. What if I don't take enough to blind me, but get brain damage? But if I let things go on like this, sooner or later suicide is going to look reasonable. I won't let that happen.

I'm on my own here. I can't tell anyone. Not Mom. Not Dad. Not Leila. Certainly no doctor. No one would understand. How could they? The world looks normal to them. To me, it looks confusing, hostile, frightening—everything crowding me, closing me in. To most people, the world is what they see. They can't imagine anything else. But that's not my world. It was once, but not anymore.

After turning all of this over and over in her mind for days, it suddenly dawned on Kathy that whenever she thought about the bottle of methanol under her bed, the bottle that offered a way back to the world she had known most of her life, she could hardly hold back a smile. The world looked much better when she thought she might never have to look at it again.

60. *"He can hide, but he can't run"*

Travis—Week 33, Wednesday

Jim Russell and Tom Fox were waiting when Travis arrived for their Wednesday meeting. He tried to give the judge's order to Russell, who simply held up his left hand, palm forward, and pointed to Fox with his right. Travis handed it to him, and there was silence for several minutes while Fox studied it.

Finally, Fox spoke. "This is quite limited in scope. We can tell you if your suspect was in the trial and whether or not he regained his sight. If he did, we have to give you his medical records that pertain to that only—nothing else. We can do that. But because we're dealing with Protected Health Information as defined by the Health Insurance Portability and Accountability Act, we have to tell Mr. Osborne that we've given you copies of his records."

"I didn't see anything about that in the order."

"It's not in the order; it's required by HIPAA regulations. To get those waived, you'd need a federal court order. Judge Brown is a Texas District Court judge and has jurisdiction over state law. Even if he were to amend his order, he doesn't have the authority to waive that regulation. If he tried, we would contest it. For us to be out of HIPAA compliance on any trial could have serious consequences for all our other ones. We would have no choice but to contest a waiver granted by a state judge. It may not make any difference to you whether we inform Mr. Osborne or not, but if you think that would compromise your investigation, you need to talk to a federal judge."

Travis considered this for several seconds before speaking. "I would prefer not telling Mr. Osborne anything, but I think he already knows he's a suspect, and I think he's just pretending that he's lost his sight again. Giving him notice that we've got his records might actually work in our favor. It could either make him sit tight and keep up his pretense while we continue investigating, or if he really did what I think he did, it could spur him to do something that would confirm our suspicions, like running away. He can hide, but he can't run." Travis turned to Jim Russell. "All right, what can you tell me about Mr. Osborne?"

61. Reckonings

Paul—Week 34, and after

WHEN THE TITLE IX HEARING for Paul was held, probably all that saved his job was the fact that no one in the administration was aware of any problems with OGF83. Technically, the school held the rights to the drug, and didn't need to keep Paul on in order to profit from it. Whether he remained on the faculty or not, he was entitled to 40% of the net income from licensing, but neither Paul nor the University would make any money from OGF83 unless it received FDA approval and was successfully marketed. Any profits from the drug were strictly theoretical at this point, and if they ever did materialize, the University would benefit regardless of whether Paul remained on the faculty or not. Still, everyone knew it would look bad if the school were to reap huge profits from the work of a faculty member who had been shit-canned for sexual harassment. Especially one who might well be in line for a Nobel if the drug worked.

These matters were all discussed by the panel convened for his hearing. There was no question that Paul had violated University rules by failing to report his relationship with Lindsey so she could be transferred to a position under someone else. There was, however, no evidence that he had ever promised her a promotion in exchange for sexual favors. She had only told two people about their affair, and both testified that she had never mentioned anything about a *quid pro quo* arrangement to them. The panel also noted that, as Paul had pointed out, she did not actually meet the qualifications for either of the positions she claimed he had promised her.

The final recommendation of the panel was that Paul remain on the faculty after serving a three-month unpaid suspension that would start the following semester; in the meantime, he would receive additional training regarding sexual harassment and the school's policies on relationships between supervisors and employees. Lindsey, of course, was moved to a position in another department. From a pragmatic standpoint, Paul really hated to lose her; he knew it would be hard to find another technician as good. He would miss the sex, too. But her going to his wife about it behind his back was unforgivable.

Sharon felt the same way about Paul, and did not let him off as easily as the school had. Paul wanted to try to save the marriage, though he had to admit to himself it was more because he was reluctant to concede failure than because he felt their marriage was strong. Sharon had long resented having to hold two part-time jobs just to keep her career limping along. A Minnesota native, she had never liked Texas, and when her former mentor at the University of Minnesota helped her find a non-tenure-track position in psychology there, she immediately filed for divorce and moved back to Minneapolis. With no children involved and Sharon almost desperately eager to leave Texas, the divorce would not be a protracted affair. In exchange for two-thirds of the money in their joint savings account and mutual funds, Sharon agreed to relinquish any claim to the house and any of its contents that she didn't take with her. Given what the house was worth, Paul figured he would actually come out ahead when it was all over. But he really had loved Sharon.

62. "Have you ever read Frankenstein?"

Paul/Travis—Week 34, Monday

AFTER LOOKING THROUGH THE RECORDS for Patient 9, Augustus Oswald Osborne, III, "Trey", Travis was convinced he was faking blindness. It had taken him weeks to regain his vision completely; it seemed unlikely he would lose it all again in less time than that. When he dropped out of the study, Trey's vision had not only shown no sign of regressing, it still seemed to be improving. *He can see, and he doesn't want me to know it.*

There was more. As the study progressed, those who interviewed Osborne had noted his irritability and bouts of anger that seemed disproportionate to the situation. Nobody had followed up on this. A report by Jim Russell that was included in the file gave the reason: None of the other nine participants, whose names had been redacted, had shown any similar behavior. One woman was having problems with depression, but neither irritability nor anger were among her symptoms. A few others seemed mildly depressed, but Russell's report suggested this could be due to their lack of response to the drug, though all had been told repeatedly not to expect much improvement, if any, in this phase of testing. Russell concluded there was no convincing evidence that the drug itself had caused any adverse psychological effects. Travis's own reading of the Osborne file left him convinced that it had.

Trey Osborne killed Steve Linscombe, I know it. He went to Lenevar that Sunday because he knew Linscombe would be there, and no one else. He wanted his old job back, and Linscombe said no. If that wasn't enough, Linscombe's knowing Osborne could see again may have threatened his disability pay, and Osborne panicked. He hadn't gone there to kill him—he just went off the rails. Then he tried to cover it up, make it look like a robbery. But he was making it up on the fly, and a lot of things just don't fit with that. He missed the money in Linscombe's pocket. He took his credit cards, but no one's used them. Linscombe's phone pinged towers from here to Tulsa, then went dead. Osborne could have tossed the damned thing in the back of someone's pickup, but probably hid it somewhere so they wouldn't even know it was there. Now he's playing blind, figuring no one could suspect him. He seems reasonable now, but everyone who saw him in the clinical trial talked about his temper and how pissed off he seemed when he quit.

Trey Osborne is a walking time bomb. I think that drug is involved, whether Jim Russell does or not.

Travis decided to tell Paul Lazarus what he had found in Osborne's file, regardless of any laws regarding confidential medical records. Of those who might actually be able to do something about the drug, only Lazarus seemed to suspect that it could alter someone's behavior. Travis called Lazarus at home that evening.

"Hello, Dr. Lazarus? This is Detective Sergeant Jim Travis; we spoke not long ago. I was trying to get information about a patient in the clinical trial of your drug."

"Of course. I'd hardly forget that. I'm afraid I still can't tell you much of anything."

"I know. I've already got the information I needed. I'm calling to tell you some things I've found out that you really ought to know. I got a court order for the medical records of the patient I was interested in. There were some summaries in the file that included information about some of the other patients, too."

"You know you can't tell me what's in confidential medical records...."

"I know that. But regardless of confidentiality, if I think someone might be in danger, I have an obligation to warn them. What I saw in the file suggests to me you need to be careful if you hear from Patient 9, who dropped out after he got his sight back. His name is Trey Osborne—'Trey' is what he goes by, anyway—and he may have some serious problems with anger. I can't tell you what I'm investigating him for, but you know what department I'm in. Several people who saw him in the clinical trial remarked about how angry he would get over minor things. That Russell guy doesn't think Osborne's anger had anything to do with the drug, but some other people there do. I remember you told me about losing your temper yourself, and how you thought the drug might make someone impulsive. If this guy's pissed off all the time and he did what I think he did, you don't want to be on the wrong end of one of his impulses."

"Why would he be a threat to me? He doesn't know me."

"Think about it, Doctor. You're a smart man, but you're not around the kind of people I see all the time. This guy's angry about something. He can see again, but he's not acting like he's happy about it. Don't you think he might hold you responsible? You created him, and maybe he'd like to talk to his creator. Have you ever read *Frankenstein*? The book, where the monster's smart and can talk, not the movie. I don't know if this guy will contact you, but if he does, you need to be careful. He might be dangerous."

"You really think so?"

"Yes I do. If you hear from him, call me, please. My office number is on the card I gave you, and I wrote my cell number on the back. I'd like to know about it right away if you hear from this guy. If he shows up unexpectedly, call 9-1-1 and say someone's stalking you. Just don't let him know."

"You think it's that serious." Paul simply said it flatly; it wasn't a question.

"I wouldn't be calling you if I didn't. I know you're not supposed to tell people what's in someone's medical records, but my duty to warn you outweighs that. I haven't told you anything I'd be afraid to explain to a judge or a D.A."

"Have you talked to him? Has he actually threatened me?"

"I haven't since I got a look at his records, though I will talk to him soon. And no, he hasn't threatened you, as far as I know. But I thought I should warn you anyway."

"You think he's stalking me?" Paul was having a hard time thinking of himself as being in danger.

"There's no evidence of that. I'm just trying to be careful. Look, you may never hear from him at all, or he may just call you and not try to meet you face-to-face. But if he ever gets in touch with you, I'd like to know about it, please. If you do meet with him, try to do it someplace public."

"Well, I appreciate the warning. You really believe it's this serious?"

"I could be wrong about this guy. I hope so. But I don't think so. I thought if I didn't warn you about him, it might bother my sleep. I've been a cop for eighteen years, I've worked Homicide for eight. Not much bothers my sleep anymore."

"That sounds serious. Thanks for telling me. I have your card. If I hear from him, I'll definitely let you know."

When Paul hung up, he tried to make sense of what he'd just heard. *Travis works in Homicide, so he clearly suspects this Trey guy of murder and thinks he might be looking for me. Why would he be looking for me? What could he get from me?*

And then it hit him. *Whatever he did, he thinks the drug might have caused it. And who would know more about the drug than the man who made it? Is he angry and looking to get even? Is he trying to get help with side effects? Or does he want me to back him on it if he tries to blame the drug? That's got to be it.*

63. Suspicion

Trey—Week 34, Friday

That Friday, Trey's doorbell rang. He grabbed his cane when he went to the door and, before slipping dark glasses on, peered carefully through the peephole. A letter carrier with an electronic pad was there.

"I have a registered letter for Mr. Osborne." He looked at Trey, who kept his face tilted slightly upward, as though the man at the door were several inches taller than he actually was. "Can you sign for it?"

"If you'll put my finger on the place you need me to sign."

"It's electronic; you can use your finger or this stylus to sign right... here", he said, placing the stylus in Trey's hand and guiding it to the pad. "Don't worry about trying to be neat."

"I won't. I'm used to signing things blind. I haven't just signed away my firstborn son, have I?"

The postman laughed. "No, you just signed for this letter." He pressed it into Trey's hand. "You got it?"

"Yes. It's a thick one. There's probably a Braille copy in it."

There was. There was also a copy in plain text, which was the copy Trey actually read once the postman left. It informed Trey that, in compliance with an order from Judge Lester Brown, Cardon had given the police certain medical information pertaining to his participation in the OGF83 trial. The letter didn't say it explicitly, but Trey knew that Cardon would have told the police he had regained his sight and, as far as they knew, could still see, though they had not tested his vision since he withdrew from the trial.

So the secret was out now; Travis knew that at one point Trey had regained his sight. He would strongly suspect Trey could still see, and he would know that if Trey could see, he had been trying to hide it. That alone would move him to the top of the list of suspects in Steve Linscombe's murder. But even if it did, what did they really have on him? They couldn't be sure he hadn't lost his sight after quitting the trial. He might be able to keep up the pretense that he was blind for a while longer, if necessary. If he couldn't pull it off, he could claim he had just been trying to keep his disability pension. Fraud, yes, but a long way from murder.

That guy Travis could probably arrest me on fraud charges right now if he wanted to. But that's not what he's interested in. He didn't come by because he was investigating a fraud case; he's investigating a murder. If he went to the trouble of getting my medical records, he definitely thinks I'm a suspect. But if he had enough evidence to tie me to the murder, he'd have arrested me by now. All he has now is suspicion. What can he actually do? Probably nothing except ask me where I was the day Steve Linscombe was killed. Maybe he'll just keep an eye on me and wait to see if I do anything suspicious, like trying to dispose of evidence, or skipping town. I've already gotten rid of anything that could tie me to Steve's death. To vanish suddenly would be admitting guilt, at least to a fraud charge. I don't want to be arrested for that, either. Best to lay low and assume the police will be watching. I wonder if they've already started.

Trey walked to his front window, carefully parted the blinds, and looked up and down the street. Everything looked the same as always.

64. Sunday Night and Monday Morning

Kathy—Week 35

KATHY CHOSE SUNDAY NIGHT AS the time that would cause the least disruption for the people around her; she expected to be in the hospital only a few days. She would play at church that morning as usual—if she got out of the hospital soon enough, she might be back for next week's service. If Leila didn't cancel any performances, she would have until Tuesday evening to find a substitute pianist—one of her students, perhaps. Leila was a pretty good pianist herself and could both play and sing if she had to, though Kathy wouldn't want her to get used to it.

At 9 p.m., Kathy would drink a half-ounce of methanol, just one tablespoonful, in a glass of water. *Enough to blind me; not enough to kill me. No guarantee either way, but it's the best I can do. I might cheat upward—three-quarters of an ounce, no higher. I'll go to bed at ten; I don't think I'll sleep much. At seven, I'll go down and say I need a doctor; they'll be up by then. I'm sure I'll have a blinding headache....* She laughed aloud. *I bet that's the first time I ever used that phrase. I'll tell them I drank methanol and to call an ambulance. I'll also leave a note on my bed in case I pass out. If my headache gets so bad I can't stand it, I'll call for help sooner, but I've got to give the methanol time to work.*

By nine that evening, everything was ready, but nothing went precisely as planned. At the last minute, Kathy added another teaspoon of methanol to the tablespoonful already in the glass. She held the glass in her hands for several minutes, working up the courage to drink it. She finally gulped the contents down, then checked the time with her talking watch: 9:23 p.m. Behind schedule, but not too far.

She tried to lie down, but sleep was out of the question. She put on headphones and tried to listen to an audiobook of Jane Austen's *Sense and*

Sensibility, finding the title dryly ironic under the circumstances. *I'll have one less sense when this is over; hope I'll still have sensibility.* She had a hard time concentrating, but because that started immediately, she thought it was probably anxiety, not the methanol. A couple of hours passed before she experienced the first clear symptom of the drug—slight dizziness. In another hour or so she began to feel some nausea, but she fought the urge to vomit. *I've got to keep as much down as I can until it's absorbed. I drank close to the minimum I need. I can't throw it up. Got to hold on.*

She stopped the audiobook shortly after midnight when she realized she couldn't remember anything she'd heard in the last ten minutes. About 1 a.m., her dizziness abated. She began pacing up and down beside her bed. Agitated behavior is one symptom of methanol poisoning, but she paced mostly because she was afraid she'd fall asleep and not wake up.

Shortly after two, her nausea got worse, and she finally had to throw up, bent over her trash can; the urge came so suddenly she couldn't make it to her bathroom. *Hope there's no methanol left by now.* She cried as she wretched over and over until nothing more came out.

The vomiting ended, but it triggered stabbing abdominal pains that came suddenly and vanished just as quickly. The first flash of pain doubled her over and caused her to cry out, though she kept her voice down. Successive pangs followed no rhythm she could discern. No matter how she clenched her stomach muscles, or what position she curled up in, the pains kept coming, stabbing like daggers. Gasping and cursing under her breath with each assault, she didn't notice until she vomited again into the trashcan by her bed that her head was starting to ache. The pain got steadily worse, growing so intense it almost made her forget how much her stomach hurt. She finally lay back and closed her eyes; she would risk passing out if it would stop the pain. But she wouldn't get off that easily; the throbbing in her head grew worse, falling into sync with her pounding heartbeat. When she at last opened her eyes, though, she suddenly felt a flash of hope. *Everything's getting blurry!*

Her head began to feel as though it were being squeezed in a vise, the former throbbing devolving into a continuous, drawn-out agony. By 4 a.m., she was wondering how much longer she could stand it; she'd never felt such pain. Though the blurring in her vision was still there, it had gotten no worse as far as she could tell. She had to hang on. She began pushing the button on her watch to hear the time more and more often, though she tried to hold back, because every time she pressed it and found that only a minute or two had passed since she last checked, she felt more tears on her cheeks, and it was hard to tell how much her vision had blurred if she was crying. *I won't make it to seven. Try to hang on till 5:30. Just till 5:30. God, it hurts. Just till 5:30. They'll be getting up then.* Just before 5:30, keeping one hand on the wall, the other clutching her stomach, she staggered down the hall to her parents' bedroom and waited, doubled over and sobbing quietly, until she heard their radio come on. She opened the door and stumbled in, falling to her knees, before they could even turn a light on.

"Mom! Dad! Call an ambulance. Please! I drank methanol. Tell them.... I don't think I can.... There's a note.... My room." She heard her mother cry, "Kathy! What?" Then she doubled over and vomited again before passing out just as she felt her father grab her shoulders from behind. Her last conscious thought was that she hadn't seen the bedroom light come on.

65. "If I want your help, I'll ask for it"

Trey—Week 35, Monday

The Monday after he received the registered letter from Cardon regarding release of his medical information, Trey was still weighing its implications. He was sitting at the breakfast table that morning around 9 a.m. when the doorbell rang.

"What the fuck?" He snatched up his dark glasses and cane and walked to the door. He looked carefully through the peephole and was surprised to see Jim Russell on his doorstep. He was glad he had looked, because if he'd opened the door without checking and saw Russell standing there, he'd have given away his deception immediately; he would almost certainly have been visibly startled. Composing himself, he carefully opened the door.

"Yes?"

"Mr. Osborne? This is Dr. Russell, from the trial?"

"I recognize your voice. What do you want? I got a letter saying you'd given my medical records to the police. Why?" Trey's tone was openly hostile.

"Not all of them. Just from the time your eyesight came back until you dropped out." Russell paused, surprised to see the dark glasses and cane. "What happened to your eyes? Are you really blind again?"

"Yes. Seems the cure wasn't permanent."

"Why didn't you let us know? We might have been able to help. We could still try a second dose, a larger one. That was part of the protocol. Why didn't you come back when you started losing your sight again?" He was genuinely shocked that someone could let themselves slide back into blindness without doing anything to stop it. Then he looked at Trey's face more closely, and realized that in the bright morning sun he could see Trey's eyes behind the dark glasses—not perfectly, but well enough to be certain that Trey was looking right at him; his eyes were focused. Trey was lying; he wasn't blind at all. Confused, Russell decided to press on. "I came to ask if you'd rejoin the trial. We might be able to help you."

"You sic the police on me, then want me back in the trial? You think that's how to get me back?" Trey practically spat the word, "sic".

"We had nothing to do with that. The police got a court order. We had to comply or be held in contempt."

"You ought to be used to that." Trey's tone was venomous.

Russell ignored that. "The police didn't tell us what they were looking for, or why. If they think you've done something wrong, we might be able to help you, if you come back to the trial. We're beginning to think OGF83 might have some psychological effects we didn't know about. If you come back, maybe we can get the police off your back."

"Sounds like blackmail to me." *If the trial doctors check my eyes, they'll know I can see. And that damn detective will know I've been hiding it.* "If you think there's some harmful effect of the drug, don't you have to tell me about it, whether I'm still in the trial or not?"

"Of course we do. Right now, we're not certain about any harmful effects except headaches. But some people think it might have psychological effects, maybe subtle ones. You could help us find out if that's true. If the police arrest you for something, and we find the drug does have psychological effects, that could help you, don't you think?"

"No one's accused me of anything. I don't know what the police are looking for. Didn't they tell you when they went after my records?"

"No, they didn't. They just said you were under investigation. It might have something to do with the disability pension you told me about, I don't know. We never said anything about that to anyone, including the police. That's none of our business. But if all of this is about your pension, we might be able to help you."

Trey could see the advantage of being backed by the people at Cardon. But right now, the risks seemed to outweigh the possible rewards. If he re-enrolled in the trial, they would know he could see, and the police would know he'd been concealing something. They would probably come after him for fraud. If he didn't go to jail; he would certainly lose his pension, with nothing to replace it. The people at Cardon would have a vested interest in explaining away any psychological effects of the drug. They'd be more interested in covering their asses than helping him. Maybe it would be better to leave them uncertain about what the drug had or hadn't done. He needed time to think all this over, and he couldn't do it standing in his damned doorway.

"Look, I think you've helped me quite enough for now. If I decide I want to get back in the trial, I know how to reach you. I'll have to think about it."

Russell had one more card to play. "If we can't get you back in to examine you, I'm not sure how much support we'd be able to give you in any legal proceedings. We don't know what the police are after. If they arrest you, we can't help you much if we don't know what's been going on with you. We'd need to have a psychologist evaluate you. You'd have to be in the trial for that. It would really be in your best interest to come back."

"I'll decide what's in my best interest!" Trey snapped back, almost snarling. "That sounds like blackmail to me. You'll only help if I'm your guinea pig? I don't think so. When I first signed up, you went on and on about informed consent. Well, I'm informing you now that I'm not giving my consent. If I change my mind, I'll let you know."

"It might be too late if you wait until the police get in on it."

Trey could feel his anger rising even more. "You know, for someone who's obviously smart, you say some pretty stupid things. You're like one of those goddamned salesmen—'You have to decide now or the offer's off the table.' I don't like being pressured and I don't like being threatened. I think... you need... to leave."

"Look, I'm not trying to threat...."

"NOW!" Almost reflexively, Trey turned his head slightly to the right and spat explosively.

Russell raised his hands, palms forward, and backed up. "All right. All right. I'm going. I was only trying to help."

Trey only held back only because he knew beating the shit out of Russell would prove he was feigning blindness. "If I want your help, I'll ask for it."

66. *"You couldn't just leave it alone...."*

Trey—Week 35, Tuesday

AFTER RUSSELL LEFT, TREY WAS trying to decide how far he should go in pretending he was blind, when the mail arrived. In it was a notice that he had to renew his car registration. He could do that by mail; what he couldn't do by mail was get the car through the annual inspection required for the renewal. If he asked his brother or sister to do it, as they had before, he would either have to enlist them in his conspiracy, which could get them in trouble, or else convince them he was blind again. It would be easier simply to do it himself, as long as he made sure no one was watching when he slipped out to get the car inspected.

About 10:30 the following morning, he took a walk to reconnoiter, wearing dark glasses and swinging his white cane, doing his best to walk the way he had when he was blind. As usual, all his neighbors seemed to be at work. Two blocks down, two Hispanic men were mowing a lawn and blowing leaves into a pile. The only other person on the street was a woman pushing a baby stroller. Nobody spoke when he passed. After walking two blocks, he decided the coast was clear and went home.

He backed his car out and drove southwest, toward a poorer area of town, to minimize the chance of running into anyone he knew. He had no particular service station in mind; he would just look for one with a "Vehicle Inspection Station" sign. As he drove down McAllen Street alongside Green Bayou and approached the stoplight at Cantwell Drive, he spotted a station a block down Cantwell to the right. As he braked for the red light, he glanced briefly down at the passenger seat to make sure he had the necessary paperwork with him. He had almost come to a stop when he felt a slight bump as his car hit the one ahead that was already stopped at the light.

"Shit!" he said aloud. He quickly backed the car up eight or ten feet and stopped. By the time he opened his door, the other driver had already gotten out and was walking toward him. He did not look happy. There was no one else nearby; they were stopped in front of an abandoned and graffiti-covered convenience store.

Trey got out, slipping the gun that he'd placed on the seat beside him into his pocket, almost by reflex; with the car door between them, the approaching man couldn't see that. Trey saw immediately that there was no apparent damage to the other car; he had almost come to a complete stop before bumping it. A quick look at the front of his own car showed no damage there, either, except possibly a small dent on the license plate frame, which might have been there already.

The other driver was now about four feet away. He was a couple of inches shorter than Trey, but at least as heavy. It wasn't all muscle, though his arms were thicker than Trey's; a large paunch hung over his belt. He was in his 50's, at least, and looked like a heart attack awaiting its moment. He also looked belligerent.

Trey spoke first. "Sorry. I'm afraid I got a little careless there. But I don't see any damage to your car. Mine, either."

The reply was not reassuring. "You need to look where you're going. I was just sitting there. The light was red." He pulled out a cell phone and took a picture of the rear of his car and the front of Trey's, then one of Trey, then put the phone back in his shirt pocket. Trey was annoyed, but didn't object.

"You're right. I do apologize. But there was no harm done, as far as I can see."

"Yeah? Well, I'd like to see your license and insurance. It was your fault! No question about it."

"Yes, it was. I said I was sorry. Let's not make a big thing out of this. There's no damage. There's no point in getting cops or insurance companies involved."

"Yeah, well, what if I find some damage later that didn't show up right away? I'd like to see your driver's license and insurance."

"You really think that's necessary? There's not a single scratch on your car. I can't see any damage at all."

"Yeah, you said that. I still want to see your driver's license and insurance."

Trey was beginning to get pissed off. "Look, there's no need to make a federal case out of this. Your car's not damaged at all. Mine either. Why don't we just forget this whole thing ever happened?"

"Hey! You ran into me, dumb ass. If you don't show me your license and insurance, I'm going to call the cops." He pulled the phone from his shirt pocket.

It was the "dumb ass" that did it. Trey stepped back and with one quick move drew the .38 revolver he had frightened the texting woman at the stoplight with. He held it just above waist-level, pointed at the man.

Trey's voice started at normal volume but got louder as he went on. "You goddamned motherfucking asshole! I'm sick of jerks like you! You couldn't just leave it alone, could you? Put that goddamned cell phone down on the hood of my car! Then just turn around, get back in your fucking car, and get your ass out of here! Don't look at me! Don't even look at my car! Just go! NOW!"

The man hesitated, but put his phone down on the hood of the car when Trey raised his gun higher. To Trey's surprise, the man didn't really look afraid; his face was instead twisted into a snarl of impotent rage. "You won't get away with this!"

"Go!"

As the man turned and started back toward his car, he suddenly moved his right arm in front of his body, where Trey couldn't see his hand. Trey instantly realized the man was reaching across his body. *The stupid son of a bitch is pulling a gun!* He had been carrying a pistol under his untucked shirt in a holster inside his waistband, positioned for a cross-body draw from left to right. Trey could have seen the bulge of the gun if he'd been looking for it.

If the man had spun to his left in turning around, Trey wouldn't have seen the gun until it was already pointed at him, and the man might have had a chance. Instead, he whipped the gun back across his body as he spun to his right to face Trey, the gun in plain sight as he whirled around. But Trey already had his own gun aimed straight at him, and he fired when the man was nearly through his turn, but before he could bring his gun to bear. The bullet passed through his upper arm and into his chest, breaking a rib. It hit nothing vital, but its impact and the pain almost made the man drop his gun. He managed to hold on to it, but his arm dropped, leaving the gun pointing downward. He tried to raise it to fire, but couldn't. He managed to get off one shot, but the bullet ricocheted off the pavement about a foot to Trey's left, sparking fragments of concrete that struck Trey's ankle, but didn't penetrate his pants leg or sock.

Though Trey had just been shot at, he felt strangely calm as he fired again. The momentum of the man's spin had carried him further around than he intended, so he wasn't quite facing Trey dead on when the second shot hit. The bullet entered his chest slightly left of center, just missing his heart but nearly severing his descending thoracic aorta. His legs buckled under him and he pitched forward and to his right, landing on his hands and knees, his gun clattering on the pavement as he fell. The blood gushing into his chest cavity above the diaphragm kept him from drawing a full breath; his blood pressure dropping rapidly, he lost consciousness within seconds. The blood pulsing from the wound puddled on the pavement.

Just after Trey fired the second shot, a white Ford F-150 drove past in the next lane, swerving away from the man hunched over on his hands and knees. The startled driver slammed on his brakes as he drove through the intersection. Trey looked up from the man bleeding in the road and saw the stopped truck about fifty feet away. He did not want any gawking witnesses; he fired at the truck, but rushed the shot and missed entirely. The driver, realizing his danger, stomped on the gas so hard his tires screeched, the truck fishtailing as it took off, the driver trying to put as much distance as possible between himself and the man with the gun.

Trey grabbed the cell phone off the hood of his car and shoved it in his left front pocket. He dropped his gun on the passenger's seat as he got in the car and backed up a few feet so he could cut through the parking lot of the derelict convenience store. Otherwise he would have had to drive around the dying man's car, and the light had turned red again by then. Trey pulled out behind a car that had just passed through the intersection on the cross street, Cantwell Drive. The driver had to have seen the man crumpled face-down on the pavement, so Trey knew at least two witnesses had seen the aftermath of the shooting, if not the shooting itself. He accelerated and pulled up close behind the car, keeping his head low so the driver couldn't get a look at him in his rear-view mirror. Trey wanted to unnerve the driver, and it worked; barely slowing for the turn, the car took a hard right at the next intersection and accelerated, while Trey kept going straight, letting his speed drop to about forty miles per hour.

Trey figured at least one of the two witnesses would already be calling 9-1-1 on a cell phone and trying to describe his car. He couldn't be sure there were no other witnesses, though he hadn't seen any, but he was certain the police would be on the way there soon, if they weren't already. They would be looking for a silver car fleeing the area, probably at high speed. He slowed to thirty miles per hour and looked around. The nearest car behind him was nearly two blocks away. He decided not to flee at all. He turned right on the next street, and when he spotted a Jack in the Box on the left a half-block ahead, he turned in and drove around to the back. Two parking spaces not visible from the street were also out of the field of view of the drive-through window camera; he pulled into one. He took out the dead man's cell phone and was dismayed to see it was an iPhone; he probably couldn't get at the pictures, and he couldn't just take out the battery to kill any signals that could be used to track him. He looked around quickly to make sure no one was nearby, then backed the car up a foot or two. He put the car in park, and got out, wiping the phone with his pulled-out shirttail to remove any fingerprints before dropping it on the pavement and pushing it in front of the left rear tire with his foot. He got back in the car, lowered his window, and drove forward until he heard the phone crunch, then stopped and raised the window, leaving his car sitting on top of the smashed phone.

He pocketed his gun as he got out of the car and walked toward the Jack in the Box, stopping to pull a local free weekly from a box in front; Trey intended to sit for a while. Once inside, he ordered both a large cup of coffee and a bacon cheeseburger combo with a soft drink, found a corner booth by the front window, and settled in with his food and his paper.

He was only about five blocks from the scene of the shooting. He could hear sirens not far off, and saw two police cars, lights flashing, pass by. Before he left the restaurant a little over an hour later, he had seen several other cruisers pass by in both directions, but by the time he finally walked back to his car, he hadn't seen one in at least fifteen minutes. If there was a dragnet out for his car, it had already moved on. He finished his meal, his coffee, and the paper, then went to the restroom and used napkins he carried in to wipe off the gun before he slipped it inside the folded paper. He then strolled out to his car, dumping his trash, but not the paper, in a bin on his way out. Walking to his car, he passed close to the dumpster behind the restaurant and casually tossed in the gun with the paper folded around it. He was confident no one was paying any attention to him. After starting the car, he looked around once more to make sure no one was watching, then rolled back and forth twice over the fragments of the crushed phone before pulling out of the lot and turning homeward. He saw no police cars at all on the drive home.

Once home, Trey was annoyed that he hadn't been able to get his car inspected. He would have to try again soon. It wouldn't do to be pulled over for something as trivial as an expired sticker.

67. "...I'm pretty sure he can still see"

Travis—Week 35, Wednesday

TRAVIS WAS UNCERTAIN ABOUT HIS next move. He knew Trey Osborne had regained his sight before he dropped out of the clinical trial, but now acted as though he were once again blind. He felt certain Osborne was faking. If he were, he would be a suspect in the murder of Steve Linscombe—but Travis didn't have a shred of evidence connecting Osborne with Linscombe's killing. Osborne could well be lying simply to protect his disability pension. Travis had a feeling that pension could be the connection between Osborne and Linscombe's murder. Once Linscombe found out Osborne could see again, he might have threatened to get it revoked, giving Osborne a motive for killing him.

But this was all conjecture. Travis needed to talk with the head of Homicide, Detective Captain Cole Reed. Reed knew the Linscombe case had reached a dead end. None of Travis' interviews with current or former Lenevar employees had turned up any viable suspects, apart from Trey Osborne, and he was a very long reach. Reed had been skeptical when Travis first mentioned his suspicions concerning Osborne, so he wasn't very sympathetic when Travis asked for a meeting and brought Osborne's name up again.

"Damn it, Jim, what you've got on this guy doesn't even qualify as circumstantial evidence. You know he regained his sight at one point, but no one's examined him since he quit the drug study. He either lost his sight again after he quit, or he's pretending to; no one knows which. If you had enough evidence for a murder charge, you could force a medical exam, but you don't even have enough for a search warrant, not on a murder charge. Your suspicion that he can see probably wouldn't even be enough to get one on a fraud charge. You'd need a picture of him driving or something. We do homicides, not fraud. As far as I'm concerned, if Osborne's collecting a pension fraudulently, that's between him and his employer. Tip *them* off, and let them follow it up if they want to. Give a private investigator something to do. I don't want you spending department time on this."

"I understand, sir. But as weak as the case is, Osborne's the only even half-decent suspect I've got in the Linscombe case. If we can't investigate Osborne, that murder's gonna be a cold case twenty years from now."

"Seriously Jim, even if you can prove this guy's lying about being blind, you've got nothing that would link him to that murder, except your own suspicion. It's not enough. You've got other cases to worry about. Forget this guy. You won't, though. I know you. All I can say is, don't waste any more department time on him. If you do any more follow-up on him, you make damn sure you follow all the rules. But you do it on your own time, not ours. Is that clear?"

"Yes, sir. I understand."

As he stood to leave, Reed stopped him. "Jim, you're a damn good detective. If you think your guy did that murder, I wouldn't bet against it. You just don't have enough evidence. No fingerprints. No DNA. No witnesses. No weapon. And anyone smart enough not to leave the first three would have gotten rid of the weapon by now, so even a search warrant wouldn't help. Go solve some other killings. God knows we've got enough of 'em."

"Yes, sir."

But Travis couldn't let Osborne off the hook. He was hiding something more than the fact that he could see.

That afternoon, Travis was sitting at his desk, going through the file on another open case, when his phone rang; it was Jim Russell.

"Hello, Detective Travis? This is Jim Russell, from Cardon Clinical Testing?"

"Of course. What can I do for you, Dr. Russell?"

"I went by Trey Osborne's house yesterday to see if I couldn't talk him into returning to the clinical trial, and I thought you might be interested."

"Was *he*? In getting back in the trial, I mean."

"No. He got pretty angry, actually, which I guess shouldn't have been a surprise, given his behavior before. I believe he thinks I've been, um, colluding or... conspiring with you, that's probably a better word, I think. He was upset that we gave you his records."

"Does he know you had to?"

"I tried to tell him that. I don't think it made any difference. But there was something else I thought I should tell you."

"What's that?" Travis's tone was almost bored.

"I can't prove it, but I'm pretty sure he can still see."

Travis bolted upright in his seat, not bored now. "Really? What makes you think so?"

"I was standing on his porch and he was in his doorway. This was about 9 or 9:30 in the morning and the sun was pretty bright. It was in his face. He had on dark glasses, but I could still see his eyes. I'm pretty sure both of them were focused right on me the whole time."

"So it was just your impression that he was looking at you?" Travis relaxed in his seat.

"Well, after we talked a few minutes, he told me to leave, and when he did, I think he aimed a gob of spit so it just missed my foot. It looked like he was aiming, to me."

Now Travis was bolt upright again. "He spit? Just... spit? And he was really pissed off?" He thought instantly of the woman at the stoplight, and Steve Linscombe.

"Yeah, I'd say so. But if he'd wanted to hit me, he could've just spat straight in front of him; I was standing right there. I think he wanted to miss. I'm not sure what kind of message he was trying to send."

"That he wanted you out of there, I'd say. Is that all?"

"No. I looked through all his records and interviews before I went to talk to him, and I noticed he said he never needed a cane to get around in his house, because he knew where everything was. But he was carrying one when he answered the door. That may or may not mean anything; maybe he thought he might have to go outside."

"He was carrying one at the door when I went there, too. It may not mean anything. But who knows?"

"Cane or no cane, I'm pretty sure he can still see. I don't know what he told you, but if his eyes have regressed at all, it hasn't been to the point where he's blind again. I thought I should tell you."

"It fits with my own impression when I talked to him. I appreciate your telling me."

When he got off the phone, Travis thought about Osborne spitting at Russell's feet. Did this guy spit every time he got mad? Someone spit in Steve Linscombe's office, though he wiped it up. Could Trey Osborne be the pissed-off man who spit when he threatened a woman at a traffic light? If there was a pissed off psychopath running around loose, was it Trey Osborne?

Whether Travis got Osborne for fraud or murder, the first thing he would have to do is prove that Osborne could see. Even if he had to do it on his own time.

68. Calm, or Cold-Blooded?

Trey—Week 35, Wednesday

THE ONLINE EDITION OF WEDNESDAY'S newspaper reported the shooting on McAllen Street, but the story was just two paragraphs long and included no description of either Trey or his car. It called the shooting a probable road rage incident. When he read that the local Crime Stoppers chapter was offering a thousand-dollar reward for information, Trey laughed. *Is that all? That fat fuck wasn't a pillar of the community, was he? I think the reward for information on Steve Linscombe's killer is up to fifty thousand now.*

Unless a surveillance camera near the scene had photographed him, Trey figured he had a good chance of getting out of this one. But there were no stores on the left side of the road, just the concrete-lined Green Bayou—named before the Corps of Engineers got hold of it. No reason for cameras there. The convenience store on the right corner, where the shooting occurred, was abandoned. The building on Cantwell Drive opposite the abandoned store faced a parking lot and had no door facing the street, so it seemed unlikely there would be any camera on that building covering the intersection. Neither of the two potential witnesses could have given the police a good description of Trey. The guy in the white truck had only stopped for a few seconds before he got shot at and got the hell out of there. Maybe he could pick Trey out of a line-up—but Trey would have to be a suspect to get in a line-up. The guy driving by on Cantwell probably never got a good look at Trey; by the time that car passed through the intersection, Trey was already in his own car. Trey couldn't decide whether he was being calm or cold-blooded when he decided not to race away from the scene at high speed; whichever, it worked.

Though he knew he could expect to hear from that detective soon, Trey didn't think there was any way Travis could connect him with yesterday's shooting. No real witnesses, no physical evidence. The same as with Linscombe.

Trey still had to worry about being charged with fraud if Travis could prove he could see. For now, he needed that pension; he would have to keep up his pretense. *How long will they keep at it if all they can get me for is fraud? It's not even that much money—I really was blind for three years. But Steve Linscombe's case isn't going away for a while. I'll have to keep an eye out for that goddamned detective.* Trey laughed out loud. *I'm sure he'd appreciate the irony in that.*

69. Pursuit

Trey/Travis—Week 35, Thursday

Whenever Trey had to drive somewhere, he usually waited till night. He would first walk around the block he lived on, swinging his white cane, to look for anything suspicious before he took his car out. If he saw any cars parked either on the street or in someone's driveway that weren't there every night, he stayed home, even if he had an errand to run.

In fact, he had spotted Jim Travis' car a couple of times during his walks, without knowing whose car it was. As soon as Cardon verified that Trey had regained his sight, Travis had begun checking up on him in the evenings, hoping to catch him out. He couldn't watch every night, and he had to try at different times, since he never knew when Trey might leave the house. He did note Trey's nocturnal walks, and assumed he was reconnoitering, but he never saw him go anywhere afterward. He couldn't be sure Trey simply didn't go for evening walks every night. If he really was blind, it probably wouldn't make much difference to him what time he went for a stroll, day or night; it was a safe neighborhood.

The Thursday after his talk with Cole Reed, Travis didn't arrive to take up his station near Trey's house until about 9:30. Before finding a place to park, he drove past the house and happened to see Trey just as he was going in the front door after one of his walks. Trey did not turn his head as Travis passed. *This guy's smart. He knows if someone were watching him, they'd look for that. Must be hard to keep your guard up all the time.* Travis quickly drove around the block, stopped three houses down from Trey's on the opposite side of the street, and parked behind a car that was there most nights. He had settled in to wait when he saw a sliver of light appear at the front of the house and rapidly widen.

The garage door was opening.

Travis pounded the steering wheel and said out loud, "Got you, you bastard!" He watched as a light-colored sedan backed out and started up the street away from his car. He couldn't be certain it was Trey driving; he would have to follow and wait until the driver gave him legitimate cause to make a stop. He had checked, and knew that Trey still had a valid driver's license. Even if Travis stopped him now, the most he could pin on him would be fraud, and he had a bigger score in mind. For now, he just wanted to be sure Trey was the driver.

Travis's unmarked police car could be driven without any running lights, and he kept them off as he pulled out behind Trey's car. He waited until Trey had turned out of sight before he switched his headlights on and followed at a discreet distance. The lighter traffic this time of night was both a blessing and a curse—there were few cars to get between his and Trey's, which made him easier to follow, but more likely to notice it. It was soon clear that Trey was either aware he was being followed, or was trying to spot anyone tailing him. At one point, he took a right turn off McLemore Avenue, a left, another left onto Pickens, and a right, ending up back on McLemore going the same direction as before. Travis drove the entire block on Pickens with his lights off, hoping to throw Trey off. He briefly pulled over to the curb after the second right, then turned his lights on and pulled out again, to make Trey think a different car was behind him now.

Trey was not fooled. He had spotted the darkened car on Pickens in his rear-view mirror and seen it pull over and then out again on Mc-Lemore. Trey routinely used driving patterns like the right-left-left-right sequence to spot anyone trying to follow him, and he was now certain someone was. He assumed it was a policeman, though he had no way of knowing he had become Travis' obsession. Trey thought it might be a private investigator hired by Lenevar to prove he wasn't blind anymore; Travis could have tipped the company off after he got Trey's clinical trial records. Trey was more worried right now about the possibility of a fraud charge costing him his pension than he was about being charged with Steve Linscombe's murder; he'd disposed of any evidence that could connect him with that. But he knew he was a suspect; that killing was what had triggered this cat-and-mouse game. If the police thought he had shot the guy at the intersection the other day, they would have already arrested him.

Why won't these motherfuckers just leave me alone, goddamn it! I need to get rid of this son of a bitch! I can't just go home with him still tailing me.

There was a 24-hour drugstore a couple of blocks ahead, and Trey pulled into the nearly empty parking lot—both to get a look at the car following him, and to pick up a few things at the drugstore, which had been his original intention in going out that night. He parked in a spot to the left of the store, away from any lights, and waited. Sure enough, a car soon cruised slowly past. Trey knew that only the car following him had been reasonably close behind when he pulled in. He could see as the car passed that it was a largish four-door sedan—probably an unmarked cop car. Figuring the driver would turn around and come back, Trey got out and walked hurriedly to the front entrance of the store, stopping just inside to look back. Sure enough, a large four-door pulled into the lot and drove around to the right side—almost certainly the same car. A mixture of fear and icy fury rose in Trey as he suddenly realized he might have trapped himself—the cop would be watching the door, the only public entrance. There had to be a back door, a freight entrance. Trey headed for the back of the store and looked for a door marked "Employees Only". There were two. The one opening behind the pharmacy counter wasn't accessible. But the other, further down on the back wall, turned out to be unlocked—probably an oversight, he thought, but maybe fire regulations required it. Either way, it was a break for him. He pushed through it and found himself in the stockroom. He was heading toward an exit sign in the back when he suddenly heard, "Hey! You can't be back here! If you're looking for a restroom, there's one up front!"

Thinking quickly, Trey approached the man, who seemed to be the manager and looked fairly young—barely past thirty, if that. Trey held his hands out in front of him, palms out, imploring. "Please, you've gotta help me! I'm being followed! There's a guy waiting for me in the parking lot. He thinks I've been screwing his wife, but I haven't! We just had to work late a lot. I need to go out the back way. Please! Is there an alarm?"

"Yes, there is. I should call the police.'"

"No! That would only make things worse!" Trey looked frantic. "If I get the cops on him, he'll come after me later for sure! If I can go out the back door, I can get away and get his wife to help sort all this out. Could you just let me out without setting off the alarm? He's waiting for me to come out the front door. If I can give him the slip for now, I'll get his wife to talk some sense into him. I've never touched her. Really! Can you help me out here?" He spread his hands out in front of him, imploring.

"I'm not supposed to open the back door. There could be someone waiting there."

"Don't you have a camera in back?"

"Yeah, we do. Let me look." That idea seemed to reassure him. There was a monitor on the wall near the back door. The surveillance camera showed nobody out back.

"Do you think he might follow you back here?" Now the manager looked dubious again. He certainly didn't want two strangers in the stockroom.

"No, I saw him waiting in the parking lot for me to come out the front door. If I can get out the back door, I can give him the slip. You could lock the employee door I came through and call the police if he comes in the store and starts anything."

"You've never touched his wife?" Whether he had or not seemed to make a difference to the manager.

"No! I wouldn't do that! I've got a wife and kids." Trey looked shocked at the very idea.

"Okay." The man walked over to the rear exit, pulling a key ring from his pocket. "Come on. I'll lock it behind you." He used a key to turn off the alarm and opened the door a crack, looking out carefully, half expecting to find an accomplice waiting despite what the monitor showed. He knew he was grossly violating store policy, but Trey really seemed scared. "Okay, come on." For an instant, Trey considered shooting the man once he opened the door, but the clerk behind the counter had certainly seen him come in, the store's security cameras would have filmed him, and the cop outside would hear the shot.

In his hurry to get the door closed, the manager almost shut it on Trey's foot as he slipped out. The back of the store wasn't completely dark, but there were deep shadows, and Trey stayed in them as he edged along the wall to the corner and peeked around it. Sure enough, a lone car parked across two spaces was turned toward the front door. It was about thirty feet from the sidewalk along the side of the drugstore and about twenty feet in front of the corner where Trey crouched. The driver was alone, with his window down about a third of the way. The engine was running, but all the lights were off.

If Trey waited long enough, the driver would probably get impatient and go in the store to look for him; he could get to his car and drive away before the guy knew what was happening. So he crouched by the corner and waited. Five minutes passed. Then ten. *Goddamn! How long will he wait?* A few minutes more and Trey was out of patience. *Nobody would stay that long in a drugstore this time of night! What's this guy waiting for? Why doesn't he go inside to check?* His legs were cramping; he couldn't squat any longer. He stood up. *Goddamn it! I'm not waiting any longer for this bastard!*

He reached in his pocket and pulled out his .38 caliber snub-nosed revolver, the second of the two he'd bought at the gun show, cocking it as he slipped around the corner. *Silence. Surprise.* Crouching low, he moved swiftly and quietly, grateful his running shoes helped muffle his footsteps. The driver didn't move as Trey drew closer. Trey didn't recognize Travis in the dim light, but it didn't matter who he was. Trey raised the gun and aimed carefully; he would have to shoot through the glass in the driver's-side window, which wasn't down far enough to give him a clean shot over it. The muzzle of the gun was about two-and-a-half feet from the man's head when Trey fired. There was a loud, sharp bang and a web of cracks appeared around the hole in the window. Trey had expected the glass to shatter, but almost all of it remained in place; he couldn't see through the glaze of cracks. When he straightened up and looked over the top of the glass, he could see the driver's head slumped forward. Trey couldn't say for sure the man was dead and thought about firing again, but a second shot would attract more attention, and seemed unnecessary—even, somehow, disrespectful.

Trey kept his head down as he ran to his car, got in, and drove away at a normal speed. He made one detour on his way home, stopping at Green Bayou to wipe any fingerprints from his revolver before tossing it in the middle of the channel, where the water was at least fifteen feet deep.

Trey didn't know it was Travis he had shot, or that Travis had been following him on his own time and hadn't told anyone he would be doing it. No police burst through the door that night, or the next morning. When Trey went online to check the news, his heart almost seemed to stop when he found it was Travis he had shot, and that he was in grave condition, but not dead. Now he cursed himself for not firing that second shot. If Travis ever regained consciousness, he would point them straight at Trey. They would probably come for him before long anyway—surely Travis had told somebody about his suspicions.

Whether the detective lived or died, Trey knew it was only a matter of time before he would be a suspect. He had options—he could continue to feign blindness; he could run; or he could assume he would be arrested and start planning his defense.

If I run, they'll catch me sooner or later, and my chances in a trial drop to zero. What's left? Either I can try to raise doubt that it was me who shot the cop, or I can claim I wasn't responsible for my actions when I did it. Forget the first one. There's a witness from the drugstore and my picture's got to be on the store cameras. There's a good chance they've got my license plate on camera already, though if that's the case, why haven't they busted my door down yet?

Claiming I'm not responsible might work. I mean my whole police record up to now is—what?—two speeding tickets? No history of violence after a few fistfights in high school. So why am I suddenly violent now? It's got to be the drug. If it could make my optic nerves grow back, what else could it be doing in my brain? What else could it affect besides eyesight? I've had a short fuse lately. I bet the drug is causing that. I need to talk to the guy most likely to know. I think I know how to find him.

70. Like a Knife in His Own Heart

Paul/Trey—Week 35, Friday

HIS SUSPENSION HAD NOT YET started, and Paul was working late more often now, since he had to do everything in the lab himself. Besides, Sharon had wasted no time moving out, so there was no reason to rush home. When he came home this Friday evening after dark, the porch light was off. Never knowing when he'd come home, he usually left it on, and thought he had that morning, but he didn't always remember to. Without it, the darkness was near-total as he felt for the doorknob and fumbled to get the key in the lock. He jerked backward, startled, when a voice came from the black void to his left near the end of the porch, where a support pillar, ten bricks wide, blocked almost all the light coming from both the nearest streetlamp and the neighbor's yard lights, making the far end of the porch seem like a black hole, swallowing all light, whenever the porch light wasn't on.

"Not easy in the dark, is it? I didn't want any light while I was waiting, so I unscrewed the bulb. Not long ago, whether it was light or dark made no difference to me, but it does now. I believe I have you to thank for that."

A figure moved toward him from the end of the porch; Paul seemed to sense a presence before he could see it, as though the darkness itself had mass.

"You're Trey, aren't you? I've been thinking you might show up sometime."

"You've heard of me, huh? Don't worry. I didn't come here to hurt you. I don't hurt people unless I'm provoked. Though it takes less to provoke me these days than it used to. I think you might have something to do with *that*, too."

"I won't try anything. I've got no reason to. I was hoping I'd get to talk to you. My drug gave you your sight back. I want to know what that's like. Let's go inside. If I can get this door open...." Paul groped for the doorknob again and finally got the key in.

Once inside, with the lights on, Paul could see that Trey had a gun pointed at him, a semi-automatic.

"You don't need that." He pointed to the gun. "I'm unarmed. And why would I want to hurt you? You're my biggest success. I *dreamed* I'd get to see this."

"I don't know what you might have heard about me. The police may be looking for me. I can't take any chances."

"Okay, but could you please not point that at me? What do you want me to do? You want to know something about the drug, I guess?"

"Yeah, I'd like to know what else it might do besides curing blindness. Let's sit somewhere we can talk. Your kitchen table, maybe?" He paused. "You're not expecting anyone, right? Your wife or something?"

"No, no one's coming." Paul gestured toward the kitchen. "This way."

When they got to the table, Paul sat first. Trey went around to the opposite side, never taking his eyes off Paul. He felt for a chair, pulled one out, and sat down with his back to the wall; a few feet to his left was the doorway to the den. A double window overlooking the backyard was on his right. Paul sat with his back to the kitchen. A counter directly behind him formed a divider about three feet high between the kitchen and dining areas; it connected with a counter at right angles to it that ran along the wall to the kitchen sink, then continued to the corner and along the back wall to the stove.

Trey turned his chair at an angle to the wall and pulled it a couple of feet further down from Paul. He laid the gun on the table, pointed toward the opposite wall, angled in Paul's direction but not aimed right at him. Trey rested his right elbow and forearm on the table, with his hand resting on the grip of the gun. He wasn't holding it, but he could snatch it up instantly.

"You said you thought I might show up sometime. Why? Who told you about me?"

"A detective came here asking about patients who'd had the drug. Travis. Detective Travis. He left his card. He asked me to call him if you ever contacted me."

Trey seemed to stiffen at the name. "Have you seen the news today? That guy got shot last night. He's still alive, last I heard, but maybe not for long. Why did he want me?"

"No! He was shot? Damn! I just talked to him last week. Damn! He came by here asking about you, though he didn't mention your name the first time. He'd heard that someone who took the drug could see again. He thought I could tell him who you were, but I couldn't; I didn't know. I had heard about you, but the guy who gives me updates on the trial never uses anyone's name. He did tell me one patient got his sight back, then got angry and dropped out, he didn't know why, but he never mentioned your name. I guess he had to give it to the police, though, because when Detective Travis called me later, he told me who you were." He paused. "Who told you about *me*? How'd you find me?"

"Wasn't hard. There's a newspaper interview online where you talked about your drug. Once I knew your name, it only cost me about $30 to find out a lot about you, including where you live. Hell, I know you have a brother and two sisters. I could've gotten their addresses if I'd wanted 'em. I could have looked up your criminal record, if you have one. That costs extra, though."

Paul shook his head. "Privacy really *is* dead, isn't it? ... Why were you mad about the trial? Why did you quit?"

"I was just pissed off at all the bullshit—all the tests, all the questions. I got fed up with their attitude. I seem to have a short fuse lately. Shorter than it used to be, anyway."

"And you think the drug is causing that?"

"Yeah, I do." Trey paused. "I've... hurt some people, and I don't think I would have done it back before I went blind. I mean, I had a temper, yeah, but I could hold it back, you know? Not anymore. Something's changed. I don't think I'm any more pissed off than before, but I used to hold it in better. Not now."

His gaze shifted around while he talked. He sometimes looked straight at Paul, but more often looked down or off to the side, as if the answer to all his questions might be there, if he could only see it. He went on.

"I don't think a day's gone by since I was a kid that I haven't fantasized about killing somebody over something, just for a second. Like idiot drivers. People who cut in line. Politicians. I can remember back in third grade wanting to kill someone who shoved me out of a seat in musical chairs. I mean *kill* him. You ever play that? We did a few times when it was raining and we couldn't go out at recess. The *teacher* ran the music, believe it or not. Do people still play that? Probably not. It's a sick fucking game when you think about it. Gets you ready for real life, I guess...." His voice tailed off, and he seemed to look off in the distance. Then his head jerked abruptly and he looked straight at Paul, as though he'd just remembered Paul was there. "Someone pisses you off, and for a second, you want to smash his face in, just grind his head on the pavement. Of course you don't. But you *want* to." He paused, a faraway look in his eyes again. "I don't know, maybe it's just me. I don't think I get those impulses now any more than I used to. But I never acted on 'em. I mean, I hadn't even been in a fight since high school."

Paul knew he had to keep the guy talking while he figured out what to do. "But now you have?"

"Yeah, with some asshole in a bar. The guy was asking for trouble. He got it. I could have walked away. I would have before. Not now." He looked directly in Paul's eyes. "I think your drug's causing that."

Don't argue with him. "Do you get that angry every day?"

"Not every day, no. Only when I'm around people." Trey laughed sarcastically. "So I don't get pissed off enough to kick someone's ass *every* day. Not unless I listen to the news." He laughed again, a short, mirthless chuckle. "Happens a lot when I'm driving, and I don't even drive that much. So many idiots out there, and they all have cars. They probably don't piss me off any more than they used to, but I react to it more now. I think your drug did that. Is doing that."

"So you've always had impulses, but you're more likely to act on them now."

"Yeah, I think so. I only seem to act on the bad ones, though."

Trey looked down at the table for some seconds, massaging his temples with his left hand. Paul couldn't see whether his eyes were closed or not, but his right hand was still on the gun. He suddenly looked straight at Paul. "Look, I haven't hurt anyone unless they threatened me. Like the idiot I bumped into at a stop light the other day. He would have killed me! Asshole drew a gun. He could have walked away, just walked away! There wasn't a scratch on his goddamn car. He had to argue. He was taking pictures! I took his goddamned phone and told him to get his ass out of there. He draws a gun, like he's a goddamned cowboy or something, and mine's already pointed at him! When I saw him do it, I wasn't scared, just shocked he could be that stupid. He deserved to get shot. He'd have killed me. But people don't have to try to kill you to be a threat, you know? They can threaten something you need....." The sentence seemed to drift off, then his face suddenly twisted into a mask of rage. "That's self-defense, too, as far as I'm concerned. I don't give a shit what the law says."

Paul said nothing. There was no point in arguing. *How many people has this guy hurt? Did he really kill someone?*

Trey went on. "I'm not the only one who took your drug. What about the others? Can anyone else see now?"

"One woman can, but she'd been blind a lot longer than you, and she's had a lot more trouble. She's having a hard time learning how to see again. You didn't have to do that, did you? Learn how to see again? She'd been blind too long, I guess. She thinks the drug's changed her, too, made her depressed. We didn't expect anything like that. The test animals all seemed normal. As far as we could tell, all the drug did was restore their sight. Now we think it might cross into other parts of the brain."

"You didn't know it could do that when you started testing it on people?"

"We didn't really understand how it was regulated. It normally triggers optic nerve formation, and that's all it seemed to do. Now we think it might be regulated by how fast it's broken down. If it stays around just long enough to do its job, like it does in the embryo, it doesn't affect anything but the optic nerve. But in adults, it breaks down in seconds, way too fast to do anything. To use it as a drug, we had to change it so it wouldn't break down so fast, and it seems having it around too long may turn it loose to do other things. In all the animal tests, even the stable drug we gave you didn't seem to affect anything but vision, as far as we could tell. But we may have missed some things. It didn't change any behavior we could see, but rats and monkeys can't tell you how they feel. You only get that from humans. Even then it's hard to be sure it's the drug." He paused for several seconds. "In hindsight, we probably should have waited till we knew more before we gave it to people. But all the tests were so promising. And it did give you your sight back. We just didn't know about the side effects."

Trey snapped back immediately. "So making me blow up, that's just a side effect? Do you know how many people I've...?" *Wait. Don't tell him too much.* He paused, drew a deep breath, then said more calmly, "How many others like me are there? Only two of us got our sight back, but what about the other stuff?"

"You're the only one who's gotten mad enough to hurt anyone, as far as I know. I mentioned the woman who can see now getting depressed. I think I may be more impulsive now, but the one time I blew up, all I did was yell in a meeting. I didn't hurt anyone." He smiled. "May have killed my career, though." Trey didn't seem to get the joke; his brow furrowed.

"Wait a minute. You took it, too? Why? You couldn't have been blind."

"I didn't take it on purpose. I breathed some in when I spilled a batch I was making. I don't know how much. But I've done a few things since then I wouldn't have done before."

"Like what?"

"Acting more on impulse, like you. Not so much angry ones, except at that one meeting. But I'd never cheated on my wife before, and suddenly I'm screwing my lab tech. We worked together for years without even flirting. The first time, it just happened all of a sudden. She'd breathed in some of the drug in the same accident I did. Probably not as much as me, but I think it might have affected her, too. I nearly lost my job over that. I did lose my wife. She didn't believe me when I said the drug might have caused it."

"Yeah, well, that's not like getting mad enough to kill someone. It has to be the drug. I know I'm losing my temper more."

Paul could see where this was going. *He's actually killed someone, and he wants to blame the drug, and he wants me to back him on it. But he was a psychopath to start with. He said he's wanted to kill people since he was a kid.*

Paul had to stall for time. *Keep him talking.* "Look, I feel bad about what's happened to you, but how can I help? What is it you want me to do?"

"I want to know if the drug is doing this. I want to know if anyone else is going through the same thing. From what you've told me, I think the drug *is* doing it, and I'm not the only one affected. If a drug causes you to do something, seems to me they should blame the drug."

"If you get drunk and kill someone, you still go to jail. You're still responsible."

"Yeah, but they figure you *chose* to get drunk. Maybe you're an alcoholic and didn't really have a choice, but they still act like you did. Don't they say it's a disease? Seems like they want it both ways. They call it a disease but treat it like a moral failure. And some people are okay when they take drugs their doctor gave them, but not when they're off their meds. If they kill someone then, are they morally responsible? What if they don't take their medicine because they can't afford it?"

"Whether they're responsible or not, we still lock them up. The only difference is where."

"But if it's a sanitarium or whatever, we don't blame them the same way, do we? And if they're cured, we don't keep them locked up. Now turn that around. Say a drug made them crazy, and without it, they're not. Doesn't the reason they took the drug make a difference? What if a cancer drug did it, not something you get high on? Who's responsible then? I didn't take your drug to get high. I just wanted the chance to see again. No one knew what else it might do. You said so yourself. That's different from hurting someone if you've been drinking or smoking crack. I didn't know the damn drug would make me hurt people."

"Did it, though? No one else who took it has." *Oh, shit. That might piss him off.*

Trey didn't take the bait Paul had inadvertently dangled. "From what you said, it has different effects in different people."

"That's true. So people might believe the drug made you do something, but it would help a lot if someone else who took it did the same thing."

"You said it made *you* more impulsive."

"I think it has. So that's two of us. The woman who has trouble seeing might help, too. She's a musician, and there's times she has a compulsion to keep playing when she's supposed to stop. So that makes three of us. We've all had problems with self-control, even if it takes different forms.

The more of us there are, the more likely they'd believe us." *OGF83 didn't make this psychotic bastard kill anyone. But I need to make him think I'm on his side and he's better off with me alive than dead. And I need to get that gun away from him.*

An idea suddenly occurred to Paul. "Do you mind if I get a drink of water? Or I could make some coffee."

"Why, so you can throw a pot of hot coffee in my face? I've seen that trick in movies." Trey's tone was suddenly hostile.

"I wasn't thinking anything like that, really. Look, you've got a gun pointed at me. I may seem calm on the outside, but my heart is pounding like a hammer. My mouth is really dry right now."

Trey looked skeptical, but after a pause said, "Okay. Water's okay. Don't do anything stupid." He picked the gun up and rotated his wrist to shake it in Paul's face. Then he laid it back on the table, his hand still on the grip.

As Paul got up, he thought about making a break for the front door. *No. I wouldn't even make it out the kitchen.* He walked to the cabinet above the sink where he kept glasses and coffee cups and opened it, moving slowly. *I need a distraction, something that'll startle him, make him duck and cover his face and leave the gun on the table—he's got his hand on it, but he's not actually holding it.* Paul kept talking as he slowly reached in the cabinet.

"I'm just getting a glass." He held one up to show Trey. "Okay? Just a glass." He pulled out one actually made of glass; there were plastic cups in the cabinet, too, but he needed something that would hurt if it hit or shatter if it missed. He turned the faucet on, letting the water run for half a minute. "Just letting it get cold," he explained. He was actually letting it get hot; he had pushed the faucet lever all the way to the left. When the water was running as hot as it would get, he filled the glass and took a sip from it, even though it burned his lips; Trey had to believe he was drinking it. *Grabbing the gun won't be enough. I'll lose if we wrestle for it. He's bigger than me. I have to knock the gun away and get to it first.*

A thought occurred to Paul, one he knew should have chilled him, but didn't: *If he gets in a courtroom and says OGF83 made him a killer, it'll be a circus. Whether the jury buys it or not, it would wreck everything. I can fix the drug, I know I can, but if people think it could make you a killer, it's all over. I can't let him do that. I can't let him leave here. If I get the gun, I'll have to shoot him and say it was self-defense, whatever he does.*

At that instant, Paul's glance fell on the wooden knife block that sat on the counter near the sink, to the right of the coffee maker and slightly further back. In the shadow of the cupboard above, it was easy to overlook. Standing at the sink, Paul was directly between Trey and the knife block; Trey couldn't see it at all from where he sat.

The only expensive knife Paul had, a chef's knife with an eight-inch blade, was alone in the block's top slot, which was actually intended for a cleaver. Paul never needed a cleaver, so he kept his best knife there instead. With the knife in a wide slot at the top of the block, his chances of getting it out fast were much better. There was only about four inches of clearance between the top of the knife handle and the bottom of the overhanging cupboard, but there was nothing he could do about that. The block was canted at an angle, giving him just enough room to pull the knife clear. He would have to make a clean draw; if he hit the block or knocked it over, it would slow him down and get him shot.

The distance from the block to Trey was daunting. Paul estimated ten feet, maybe eleven or twelve. It would probably take at least three seconds for him to get to Trey. If he couldn't startle him, make him forget the gun for an instant, it wouldn't take more than two seconds for him to snatch it up and fire. Every move would have to be perfect.

From out of nowhere, Trey suddenly said, "You think I should turn myself in?"

It broke Paul's train of thought. "Don't you? Aren't the police after you?"

"One of them was. Not anymore." Trey kept a straight face; he wasn't trying to joke about it.

So he shot Travis! How many people does that make? At least two. "What do you mean?"

"Nothing. Forget it." He hadn't intended to say anything about the cop; it just slipped out. He paused. *Was ambushing that cop an impulse?* "Do you think the drug affects your judgement? Not just makes you impulsive, but makes you forget the consequences? Is that the same thing?"

"Hmm." It wasn't a drawn-out, "Hmmmm", more like a short grunt, as if Paul had encountered a new idea. "I don't know. If you do something impulsive, you're not thinking about consequences, are you? If you thought about it and did it anyway, it wouldn't be an impulse anymore. Would it?" He wasn't just asking rhetorical questions.

"Couldn't the drug screw up your judgement about that, though?"

"I don't think so. I believe my thinking's as clear as ever. If I'd thought about what fucking my lab tech would lead to, I probably wouldn't have done it. But I didn't think about it. Not the first time, anyway. We just got caught up in the moment."

"But then you kept it up. It wasn't impulsive anymore, then, was it? You really don't think it affected your judgement?"

"No. I knew it was risky. You can't foresee everything. I never thought she would call it sexual harassment. I didn't see that coming."

"You say that, and you still think it didn't affect your judgement?"

That brought Paul up short. *Walked right into that one.* "Ouch. Good point. But that's hardly the first time I didn't see something coming when I should have. I can't blame the drug for that. Do you think it's affected your judgement?"

"Maybe. I'm just thinking about things I've done that seemed right at the time, but don't now. Things I wouldn't have done before."

I won't let you blame the drug. "What kind of things?" *Keep him talking.*

"Nothing I wanna talk about."

Paul looked over at Trey, who seemed to be staring out the window to his right, his mind on something either far away or deep inside. *Do it now.* Paul moved the glass of water from his right hand to his left and almost casually turned his back on Trey, edging toward the knife block, hoping Trey would keep staring out the window. *Now!* Paul suddenly erupted, grabbing the knife and pulling it cleanly from the block, spinning to his left as he hurled the glass of water backhanded toward Trey's head. He dropped into a half-crouch as he brought the knife around in front of him, his movements partly hidden from Trey by the counter between them.

His momentum and the fact that he hurled the glass with his left-hand made it impossible to aim accurately. It missed Trey's head and shattered on the wall behind him, sending water and shards of glass flying, some of both hitting Trey. Startled as the glass flew by, he ducked several inches and raised both hands to shield his face, leaving the gun on the table.

He instantly saw his mistake and grabbed for the gun. But flinching had cost him critical time, and bought it for Paul, who covered the distance between them in two enormous steps, almost leaps, around the counter and table. He brought the knife in a vicious arc across his body toward Trey, the flat of the blade almost parallel to the floor. He reached out and tried to slam his left hand down on the gun, but Trey snatched it away first; Paul's hand smacked the tabletop with a resounding thwack.

At that instant, time all but stopped for Paul. He could see everything with crystalline clarity—the sparkle from shards of broken glass on the table, drops of water running down the wall, the five o'clock stubble on Trey's cheeks. He felt a Zen-like calm; he was somehow both audience and actor in a slow-motion movie, the knife in his hand arcing slowly toward its target as Trey rose halfway from his chair, seemingly without urgency, and raised the gun—carefully, deliberately—aiming straight at Paul. Even staring at the gun, Paul felt no panic; he seemed to have all the time there was to watch the scene unfold. He had put the sequence in motion; there was nothing further he could do. All sound had stopped with the slam of his hand on the table; he was astonished to feel, not hear, an involuntary cry ripped from his own throat. He did not know why he cried out—there was no chance Trey could miss, but it hardly seemed to matter. He was a detached observer, looking on from somewhere outside himself, watching as Trey pulled the trigger.

But there was no bang, just a click, the first sound Paul had heard since his hand slammed the table, and somehow the loudest sound either man had ever heard. Since getting rid of the gun he killed Steve Linscombe with, Trey had fired nothing but revolvers; with the gun loaded, all he had to do was pull the trigger. But this gun was a semi-automatic, and he hadn't racked the slide after inserting the magazine; there was nothing in the chamber. Pulling the trigger did nothing. Trey let loose a loud, drawn-out, "Fuck!" that mixed shock, fear, and anger, all in one.

Abruptly, time started again for Paul; everything seemed to happen at once. Trey's wide-eyed look of shock when the gun failed to fire instantly became a grimace of pain as the knife blade slid between two ribs, plunging deep into his left side. The knife had a razor edge and would cut meat with little pressure, but Paul grunted as he used all his strength to shove it in Trey's side to the hilt. The effort was pure overkill; he could have been cutting through water. When the bolster of the knife slammed into Trey's left side like a punch, cracking a rib, all of Paul's weight was behind it, and the eight-inch blade was in as far as it would go.

Paul's momentum knocked Trey back into his seat. With his left hand, Paul slammed Trey's gun hand down on the table. Paul felt Trey's hand go slack, but kept it pressed to the table. Trey slumped forward with a guttural groan and tried to twist his body around to relieve the crushing pressure in his chest as blood spurted from his partially severed aorta into his chest cavity. The knife had also pierced both lobes of Trey's left lung; he gave a convulsive cough, spraying blood over their hands, the gun, and the table. Blood gushed from his side where the knife had gone in, soaking his shirt and pants, running down the chair legs and onto the floor. Grimacing in pain, Trey barely managed to gasp, "I needed you."

Paul almost snarled. "What for? To help you fuck up everything I worked for? No! My drug didn't make you a killer!"

For an instant, Trey seemed to smile faintly. "And… you…?" He hoarsely whispered, barely audible, then grunted as he let go of Paul's hand. Paul let up on Trey's slack right hand, then let go of the knife and backed away, leaving the handle protruding grotesquely from Trey's side. Trey waved his left hand weakly toward Paul, with his index finger raised, though he couldn't quite curl his other fingers completely into his palm. He grimaced again and coughed another spray of blood. A thin red trickle ran out the corner of his mouth as he turned his head to the left and laid it on the table as though he just wanted to rest a while, his eyes half-open. His left hand dropped to the table as well, index finger extended.

Trey's pointing finger felt like a knife in Paul's own heart. "No!" Paul shouted angrily. "*You* caused this! You wanted to kill people before you ever took the drug. You said so! It didn't make you do anything. It let you see!"

But Trey no longer saw anything. He coughed blood once more, weakly, then gave one long, drawn-out sigh and didn't move again.

Breathing hard, Paul stood and watched more than a minute for any sign that Trey was breathing, then felt for a pulse. Nothing. Paul stood over him for several more minutes, almost daring him to breathe, then walked to the kitchen sink and washed the blood off his hands with dish soap. Paul calmly got out his phone and called 9-1-1. He told the dispatcher it was too late for an ambulance, though he knew she would send one anyway, then walked into the front room and stood at the window, waiting for the first car to arrive.

Paul replayed in his head everything that had happened since Trey's voice emerged from the darkness on the porch. *How many people did this guy shoot? At least two, maybe more. If he were alive, he'd hurt more than that. OGF83 would never be approved if the FDA thought it could drive you mad, make you a killer. But he was a psychopath already. He had violent impulses even before he went blind, he said so. It wasn't the drug. Even if it was, I can fix it, I know I can. I can make it break down faster, keep it from spreading. It'll cure blindness in thousands of people, millions. I couldn't let him wreck that. I didn't want to kill him, but I'd do it again if I had to.*

Sometimes, he thought, *you just have to trust your impulses.*

71. *"I was hoping for that"*

Kathy—Week 36

Kathy's note explaining her apparent suicide attempt was meticulous. *I'm not trying to kill myself. I just want to be blind again. Nothing I see makes sense; it just makes me miserable.* The note detailed what she had taken, how much, and when. It was slightly off only because she had typed it in advance—it didn't mention the extra teaspoon of methanol she added at the last minute, and it gave the time she drank it as 9 p.m., though it actually was slightly later than that. It still gave her doctors more than enough to go on. They administered fomepizole, though most of the methanol had already been metabolized by then, so it didn't help much. They started dialysis immediately, which may have helped more, even though she drank less than the thirty milliliters usually considered the threshold for dialysis—they didn't entirely trust the note, and the time lapse since her dose dictated aggressive therapy. She was then put on a ventilator and a bicarbonate drip.

She avoided serious brain damage, except to her optic nerve. The ophthalmologist who examined her on her second day in the hospital pronounced her blindness irreversible.

She had gotten exactly what she wanted.

When she got out of the ICU, her parents insisted on a private room for her, paying extra up-front and out-of-pocket. The hospital administrators had misgivings, but gave in, with the proviso that her room be next to a nursing station so someone could check on her three times each hour. Rachel Abramowicz, a psychiatrist called in to assess Kathy's state of mind, was astonished to find her not depressed at all.

"Could you help me understand why you would want to be blind?"

"You can't. Nobody could who hadn't gone through what I did. When I woke up and couldn't see anything, I felt so relieved, I laughed out loud. Shocked my mom, I'll tell you. She thought I'd wake up moaning or something. The only thing seeing did was make me miserable. Just a mess of colors and shapes. No order. No pattern. Every time I turned my head, it all changed. Everything closing in on me, everything right *there*. I couldn't block it out as long as my eyes were open. I felt paralyzed. I could hardly make myself move. No matter where I turned, I thought I'd walk into a wall. And it never got any better." Kathy propped herself up on her right elbow, then reached over and fumbled on the nightstand for her dark glasses. She found them before the doctor could get up and get them for her, and slipped them on.

"Couldn't you just close your eyes when you walked?"

"No! You can't walk around squinching your eyes shut all the time; you have other things to worry about. You know why blind people like me wear dark glasses? Your eyes move around on their own and it bums people out. Forget all that other shit you hear. If you're nerve-blind and can't see anything at all, you don't need dark glasses. I never got sunburned eyeballs in my life, and why the fuck would I care about cataracts? You cover up your eyes for other people; it doesn't do a damn thing for you. But when my sight came back, I had to cover them up for *me*. I needed glasses that block everything because I knew what was waiting when I took them off—a flood of colors and shapes would hit me all at once, and I couldn't make sense out of any of it. I couldn't pick out objects, or even if I could, I couldn't tell how close they were. I couldn't even recognize my own mother's face. And the longer I let it go, the worse my hearing got. Maybe I'm too old for my brain to rewire itself for seeing. I was just a kid when I went blind. My brain could still change. But now? The parts used for seeing when I was a kid probably handle hearing now. If they tried to switch back, I don't think they'd work right for either one. If I can't trust my eyes, and my hearing goes, what then? I had to do something."

"But you were depressed, and that may not have been caused just by your problems with seeing. The drug you took seems to have psychological effects nobody knew about."

Kathy leaned back against her pillow; the back of the bed was raised as high as it would go. "I know that. I can't be sure my fucked-up eyesight caused my depression, but now that I can't see at all, I think that's where most of it came from. I know what I did seems crazy, but do I really seem crazy to you?"

"'Crazy' isn't a medical diagnosis, but there's nothing in your chart and nothing I'm hearing now that would make me think you're delusional or suffering from any psychosis. But depression is a mood disorder, it doesn't come with delusions. The fact remains, you tried to poison yourself."

Kathy turned sideways, leaning on her elbow again. "But I didn't try to kill myself. I knew the amount of methanol I drank wasn't enough to kill me. I waited until the drug had time to work, then I told my parents I needed to go to the hospital. I knew I wouldn't die. There was a chance I would damage more than my optic nerves, I knew that. But I had to risk it if I wanted to be blind again. I didn't have the nerve to gouge my own eyes out or something, like Oedipus. I just couldn't face the pain. ... You know about Oedipus, right? Of course. You're a psychiatrist; you know the Oedipus complex."

"I don't put much stock in Freud, but, yes, I know who Oedipus was. I'm glad you didn't gouge your eyes out. But you're lucky. Methanol kills a lot of people."

"I know that. I knew it was a gamble. But I got what I wanted. I'm fine now."

"So you don't feel like hurting yourself at all now?"

"No, not at all. Look, I know most people won't understand why I'd rather be blind. But they haven't been through what I have."

"I'm still worried there might be other psychological effects of the drug you took. If there are, you might not realize it."

"Look, I know the drug had psychological effects. The guy who made it told me he thinks it might make you more impulsive. But drinking methanol wasn't impulsive. It took planning."

"Most people would find the idea of planning something like that irrational. You would have to be in a deep depression or...."

Kathy sat back and threw both her hands up. "I *was* depressed! Horribly! But I knew what I had to do to stop it. It was completely rational. I knew I couldn't get a doctor to blind me painlessly, and all the options besides methanol would have been too painful, and disfiguring, too. Gouging my eyes out, putting acid in them, whatever. I wouldn't have been able to do any of them. Drinking methanol was a calculated risk, and I took it"

"But do you think that was the only way to stop your depression? There are things we can do to treat depression."

"None of them would have worked. I've been taking Welbutrin, you know. Isn't that in my chart? It didn't fix anything. I saw—you just can't get away from that expression, can you?—I saw what I needed to do, and I did it, and it worked. The depression I had isn't the kind you can treat with a drug. It had one cause, and that's gone, and so is it."

"You don't feel depressed right now. Are you sure you'll feel the same way tomorrow?"

"I think tomorrow I'll feel exactly the same way I've been feeling since I woke up and couldn't see anything. Relieved. Happy. I'm sure I'll have ups and downs, just like anyone. If I get depressed again, maybe I'll need your help then. But right now, I don't. I feel fine. I appreciate your concern, but all I really need now is to get out of this hospital and back to my life."

"I'd like you to come by my office at least once a month for a while, or I could refer you to another doctor if you'd like. Please think about it. From a psychiatric standpoint, I see no reason to keep you here. Your doctors say you're physically okay, aside from being blind. That's probably permanent. But you knew that."

"I was *hoping* for that."

72. The Lazarus Effect

Paul/Kathy—After

PAUL'S KILLING OF TREY OSBORNE was clearly self-defense—Trey's hand was still on the gun when the police arrived. Paul was quickly no-billed by a grand jury. Video from the drugstore the night before Trey's death left no doubt that he shot Jim Travis—who survived, though he faced an arduous rehabilitation process. He lost his left eye, and it would be weeks before he could walk again, unsteadily; he would need months of speech therapy. He vowed to be back at work within the year, though, and no one who knew him would bet against it.

There was no evidence connecting Trey to Steve Linscombe's death; the case remained open, with no suspects. Paul told the police about Trey's claim to have killed a man at a stoplight, but they couldn't definitively place Trey at the scene; the case remained officially unsolved. The secrets of any other crimes Trey might have committed died with him.

Cardon Clinical Testing and Southeast Texas State University quietly canceled the OGF83 trial, citing possible untoward reactions caused by the drug. Paul Lazarus was soon trying to create a new version that would act on the optic nerve and nothing else. Hopes were high.

Xi Lin left the University soon after her transfer from Paul's lab. There were rumors she returned to China; no one at the school knew for sure.

* * *

After her release from the hospital, Kathy was soon able to pick up pretty much where she had left off. Leila was thrilled to get Kathy back—the old Kathy. It took a few weeks to get her playing back to the same level as before—whether because she was out of practice or because there were lingering effects from the methanol, no one could say. But her mood was much better—the darkness had lifted, blindness be damned.

Kathy was thrilled to have her old life back, so she was both startled and dismayed one morning three months after leaving the hospital when her mother clicked the light on in her bedroom and Kathy saw the flash. She quickly arranged to see her new ophthalmologist, Dr. Anika Srinivasan—she couldn't face Dr. Stark again after she blinded herself.

After hearing Kathy's history, Dr. Srinivasan had her undergo an MRI scan of her brain. The doctor could hardly contain her excitement when she met with Kathy to go over the results.

"Believe it or not, that drug you took still seems to be working after all this time. Your optic nerve appears to be repairing itself. You might be able to see again soon!"

It took a few seconds for the words to sink in. Kathy suddenly felt a crushing weight in her chest; she could barely breathe. The muscles in her face quivered as she tried to hold back a sob, but she finally let go, tears streaming down her face. Her eyes just then were useless for seeing. But they worked fine for crying.

Acknowledgements

THE SEEDS THAT GREW INTO *Unblinded* germinated in the mid-1970s when I first read of Marius von Senden's remarkable book, *Space and Sight*, about the experiences of people blind from birth who gained their sight after surgery for congenital cataracts, as described in Annie Dillard's luminous *Pilgrim at Tinker Creek*. The idea of basing a story on similar experiences stayed in the back of my mind for over 30 years. I first sketched out episodes for it in 2011, and began working on it seriously in 2016. I am indebted to four people for advice and support during *Unblinded*'s long gestation. Gina Panettieri and Tia Mele of Talcott Notch Literary Services generously provided valuable feedback on an earlier draft of the book at a time when I thought it was finished, leading me to rewrite it almost completely. While line-editing the resulting manuscript, Stephanie Jaye Evans made many valuable suggestions that led to this substantially revised final version. Above all, I am grateful to my wife, Sara Munson, who proofread earlier drafts and suggested several improvements in the manuscript, while providing encouragement and support throughout its writing. Any flaws remaining are entirely my own.

About the Author

AFTER GRADUATING FROM THE COLLEGE of Charleston (South Carolina) with a B.A. in Biology, D. Michael Hallman worked for several years in a DuPont textile factory, then as a research technician in a pharmacology laboratory at the Medical University of South Carolina. Resolving to kill himself by degrees, he then earned a master's degree in Epidemiology from the University of South Carolina and a Ph.D. in Biomedical Science (Human Genetics) from the Graduate School of Biomedical Sciences at the University of Texas Health Science Center in Houston, Texas. Working as a genetic epidemiologist, he has held faculty positions at Tulane University and the University of Texas School of Public Health. He now lives in Houston with his wife, Sara, and nine rescue cats.